THE DEATH OF
DELGADO
AND OTHER STORIES

The Death of Delgado and Other Stories
Copyright © 2015 by Rod Miller

ISBN: 978-1-942428-54-1

Cover design by Kimberly Pennell
Interior design by Kelsey Rice

THE DEATH OF DELGADO

AND OTHER STORIES

Rod Miller

𝑃
Pen-L Publishing
Fayetteville, AR
Pen-L.com

CONTENTS

A BORDER DISPUTE

Originally published in the Pocket Books anthology Lone Star Law, *edited by Robert J. Randisi, "A Border Dispute" was a Finalist for the Western Writers of America Spur Award in 2006. The story inter-twines two tales—one present day and the other from the past. As the modern story unfolds from beginning to end, the old story unfolds from end to beginning.*

———— ◆ ————

The walls of the gorge lit up briefly in the lightning flash. Although it was but midafternoon, heavy clouds and high cliffs blocked enough light that it was dark as late evening along the river's course in the canyon's bottom.

Knowing it was a matter of minutes until the clouds burst, the man in the canoe started watching the walls for a place to put ashore.

Not that he minded getting wet. But the tons of water the storm was dumping on the desert were already pouring down feeder gorges and into the river and the coming high and white water was more than he cared to tackle in a cheap open canoe. His cargo was much too valuable to risk. And so he scanned the shore as he slid along on the current.

Not that there was shore to speak of. But that was why he was on this stretch of the *Rio Bravo*—Rio Grande, the gringos called it. Smuggling drugs across the border wasn't the cakewalk it once was, so the commerce was forced into ever more inventive avenues and isolated places.

The so-far successful method that brought him here was simple. Get to a place on the Mexican side of the river where you can get yourself, your cargo, and a cheap canoe over the rim of one of many canyons downriver from the Big Bend country and float lazily downstream for a few days or even a week to reach another semi-accessible pre-arranged place on the American side, set the canoe adrift, and climb out of the canyon with the cargo.

So far, it had worked. The buffoons in the Border Patrol and the D.E.A. idiots could not comprehend this offset fashion of fording the river and

1

so concentrated on more conventional crossings. But, he feared, the *Rinches*—the derogatory border Spanish term for the Texas Rangers—were wising up and he might soon have to come up with a new and equally devious plan or he could wind up in some Texas *juzgado*.

His eyes picked up a dark cleft in the cliff's face just a few feet above the water and he backpaddled to slow and turn the canoe, pushed himself back upstream a few yards with a dozen deep strokes, then pivoted again and allowed the canoe to drift downstream as he used the paddle to force it against the wall.

When he again spied the slender opening he grasped jagged rock and stopped for a closer look. The canyon hereabouts was riddled with caves, but not many were accessible without serious climbing and he had neither the time nor inclination for that. So he sought shelter that was above the high water mark and no higher.

This should do fine, he thought.

With a couple of lengths of bright yellow plastic braided rope he lashed the canoe securely fore and aft to rock outcroppings. He rummaged through one of the watertight plastic chests that filled the canoe and selected a blanket, a battery-powered fluorescent lantern, a water bottle, and a lunch sack full of cold tamales and tortilla-wrapped frijoles. He fashioned a makeshift sling from the blanket and, with the food and lantern in its pouch, scrambled the few feet up the cliff to the narrow opening.

Once through the crack, he sat back against the wall for a moment to catch his breath. A thunderclap rolled through the canyon, shattering the sky, knocking the storm loose into the gorge. The sound of heavy raindrops splattering off rocks and pocking the river made him glad he was out of it.

Even in the dark he sensed the cave was a small one and sang a few lines of a favorite *corrido* to see if the echo agreed. It did.

The smuggler slid a few feet further into the mountain before unslinging the blanket. He set the lunch sack aside and stowed the lantern between his thighs and wrapped the blanket around his shoulders before punching the button to activate the lamp.

He did not realize how accustomed his eyes had become to the dim until the painful glare of the light. His face wrinkled in a squint and a hand raised instinctively to shield his eyes. Then his vision cleared and he let loose an inadvertent gasp, nearly a scream.

Sitting next to him, no more than a foot away, was a rack of bones and stack of litter that had once been a man. Another skeleton lay on the floor nearby. The smuggler, whose line of work had occasioned his seeing no small number of dead bodies, and even watching a goodly number who were alive become dead, was nevertheless startled and shocked and left temporarily lacking the ability to breathe.

———◆———

Calderón died instantly in a powder flash and, since he saw it coming, it would be incorrect to say that he never knew what hit him. Another cliché often applied to such instances may, however, be true: he never felt a thing.

That cannot be said of the other man, Butts, whose death was both lingering and painful.

And although it violates the order of their dying it is yet true that Calderón killed Butts, and then Butts killed Calderón.

———◆———

The smuggler considered bolting the cave and braving the storm, but curiosity got the better of him once composure returned. He studied the bodies—corpses—skeletons—and wondered how they came to be dead in this out-of-the-way place.

It was clear they had been dead for a long time. A long, long time. Little remained in the way of flesh—the odd strip of jerky clinging here and there the only evidence that meat and skin once covered the bones.

Since the skeletons were largely intact, the place must be protected from predators, at least large ones. He assumed bugs and worms and rodents had done the scouring.

A sizable chunk of bone was missing from the upper forehead and top of the skull of the man seated beside him. The side of the head of the other man, the one curled on the floor next to the black smudge that must have once been a fire, was dented and cracked. That says something, he thought.

———◆———

Butts knelt next to the small fire, kindled from rats' nests and twigs and a few pieces of driftwood he'd collected from where they'd been lodged in the rocks near the cave's entrance. The fire would never burn long enough to dry them, but the spindly flames provided a bit of light and took the edge off the chill.

It wouldn't matter if they were still wet come morning, anyway, he thought, since it would be back in the river for the both of them until they could find a place on the left bank to climb out of the canyon. He fed the fire a few more twigs and turned toward Calderón in time to see the rock in the Mexican's fist the instant before it smashed into his head with a dull crack like a stick of wood snapping underwater.

The blow rattled Butts to the soles of his boots, but as his eyes blurred and his ears buzzed and his brain bled, he managed to unholster his Colt and, with the last remnant of strength in his arm and hand, bring the weapon to bear and fire. Calderón, weak from the flight and the fight and the fall and the float, had barely managed to lift the rock, no bigger than the crown of his lost *sombrero*, for a second swipe at the fallen Butts when the heat of the muzzle blast withered his eyelashes and the bullet ripped a peso-sized chunk out of his head.

As soon as Butts fired the shot, the weight of the gun carried his hand to the cave floor and he instinctively curled into a fetal position. The noise inside his shattered head drowned out the sound of his whimpering. Pain squeezed at his skull and the blood poured both into his head and out of it, eventually washing away all awareness and finally life itself.

———◆———

Not much left in the way of clothing, the drug runner noticed. Practically all the fabric, it appeared, had been unraveled and hauled away string by strand. Most likely, he thought, to line rodent nests. Dried and cracked remnants of leather boots remained. Rusted spurs said both had been horsemen.

Other metal objects survived. Corroded buckles and tarnished brass cartridges in a gunbelt around the body on the floor. A rusty old revolver wrapped in finger bones. And, still surrounding the thin bones of the men's wrists, a pair of handcuffs.

The cuffs linked the right wrist of the man leaning against the wall to the left wrist of the man on the ground. That, and the fact that the downed man held the gun, led the smuggler to the obvious conclusion that the one seated next to him had been the prisoner of the other.

But what the hell were they doing here, in this miserable cave in the bottom of a river gorge with no way out? As he mulled it over, his eye caught something else. There, wedged in the dust under a rib bone was a dull metal disk. He wiggled it out of the dirt and brought it closer to the light.

He could see, after rubbing off a layer of grime, that it had once been a silver peso. But its face had been crudely hammered smooth and a series of wedges punched out to create the shape of a star within a circle, around which was stamped the words TEXAS RANGER.

Rinches! he realized. This dead *pendejo* was one of the *Rinches*!

———◆———

Butts clung to the rocks with one hand while the other fist held a twisted handful of Calderón's shirt collar. He was further encumbered by the Mexican's heavy *mochila*, an oversized set of saddlebags, slung over his shoulder. Both men sputtered and spat volumes of water back into the river where it belonged. Calderón had the worst of it, in turn hacking water from his lungs and spewing it from his stomach.

"Stay afloat, Calderón. I can't keep you from drowning by myself."

"Why don't you just let go?"

"You ain't getting off that easy you thieving sonofabitch. I'll watch you rot in a jail cell and enjoy every minute of it."

The Mexican made a half-hearted attempt to tread water while the Ranger looked over the rocks above. The canyon walls were rough and jagged, nearly vertical. Caves and shelter rocks were visible in the cliffs, but he could not see a way to get to them. Then, just before casting off to float downriver and try again elsewhere, he spied a dark cleft in the rock a few yards upstream. Maybe, just maybe, he thought, it was within reach and might offer shelter from the coming night.

"Come on. Upstream," Butts said.

"*Qué*? What do you want?"

"There," the Ranger gasped, pointing out the cave. He hacked up and spit out another gob of slimy water. "Climb. Get out of this damn river."

Butts pulled Calderón through the water and spun him toward the rocks. The Mexican clawed for holds and between the two of them pushing and pulling they reached the spot below the cave. The Ranger jerked upward on Calderón's shirt, lifting him higher in the water.

"Up," he said. "*Arriba.*"

The Mexican barely had the strength to struggle the few feet up the face, and it was almost more than Butts could do to pull himself along behind and prod the prisoner at the same time. As Calderón disappeared into the narrow crevice, the Ranger called out to him.

"Calderón!"

He waited a moment, stuck to the rock like a lizard, then called again, louder this time.

"Calderón! Poke your ugly face out that hole!"

The Mexican's face slithered out the crack like a tortoise poking its head out of its shell.

"*Qué?*"

"Here. Grab these."

Butts pulled as many sticks and twigs of driftwood as he could find out of the rocks and shoved them upward, one at a time. Calderón took them and pushed them into the darkness behind him. Having scavenged all the wood at hand, Butts scrambled that last few feet up through the rocks and followed his prisoner into the cave. Before he even sat down, he clamped handcuffs around Calderón's wrist and fastened the other end to his own.

"What the hell, man?" Calderón said. "You think I'm going somewhere?"

Butts did not reply, merely dropped to the ground in a heap of fatigue and sucked in a few ragged breaths.

"Unhook these bracelets. I don't want to spend the night chained to no damn Ranger."

"Shut up. It ain't like you got any choice in the matter."

"Where am I going to go? I been chased halfway across *Tejas*. I been beat up. Fell off a cliff. Nearly drowned. I ain't got the strength to break wind and you think I'm going somewhere? Besides, you know I can't hardly swim anyhow."

Butts ignored Calderón. Or pretended to. He did not believe for a minute that the Mexican was anywhere near as bad off as he let on. Besides, the Ranger had experienced all the same troubles his prisoner had and doubted he himself had the strength to stop an attempted escape.

After a brief moment of blessed silence, the prisoner piped up again. "Hey, Ranger—what's your name?"

"Butts."

That drew a chuckle. "Butts? What kind of name is Butts?"

"My name. The one I got from my daddy. The only one I've got."

"What, gringo, you don't got a first name? Everybody just calls you Butts?"

"That. Or C. W."

"*Qué?*"

"C. W. Them's my initials. I go by C. W. Butts."

"What's that stand for, C and W?"

That drew a chuckle from the Ranger. "Clarence. Clarence Winthrop. Clarence Winthrop Butts."

Calderón laughed. "*Madré de Dios*! No wonder you like C. W. How come you know my name?"

"Hell, you're famous, Calderón. Either a hero of your people or the most hated man in West Texas, depending on who you ask. I've known your name these ten years since I been with the Rangers."

A fruitless chase after the Mexican had, in fact, been the first assignment Butts was given as Ranger. Butts was detailed to the Rangers' Frontier Battalion, which had but a few years earlier captured the notorious murderer John Wesley Hardin and killed the outlaw Sam Bass. The day of his enrollment in July of 1882, the tenderfoot Butts was sent out with a posse to chase down Calderón and his *bandido* gang after they had robbed an express shipment out near Marfa.

But the robbers won a long hot miserable race across the desert and crossed the border before the Rangers could overtake them. Butts had spent a goodly portion of the intervening decade trying to stop the Calderón gang's robberies and killings across West Texas, but the Rangers always seemed to be a day behind the bandits.

"I been on your tail now and again over all that time."

Again Calderón laughed. "You must not of got too close, Butts, or I would know who you are."

"Maybe so. You are a slippery little bastard, I'll give you that."

"*Claro*. But outsmarting gringos is no big thing. It has been an easy life, robbing those who stole our country. It is like—how do you say it?— taking candy from a baby. Beating you people is almost too easy."

"That maybe was true once, but those days are over now. You make the same mistake my daddy said caused the Confederacy to come out in second place—thinking that winning battles is the same as winning a war."

"What are you talking about, Butts? I have good English but I do not understand what you say."

"I'm saying you may have won some battles by getting away up till now. But now you're mine, and that means you done lost the war."

Both men sat quietly for a time, then Butts unslung the heavy saddlebags from his shoulder and tossed them back into the cave where they lit with soggy clink. As his eyes adjusted to the dim light he spied a wad of grass that had once been a nest for rats or mice and picked it apart into a small pile in front of him. Other, similar wads were within easy reach and he retrieved a few of those and piled them nearby.

Finding a likely looking piece of rock, Butts next pulled his pistol from its holster and glanced the stone against the metal at the bottom of the grip to see if he could raise a spark. He could. Soon, the dry grass sparkled and smoked and glowed and a few gentle breaths coaxed out a flame.

"Thank God for Samuel Colt," Butts said, holstering his revolver as he added progressively larger twigs to the fire. He knew the fire would be short-lived. But he did not know that within minutes, more than a fire would die in this cave.

————— ◆ —————

Curious about the rest of the story, the smuggler hoisted up the lantern and cast his gaze into the dark corners of the little cave. At first he saw only evasive movements of rodents and insects hiding deeper in cracks and crannies but in due course his eyes picked out a curled and cracked hunk of leather in the shadows.

Stepping gingerly to avoid splintering the bones on the floor, he followed the lamplight to the discovery and dragged the heavy bag away from the wall and into the cave's center. It looked to be of the same vintage as the bodies and about as intact. It was, he decided, a mochila of the type he still saw used occasionally by the *vaqueros* of his homeland on the opposite shore. Smaller than a kyack for a packsaddle but bigger than the saddlebags of Texas cowboys, a mochila was cut to fit over a saddle horn and cover all or part of the seat. Pockets or pouches were sewn on the sides for carrying whatever the rider wanted to take along.

And what, exactly, the smuggler wondered, was this one carrying?

The mochila was dried out and some of the leather strings that stitched it together had rotted through. Parts of it were gnawed away. But the pouches still held whatever they held. He shifted it around to get to one of the buckles to find out what and as he tugged the strap to free the buckle prong, it broke in his hand. Peeking in through the lifted flap, he caught the dull glint of metal.

His heart skipped a beat and his lungs involuntarily gasped for air. In the exuberance that followed, he tore loose the other pocket flaps and shook free a trove of tarnished silver coins and glowing gold coins that clinked into a pile on the floor of the cave, followed by the dull thud of a quartet of shiny, good-as-new, gold ingots.

———◆———

Butts knew the bandit was his when he saw Calderón abandon his spent horse, leaving the broke-down animal quivering and dripping sweat and sucking wind at the rim of one of the many rocky canyons hereabouts that dropped into the bigger canyon of the Rio Grande.

From a distance, he watched the robber strip the mochila and head down the deepening gully afoot. Calderón attempted to spook the horse away, but the scrub had hit bottom and stood unfrightened, spraddle-legged with head sagging. The Ranger's horse was also tired but, being accustomed to better feed, had held out just enough longer to run the Mexican mount into the ground.

Turning his horse in the downhill direction of the gully Butts pushed hard along the rim for better than half a mile, figuring to get ahead of the bandit before dropping into the canyon for a surprise attack.

The plan worked. Concealed behind a rock outcrop at the side of the narrow draw, Butts watched for some minutes as Calderón hustled downhill, dodging boulders and scrambling over drop-offs into the shallow hollows at their bases where storm runoff would puddle and churn before heading again downhill to the next short fall.

Having been the object of the Ranger's pursuit for several long hours and many hard miles, Calderón assumed Butts was still coming after him so he spent as much time looking behind him as ahead. And so it was unnerving when Calderón turned from one such backward glance to find himself stood up by the barrel of a revolver mere inches from the end of his nose.

Too startled to react, the Mexican did not even breathe until Butts spoke.

"Don't you move, you greaser sonofabitch, or I'll shoot you dead, sure as you're born. Get them hands up, real slow."

As Calderón complied, Butts pulled the bandit's pistol from its high-riding, cross-draw holster and threw it into a jumble of rocks on the steep side of the canyon.

"Now, sit down. Drop right straight down on that skinny butt of yours and don't try anything cute."

Keeping his pistol trained between the man's eyes, Butts squatted before him and patted around for the knife he knew would be concealed in his boottops. He found it and tossed it away.

Butts then holstered his pistol and looked to where he had tucked a pair of handcuffs under his gunbelt, his brief inattention prompting the prisoner to reach behind his head and slide a thin-bladed knife out of a scabbard concealed between his shoulder blades.

Calderón's sudden movement caught the Ranger's attention and he instinctively took a backward step. The resulting accident is the only thing that saved his life. Butts stumbled and tripped when his heel caught on a rock and he fell flat on his back. Unable to stem or shift the momentum of his thrust, the bandit's blade sliced only desert air as he followed its path over the top of the fallen Butts, likewise stumbling and landing half in the dirt and rocks and half atop the lawman.

Quick as spit on a hot griddle, Calderón scrambled off Butts and to his feet and looked around desperately for the knife jarred loose in the fall. Butts saw it first, and grabbed it up from where it had landed almost in his hand. He flipped quickly to his knees and braced for the Mexican's next attack, but Calderón instead turned and loped off downhill. The knife clattered in the rocks as Butts flung it away and took after him.

Even with the heavy *mochila* Calderón carried, Butts figured he must have a thirty pound advantage over the outlaw, who, while short and skinny, was likewise wiry and cagey. And had it not been for dumb luck, he knew the Mexican's knife would already have cut him to ribbons. So while his pursuit was vigorous it was not without caution.

It took another accident to again stop the chase. An unfortunate step wedged Calderón's foot between boulders, impeding his stride just enough to stretch him out face first among the muddle of rocks in the bed of the dry watercourse. Butts was upon him before he could recover and, with all the force he and gravity could muster, dropped a knee into the middle of the man's back.

Rather than disabling the desperate bandit, the capture inspired him and Calderón flipped to his back and unleashed a vicious knee which landed swift and square in the Ranger's crotch, expelling his breath more effectively than the Ranger's knee to the Mexican's back had.

Calderón exploited his advantage by crabbing out from under the Ranger and landing another ferocious kick to his ribs. Butts automatically reached for his pistol as the blow rolled him, but could not accomplish the draw as he had affixed the safety strap over the gun's hammer to secure it during the chase.

Now it was his turn to scramble out of the way on elbows and bootheels as the Mexican attempted to brain him with a rock. Again, Calderón's momentum carried him to the ground and again Butts took the opportunity to leap astraddle his back. He immediately grabbed Calderón by the wrist and wrenched his arm behind his back, forcing the hand painfully upward. Then, for good measure, he landed a few kidney punches.

Butts relaxed slightly when the Mexican sagged limp below him and again he reached for the manacles. In the instant he loosened his grip on Calderón's wrist to replace it with a cuff, the bandit exploded upward and again scrambled out of the Ranger's grasp and down the draw.

He did not get far, soon skidding to a stop. His next step would have carried him into empty air with nothing between him and the river below but a sheer drop of some thirty-five feet. Lacking the Mexican's knowledge of their current situation, Butts did not stop as Calderón had, instead launching himself with a mighty leap, the force of which barely diminished as he wrapped his arms around the bandit and carried them both out into the chasm.

Although Calderon knew what was coming and so his scream came first, Butts soon overcame the disadvantage and his yell surpassed the Mexican's on all counts—length, intensity, and the quality of the profanity. And he did not stop the scream until it was replaced in his mouth by river water.

The shock of the landing tore the pair apart and when Butts surfaced he saw that Calderón was in a bad way, his slight frame lacking the buoyancy to keep himself and the heavy mochila above water. Besides, the bandit evidently lacked swimming skills beyond the ability to thrash around enough to break the surface from time to time and gasp a breath as the river pushed them along downstream.

A few powerful strokes carried Butts across the current to where the Mexican floundered and he wrapped his arm around Calderón's neck to hold his head above water. Calderón, of course, misinterpreted the action as another attack and objected violently. Butts increased pressure on the bandit's throat to dampen his struggling and yelled into his ear instructions to hold still. Either fatigue or lack of oxygen or the Ranger's yelling finally calmed Calderón and he relaxed and allowed Butts to keep him afloat.

"Damn it man, here I am trying to save your life and here you are trying to drown us both. You're going to have to shed them saddlebags or they'll drag you down."

"Are you *loco*? This mochila is why I have been running from you and why you have been running after me. And now you want me to dump it in the river?"

"No, you fool. I'll carry it. It won't weigh me down near as much as it does you, you skinny little bastard. Give it over then we can figure how to get out of this damn river and back on dry land."

———◆———

Quarter Eagles. Half Eagles. Eagles. Double Eagles. Spanish Reals. Silver Dollars. Gold Dollars. Silver Pesos. Other curious coins the smuggler had never seen nor heard of. But he knew enough to know that the metal the coins contained far exceeded their worth as minted currency.

And then there were the gold ingots, whose value he could not, dared not, even imagine.

He passed the time stacking, restacking, dividing, subdividing, combining, separating, shuffling the coins.

There were worse ways to pass a rainy night, he thought.

———◆———

All the success Calderón had enjoyed eluding the Rangers over the years ended by sheer happenstance; one of those ugly coincidences life throws at one from time to time in order to keep one humble.

Butts and a couple of other Rangers happened to be laying over in the railroad town of Sanderson on a trip from Fort Stockton to Langtry. Word came down while the men were enjoying a rare hotel breakfast that a bandido gang had waylaid the morning eastbound a few miles outside of town and made off with a bank shipment—not a tremendous haul, but a significant one.

Even before their abandoned breakfasts had gone cold the Rangers were armed and mounted and on the trail.

Calderón did not imagine that pursuit would come so quickly, so the Rangers surprised the bandits squatting around empty money sacks dividing the take for easier transport. Had they done so in concealment, it is likely the lawmen would have captured them then and there. But the Mexicans had stopped on a wide and dusty dry lakebed and so saw the Rangers coming from a good way off.

They quickly stuffed the loot back into bags, into pockets, into pouches, into saddlebags, into mochilas, even inside shirts and the crowns of sombreros and clambered aboard their horses and lit out across the flat. But the Rangers were better mounted and the gap between the three of them and the five bandits closed with every stride.

The pursued and pursuers started exchanging optimistic gunshots while still outside pistol range, and kept up the fire until the distance closed to effective range. Whether the Ranger riding next to Butts meant it or whether it was a fluke—a subject of much discussion in Ranger circles for years to come—the fact remains that he placed a bullet directly through the back of the neck of one of the retreating bandits, evening up the odds some by making it three after four.

Shortly after the bandit fell, the group split in two, with three staying together and the other striking off alone. Butts signaled the other two Rangers to continue after the group of three, knowing they could improvise in the likely event the bandits split up again later. He veered sharply southward following the lone rider. Already, he sensed victory—sensed, at least, that the chances of catching the bandit were heavily in his favor. What his chances might be once he caught up with him he could not say.

Off the flats and onto more rugged terrain, the pace of the pursuit slowed. But still Calderón drove his mount furiously. He knew the river was ahead. And he knew it cut through one deep gorge after another through this country, most likely putting it and the border beyond reach. But if his horse held up, he knew the off chance that he would hit the river at a place he could cross was the only chance he had.

———— ◆ ————

The rain had stopped sometime during the night and by midmorning the worst of the gullywasher had passed and the Rio Bravo was back to its normal flow.

He was nervous, tense, wound tighter than his usual state of alertness while at work. Which is to be expected, perhaps, given that yesterday's unlikely events had made this far and away the biggest payload of his career—even if he jettisoned the contraband drugs. So, even though the chances of someone in law enforcement spotting him on this rugged, lonely stretch of river were practically nil, the smuggler nonetheless kept a sharp eye on the cliffs above the left bank. He did not think he would spot a Border Patrol officer up there, or a D.E.A. agent.

But those Rinches, he thought. Those damn Rinches. It's hard to get the best of the Rinches.

JUST LIKE TULLY SAID

Once upon a time, Amazon.com had a program called Amazon Shorts that digitally published short fiction in a variety of genres, including Westerns, and including "Just Like Tully Said." The program disappeared, but this story survived. In fact, it grew. Tully became Rawhide Robinson, the title character in two novels, Rawhide Robinson Rides the Range *and* Rawhide Robinson Rides the Tabby Trail.

———————•———————

Sparks streamed into the sky like an upside-down rain shower as trail boss Enos Atkins stirred up the coals and tossed another skinny log on the campfire. With supper on the inside of the drovers and sleep not yet upon them, it was time for a song, a poem, a story, to put the lid on the day and uncork the night.

"Say Tully, this your first trip up the trail?" Enos asked, knowing that with Tully Prater that one simple question would get the evening's entertainment rolling and keep it going into the wee hours. The man had a penchant for storytelling and no shortage of tales to tell.

"Oh, hell no," Tully said. "I went up the trail with a herd a few years back. We were bound for the railhead at Ellsworth, Kansas with a sea of beeves belonging to Mr. Ford Fargo of the Double-F-Slash Ranch. Thing was, though, I never made it to Kansas, as misfortune set in along the way as has often been the case with me."

Tully let the statement lie there like an unbranded calf, knowing it was only a matter of time before one of the hands grabbed it.

"So what the hell happened?" McCarty blurted, ending the uncomfortable pause.

"Well, we was crossing the Canadian River in a rainstorm, trying to get them cattle across before the water got too high. I was on the far bank soaked from the soles of my boots to the crease of my hat, keeping the critters bunched once they climbed out of the water, when this one old mossy horn bunch quitter started swimming upstream. I followed along with him, knowing he'd come ashore once he figured he was clear of the herd and could make his getaway.

"Thing was, though, when he tried to get to dry land he got bogged. That river along there is awash in quicksand and that nasty old steer had found him some of it. So I punched a hole in my catch rope, figuring to land a loop around his horns and drag him out of there. It took me two tries, but I snaked a long loop around his big old rack. He wasn't none too happy about that—snorting and blowing and bellering and waving them antlers around like he wanted nothing better than to poke one of them in my eye.

"But I started in to hauling him out of there just the same. Thing was, though, the lasso rope I was packing was an eighty-foot Mexican gut line, and you all know how a rawhide rope acts when it gets wet. That old horse and me kept pulling and that steer kept sinking and that reata kept stretching. Well, we just kept on pulling and pulling and pretty soon we was out of sight and out of earshot of the river, the herd, and that steer. Stretching and stretching we went, and before you know it, what with the rain and all, I lost all track of time and distance and just kept on riding.

"All of a sudden that rope went slack and before I even had time to realize that the steer had come unstuck, here he comes sailing through the sky and flies right over my head. Now, not being one of them cowardly California-type dally ropers, my reata was tied hard and fast to the saddle horn, so I figured there'd be hell to pay when that rope pulled tight.

"Thing was, though, that gut line was so soaking wet and stretchy there never was much of a jerk. When that steer hit the end, it just started stretching again, and soon enough it yanked that horse right off the ground and sent him a-sailing through the sky. And, being firmly planted in the saddle at the time, I was along for the ride.

"We just kept swapping ends, spinning around and around up there like one of them bolo things them gauchos down in South America throws, and me not knowing when it would ever end. After a while, the rain let up as we flew on beyond the storm, and soon the sky cleared and the sun started shining.

"I had no idea where we were or how much country we had flown over. Finally, though, I recognized the Rocky Mountains and noticed we was flying right toward Pike's Peak, way the hell and gone up there in that Colorado country. Damned if we didn't fly right past that craggy old jaggedy old pointy old mountain peak, that steer on one side and me and the horse on the other. Then, as you might imagine, we reached the ends of the rope and started spinning around that mountain in opposite directions, with the rope wrapping around and around that peak tighter and tighter, just like some Californio taking his dallies.

"So when the rope finally ran out we all—me and that horse and that steer—ended up clinging like spiders to a wall on the steep sides of that rocky peak wondering what to do next. Thing was, though, that rawhide rope was drying out fast, shrinking up around that mountain top and squeezing it tighter than a crib girl on payday. Before you know it, I'll be damned if that shrinking rope didn't pinch the top right off that great big mountain. Squoze it plumb off and sent that peak rolling down the mountainside busting into ever-smaller pieces until it was all gone. And that ain't no lie."

"Tully, you're so full of shit your eyes is brown!" one of the cowboys said.

"Doak," Tully replied, "have you ever seen Pike's Peak?"

"No, I ain't. What the hell's that got to do with it?"

"Any of you boys ever seen that mountain?" Tully asked.

"Hell yes, I seen it," Enos said.

"What's the top look like?" Tully asked.

"Well, it's just kind of bulgy and rounded, looks sort of smooth-like."

"It ain't all steep and jagged, with a big old pointy top?"

"No, Tully, it ain't."

"You see," Tully grinned. "It's just like I said!"

"Oh, B.S. Tully! That don't mean—"

"Doak!" McCarty interrupted. "Just shut up and let Tully tell his story. Go ahead on, Tully."

"So, anyways, while we was sitting up there, I noticed that all around us on that brand new mountaintop was these big yellow hunks of what looked to me to be pure gold. With the sun going down, it was all sparkly and shiny and flashing yellow light for miles in every direction," Tully said. "I'll tell you, it looked right pretty, glowing like that in the sunset, sending off all them golden rays.

"Well, I gathered up what I could stuff in my saddlebags then I sacked out for the night, figuring I'd ride down off that mountain come morning and see how and where to stake me a mining claim."

And Tully talked on.

"Thing was, though, when I opened my eyes there was prospectors everywhere, crawling all over that new Pike's un-Peak like flies on a pasture flapjack. And there was so many claim stakes sticking out of that mountain it looked like a porcupine. Fact is, it reminded me of that one time I got all shot full of arrows by the Commanches—but that's another story."

"Oh, dammit Tully, I ain't listening to another word of this!"

"What's the matter, Doak," Tully asked, "ain't you never heard of the Commanches?"

"No! I mean, yes! But that ain't what I'm talking about. I mean that other stuff, about the gold."

"Oh, I see. What you mean is, you ain't never heard of the Colorado Gold Rush."

"Of course I have!" Doak said.

"And didn't you ever hear that saying, 'Pike's Peak or Bust'?"

"Sure I did."

"See, Doak," Tully grinned. "It's just like I said!"

"Bullshit."

"Doak, Tully, you two stop your damn arguing," Enos said. "Doak, you shut up and let Tully tell his story. Tully, you shut up and talk."

"Well, okay then. Anyways, as I was saying, I got to talking to this one old prospector name of Sourdough Saleratus and he allowed as how all the good claims thereabouts was already taken. Too crowded for his taste, besides. But he said he knew of some promising terrain over in the Arizona Territory, and that if I'd use what gold I had gathered up there on Pike's Peak to grubstake us, he'd take me along and we'd be equal pards all the way, fifty-fifty.

"So I did and we did—we loaded up on supplies and such equipment as we'd need and me and old Sourdough Saleratus set out for Arizona Territory to strike it rich. That's some country thereabouts. Not much water to be found, and about the only thing that grows good is rocks. Why, there's whole mountains made out of one hunk of sandstone. And that ground's so hard I doubt a herd of stampeding elephants would leave a trail. But old Sourdough Saleratus got us through—or, I should say, got us to where we was heading, which wasn't through at all, but right out in the middle of all that desolation. And so we set in to prospecting."

And Tully talked on.

"I'll tell you boys, I never worked so hard in all my born days. I'd dig and dig and dig and that old man Sourdough Saleratus would wash and wash and wash. Then we'd start over again. Old Sourdough Saleratus seemed to know what he was looking for. He'd swish and he'd swish that pan and eyeball every speck of every shovel full I dug. Thing was, though, he never did see what he was looking for. We never found a trace of any minerals whatsoever. All me and Sourdough Saleratus got for all our work was a big damn hole in the ground. Hell, you can still see it, if you care to, and that ain't no lie. Any of you boys ever hear of the Grand Canyon?"

"Tully, damn you!" Doak said.

"Ain't you seen it, Doak?" Tully asked.

"No, I ain't seen it. And you ain't neither, if you ask me. I'll bet a dollar and a drink at the end of the trail that none of us has seen the Grand Canyon—including you, Tully."

"You lose, Doak—I done been to the Grand Canyon," McCarty said.

"Well, tell them what it looks like, then!" Tully said.

"Oh, it's big. That sucker stretches for miles. And not only is it long, it's deep. And it's got all these other canyons hooked into it, ever' one of 'em deeper than anything you ever saw. And if you look way, way down in the bottom from some places up there on the edge, you can see that there's a stream down there. Looks like a little bitty old creek, but they told me it's a big old river. Biggest damn hole I ever saw, that Grand Canyon."

"See, Doak, it's just like I said! Anyhow," Tully continued, "my old pardner Sourdough Saleratus finally decided the whole thing was a big bust and we was running low on supplies anyhow, so we headed back to Colorado. Boys, I'll tell you, you ain't never seen anything like it. While we was getting nothing but blisters and sore backs over there in Arizona, them miners in Colorado was striking it rich every time they turned over a rock. Seems like there was mines up and down the sides of every mountain in every canyon. And all that gold had sure drawn a crowd. Miners was thick as seeds in a chili pepper, scrambling around all over them slopes. Thing was, though, with all them miners showing up so sudden like, there hadn't been time for proper towns and conveniences to keep up, so there was a surplus of mouths to feed and a shortage of food to put in them."

And Tully talked on.

"Well, I got me an idea. A good one for a change, as it turned out. See, I still had that big old steer trailing along at the end of my lasso rope—he was pretty well broke to lead by then—and looking to me right then like nothing more than a sizzling stack of high-priced beefsteaks."

"Tully, that just can't be!" Doak hollered.

"Why Doak, I don't recall seeing you thereabouts," Tully replied. "Was you in the Colorado Rockies in them days?"

"No, of course not! But what's that got to do with it? There's no way that steer—"

"Doak, dammit, shut up! I want to hear the rest of Tully's story," McCarty said.

"Where was I?" Tully wondered. "Oh, yeah. Well, I figured to hold me a raffle and sell off that old steer at five dollars the ticket, which is just what I did. I had some advertising fliers printed up and went around to all the towns and camps thereabouts, inviting one and all to buy a chance at being the lucky winner. Hell, you can't even imagine how many folks ponied up! You'd have thought a whole damn herd—instead of just one old beef—was up for grabs the way them miners shelled out. They bought up them tickets faster than I could keep track of. I don't mind telling you boys, that critter fetched a pretty penny—more money than I had ever even imagined, let alone held in my hand."

"Well hell, Tully," Enos said. "I never had you pegged for a rich man."

"Yeah! If you're so damn rich how's come you're out here with us all, acting like a common saddle tramp?" Doak asked.

"Oh, I had that money in my hands, all right," Tully said. "Just like I told you, boys. Thing was, though, I didn't hang on to it too long."

Again, Tully let the silence stretch until McCarty snapped with the tension.

"C'mon! Tell us what happened, Tully!"

"You know, boys, ever since I was a little shaver, I always dreamed of owning me a spread. And now, by damn, I had the means to make that dream come true. So me and that old horse and all that money headed back down the trail to Texas, where I intended to become a cattle baron. I stopped off at the land office in this little town away out in West Texas and traded all that hard-earned cash for title to a million or two acres of wide-open spaces. I put every penny I had into land, see, on account of I figured I could chouse enough cattle out of the brasada to stock it, and round up enough wild horses to do the chousing."

And Tully talked on.

"I hired me a crew—a colorful bunch of characters, names of Jefferson and Nacho and Eagle Beak and Bok Choy—and we headed out to the ranch. We looked the place over, then looked it over again, finally deciding on the best location for a headquarters. We didn't even think about putting up a house—the most important thing being corrals and pens and paddocks and such to get us started in the cattle business.

"Punching post holes in that caliche was no small job, I'm here to tell you. Every hole we dug took a goodly amount of sweat, and we had a goodly number of post holes to dig. But me and Jefferson and Nacho and Eagle Beak and Bok Choy got it done.

"Thing was, though, we'd just bedded down for a good night's sleep after the day we dug the last post hole when the wind came up. Now, any of you boys as has been to West Texas don't need me to tell you how the wind can blow out there. It blowed and it blowed all the night long. Me and Jefferson and Nacho and Eagle Beak and Bok Choy huddled under the wagon the whole night through while that wind whipped around us, and I'll tell you we like to been sanded smooth from all the grit in the air. We was all spitting mud pies, for sure."

And Tully talked on.

"Come sunup, we scraped all the dirt and rocks out from under our eyelids and took a look around. I coulda cried. Fact is boys—and it don't shame me none to admit it—I did cry. Bawled like a newborn baby that's just been smacked on the backside. And you would have cried too, I daresay, if you saw what me and Jefferson and Nacho and Eagle Beak and Bok Choy saw. Thing was, see, when the sun went down I had been a budding cattle baron. When the sun came up, I seen that circumstances had once again placed me firmly among the penniless."

Some of the boys around the campfire that evening swear to this day that they saw Tully Prater wipe away a tear. Others hold that he was merely rubbing tired eyes, as the hour was late and the time for reasonable drovers to be asleep had long since passed. In any event, it took a few minutes for the man to collect himself and carry on with the story. This time, none of the boys doubted his word—at least out loud—or pushed him to proceed.

In his own good time, Tully talked on.

"You shoulda seen it boys. It was a sorry sight. My whole damn ranch had done gone and blown clean away in all that wind. I shit you not, every square inch of every acre of my cattle empire had up and relocated to somewheres down in Old Mexico. The whole damn ranch just peeled up and flew plumb away. The only piece of land left with my name on it was that little patch there under the wagon where me and Jefferson and Nacho and Eagle Beak and Bok Choy had huddled in the windstorm, where I guess we held it in place firmly enough to keep it from gusting off with the rest of the ranch.

"I'll tell you, it was so bad there wasn't even a trace of the place. Why, so much had blowed away that all them post holes me and Jefferson and Nacho and Eagle Beak and Bok Choy had dug down into the ground were now sticking up out of it! Every one of them, poking up all over the place as high as they used to be low!

"Well, having run plumb out of options, I hitched up the team and drove all around where my ranch headquarters was supposed to be while Jefferson and Nacho and Eagle Beak and Bok Choy cut off all them post holes at the bottom and stacked them in the wagon. Then we hauled that wagon load of post holes into town, where I sold them all to the storekeep. I convinced him that since they were brand new and in good shape, he wouldn't have much trouble shifting them to settlers coming into the area. Seeing as how I was in a fix, he also took the team and wagon and saddle horse off my hands.

"Thing was, though, every penny them post holes and my outfit brought was just barely enough to cover wages for Jefferson and Nacho and Eagle Beak and Bok Choy. And that left me with nothing to my name but the saddle on my shoulder.

"So there I was, walking down the road kicking horse turds when I run onto you all gathering up this herd. You boys know the rest."

PLAY DEAD OR DIE

Author, editor, and publisher Troy D. Smith put together an anthology of stories to benefit Stranding Stone American Indian Cultural Center in Monterey, Tennessee. Tales from Indian Country *includes my story "Play Dead or Die." While a work of fiction, it is based on the real-life experience of a young Shoshoni boy during the Bear River Massacre, the worst Indian killing by the United States Army in the history of the West.*

———— • ————

The icy ground burned Da-boo-zee's skin—his clothing offered little protection from the hard-frozen earth or the bitter wind blowing through the Shoshoni winter camp.

The place, that is, where the camp used to be.

Since the *toquashes*, the soldiers, showed up this morning his village had disappeared. Stains of many colors dirtied the snow. Black from ashes of burned lodges and scattered cooking fires. Purple from dried berries dumped and trampled. Brown mud from marching boots and fleeing moccasins.

And red.

Everywhere, red; the spilled blood of his people smeared the snow along the banks of Bear River.

Da-boo-zee had trouble keeping his eyes closed—even though his grandmother told him he must pretend to be dead. But the wind stung, the smoke burned. And, for curiosity's sake, he just couldn't help peeking.

———— • ————

The army attacked before sunrise, splashing across the icy river and charging across the snow. The Shoshoni men fought bravely, turning back the first attack and killing more than a dozen soldiers. The camp was

23

a good place for a fight, tucked into a shallow ravine where Beaver Creek came out of the hills and meandered to the river. Willows lined the steep sides, offering protection from the wind—and from attacking soldiers.

It was a favorite place for The People to spend the winter. There was water aplenty, and fish in the river. The children slid down the snowy hillsides for fun, riding sleds of stiff rawhide from deer, elk, and buffalo. They played stickball and chase games on the pastures where hundreds of Shoshoni horses grazed. There was good hunting—at least there had been before the white settlers came. And the villagers liked to soak in steamy hot springs near the village.

It was a peaceful life. Mostly, the Shoshoni got along with the thousands of white people traveling through their land, and with the hundreds of settlers who came and stayed. But there had been clashes, and people on both sides had been killed. Just a few weeks ago, Shoshoni men from another band killed a white man near Da-boo-zee's village. The soldiers had come from their fort near Salt Lake City to get revenge.

And, Da-boo-zee could see, each time he stole a glance, they had gotten it.

———•———

For weeks, The People had been celebrating a Warm Dance to send winter away and bring better weather. Hundreds of Shoshoni from other bands had come, feasting, playing games, and enjoying one another's company.

But the killing of the white man spoiled the fun and many fled in fear. When a tribal elder dreamed that soldiers would come and kill The People, others went away.

The leaders of Da-boo-zee's band believed they could make peace with the soldiers. But other men wanted to fight and prepared for war.

At fourteen, Da-boo-zee was too young to be a warrior, although his uncles had already taught him to use the bow and arrow, to fight from horseback, even to shoot the few long guns the band owned. But his bravery and courage were yet untested, and it would take time and experience to be welcomed into the warrior ranks.

So, when the soldiers attacked this morning, Da-boo-zee stayed in the village, running from lodge to lodge awakening people and urging them to take shelter in the willows and brush, or escape up the hills. But it was cold—below zero—and windy. And there was little time.

"Hurry, you must get away!" he shouted to frightened women and children huddled in their lodges. They struggled out of warm robes and dashed into the cold winter morning, only to be cut down by bullets buzzing through the air like angry hornets.

The women and children milled in confusion, Da-boo-zee and others urging them on. But everywhere they turned there were soldiers, firing down at them from the hills, or standing on the banks of the ravine, shooting into the village.

The Shoshoni fighters used up most of their ammunition fending off the first attack. After that, it was bows and arrows and tomahawks against guns.

Soldiers surrounded the camp and pressed in, pushing the Shoshoni one way then the other. Some soldiers kept their rifles, using bayonets when frozen fingers could no longer reload the guns. Others threw rifles aside and drew revolvers, shooting down everyone they saw with shot after shot after shot.

With nowhere to turn, bewildered Shoshoni swarmed in confusion, looking for any avenue of escape. They were shot down trying to climb the steep hills. They were shot down hiding in the willows. They were shot down crossing the river, or hiding in the water under its banks. Bodies floated downstream, blood turning the water red.

Da-boo-zee's older brother tried to rescue his wife by pulling her up onto his horse and riding for the hills. But a bullet from an army rifle struck between her shoulder blades and she fell from the horse, dead.

Sagwitch, Da-boo-zee's father and one of the chiefs, was wounded. Twice he tried to ride away, only to have his horses shot. He finally escaped across the river when another man gave him his mount, then held onto the horse's tail to be towed to safety himself.

Other members of Da-boo-zee's family were also shot—some killed. The bodies of aunts and uncles, cousins, friends, littered the ground. Women, children, even babies had been slaughtered. Chief Bear Hunter had been beaten, whipped, and shot, then killed by a bayonet heated in the flames of a burning lodge and shoved in one ear and out the other.

Da-boo-zee himself was wounded. Blood from his shoulder, torn by a bullet, stained the front of his buckskin shirt and was frozen stiff and hard against his skin.

Old men, children, mothers carrying babies, cried out in surrender but their cries were ignored. In many places on the battlefield, you could not take a step without stepping on one of the fallen People.

———— ♦ ————

"We will lie here, among the dead," his grandmother said. "Do not move. Do not open your eyes. When you hear the soldiers near, do not even breathe. Do this, or you will die."

And so he lay on the frozen ground, as still as he could. He did not know how many of The People lying near him still lived. He heard wailing and crying, howls and whimpers—but with each gunshot, another voice fell silent as the soldiers killed everyone they found alive.

"Stay still, Da-boo-zee," his grandmother whispered when discomfort caused him to stir. Then a shot was fired and he heard her no more.

A soldier's boots came squishing and squeaking through the mud and snow and a shadow fell across Da-boo-zee's face. When he could stand it no longer, the boy opened his eyes. All he could see was the barrel of a gun, inches away and pointed at his face. He closed his eyes, expecting a blast of gunpowder to be the last sound he heard on earth.

But no shot was fired.

Again, he opened his eyes and the soldier standing above him came into focus. The man raised his weapon, again aiming at the boy's head. Again Da-boo-zee closed his eyes.

Still, there was no shot.

He opened his eyes a third time, and again the soldier aimed the revolver at him.

"This will be it," Da-boo-zee thought as again his eyes fell shut. "Now I will die."

He did not flinch. He did not cry. He did not beg. He did not run. "If I must die," Da-boo-zee thought, "I will die like a brave Sho-shoni warrior."

And so he waited.

After what seemed an eternity, the soldier walked away. The reason for his mercy can only be guessed at, for few of his comrades showed any that day. They killed some 300 of Da-boo-zee's people. The small number who lived were left to die in the cold without food or shelter. The soldiers even stole their horses and drove them away to Salt Lake City.

Da-boo-zee gathered that night with other survivors around a warming fire on the bluffs above the river bottom and the destroyed village. He lived for many more years, becoming a chief and respected elder among the Shoshoni. He never stopped telling the story of the miracle of his life and the massacre at Bear River.

"The People," he would tell the children, "must never forget."

NO LUCK AT ALL

When "No Luck at All" appeared in the 2006 Berkley anthology Texas Rangers, *edited by Ed Gorman and Martin H. Greenberg, it drew an angry e-mail from a reader. Unhappy with the ending, he asked, "Doesn't the reader deserve a more fitting and satisfying conclusion to the story?" I could only answer with a quotation from Ecclesiastes: "The race is not to the swift, nor the battle to the strong . . . nor yet favour to men of skill; but time and chance happeneth to them all."*

———•———

"Get them boots."

Responding to the mumbled command, one of the dismounted killers tugged the boots off the body while the other piled loot—a rifle, a brace of pistols, odds and ends of clothing and camp gear—onto the pack mule.

The leader sat astride his pale horse above the bloody destruction and studied the worn badge in his hand. With the ball of his thumb he rubbed off a fine layer of dust and read the words TEXAS RANGER before tucking it into a vest pocket.

As the corpse cooled in the desert heat, the plunderers turned their attention to stripping the tack off the dead horse. Less than a week had passed since the horse and rider came into the country, sent to exterminate this swarm of locusts who picked clean everything in their path.

———•———

"Near as we can tell, there's just three of them. But they don't leave anything in the way of witnesses," the sheriff told the Ranger. "By the time they ride off, there's hardly a thing left for the coyotes and vultures, let alone anything in the way of explanation. We don't know who they are. Or where they came from.

"There's a lot of empty land around here and folks is spread so far and wide that no one ever sees them, only what they've done—and then not until it's too late to do any good. But they've been killing and robbing on both sides of the border since springtime. Now and then, some of their plunder turns up in shops down in the border towns, usually brought in by Indians for barter. But nobody believes these killers is Indians—too savage, even for them. Most likely they themselves got the stuff in trade from the thieves."

The Ranger sat quiet, letting the sheriff lay out his tale. He suspected the man was more interested in talking about the bandits than tracking them down. A hotel dining-room table separated the two. It is hard to say whose jaws were working harder—the Ranger, enjoying his first hot meal in days, or the lawman, talking.

A pounding on the door in the middle of one night is what started the sheriff's story. A scared muleskinner had left his teams and freight wagons in the street to report a bloody mess on the trail into town. The sheriff gathered a posse and got there in the early morning, but it was clear they were about a day late to do the family any good.

The Mexican family, it appeared, was on the way to market to trade loads in a donkey cart when set upon. Dried chilies were trampled in the dust and beans and corn were strewn about.

The people had fared no better than their goods. The man and his wife were tangled together in a bloody heap, stripped of their clothing with throats cut. Each was punctured with numerous stab wounds, and from the mutilation of the young woman, the sickened posse imagined unspeakable atrocities she must have suffered before being dumped in a pile with her husband.

But their greatest horror was for the child.

Little more than a baby and of a sex now indeterminable, it was tied to the wheel of the cart—hung there as a target for knife-throwing practice. They could imagine the steel spinning toward its mark; almost hear the blades repeatedly striking home. What they could not imagine was the why. A mere child. A baby. Of an age and innocence that could not possibly have given offense. What manner of men were these?

The only shot fired there had been the one that blew a hind leg off the donkey. Still harnessed to the cart, it appeared to have bled slowly to death, hobbling in circles hauling its grisly load until falling dead in the shafts.

Coyotes had visited in the night, and the destructive work of flies was well on its way. Buzzards wheeled overhead, patiently waiting their turn.

The sheriff and his helpers hoped to end the desecration by burying the family in a common grave deep enough to discourage scavengers; the donkey's carcass left where it lay as a distraction.

Meanwhile, the best tracker from the posse cast about for a trail to follow, but any trace of the killers was indecipherable, as they looked to have come and gone along the same road as their victims, the freighters, and any number of others since rain had last erased the road.

"There's no telling even which way they went, Sheriff," the tracker reported. "But it looks as if there were three of them, from the footprints around the bodies. I'd guess they had three, maybe four horses. And a mule for sure."

"Pack animal," suggested another posse rider. "For hauling off their plunder. Who knows what they stole from these Mexican farmers. Probably everything they'd been able to scratch out of the dirt all this year."

"Hmmmph," the sheriff grunted. "Wouldn't be none too difficult to find somebody more worth robbing than these poor souls were."

"They did this just for sport," someone suggested as the posse started the slow ride home.

———— ◆ ————

"I've got to be honest with you," the sheriff told the Ranger, bringing his tale to an end. "I'm not entirely sorry we couldn't find a trail to follow. I'm not sure I'd want to meet up with that bunch."

The sheriff told the Ranger other stories of the destruction the killers had spread across the land, stories other lawmen had told him and reports he'd heard through the grapevine: of a ranch hand shot and stripped and tied to his horse's tail to drag for days; a family of homesteaders stewing in a stock tank, their shack burned and animals slaughtered; the town marshal who went hunting them and ended up dead and dangling with his hide peeled, hung head down from a cottonwood tree in a river bottom; the old Indian staked out naked to die slow in the sun; the two Mexican soldiers found hacked to pieces and impaled to scrub trees on their own swords . . . .

There were others. The marauders cared not who their victims were. It seemed no one who crossed their path survived the encounter. As a result, they were not concerned with stealth or subterfuge. They rode where and when they pleased and killed at will. The only consistency was the thievery.

"Like I said, where that stuff ends up is anybody's guess. Little bits of it shows up now and again amongst traders and shopkeepers, but the trail that it took to get there is a tangled one—a swap here, some barter there, and it's changed hands a time or two 'fore anyone recognizes it for what it is. It seems most of it comes through the Indians, but they won't say how or when or even if they laid hands on it.

"My guess is these bandits steal for the hell of it, carrying off anything they think they can get shed of easy. Then they burn or ruin what they don't want, destroying it for entertainment. But, if you was to ask me, I'd say it's the lives they're after. Leastways they've yet to not take one when they had the chance, far as I can learn."

That thought laid there on the table between them for a quiet moment until the sheriff spoke again.

"Well sir, I sure am glad they saw fit to send a Ranger out here to deal with this. If there's anything more I can do to help—anything at all—don't hesitate to call on me. It's getting late and I guess I better be making my rounds. And I suppose you're wanting to hit the hay so as you can get an early start hunting those varmints down," the sheriff said as he rose from his seat. "Finding them out there in all that empty ain't going to be easy, but maybe you'll get lucky."

Later, up in his room, the Ranger allowed to himself that luck would have little to do with it. Leastways that was his experience. It was more a matter of work, and now was as good a time as any to get to it. He retrieved his saddlebags from where they hung over the back of a chair and found in them a stub of a pencil and a folded piece of foolscap, which he smoothed out and studied.

On the paper was a hand-drawn map of the country thereabouts, one he had sketched from memory of earlier visits. He had no illusions about its accuracy for scale or detail, but was confident that the relationships among major features—mountains, canyons, passes, streams, roads, main trails, and such—were essentially correct.

Sprinkled around the map were a number of Xs, where, according to the reports he had been given when he took on this assignment, the men he was after had committed their foul deeds. Next to each X was scribbled the approximate date the incident had occurred. He pored over the map, dragged the pencil lead across his tongue thoughtfully, and added a couple more Xs and dates based on what the sheriff had told him.

The marks on the map appeared to be distributed pretty much at random. The only obvious pattern the Ranger could see was that the gang avoided the scattered towns and villages, attacking only in out-of-the way places. Thinking he could link some of the incidents by time, he drew lines connecting the sites according to proximate dates. Although widely separated by both distance and time, the crime scenes did tie together somewhat as a result of the exercise.

He learned that the killers tended to zigzag through the country, wandering across low mountain ranges or onto neighboring drainages between strikes, always working more or less toward the Indian lands and the border. This seemed sensible for the bandits, he thought, keeping them several steps ahead of detection and allowing them to increase their load of loot as they neared the tribes and the border traders where they could market the goods.

But he believed, as the sheriff did, that the money derived from the thievery was but a sideline for this bunch. There were easier ways, quicker too, to load up on plunder for profit. No, it wasn't money that drove them. It was blood lust, pure and simple. Something in these men was twisted like discarded fence wire to where they took satisfaction, pleasure even, in cruelty and killing.

The loose pattern he discerned in the scratches on the map suggested that if he headed west and a little south and over the mountains toward the river on the next broad plain, he would be closer to his quarry.

Just how close, he could not know.

———— ◆ ————

After a few hours of restless sleep and a tasteless breakfast, the Ranger headed for the livery stable.

"Morning to you," said the hostler. "Yours must be that white gelding that came in late yesterday. My partner said you'd be along early. Well, your horse is fed and watered. I gave his feet a look-see. Whoever tacked on those new shoes did a fine job. He's ready and waiting for the saddle in that third stall there. A man's lucky to have a horse like that."

As the Ranger rode out of town, the day was starting on a small ranch some forty miles west of there. The place was tucked into a bend of the river where the extra moisture supported enough acres of grass to keep a small herd of scrub cattle alive. Away from the water, feed was scarce so the nearest neighbors were about five miles away up- and downstream. Only the man and his wife were left to work the ranch—their children grown and gone—and, in fact, the two of them were about all the place could sustain.

Watching the sun rise over the far horizon, the woman made her way to the small barn, milk bucket in hand, while her husband of forty-three years walked toward the pasture to check his bunch of spindly cows.

From the lows bluffs above, three mounted men looked on.

"Damn!" said the one on the black horse through a snaggle-toothed grin. "Them folks down there, their luck has plumb run out. But us—well boys, we're in luck."

Silence returned as they studied the layout. Then the leader of the band offered his opinion.

"Luck ain't got nothing to do with it," he said. "Any man that puts his trust in luck is a fool." With a cluck of his tongue and a lazy poke of spurred heels into his mount's belly, he started down the trail toward the ramshackle homestead.

Luck, he thought. Do these dolts believe luck has anything to do with keeping them living high instead of swinging from the end of rope? He hacked a gob of yesterday's trail dust from his throat, leaned out over the horse's shoulder and spat on the ground, figuring that if these idiots that had thrown in their lot with his believed luck was involved, they were dumber than he thought.

Slowly, even casually, the horsemen made their way down to the river bottom and rode into the trampled hardpan yard among the few tumbledown buildings.

"Go get him," the leader muttered, lifting his chin in the direction of the rancher walking the pasture. The rider on the big sorrel turned and rode off on the errand. The third man dismounted, tied his black and the pack mule to a fence rail and walked to the barn.

Inside, unaware, the woman leaned her forehead into the cow's flank squeezing streams of milk into the pail, lulled by the rhythmic squirts.

The marauder grabbed her by the shoulder and flung her across the milking stall and into the wall. She did not even have time to scream before his booted foot landed in her ribs, forcing her breath away. With a smile, he picked up the pail, stuck his face inside, tipped back and drank deeply of the warm, foamy milk.

Outside, the other rider drove her husband back toward the yard, urging him along with a stock whip as he stumbled along sucking wind and struggling to keep his feet. They stopped near the waiting leader, still sitting his horse so calm and quiet you could imagine him dozing off.

The rancher, worried and frightened, fought for air as he asked "What do you want? Where's my woman?"

The man who had driven him in laughed maniacally and popped the back of the old man's head yet again with the stinging lash of the whip.

The leader did not respond or even react.

"What is it? What do you want?" the rancher cried, nearing hysteria.

This time, the leader answered: from beneath his black duster he raised a shotgun and let go with a blast to the man's belly. The load of shot crashed the old nester into the corral fence. Tangled in the rails, he hung there helpless and witnessed the wasting of his life's work as he slowly, slowly bled out.

Meantime, having drunk his fill, the raider in the barn swung the bucket by its bail until it stopped suddenly against the woman's head. He slit the cow's throat, watched the hot blood spill and puddle onto the packed dirt floor. As the cow weakened and dropped to its knees, he dragged the woman outside. Dropping her in the dust and landing another kick in the ribs for good measure, he made his way to the house.

As he threw pots, pans, trunks, boxes, clothing and anything else he laid his hand to out through the door and windows, his partner with the stock whip entertained himself chasing chickens and popping off their heads with a snap of the lash.

After amusing themselves for more than an hour with plunder, torture, and, eventually, the murder of the old woman, the three piled their pick of the spoils atop the laden mule.

Figuring the smoke plumes would soon enough bring neighbors nosing around, the killers rode out of the haze and stink of the ruined ranch, splashing through the shallow water of the slow river, across the flood plain, up the eroded escarpment, and onto the empty desert.

With the riders on the sorrel and black horses behind and the pack mule bringing up the rear, the man in the black duster set a course a little south of east.

He figured to top the low range of distant mountains and follow an easy, narrow canyon he knew of down the other side. By the middle of the morning, he reckoned, they'd take to ground somewhere in the hills off the canyon while he mulled over where to strike next, after which they would call this trip good and ride southwest again, back into the Indian country and no-man's land along the border to relax for a spell.

If things got too boring, he could always slaughter himself a savage or two.

———— • ————

The Ranger chewed over his situation along with a hunk of jerky. After the day's ride, he had camped on a rise, just out of sight of a trail he had followed up a ravine that had become a canyon as the hills rose around it. Soon, he'd ride the rest of the way up that canyon. Soon. But not just yet.

That sheriff back there wasn't a coward, he decided—nor were his cohorts in the towns roundabout. He—and the others—did a passable job dealing with criminals and lawbreakers. But fighting evil like this was something else again. The perpetrators of this reckless thievery, this wanton destruction, this wholesale slaughter were beyond understanding, let alone facing. Even he had not wanted the job. When the assignment came down, he told the captain he could not do it, that it was too much for one man.

"You're right," the captain answered. "But we ain't sending a man. We're sending a Ranger."

Still, the Ranger tried to beg off, claiming he was not up to it. But the captain was having none of it.

"Look, you're the best Ranger I've got. You were the best I had when we started this outfit, and you're still the best," he said. "Not to mention lucky."

But the Ranger didn't believe in luck. Nor did he view his performance as a Ranger as anything out of the ordinary. He had backed down his share of bad men over the years, sure, and rid the country of assorted vermin from time to time. In the process he had attracted a few admirers among the folk he worked for and with, even though he had never sought glory for himself.

Facing danger was part of a Ranger's job, and so was risking your life to save lives—but the wickedness he was expected to overcome this time was more than he cared to deal with. At his age, he figured his Rangering years were about used up. And his luck—if there was such a thing—was likely about used up too.

"You're nowhere near used up," the captain argued. "Even if you was, these thieves and butchers don't know it. They're likely to quit the country soon as they know you're after them. And they wouldn't be the first bad guys to do just that."

In the end the Ranger agreed, if reluctantly, to take on the task. Still, he could not help thinking these were not ordinary bad men he was sent to overcome. Ordinary men—bad or otherwise—would not—could not—do what these scapegraces did with seeming abandon. He feared there was not enough blood in the three of these murderers to atone for all the innocent blood they had shed. Even his own blood may be shed—should it come to that—in payment for their sins. And, though he accepted that risk as part and parcel of being a Ranger, he did not relish the thought.

As he sat mulling it all over and watching the sun rise, he heard someone coming long before he could see them. There was a faint, curious tinkling and clanking of metal coming down the trail he meant to go up. He smothered the small fire and crept to a place where he could watch unseen.

The three horseman he saw looked ordinary enough, if dirty and disheveled and run down. But the pack mule in tow, the source of all the noise, was something to see. More than anything, it reminded him of a walking medicine show. As the parade drew nearer, the colorful banners and clanging bells that made up the mule's precarious load became bundles of clothing and boxes and bags and pots and pans dangling at all angles from the pack saddle. Rifles sprouted from the pile like bagpipes.

The Ranger knew he had found what he'd come looking for.

———— • ————

The killers were well down the canyon when dawn broke. The leader rubbed the itch out of his eyes with balled fists, an itch that grew worse with the climbing sun. He knew the other men had been asleep more than they had been awake for more than a few miles, and even the horses stumbled with fatigue now and then. But he fought to keep his eyes open, wanting to make a few more miles before hiding out for the day.

Had he not been so determined to stay alert, he would not have noticed the hoofprints on the dusty trail where there hadn't been any before. That meant a lone rider on the way up the canyon had left the trail not far from here. A shod horse, so it was no Indian—a white man, probably, Mexican, maybe. Whoever it was didn't want to be seen any more than they did. He'd have to pay attention to the back trail now, in case whoever was out there took a notion to follow them rather than continue up the canyon.

Soon enough, the hairs in the small of his back started tingling and he knew they were being followed.

He liked to have worn out his neck craning around trying to get a glimpse of whoever was back there, but whoever it was was no dummy.

The man trailing them never revealed himself, hanging back around every turn until he could ride on unobserved. Well, the man in the black duster thought, he's up to something. Hatching a plan.

We'll just see if his plan works out.

———————◆———————

Allowing the horsemen to get a good ways up the trail, the Ranger drank the dregs of his bitter morning coffee, bundled up the last of his camp, and rode off in slow pursuit, formulating a plan of attack. He stayed nearby but out of sight for an hour or more, relying on the noise of the jangly pack mule to cover his hoofbeats.

Then, edging around an outcrop, he saw only two riders ahead—mounted on the sorrel and the black—and knew he would never carry out his plan. He felt the tremor from the bullet that hit his horse at the same instant he heard the thwack of lead pounding flesh, followed instantly by a rifle's report. As the horse buckled beneath him, he swung from the saddle and felt the scorpion sting of the bullet that killed him.

———————◆———————

The two scavengers picked the horse clean, pilfering the saddle bags and bedroll, adding even the saddle to the spoils atop the mule. Noting that the horse was recently shod, one asked the mounted leader if he should pry the new shoes loose to add to the plunder.

"Nah," he mumbled. "It's bad luck to pull the shoes off a dead horse."

AFTER THE BURNT BISCUITS

Fans of cowboy poetry are familiar with the Henry Herbert Knibbs classic "Boomer Johnson," in which a surly cook meets his doom. But what happened afterward? "After the Burnt Biscuits" is my imagined continuation of the tale. The poem is included as a prologue to set the stage. This story was published online in 2007 as part of Amazon's short-lived Amazon Shorts program.

———◆———

BOOMER JOHNSON
By Henry Herbert Knibbs

Now Mr. Boomer Johnson was a gettin' old in spots,
But you don't expect a bad man to go wrastlin' pans and pots;
But he'd done his share of killin' and his draw was gettin' slow,
So he quits a-punchin' cattle and he takes to punchin' dough.

Our foreman up and hires him, figurin' age had rode him tame,
But a snake don't get no sweeter just by changin' of its name.
Well, Old Boomer knowed his business—
he could cook to make you smile,
But say, he wrangled fodder in a most peculiar style.

He never used no matches—left 'em layin' on the shelf,
Just some kerosene and cussin' and the kindlin' lit itself.
And, pardner, I'm allowin' it would give a man a jolt
To see him stir frijoles with the barrel of his Colt.

Now killin' folks and cookin' ain't so awful far apart,
That musta been why Boomer kept a-practicin' his art;

37

With the front sight of his pistol he would cut a pie-lid slick,
And he'd crimp her with the muzzle for to make the edges stick.

He built his doughnuts solid, and it sure would curl your hair
To see him plug a doughnut as he tossed it in the air.
He bored the holes plum center every time his pistol spoke,
Till the can was full of doughnuts and the shack was full of smoke.

We-all was gettin' jumpy, but he couldn't understand
Why his shootin' made us nervous when his cookin' was so grand.
He kept right on performin', and it weren't no big surprise
When he took to markin' tombstones on the covers of his pies.

They didn't taste no better and they didn't taste no worse,
But a-settin' at the table was like ridin' in a hearse;
You didn't do no talkin' and you took just what you got,
So we et till we was foundered just to keep from gettin' shot.

When at breakfast one bright mornin', I was feelin' kind of low,
Old Boomer passed the doughnuts and I tells him plenty:
"No, All I takes this trip is coffee, for my stomach is a wreck."
I could see the itch for killin' swell the wattle on his neck.

Scorn his grub? He strings some doughnuts on the muzzle of his gun,
And he shoves her in my gizzard and he says, "You're takin' one!"
He was set to start a graveyard, but for once he was mistook;
Me not wantin' any doughnuts, I just up and salts the cook.

Did they fire him? Listen, pardner, there was nothin' left to fire,
Just a row of smilin' faces and another cook to hire.
If he joined some other outfit and is cookin', what I mean,
It's where they ain't no matches and they don't need kerosene.

----•----

First off, I've got to say that this situation has gotten entirely out of hand.
The cattle have wandered off and scattered from hell to breakfast on
account of all the cowboys quitting. So the calves are unbranded and

there's a whole summer of cow work lined up and no hands left to do it, which will have the boss all in a dither as you might imagine. On top of all that, the law is on the way here to conduct an investigation into the killing.

None of it had to happen. I can think of any number of ways it might have been different. With a timely firing the boss could have avoided this mess. The cook didn't have to threaten me in the matter of the doughnuts. The cowboys could have just peeled the black bottoms off the biscuits and made the best of it. A little patience all the way around would have gone a long ways. But none of that happened and so here we are.

Now, I admit that some of the blame rightly falls to me. For the killing, sure. And that, I guess, did set off all the other events, so I suppose I have to accept a share of the blame for those, too. But not all of it. Like as I said, others could have stepped in but didn't. Others could have reacted differently and didn't. Of course none of that changes anything and here I am.

I see that this tale is getting as twisted and tangled as a greenhorn's catch rope so just let me back off here for a minute and try to sort things out. Maybe if I just start at the beginning and lay out the whole affair you'll see that it isn't all my fault and that the batch of burned biscuits that got everyone and everything so stirred up wasn't really all that big a deal and, given the circumstances, maybe even bound to happen.

It all started this morning when I woke up feeling a little soft in the middle due to my ill-advised activities last night. Me and some of the boys had been to town and I confess I drank more rye whiskey than I ought to have and didn't get my usual ration of sleep on account of the lateness of the hour of our return.

Be that as it may, the sun still seemed unusually bright this morning and my eyes were not in the mood for all that damn shining. My hat felt like it had shrunk two sizes and liked to squeezed the top of my head plumb off. I can't describe the inside of my mouth except to deny having eaten or drank anything that tasted anywhere near that bad.

Now there ain't no way I could feel that bad on the inside without it showing on the outside, which should have alerted cookie to ride a wide circle around me. But that sort of compassion just wasn't in Mr. Boomer Johnson's nature, and that lack is what killed him.

Boomer Johnson, you see, was this old stove-up pistolero and cowpuncher who took up punching dough in his declining years. I am not the only hand on the outfit to have had a run in with the man. We all did. He should have been sent down the road kicking horse turds long ago and if he had of been, the cows never would have wandered off and we wouldn't be in this fix. But I am getting ahead of myself again.

Anyway, if the boss would have fired Boomer Johnson and hired a new cook, no one would have shed a tear. In fact, the crew likely would have raised a rousing cheer and tossed their Stetsons in the air in exuberance.

The fact is, though, the boss feared—rightly so, most likely—that firing the man would lead to a violent altercation due to Boomer's all-around nasty attitude. His habit of marking pies and stirring frijoles with his pistol barrel was part of it. And shooting holes in his doughnuts rather than taking a more traditional approach helped keep us buffaloed. Come to think of it, as often as he threatened to, Boomer never actually shot anyone so maybe it was all just bluff and bluster.

But, like as I said, I was not in the mood for any of it this morning. So after waiting my turn in the grub line I refused Boomer Johnson's offer of a doughnut and said, "No, all I takes this trip is coffee, for my stomach is a wreck."

I tell you it got so quiet about then I could hear the steam rising off my coffee. While the other cowboys looked on, Boomer threaded a handful of them doughnuts over the barrel of his smoke pole and shoved it—rather more forcefully than necessary, I might add—into my gizzard.

"You're takin' one," he says.

I let Mr. Colt make my reply. Right there in front of God and everybody, I pulled my Colt's Single Action Army Model 1873 revolver out of its holster sudden-like and shot him dead.

Of course I assume full responsibility for the death of Mr. Boomer Johnson, and will admit as much once the law arrives to conduct its investigations. Of that there can be no question. I will, of course, claim self-defense or at least mitigating circumstances. Unfortunately, all my witnesses rode away when the cowboys quit, and given the unfortunate incident with the biscuits I don't know if they would come to my defense anyway. But I am getting ahead of myself again.

Once the smoke cleared, I could see the crew all sitting there with their jaws dangling down like a bunch of adolescent boys at a girly show. No one said anything, shocked into silence as they were. All eyes were locked on the corpse of Boomer Johnson. As if on cue, all eyes shifted to stare at me. After a few eternal seconds, every one of them blinked, seemingly in unison, and dove back into their breakfasts as if nothing had happened.

Realizing the gravity of the situation and recognizing my need to be accountable for my actions, I sent the young Mexican lad who served as cook's helper to fetch the boss and told him, "Don't spare the horses." That last was meant metaphorically, of course, as the house was no more than fifty yards from the bunkhouse and cook shack. But I wanted the boy, as well as my cowboy compatriots, to realize that I was aware of the seriousness of the event and was not attempting to deny my culpability or cover up what had happened.

The boss quickly assessed the situation and wasted no time in outlining a course of action. Not a wise course, as it turned out, but you have to give the man credit for his decisiveness.

"Well, cowboy," he told me, "until we get a new cook hired around here you're it. I'm riding into town to fetch the law. One of you throw a wagon sheet over Boomer there to keep the flies off. The rest of you get to work and get them pairs gathered. We got branding to do."

I didn't protest at the time, and I guess you can call me an idiot for that. Or a damn fool, if you'd rather. Either would be an appropriate description. I am, after all, untrained in the culinary arts. I am a cowboy, fully schooled and well experienced in the ways and means of tending livestock on the range or in the pen. In the heat of the moment, I neglected to mention that the only thing I know about food is how to eat it. But as I watched my saddle pals ride out on the morning to gather the herd the hopelessness of my situation hit home.

There I was, expected to prepare supper for half a dozen cowhands, hungry from a day riding circle through sagebrush and sand, alkali and saltgrass, cedar trees and tumbleweeds. It's a hot and sweaty job that works up a healthy thirst and a hearty appetite. Speaking for myself, there have been days I was hungry enough after a gather to eat the rear end of a skunk, without salt.

So you can appreciate my situation and understand, perhaps, that the biscuit incident was only the result of my attempting to make the best of my untenable circumstance. And while it was I, and I alone, who actually burned the biscuits I believe there is blame enough to go around.

As for the cattle now scattered from Dan to Beersheba and the unbranded calves, I am willing to share the blame even though I, myself, did not light a shuck over a matter so trivial as a slight blackening at the base of a batch of baked sourdough. (Well, the blackening was not all that slight, to be perfectly honest.)

Here's what happened next. Not exactly what should have happened, or what I hoped would happen, but what happened despite my best intentions. The boy and I gathered up the breakfast dishes, including a considerable heap of pots and pans from the cook shack and from around the fire, and dumped them into a tub of water with a generous portion of lye soap and swabbed them out good.

That was my first of many screw-ups. How was I know that you don't wash a Dutch oven or a cast-iron frypan? They looked to me like they needed a good scrubbing, coated with baked-on grease and blackened by smoke like they were. In his defense, I should say that the boy tried to stop me. But I figured the kid had picked up the former cook's unsanitary habits and so I paid him no mind. Yet another in my long line of mistakes, but at least I am willing to admit it.

Afterward, the boy retired to the shade of a lonely cottonwood tree to practice trick and fancy roping while I entered the cook shack to contemplate my next move. "Shack" is an apt name, the facility being nothing more than a ten-foot square assemblage of posts and boards lashed and tacked together in a haphazard fashion. The structure contained a hole where a door ought to hang, but no windows. So it was poorly illuminated in a way that reminded me of a speckled longhorn hide—mostly dark, but mottled with patches of light of various sizes and shapes where sunshine leaked in through the gaps between wall boards and roof shingles.

Perched in the middle of the dirt floor was a cobbled-together table. Another of similar size was shoved up against the far wall, its top hidden under a heap of cooking tools, empty cans and boxes, and a jumble of dirty aprons and soiled dish towels. Against the wall to the right was a cabinet-type affair with open shelves and a couple of drawers in the middle and some doors below. Cans and bottles and boxes of all shapes and sizes littered the shelves. A sorry-looking sheep dog lay curled up against the other wall, dangerously underneath a rickety shelf covered with yet another mess of food-related containers. And that sums up the contents of the "kitchen."

Although Boomer Johnson had accomplished the task twice every day, I couldn't imagine how anyone could whip up vittles for half a dozen hungry cowboys in such circumstances. Nevertheless, I have never been one to shirk my duty regardless of the consequences. Of course had I foreseen said consequences I might have just said to hell with it and rode away.

THE DEATH OF DELGADO

A pot of frijoles was stewing over the fire outside, as it always was, so I knew one menu item was already taken care of. Beneath a fly-specked cloth on the center table was a hunk of meat clinging to what was left of the hind leg of a cow. I figured when the time came I could whittle off some slabs of that and toss them in a frypan. I rummaged around on the shelves and came up with enough canned tomatoes to go around. I had no intention of attempting a dessert. So far, supper looked simple enough—a little stirring, a little slicing, prying the lids off a few cans.

Still, there was the problem of biscuits. My ignorance of the process of whipping up a batch of sinkers was near total, so I tidied up the cook shack while I contemplated it. The house cleaning, as it turned out, saved the day. Or sent it spiraling out of control, depending on how you look at it. But the thing was this: while blowing the dust off various containers and arranging items on the shelf, I discovered Boomer Johnson's recipe for biscuits.

Please do not get the impression that the nature of my discovery was obvious. No. Like everything else associated with these unfortunate events, determining what I held in my hand was a convoluted and confusing process.

The item in question was written, and I use the word loosely, on a cardboard box that once contained powdered alum. I assume it was written in Mr. Boomer Johnson's hand. The letterforms were so crude and misshapen that they appeared to have been sketched out painfully by a pencil held between the toes of the left foot. The beginning strokes of certain letters were darkened, as if the scribe had periodically dragged the lead of the pencil across the moist surface of his tongue.

But that is neither here nor there.

With supper time drawing ever nearer, and along with it the pivotal incident in this sad tale, I figured now was as good a time as any to acquaint myself with the subtleties of biscuit mixing and baking. Cowboys, after all, expect biscuits with their beef and beans (and canned tomatoes, in this case).

The recipe was written, according to the common convention, in two sections: a list of ingredients and their quantities, followed by a brief (and in this case, downright cryptic) narrative description of assembly and cooking.

As I translated each ingredient, I located the items on the various shelves and in the dim cubbyholes of the kitchen. "Flour," in a bin behind one of the cabinet doors.

"Salt," I found in a canvas sack on the bottom shelf of the cabinet. "Sugar," in clumps and lumps of assorted sizes mixed with the granules, was in a tin canister which I located on an upper shelf. "Soda" in a smallish box nearby. "Fat" I found in a smelly crock with a tight-fitting lid, next to "Sourdough Starter" in another crockery container, this one with a flat India rubber ring under the lid and a wire loop attached to the sides of the crock to hold the lid firmly in place with an airtight seal.

One would not assume that such an innocent-sounding list of foodstuffs could wreak such havoc on a ranch and contribute to so much violence and disarray. But, I suppose, even the most innocent things can have ill effects when improperly used by unskilled hands. Those hands, in this case, being mine. Again, I am getting ahead of myself.

"Mix dry ingredients" the narrative portion of the recipe directed. That seemed obvious enough, so I did. Four cups of flour, a teaspoon of salt, three tablespoons of sugar, two pinches of soda. What was not obvious was the meaning of the "C" "T" and "t" symbols scrawled on receipt. But I discerned they were units of measure and found some spoons with similar markings stored in a smallish cup that obviously wasn't meant for coffee, and assumed—correctly in this case—that these were the proper measures. No mention was made of "sifting" but I have since learned that this step, which experienced cooks perform as a matter of course when preparing baked goods, would have eliminated the troublesome lumps.

Next I attempted to "cut in the fat." A pocket knife is not the proper tool for this task, I have since learned, but what do you expect? Ask a cowboy to "cut" something, anything, and he'll automatically pull a buck knife out of his pocket. When my buck knife proved useless for the task at hand, I tried a kitchen knife but it was no improvement.

The next instruction said "Stur (sic) in Starter." I dumped in the three-and-a-half cups the recipe called for of the bubbly mess from the crock and stirred until I had a stiff gelatinous blob that couldn't have been stirred any further even with assistance from a team of draft horses.

So I advanced to the next task outlined, which was "Nead (sic) and roll out." Having seen this accomplished by numerous cooks on countless occasions, I knew how this was done. With liberal amounts of flour to prevent sticking, I managed to get the dough spread out. I then cut out the individual biscuits with an empty sliced peaches can that seemed to be kept for that purpose, if the bits of dried and crumbly dough stuck to it were any indication.

THE DEATH OF DELGADO

In hindsight, I can confidently claim that, with a few minor exceptions, I had, up to this point, performed the task of biscuit preparation satisfactorily. From this point on, however, nothing went as intended. But I did my best. And I still contend that at least the middles of the biscuits were edible, if not as fluffy as they might have been. Even the tops, albeit hard enough to require a strong jaw to bite through, were edible. While I readily admit that the bottoms were burnt, it still seems a trivial problem; certainly not one requiring wholesale resignations. But, as seems my wont, I have again violated the chronology of events and gotten ahead of myself.

I arranged the biscuit rounds in the bottom of the big Dutch oven. My recipe, by the way, said nothing about either greasing or preheating the pot, so my failure to do so is attributable to ignorance and was totally without malice. My previously scrubbing it vigorously with soapy water was also a contributing factor in the kettle's less-than-satisfactory performance. Again, my fault, but due to ignorance rather than any desire to cause harm.

You can imagine, perhaps, (although I could not at the time) the result of placing a cold, ungreased cast-iron Dutch oven filled with biscuit dough directly into the hot coals of the cook fire.

While the biscuits baked by the fire I carved a stack of steaks from the meat on the table. This proved a more difficult task than I guessed, resulting in slices of uneven thickness. But, seeing the dust from a sizable herd hanging in the low light of the late afternoon sun, I knew the boys would be showing up shortly. And they would be hungry when they did. So I set a couple of great big shiny clean frypans on the metal rack over the cookfire, which rack was a result of the late Boomer Johnson's ingenuity. (The corpse of Boomer Johnson, incidentally, was still there under the tarp, a gruesome reminder of the morning's altercation for which I would be accountable—and rightly so—when a representative of the law enforcement system arrived. Of course it is ludicrous to seem to suggest that the body might have been elsewhere, immobility being a normal consequence of death.)

I dollopped a generous quantity of fat into the frypans, resulting in the emission of billowing clouds of smoke. But once I threw in the slabs of beef, the smoke dissipated.

Returning to the cook shack, I opened up my pocket knife and sawed open enough cans to provide what I assumed would be a sufficient quantity of tomatoes for the crew. I dumped the tomatoes into a large bowl and stuck in a big spoon for serving. The tomatoes not being of sufficient viscosity to support the spoon, I watched helplessly as its handle slid down the interior curve of the bowl and disappeared. A few minutes of probing the depths of the bowl with a fork retrieved the lost spoon and a more suitable utensil with a longer handle was located. So far as I am concerned nothing more need be said about that unfortunate, albeit minor, incident.

The steaks were smoking as I stepped out through the doorway, but as I turned them over they didn't seem to be seriously overcooked. This, however, was somewhat difficult to gauge, as the thinner sections of the meat (the result of my admittedly bad job of slicing) were rather crisp while the thicker parts were still rather soft and juicy. But, taken as an average across the entire surface, the cooking of the meat up to that point seemed to me within acceptable limits.

The cowboys, who were now dismounted (save the two selected to hold the herd and take their evening meal later) and approaching the fire with plates in hand, did not share my opinion. They expressed dissatisfaction with the state of the meat, but their displeasure did not approach the hysteria soon to be provoked by the burnt biscuits.

The beans drew no comment. I am grateful to the canned tomatoes for temporarily calming the hungry hands, even lightening the mood noticeably. For reasons I neither know nor understand, canned tomatoes have long been a favorite of working cowhands.

My cowboy friends and erstwhile coworkers were, by now, watering at the mouth in anticipation of hot, fluffy, lighter-than-air biscuits that seemed to float down one's throat in defiance of Sir Isaac Newton's law of gravity. Boomer Johnson's skill with biscuits and other baked goods was considerable, after all, despite his shortcomings in other areas. You cannot begin to imagine the depths of the cowboys' disappointment as I lifted the oven lid with a pothook revealing the biscuits within. Once, that is, the smoke cleared. As they looked on, crestfallen, I prodded the exposed surface of the biscuits with the fork I held in my right hand (the left hand still holding the pot hook with the lid dangling therefrom). The solid "tap-tap-tapping" sound was not hopeful. Still, I pried loose a biscuit and lifted it on the tines of the fork for further examination.

At that point, there was no disputing the fact that the biscuits were, in fact, burnt. May I remind you that I have never disputed the fact that the biscuits were burnt; I did not then nor do I now dispute that fact.

The entire bottom was charred black. The middle, between the rigid top and the burnt bottom, did bear some resemblance to an edible biscuit, although it could not be called "light" or "fluffy" by any stretch of the imagination. Still, I believe my efforts deserved at least the courtesy of an attempt by the cowboys to eat the biscuits. They were, after all, my friends and coworkers.

Alas, that was not to be. Not one of the four stepped forward to accept a biscuit, or to offer the opinion that the absence of biscuits for supper might be acceptable in the circumstances. Not one. Instead, it was a string of slurs and insults.

"Damn! Them biscuits ain't edible!"

"You call *them* biscuits?"

"Who the hell taught you to cook?"

"Burnt biscuits! Hell's bells!"

"Shee-it! Here I am half starved and you done burned the biscuits!"

"I'll be damned if I'll work for an outfit that serves burnt biscuits!" said one.

"I'm with you," said another. "Let's ride!"

"I'll not abide such abusive treatment for forty a month and found. I'm quitting too," said another.

"Let's tell the others," one said. "They shouldn't have to be served burnt biscuits either."

I told them I was sorry. Apologized profusely, in fact. Attempted no excuses. Accepted full responsibility. Swore I'd try harder. Offered to whip up another batch, then and there. All to no avail. All I got were mean and nasty looks as the cowboys mounted up and rode away.

Standing there in shock, I watched them disappear behind the rise between ranch headquarters and where the herd was being held, then reappear with the two hands who had been guarding the herd. The six of them were skylined there atop that rise for several minutes as they spurred up their horses into a high lope in the general direction of town.

That I ought to get mounted and attempt to hold the herd they had spent the day gathering did not, in my traumatized state, even occur to me. Nor did it occur to me to send the boy. So the cattle drifted off toward every point of the compass, each to its favorite grazing ground. The unproductive cows that would have been culled went. The hundreds of calves that would have been branded and earmarked went. Those among them of the male gender that would have been castrated went, immature testicles intact.

But the ramifications of the situation did not end there. A ranch cannot work without cowboys, and this ranch had no cowboys save me. How the boss would get the work done I did not know.

All because I burned a batch of biscuits.

All because I shot and killed the cook.

All because of a hangover due to ill-advised binge drinking and sleep deprivation.

I make no excuses. I am fully willing to assume my share of the responsibility for the events that transpired as a result—direct or indirect—of my actions. I have said so repeatedly. I do not want compassion. I request no pardon. I do not ask forgiveness.

All I ever wanted was another chance.

SEPARATING THE WHEAT FROM THE TARES

BEING A TRUE ACCOUNT OF THE DEATH
AND LIFE OF ORRIN PORTER ROCKWELL

Writer and editor Robert J. Randisi hatched a plan for an anthology featuring fictional stories about historical "good guy" figures from the Old West— the "white hats." I submitted this story about one of my favorite frontier characters who, according to some, would certainly meet that description. Others would disagree—but more on that later. The Berkley anthology, White Hats, *was published in 2002.*

———◆———

I am the last man to see Porter Rockwell alive.

In the early hours of the afternoon of 9 June 1878 he passed on to his reward in his office at the Colorado Stables where I am hostler. Since the last words to pass his lips fell upon my ears and mine alone, I feel obliged to set down the events of that day and the night previous, leaving a true and accurate record to refute the rumours and speculations concerning his death.

Having known the man over a number of years it seems my duty, as well, to set straight the facts of his life and rebut the calumny that dogs him even in death. He had not grown cold in his grave when the *Salt Lake Tribune* libeled him in its columns thus:

> The gallows was cheated of one of the fittest candidates that ever cut a throat or plundered a traveler. Porter Rockwell is another in the long list of Mormon criminals whose deeds of treachery and blood have reddened the soil of Utah, and who has paid no forfeit to the law. He was commissioned by the Prophet Joseph Smith avenger-in-chief for the Lord when the Latter-day Saints were living a troublous life on the border, and arrived in this Territory where the fanatical

leaders of the Church suffered no restraint, and the avenging angels were made bloody instruments of these holy men's will. Porter Rockwell was chosen as a fitting agent to lead in these scenes of blood.

The absurdity of these slanders is plain to all familiar with "Port" but painful to his memory even so. The true facts attest that Porter Rockwell was the finest peace officer, bodyguard, bounty hunter, pioneer, tracker, scout, and guide to ever carry sawed-off .36 caliber Navy Colt pistols in his coat pockets.

Allow me, now, to begin my account at the end.

——————— ♦ ———————

The last words Porter Rockwell spoke came in reply to a question of mine. We had talked off and on since his arrival at the Colorado Stables at about one o'clock in the morning. He kept a small seldom-used office there. Most of his time the past few years was spent at his ranch away out on Government Creek, but he occasionally came to town to visit his family and tend to the remnants of his freighting business. He sometimes slept on a cot in that office, as he did that final night.

Port had escorted his daughter Mary to watch Denham Thompson play the lead in *Joshua Whitcomb* at the Salt Lake Theatre. After seeing her home, he spent a quiet hour at a saloon before walking the three blocks to the stable to retire. He arrived here just after one o'clock. He slept a few hours, then awoke complaining of cold and a sick stomach. We talked off and on as he dozed and thrashed uncomfortably through the remainder of the night and morning. Shortly after midday, he was again taken by chills and vomiting. He struggled to sit up and pulled on his boots.

"Port!" I asked. "How are you?"

"Wheat. All wheat," he replied weakly.

He then lapsed into unconsciousness, never to awaken again in this world—to die, as the saying goes, with his boots on.

Perhaps his final words bear explanation. "Wheat" was a favorite expression of Porter Rockwell's, heard often by those who knew him. Some claim it is of uncertain origin, but I know where it comes from and what it means because Port told me. It is from the thirtieth verse of the third chapter of *The Gospel According to St. Matthew*: "Gather ye together first the tares, and bind them in bundles to burn them: but gather the wheat into my barn."

So, all that was good was by Port described as "wheat" variously meaning "all is well" or "that is good" or "everything is fine" and such like. His detractors take it further, using the scripture against him—it is the reason, they say, he killed the forty or eighty or one hundred and more they claim for him; they were but "tares" to be destroyed.

I asked Port one time about the deaths attributed to his hand. His answer was as simple and direct as the man himself: "I never killed anybody that didn't need killing."

———•———

On the day of his death, Rockwell was, in fact, awaiting trial for the Aiken affair. In the autumn of 1877 he had been indicted, arrested, and jailed for murder. Only $15,000.00 bail posted by friends kept him from languishing in a cell awaiting the term of the district court. Anti-Mormon prosecutors obtained from a grand jury with similar leanings a True Bill accusing Port and Sylvanus Collett of murdering John Aiken *twenty years before*! I heard the story from Port himself, and here is the truth of that matter.

Painted by lawyers for the government as innocent and unsuspecting travelers set upon by Brigham Young's Destroying Angels, the Aiken party was, in reality, a band of opportunistic California gamblers. Decked out in Texas hats and riding silver-studded Mexican saddles on fine horses, the party of six, led by John Aiken and his brother Tom, arrived in the Territory late fall, 1857. Hearing that the United States Army was marching to attack and occupy Utah Territory, they had set out from southern California with a considerable stake and a gambling outfit including playing cards and dice and a faro layout, intending to pick the soldiers clean.

The bunch was arrested before even reaching Great Salt Lake City. Jailed in Ogden and later transferred to the territorial capital, the Aiken party was held for two weeks or so while authorities decided what to do with them. They determined to release the Californians and escort them from the Territory on the southern route to prevent any possible contact with the approaching army. Port was assigned to lead the escort party, duly authorized by law.

"Four of us took four of them south, two of the gamblers being allowed to stay at large in the City until spring," Port said. "We was camped on the Sevier River when I was woke up by some commotion, which was our charges attempting an escape. One of them fancy men had the best of Collett and so I shot him, but he run off through the bushes with a bullet of mine in his back. Them two Aikens and the other'n was down and I figured them dead so we dumped the bodies in the river. Come dawn we rode north considering the job a bad one, but a finished one just the same."

The next afternoon, the wounded outlaw stumbled barefoot into the town of Nephi bleeding from his head and the bullet wound in his back. The local sawbones probed for the bullet, and, sure enough, it was the same caliber as Port's Colts. Later in the day, the townfolk were surprised by the arrival of another of the outlaws—this one John Aiken, obviously not as dead as believed—apparently revived by the cold water of the Sevier River. He, too, was barefoot and bleeding from head wounds. Four or five days later, the pair had healed enough to travel and asked to be driven to Great Salt Lake City. Two young men volunteered for the job.

Eight miles north of Nephi, the party stopped to water the team at Willow Creek when the door of the sheepherder's shack there flew open and blasts from a shotgun cut down the wounded gamblers. The boys lit out of there and Aiken and his traveling companion were never seen again, dead or alive.

Twenty years after the fact, Port and Sylvanus Collett were blamed in the mysterious Aiken affair on the flimsiest of evidence—or a complete lack thereof if you ask me. Port refused even to cooperate in his defense, "Wheat" being his only reply to questions from his lawyers.

Laying the blame on Porter Rockwell is not a recent development. As far back as the thirties, when the Mormons were abused and mobbed by Missouri Pukes, Port was accused of being chief of the "Danite" bands that retaliated against the mobs. Then, when Governor Lilburn Boggs ordered the Mormons evicted from Missouri *or exterminated* and an assassin attempted his life in reply, that, too, was attributed to Rockwell.

There was no credible evidence in either case, and I believe that if Port had set out to kill Boggs he would be dead today. Whether with pistol, rifle, or shotgun, his skills as a marksman were the stuff of legend—as you will see from the facts behind another of his more famous escapades, as related to me by the legend himself.

THE DEATH OF DELGADO

———— ◦ ————

The year was 1845, and the place was Hancock County in Illinois, not far from the city of Nauvoo and not long after a mob had jailed and murdered the Mormon prophet Joseph Smith and his brother Hyrum.

Port was a favorite of Joseph Smith's, appointed by him in his capacity of mayor of Nauvoo as a deputy marshal and personal bodyguard. In fact, Rockwell's long, flowing locks were the result of his association with Smith who prophesied, "Orrin Porter Rockwell—so long as ye remain loyal and true to thy faith, ye need fear no enemy. Cut not thy hair and no bullet or blade can harm thee." A true prophecy as it turned out. But I digress.

The other characters in the incident at hand were Frank Worrell, leader of the Carthage Grays, a so-called militia unit that murdered the incarcerated Smiths; and county sheriff Jacob Backenstos, unpopular in the area because the mobocrats accused him of sympathy with the Mormons.

Rockwell tells the tale:

"I was watering my horse alongside the Warsaw Road when I spies Backenstos whipping up his horses and flying down the road towards me in a carriage. Coming over the rise a ways behind was two men a-horseback. Jacob hauled in the lines in a cloud of dust and hollered to me, 'Rockwell, in the name of the State of Illinois, County of Hancock, I order you to protect me from the mob at my heels!' I had my pistols and a rifle so I told the sheriff not to worry. I didn't know so at the time, but five other men was behind the riders, coming on hard in a rig and a light wagon.

"One horseman was well ahead of the other. Backenstos hails him and orders him to halt. Instead, he pulls out a pistol. By now I seen I was facing that sonofabitch Frank Worrell so I shot him."

The sheriff later said in official reports that the rifle bullet, fired from a distance of 100 to 150 yards, tore through Worrell's chest and launched him from the saddle. The other rider, and the men in the two outfits that had by now arrived on the scene, lost heart at the sight of their leader bleeding in the dirt. Loading the dying body in the wagon, they turned tail.

"'Well, I got him, Jacob. I was afraid my rifle couldn't reach him, but it did. Only missed a little bit.' 'What do you mean?' he asks me, and I says, 'I aimed for his belt buckle.'"

———◆———

Another silent witness to Port's long-distance accuracy with his weapons was the unidentified scapegrace behind the Great Bullion Robbery of 1868. The Overland Stage, eastbound out of California, was held up in the Utah desert and relieved of some $40,000.00 in gold. The driver pushed on to Faust Station, next along the line, where Port was to board the stage as a Wells Fargo shotgun guard for the run to Fort Bridger. Instead, he mounted up and rode off on the stage's back trail in pursuit of the thief.

"He was a wily one," Port told me one time, "taking care to cover his tracks and otherwise confuse his movements. But I catched him up on Cherry Creek, two days after taking up the trail. The gold was in the ground, I figure, so I lay low keeping an eye on him. After a week or so of skulkin' around out there, he's sure he's not being followed so he sneaks off and digs up the gold. About the time the last bar comes out of the hole, I draw down on him and make the arrest without incident.

"Me, that gold, and the outlaw make our way to my place on Government Creek where I has Hat Shurtliff keep an eye on him while I gets some sleep, which I had been missing a lot of, you see. Ol' Hat, though, he fell asleep on the job and wakes up just as the prisoner clears the corral gate on one of my horses. I stagger outside whilst trying to peel back my eyelids and blink out the blur just in time to see him skyline on a little ridge east of the cabin. Them stubby Colts of mine ain't much for distance, but I fired all the same.

"Well, I figures I missed since I didn't see no evidence to say otherwise. So's I finished up my sleeping and gets things in shape at the ranch then hauls the gold on into the Wells Fargo office in Great Salt Lake City, where there's a report of a dead man found propped up agin a telegraph pole. Seems his horse had wandered off, leaving the poor soul to bleed to death from a bullet wound in the back. I never saw the body. But I suspect I'd of recognized him."

———◆———

The infamous Lot Huntington felt the effect of Porter Rockwell's marksmanship from a range close enough to look the fearsome lawman in the pale blue eyes.

THE DEATH OF DELGADO

The cause of the whole affair was The Honorable John W. Dawson, vacating Utah in the dead of night following a glorious three-week term as Governor of the Territory, during which time he had managed to aggravate enough folks high and low with his debauched behavior that he feared for his life. Which, by the way, would have been no great loss.

While waiting at the stage station, the disgraced Dawson was set upon and pistol whipped by a half dozen drunken cowboys who left him for dead and rode off into the windy winter night. Dawson survived and identified one Lot Huntington, a known petty outlaw and rustler, as leader of the gang. Local police had no success in locating the accused after two weeks of searching, at which time the story takes a curious turn.

A strong box containing $800.00 cash belonging to the Overland Mail disappeared from the Townsend Stable, along with Brown Sal, one of the finest horses in the Territory. Suspicion again centered on Lot Huntington and his crowd, who were seen leaving the vicinity and heading west. A posse was formed to take up the chase, with Porter Rockwell in the lead. The posse passed through Camp Floyd some several hours behind the bandits and rode hard through the night to Faust Station, where Port spotted Brown Sal under a shed in the corral. He takes up the tale from there, as best I remember his telling it.

"It was coming on morning and we was cold and tired and the wind was hard and bitter. But, wanting to avoid any unnecessary gunplay, I elected to surround the station and wait and see. Along about sunup, Faust himself comes out of the inn to do his chorin' and I beckons him over to where I was hidden. He tells me Huntington is in there with two others eating their breakfast.

"So I sends Faust back inside to explain the situation, figuring they'd see the hopelessness of their plight and come out with hands up as instructed. Well, lo and behold, next thing I know Lot Huntington comes strollin' out pretty as you please with a big ol' .44 caliber cap-and-ball pistol in his fist. I calls out a warning and shoots in the air but he walks on over to them corrals like he ain't got a care in the world. I rushes over to the shed just as he's swingin' onto Brown Sal bareback and I hollers out another warning. Lot aims that pistol at me but before he could fire I unloaded eight balls of buckshot from my Colt into his belly. He gets all tangled up in the fence rails fallin' off that horse and made a strange picture danglin' there and dyin'."

The other two surrendered without further violence, and Port and the posse delivered the corpse, the prisoners, the strongbox, and Brown Sal to the authorities back in the City. While unsaddling his horse minutes later, Port hears gunfire.

"With pistols in hand I ran back to where I left the prisoners with the police. 'What happened?' I asks the constable and he says all matter-of-fact, 'Tried to escape.' But I looked at them bodies close, and both was powder-burnt and one shot in the face. How the hell that happened I couldn't discern, lessen he was runnin' away backwards."

———◆———

A final incident, selected from many, must suffice as testimony to Porter Rockwell's skills as horseman and tracker. Known far and wide for his ability to handle horses no other could master and getting more miles from a mount than possible as a practical matter—with no ill effects on the animal—Port was sometimes accused of thinking more like a horse than a horse did. The upshot was a relentlessness on the trail that, combined with seeing sign where there wasn't any, made Port the first one called upon when there were rustlers to be caught.

One story, as I say, will serve. It was told to me, not by Rockwell, but by letter from Frank Karrick, a freighter who hauled goods between Sacramento and Great Salt Lake City and was the beneficiary of Port's services in recovering a herd of stolen mules. I quote his missive at some length:

> I was 70 miles south of Great Salt Lake City back in '61 when several valuable mules disappeared in the night. Upon discovering my loss in the morning, I left the teamsters to guard the wagons, goods, animals & such while I went off in pursuit but soon lost the trail in a confusion of hoofprints. Knowing no other recourse I reported the crime in Great Salt Lake City where B. Young himself suggested I enlist the support of Orrin Porter Rockwell. Upon retaining his services we repaired to the place I lost the trail, now three days cold. Rockwell examined the ground for a time and pointed out the track we were to follow. Asking how he knew,

he answered "Never mind. They've only taken the shoes off the mules. We'll just stay on this trail."

About dusk the trail again became entangled, having been crossed by a large herd of cattle. Rockwell expressed no dismay and followed up the herd. After dark, we approached the drover's camp, unnoticed until reaching the edge of the firelight where Rockwell reined up. Soon we were looking down the barrels of several firearms in the hands of the startled men in the camp, one of whom hollered "Stay right where you are or the shooting starts!" Rockwell answered in his squeaky voice "Wheat, fellers, wheat." Either the voice or the term had meaning in the camp, as the reply came back "Port! Step down and join us! Supper's soon ready and the coffee's hot."

(Note: Perhaps I neglected to mention that rough and tough though he was, Porter Rockwell's voice did not match; it being rather high-pitched and tending to break higher when excited. This fact was not to his liking. Likewise, his hands were small and well formed, almost feminine in appearance and not at all in keeping with what one might expect in a so-called "rough character." Continuing now with Karrick's report.)

After sharing the warmth of the fire through the night and a hot breakfast, both courtesy of the men moving the cattle, we rode out ahead of the cowboys as they were lining out the herd at first light. As if he never doubted their course or destination, Rockwell soon pointed out the tracks of my stolen mules. We pushed hard through the day. Near sunset, we trotted up a rise and saw a faint trace of dust in the far distance. Rockwell rustled about in his saddlebags and produced a telescope. "Two men . . . some horses . . . and mules—come on!" he said. And go on we did, with haste.

For the second time in as many evenings, we rode up on men hunched around a campfire. This time Rockwell did not wait to be noticed but instead rode right into the rustlers' camp (there can be no doubt on this point—my mules were clearly visible in the fading light, grazing on the banks of a nearby stream) with snub-nosed Colt revolver in hand.

I regret my tale lacks the excitement of a shootout (although I did not regret it at the time) but the fact is the two were visibly frightened of Rockwell and offered no resistance. They were soon behind bars, my mules back in harness, and Rockwell gone home richer by $500.00 worth of my gratitude. On reaching my destination in California, I rewarded him further with the shipment of a hand-tooled saddle and demijohn of fine whisky. I heard later he was vastly more interested in the whisky than in the saddle.

In all my years of freighting, never once did I have the pleasure of meeting a better man than Porter Rockwell. His ability as a tracker I have never seen equaled. Nor have I seen another who commanded such presence among men, as demonstrated by the gladness and the fear I saw in the faces of the cowboys and the outlaws, respectively, we encountered during our brief expedition. My gifts did not begin to repay Porter Rockwell and I consider myself ever in his debt.

Respectfully,
(signed) Frank Karrick
Sacramento, Calif.

———— ◆ ————

By now it ought to be clear to even the most skeptical that Orrin Porter Rockwell was a credit to his people and a force for law and order. I could tell more. But I fear the lies and venom would yet outweigh any further words I could put to paper.

The reports of his death by poison or by bullets or by a beating administered by various people he is said to have wronged are likewise false. He died, as I have said, in his office at the Colorado Stables in my presence. The coroner's jury, influenced by the testimony of four physicians, determined there was "no evidence of injury, nor any symptoms of poisoning" and the death a result of the "failure of the heart's action, caused by a suspension of the nervous power."

If that description is correct, it is the only time Porter Rockwell ever lost his nerve.

THE PEOPLE VERSUS PORTER ROCKWELL

It seems inevitable that editor Robert J. Randisi would follow White Hats *with a similar volume of stories about the black hats, the bad guys, of the Old West.* Black Hats *was published by Berkley in 2003. When I proposed a story showing the other side of Porter Rockwell, Randisi was reluctant—he did not want to use the same authors in this companion anthology, nor did he care to repeat a subject. But he liked this fictionalized account of actual events and included it nonetheless.*

———◆———

Now comes V. Harmon Haight, District Attorney in the First District Court in and for the Territory of Utah, appearing for the People of the United States of America, Plaintiff, seeking from this duly summoned and sworn Grand Jury a True Bill against Orrin Porter Rockwell, Defendant.

"Thank you, Mr. Secretary. Gentleman of the Jury, the oath you have taken requires you to evaluate the evidence The People will present in this matter. Your duty is to determine whether or not probable cause exists to believe the accused committed a crime. If the evidence establishes such a probability, you must return a True Bill and, thus indicted, Porter Rockwell will stand trial to determine guilt or innocence. You may also, of course, refuse to indict—but after hearing the quantity of evidence The People will present before the Grand Jury, I doubt it.

"The crime for which Rockwell stands accused is murder. Now, gentlemen, this crime is not a recent one. The victim, one John Aiken, was last seen alive on the earth in October of 1857, just one month shy of twenty years ago. The details of the crime appear dim through the dust of passing years and the evidence obscured. And, even though you will hear from witnesses who place the defendant at or near the scene of the crime those many years ago, The People will not ask you to reach your decision in this matter on testimony of those long-ago events alone. No, gentlemen, you will be allowed to evaluate the man Porter Rockwell as a whole—to determine his role in this affair within the context of a life of bloodshed and carnage. But, since it is the murder of John Aiken for which the man stands accused, the evidence in that crime shall first be presented to the Grand Jury.

————◆————

"Guy Foote, do you understand the oath you have taken?"

"Yessir."

"Very well. Tell the jury, please, your place of residence in October of 1857."

"Nephi."

"And do you recall the events that are the subject of this inquiry?"

"Yessir. I'm told you're looking into what happened to them Aikens who came through there in chains."

"What did happen?"

"Well sir, as I said, they came through as prisoners, under the charge of Porter Rockwell and some other men. I didn't know them then and I don't recall them now—"

"But you do recall Porter Rockwell. Why is that?"

"Oh, everyone knows Port. All us kids back then held him up as a hero."

"Do you still?"

"I can't rightly say as I do."

"What changed your mind, Mr. Foote?"

"It was this affair with them Aikens I'm trying to tell you about."

"Go on, then. I apologize for the interruption. Tell the jury the course of events."

"Port and his posse passed through town in the afternoon and we all turned out to see. They rode on by and, I was told later, stopped a few hours farther on and camped by the river out there, the Sevier River.

"Late in the night I was woke up by some folks talking in the public room—my folks ran a sort of hotel, see, putting up boarders and travelers. I heard Porter Rockwell say, kind of mad-like, 'we made a bad job of it boys—one of them got away.'"

"Did you *see* it was Rockwell?"

"No sir. But it was his voice, kind of high and squeaky like. Anyhow, they was gone when I woke up and I didn't think much of it. Later on, though, one of them prisoners, Tom Aiken he was, came back to town afoot with a bloodied head and a bullet in his back. He hadn't his shoes nor shirt, and was pretty thoroughly chilled. His story was that the posse had fallen on them in the night, hollering about an Indian attack, and whacking them over the heads. He managed to get to his feet, he said, and run off but was shot in the back—by Porter Rockwell he believed, as he had seen Port with a pistol in his hand—before he could make his escape. But he managed to get away in the dark and the willows, and hid out all night. Them others was killed and dumped in the river, he says. Ma and Pa put him up in a bed and Doc fished a bullet out of his back.

"Along about evening, another one of them men showed up—John Aiken this time—him, too, with a nasty gash on his topknot and barely half dressed hisself. He didn't remember nothing but waking up when he hit that cold river, and managed to stay out of sight until he thought it safe. He took to a bed at our hotel too."

"Moving along, Mr. Foote, we understand from other testimony that the local authorities opted to escort the two 'prisoners' back to Great Salt Lake City once they were sufficiently recovered. You had a role in that?"

"Yessir. Me and Billy Skeen offered to make the trip. There wasn't much on that time of year, and us being about fourteen years old, thought it would make a fine adventure."

"You weren't afraid?"

"Nah. Them two was pretty used up. They was barely in shape to travel, so no one figured they'd try anything. They was outfitted by folks in town—I remember Pa gave John Aiken an old coat he had—and we set out. About eight miles or so north of Nephi there's this place called Willow Creek; nothing there but a spring and a sheepherder's cabin, but it's a convenient watering hole where most folks stopped, as did we. While I saw to the team, Billy and them others was stretching their legs. I heard that cabin door bust open and considerable gunfire and turned and saw both them Aikens fall, one of 'em near torn in two from shotgun balls. Someone in that shack hollers out for me and Billy to just climb in the wagon and get on home."

"Do you know who it was?"

"No, Mr. Haight, I can't say as I did then or do now."

"Could it have been Porter Rockwell?"

"He might of been in there, but it wasn't him hollering. I would of recognized his voice. So I guess I can't say he was there."

"How does the story end?"

"We lit out of there as ordered and went back to Nephi. Some folks went back out to Willow Creek after we said what happened, but nobody ever saw them Aiken fellas again, nor even their bodies. They figured whoever had shot them had dumped them in the springs.

"That evening, Rockwell and another man rode into town and spent the night at the hotel. A day or two later I found Pa's old coat hanging in a lean-to we had over the back door. It was stained with blood and I counted eight holes in it. Billy Skeen saw it, too. I showed him."

———— • ————

"Mr. Secretary and gentlemen of the jury, I would like now, if you please, to read into the record a correspondence from one Albert D. Richardson of the *New York Tribune*, who visited Utah Territory in 1865 in the company of the eminent Schuyler Colfax, then Speaker of the House of Representatives in the United States Congress."

"What is your purpose in doing so, Mr. Haight?"

"Merely to show, Mr. Foreman, another aspect of Rockwell's character— to further establish a ready disposition toward violence, if you will."

"Go on, then."

"Thank you. This, from Richardson's published accounts in the *Tribune*:"

> While abroad on the streets of Great Salt Lake City yesterday I encountered the notorious Mormon assassin Porter Rockwell. The chance meeting was a frightful one, as Rockwell had me confused with Fitz Hugh Ludlow, another reporter, whom I am said to resemble, and who passed through Utah Territory some time earlier and had written in the *Atlantic Monthly* an unflattering description of Rockwell. He believed it was I who had characterized him as the murderer of one hundred and fifty men; and he significantly remarked that if I had said it he believed he would make it one hundred and fifty-one!

———— • ————

"State your name and rank, please."

"Patrick Edward Connor, Colonel, Third Regiment, California Volunteers, Retired."

"Colonel, how did you come to know Orrin Porter Rockwell?"

"In 1862, I was ordered by the President and Commander in Chief to move seven companies of my command to Utah Territory to protect the Overland Mail route against Indian depredations. And, it was understood, to keep an eye on the Mormons whose loyalty to the Union was suspect.

"I had heard of Rockwell. He enjoyed a certain notoriety throughout the West. I had even heard tales of his exploits in California in the gold rush years. But my first direct experience of the man came in the form of a report that he was riding through the streets of Great Salt Lake City as my command approached, offering any and all a $500 bet that my soldiers would never cross the Jordan River. We did, of course, and marched through the heart of the City with loaded rifles, fixed bayonets, and shotted cannon. We pitched our tents on benchland overlooking the city and established Fort Douglas among the Mormons."

"Fine, Colonel. Had you any direct dealings with Rockwell after that?"

"Considerable. If you have read your history, you know of the Battle of Bear River. I shall spare this assembly the details; suffice it to say that in the dead of winter, my California Volunteers located and attacked a camp of hostile Shoshoni Indians in Cache Valley, killing more than two hundred, destroying their camp and supplies, and recovering property stolen from settlers.

"Rockwell was instrumental in this effort. He guided us to the savages and offered valuable strategic advice for overtaking the camp. He participated bravely in the fight as well. But his greatest value came after the battle. I daresay that without his valiant service in obtaining teams and wagons to transport our wounded and unhorsed troops back to Fort Douglas, most of my command would have died in the cold and the storms."

"What is your opinion of the man?"

"Over time, I came to consider him a friend, Mr. Haight. One whom I admire greatly. I know of no better guide or frontiersman. He is, in my opinion, to use his own words in describing good things, 'all wheat.'"

"You say you became his friend, Colonel. Would you describe yourself, also, a confidante?"

"I suppose so. We have talked a good deal about his life. Given all I had heard about him, I was curious about the facts of his history."

"You're aware, I'm sure, that Rockwell was accused of the attempted murder of Lilburn W. Boggs, ex-governor, at the time of the assassination attempt, of Missouri."

"Yes. I questioned Rockwell closely about that incident one evening after we had shared a number of what he called 'squar whiskies.'"

"Would you relate to the members of the Grand Jury, please, his answer."

"He said, 'I shot through the window, and I thought I had killed him, but I had only wounded him; I was damned sorry I had not killed the son of a bitch.'"

———— ◆ ————

"Madam, we sincerely appreciate your appearance before this Grand Jury to relate a difficult incident that must still grieve a mother's soul. If you will, state again your name for the members of the Grand Jury."

"I am Eliza Scott McRae."

"Mrs. McRae, I need not remind you that you are under oath. Relate, please, the events of your life in late July and early August of the year 1861 in which Porter Rockwell played a role."

"Well, Mr. Haight, my two sons, Kenneth and Alexander McRae, were accused at that time of robbing an emigrant. I don't know but what they might have done it—they were young men and full of themselves, and had been given to occasional mischief. But this crime was more serious, so I don't know.

"At any rate, Porter Rockwell and a police officer set out to track them down and, as it was told to me, they caught my boys a ways up Emigration Canyon."

"Were your sons then jailed and brought before the court?"

"No sir. At an out-of-the-way place there in the canyon, they were gunned down with a double-barreled shotgun in the hands, I believe, of Porter Rockwell."

"Were there witnesses to this fact, Mrs. McRae?"

"None that could or would talk."

"Then why do you attribute the atrocious act to Rockwell?"

"On account of what happened next. Rockwell and that police officer rode up to my house with the boys toes up in the back of a buckboard. Port dumped the bodies into the dirt of my door yard. Then he spoke to me. He said, 'Mizz McRae, had you done your duty when raising these boys, I would not have been forced to do mine.'"

THE DEATH OF DELGADO

———— ◆ ————

"Gentlemen of the jury, in my hand I hold reports from numerous investigations The People have conducted into the affairs of Mr. Rockwell. As you see, it is a stack of considerable thickness. I will not burden you nor the record of these proceedings with a full account. It is available for your perusal should you so choose. I must remind you, gentlemen, that Porter Rockwell stands accused—formally—only of the murder of John Aiken. We do not seek an indictment for all these crimes. But allow me, gentlemen, to read out to you a few of the more notorious incidents attributed to Rockwell. And recall the old saw, gentlemen: where there's smoke there's fire.

"July, 1850; Rockwell, upon orders from Mormon leaders, cured the sick old woman Alice Beardsley of the disease of 'apostasy' by slitting her throat.

"August, 1850; an unidentified argonaut on the trail to California was decapitated by Rockwell, Mr. Scott the sheriff, and another man, merely on the suspicion that he had been a member of the Illinois mob that killed Mormon leaders Joseph and Hyrum Smith in 1844.

"April, 1851; Rockwell, leading a posse that captured four Ute Indians suspected of horse thievery, ordered the prisoners shot rather than returned for trial.

"October, 1853; a government surveying party under the command of Captain John W. Gunnison is wiped out by a band of Indians led by Kanosh. It is believed that Rockwell inspired or participated in the atrocity.

"April, 1856; the bullet-riddled bodies of Almon W. Babbit and his teamsters are found dead on the prairie near Fort Kearney, relieved of $20,000 in government funds enroute to Utah for the construction of the Territorial Capitol. Papers belonging to Babbit and stock carrying his brand are found in the possession of Porter Rockwell days later at Fort Laramie.

"September, 1857; Rockwell initiates aggression against troops of the United States Army marching to quell rebellion in Utah. Raiders, under Rockwell's command, burn forage, stampede livestock, destroy food and stores, thus endangering the lives of some 2,500 soldiers forced to winter on the high plains with insufficient supplies.

"February, 1858; Henry Jones and his mother, accused of an incestuous relationship, are mutilated and murdered at their home in Payson. It is widely known that Rockwell was dispatched by authorities to dispense this 'justice.'

"September, 1859; the sound of gunshots in downtown Great Salt Lake City led to the discovery of John Gheen, stretched out on the sidewalk with blood and brains oozing from two gunshot wounds to the head. Again, Porter Rockwell is widely believed to have been responsible for this 'apparent suicide' of a man troublesome to Church authorities.

"May, 1860; two known outlaws, Joachim Johnston and Myron Brewer, staggering drunkenly from a saloon toward a boarding house, are gunned down on the streets by an unseen assassin. Porter Rockwell is believed to have been responsible for saving the City the expense of a trial.

"December, 1866; the body of a black man, Thomas Colbourn, also known as Thomas Coleman, was found with throat slit from ear to ear. Rockwell, in this instance, was the leader of a group enforcing the laws against miscegenation.

"Gentlemen of the Grand Jury, I could continue. While much of the evidence is sketchy and covered up by those who have been in *de facto* authority in the Utah Territory these past thirty years, there is no doubt that this carnage occurred. And, I submit, there is little doubt that Orrin Porter Rockwell took part in these, and other, events attributed to his bloody hand. The most conservative estimate of the bodies in his wake runs to forty. Others place the tally much higher.

"The People ask you, as duly sworn members of this Grand Jury, to return a True Bill against this killer in one case and one case only—the murder of John Aiken. This indictment, alone, will be sufficient to bring Porter Rockwell to trial and justice; to rid our society of this scourge. Gentlemen, do your duty."

————— • —————

We the members of the Grand Jury currently seated in the First District Court in and for the Territory of Utah, believe, according to the evidence laid before us, that sufficient cause exists to suppose that he did commit the crime and do herewith return a True Bill against Orrin Porter Rockwell and order that, thus indicted, he be tried in court to determine his guilt or innocence in the murder of John Aiken.

THE DEATH OF DELGADO

———◆———

Addendum: Let the record show that on 29 September 1877 Orrin Porter Rockwell was arrested by the United States Marshall for the murder of John Aiken and delivered to the penitentiary for safekeeping.

———◆———

Addendum: Orrin Porter Rockwell did appear on 6 October 1877 before Associate Judge Phillip H. Emerson, where he was admitted to bail in the amount of $15,000, released from custody, and ordered to stand trial for murder during the October, 1878 term of the First District Court.

———◆———

Addendum: 9 June 1878; Orrin Porter Rockwell, awaiting trial for murder, died this day in his office at the Colorado Stables. Autopsy and inquest ordered.

———◆———

Addendum: 11 June 1878; Upon physician testimony and autopsy results, the Coroner's Jury investigating the demise of Orrin Porter Rockwell today brought a verdict of death by natural causes due to failure of the heart's action, finding no evidence of injury or poisoning. The body was released for burial.

THE TURN OF A CARD

While violent, action-packed plots may be the norm, there's more to Western stories—at least there ought to be. Some of us believe sixguns and shootouts are over-represented at the expense of everyday life and lighthearted tales. "The Turn of a Card" is about cowboy camaraderie, celebration, and shenanigans. And while the events it recounts may be outlandish, what happens here is at least as likely, if not more so, than stories with a higher body count. Renowned Western author Dusty Richards asked for this story for the first Cactus Country Anthology *from High Hill Press.*

———— ◆ ————

The Carson River is a stream too lazy to announce its presence. The soft flowing sound came instead from breeze-rattled cottonwood leaves on trees that shaded the watercourse.

Joshua Lonigan was only slightly more active than the river, perched as he was on a dry deadfall log massaging bare feet recently cooled in the stream. As he pulled on a sock the end gave way and two toes poured out the hole.

"Damn."

"Six bits says the same thing happens with your other sock," came a voice from under a dusty, oily, wide-brim hat shading the face of a long drink of water sitting with legs aspraddle and a cottonwood for a backrest. The voice belonged to Seth "Six Bits" Slater, a long-time saddle pal of Josh's.

"Keep your damn bet. And shut up."

"There ain't no need to be testy," Six Bits said.

"Oh, I know it. I'm just tired of being here is all."

The two were shaded up from the heat of the day, keeping casual watch over a herd of trail-weary beef cattle and waiting their turn to partake of the pleasures available up the hill in Virginia City. They had bedded the herd here yesterday and the trail boss and owner of the beeves, Texas Red

McIntyre, had given the rest of the crew liberty after instructing a pair of them to return to the herd this afternoon and relieve Josh and Six Bits.

The man knew from long experience with those two that had he given them the first shift in town, the designated second shift would never set foot on Virginia City's boardwalks.

Lonigan and Slater had come north from Texas with McIntyre some half dozen years ago. They had pushed a mixed herd of cattle to California in 1856, McIntyre having liquidated in Texas hoping to strike it rich in the gold country selling beef rather than mining ore. But they arrived on the heels of more than seventy thousand Texas cattle driven to California over the few years past. Finding prices so cheap and cattle so common you could hardly give them away, McIntyre opted instead to take up ranching, selling the steers for what he could get and turning the cows and bulls out to pasture to eat grass and reproduce and await a better market.

Texas Red established his California ranch in the Sonoma country, squatting on what he considered free range but which was, in fact, part of a Spanish land grant held by Mariano Vallejo. But the Spanish, then the Mexican, sun had set in *Alta California* and McIntyre's claim, along with many other such tenuous claims, went largely unchallenged.

Now, the influx of thousands of men to work the Comstock mines across the mountains in Nevada had created what Texas Red hoped would be a lucrative market for beef. He had visited the Great Basin on a few occasions and was of the opinion that meat would yet be in short supply there since the Comstock country offered few prospects for raising cattle—grass being so scarce that a cow was forced to graze at a high lope just to find enough to fill its belly. He did not even consider the country suitable for raising sheep—never mind the fact that those animals could probably be convinced that graze was plentiful, sheep being the only critters so stupid that their intelligence was not affected in any significant way by being killed and eaten.

So McIntyre and his two top hands, Josh Lonigan and Six Bits Slater, gathered a few more drovers and a herd of steers and lit out on the Overland Trail across the Sierra. Having arrived, Texas Red had ridden off to negotiate a sale, leaving the two cowboys behind with nothing to do but keep the herd from quitting the country.

And wait.

"See them two steers laying over there? Them ones just off from the bunch a bit?" Six Bits asked after holding his silence for a suitable interval.

Josh said, "One of them red with a brockle face and the other one yellow?"

"Them's the ones."

"What about them?"

"I got six bits that says the yellow one gets up first."

"Covered."

As if on cue, the brockle-faced steer shook his long-horned head, shifted his grass-fat belly, hoisted up his hind legs and paused for a moment on the props before levering up the rest of his body.

"That's one more you owe me," Josh said.

"That it is. I trust you're keeping a tally. As you well know, I am not a man to welch on his bets."

He was a man, however, who would wager on anything, anytime, and offer a double-or-nothing bet when he lost. Josh had long since given up keeping track, figuring that Six Bits owed him more money from lost wagers than the cowboy would earn in wages in two lifetimes. But indulging your best friend's gambling habit is all part of the deal isn't it? That, and keeping him from getting in too deep when the stakes were higher than six bits and the others in the game less forgiving.

Two of the other drovers eventually made it back, worse for wear but feeling no pain, to give Lonigan and Slater their chance at the town. The eager pair reined up at the edge of Virginia City just at sundown and commenced staggering back and forth across C Street in their intended attempt to visit every saloon along its length.

C Street slashed across the steep face of Mount Davidson creating Virginia City's main boulevard. Cobbled-together shacks tumbled down from the slope above; downhill sprouted headframes of the richest silver mines ever known. In between, C Street rollicked day and night. Drinking establishments, opium dens, gambling houses, music halls, mercantiles, billiards parlors, haberdasheries, whorehouses, barber shops, restaurants—any and every appetite itching a man could be scratched several times over along this chaotic, raucous, decadent dirt road.

Before the night was finished—but not long before—Josh and Six Bits had made the circuit, ending their quest in the crowded, noisy, smelly C Street Saloon and Entertainment Emporium. The ramshackle saloon sat at the northern reach of C Street, the first or last place anyone coming to or leaving town on the main road north would encounter. Josh swayed gently against the bar, grateful for having it there to hold up himself and the considerable load of whiskey he carried.

THE DEATH OF DELGADO

The bar graced the north wall of the saloon, staggering back from the front doors along most of the building's narrow length. An out-of-tune piano, whose saving grace was its ability to jangle loudly if not melodically, filled the space from the end of the bar to the back wall. A battered door hung over a passage cut through the center of that wall, behind which were three narrow curtained-off cribs where saloon girls served up their own brand of intoxication.

Front-to-back along the south wall marched three scarred tables surrounded by rickety chairs. Next came a faro layout, abandoned at the time in favor of the game at the poker table in the back corner.

Here, Six Bits Slater was engaged in his favorite pastime. Granted, the man would gamble on anything and play any game. But the ever-more popular card game called poker was his preferred means of disposing of any money he happened to have. Faro, he often told Josh, was a fool's game where you played only against the house and the house held the odds.

Poker, though, that was different.

Slater liked the fact that every player at the table played against every other, with no one, including the house, having an advantage. Hell, you didn't even need the house to play poker. But the house was in tonight's game, in the person of Calvin Wiley, proprietor of the C Street Saloon and Entertainment Emporium.

He was a man gone soft and fat, given to perfumed hair oils and barbershop shaves and suits more suited to the elegance of a riverboat than the dingy environs of the Nevada desert. Still and all, his pretensions in dress and grooming could not disguise the fact that he was but a crude Missouri Puke belching and scratching and hacking and spitting his way down the social ladder he wanted so desperately to climb.

Tonight, he was financing his affectations at the expense of Six Bits Slater. Through the course of the night and a run of luck the length of C Street, Slater had managed to turn his forty-dollar wages into the princely sum of eighty-four dollars. But two hours across the table from Wiley had reduced him once again to poverty.

Slater considered the cards in his hand. His three-card draw had helped the pair of queens he got in the original deal. The king of clubs was worthless to his purpose so he pulled it from the center of the filled out hand and placed it behind the other cards. But the other two drawn proved more useful—a pair of threes.

Queens and threes. The way the cards had been falling on this table that ought to be a winner, Slater thought. So when the bet made its way around the table, he raised the stakes just enough to let the players know he was serious but not enough to scare them off. The next player saw the raise and the bet came to Wiley.

"Here's five," he said, tossing a gold piece into the pot for the call. Then he counted out a stack of coins and slid it to the center of the table. "And here's fifteen more."

You could almost feel the breeze from the poker hands hitting the table as every player in the game folded.

Except Six Bits Slater.

He scraped together every coin he had and borrowed a gold Eagle from Josh to see the bet. Wiley could have raised again and forced Slater out of the game, but, being a sporting man he said, instead, "What you got, cowboy?"

Six Bits fanned his two pairs onto the felt and reached confidently toward the pot.

"Hold on there," Wiley said.

He closed up the fan of cards in his hand and placed the stack face up on the table. Then, with his index finger, he slid the cards aside one by one to reveal a full house—sixes and tens.

When both of Wiley's hands hit the tabletop to rake in the pot holding the last of Slater's money, Six Bits took the opportunity to shove the barrel of his pistol under the gambler's well-trimmed moustaches, drawing back the hammer as he did so.

Slater said, "Now *you* hold on there, you sonofabitch."

"What the hell's the matter with you cowboy?" Wiley said as Slater rose to his feet. "Can't stand to lose?"

"Oh, I can stand losing, all right. It's part of the game. What I can't stand is being cheated."

The word "cheat" prompted a wholesale scraping of chair legs across the plank floor as the other players vacated the table. The commotion drew the attention of the crowd and silence rippled across the saloon until the only sound in the room was the tick-tock-tick of a wind-up wall clock above the bar and the noise of C Street seeping in through the swinging doors.

Wiley appeared unruffled but beads of sweat appearing on his forehead betrayed his anxiety.

"Holster that gun and get out of my saloon, you sorry bastard," he eventually said, prompting the exhalation of so much held breath you'd swear the flames in the lamps flickered.

"I ain't no bastard," Six Bits said. "I just can't locate my folks."

That prompted titters from a few patrons, but the laughter was soon swallowed by the tension.

"Get out."

"I won't do it. Not before I kill you."

"You'll hang if you do."

At that, Six Bits laughed. "Hell," he said, "nobody would convict a man who killed a card cheater and you know it."

"I am not a cheater and you know it."

"You're not only a cheat, you're a liar. You've got so much pasteboard stuffed in your sleeves and cuffs and pockets you'd likely catch fire if you got too close to a flame."

Wiley's only response was that the beads of sweat on his forehead grew so heavy they succumbed to gravity and commenced rolling down the fat gambler's face.

Six Bits cast a glance toward his friend at the bar.

"Come over here and clean him out," he said, and Josh Lonigan pushed himself away from the bar and walked over to the poker table, his footsteps ringing hollow through the saloon.

Josh peeled back the gambler's jacket cuffs and shirt sleeves, revealing hidden cards up both arms. Cards were pulled from Wiley's watch pocket and another was revealed when Josh jerked the vest open, popping off buttons in the process.

Six Bits said, "You said you ain't been cheating, you lying sonofabitch. What do you say now?"

Wiley sat and sweated in silence.

"Kill him," one of the other card players said, triggering assenting murmurs through the crowd, many members of which had come to the realization that Wiley had likely been skinning them right along.

"I ought to. But being a betting man, I got a better idea. You game for an honest wager, Wiley?"

"What's the game?"

"Five-card stud poker. That way we can keep your grimy mitts off the cards. One hand. He deals," Six Bits said, inclining his head toward the card player who had encouraged Wiley's death.

"What's the bet?"

"Well, here's how I see it. About the only thing I hold just now is your life in my hands. I'm willing to bet that against something you got—the title to this hell hole."

"You crazy?" Wiley sputtered. "You want me to risk my saloon on a poker hand?"

"That's up to you. Worthless as your life is, it ought to be worth more than this place."

"I guess I got no choice in the matter."

"I guess that's right."

Six Bits asked Lonigan to cover Wiley, holstered his pistol, sat down, then waved the designated dealer toward an empty chair.

"Deal," he said.

The man gathered up all the cards from the table, including Wiley's holdouts, and pitched the lot into a spittoon. The crowd pressed close to the table, forcing the bartender to elbow his way through with a fresh, sealed deck. The dealer unwrapped and shuffled the cards three times then slid the stack toward Six Bits for the cut.

"Let Wiley cut them," he said. "I don't think he can sully the cards just by cutting them."

Wiley lifted off the top two thirds of the deck and set it aside. The dealer put the bottom stack on top with the comment, "Cut 'em deep, sleep in the street," which drew a nasty stare from the still-current proprietor of the C Street Saloon and Entertainment Emporium.

Hole cards hit the felt followed immediately by a face-up ten of diamonds to Wiley and the ace of hearts to Slater.

Six Bits did not peek at his hole card.

Wiley cupped his hand around his and rolled back a corner to reveal the jack of clubs.

"Now you've looked, get your slippery hands away from them cards," Six Bits said.

Wiley complied.

"Ace bets," the dealer said.

"There ain't no bets but the one, you dumb shit!" Wiley said, stress evident in his voice if not his demeanor.

"Queen on top of the ten," said the dealer of Wiley's growing hand, "possible straight."

Then, "Eight of spades to go with the still-high ace."

The players contemplated the cards for but a second before the next addition lit on their respective piles.

"Nine of hearts to Mr. Wiley. Straight still possible," the dealer said.

"Six Bits gets the three of spades. Ace high still the betting hand."

Wiley knew he had the jack of clubs in the hole and wished to hell he could somehow slip a king or an eight onto the deck to complete the straight. Were he the dealer, it could be done. But this, damn it all, this was an honest game and he felt himself at a disadvantage.

Then, "Nine of clubs. Busted the straight, but a pair of nines showing."

And then, "Seven of clubs to Six Bits. Pair of nines the high hand. Anything better?"

Wiley flipped over his hole card.

"No help from the jack. Pair of nines still on top."

Six Bits Slater made no move to turn his hole card, choosing instead to watch runnels of perspiration creep down Calvin Wiley's face. After ten seconds that stretched into eternity, he reached down without averting his eyes and slowly overturned the card. From the crowd's reaction, he knew it was a good one.

The dealer said, "Ace of diamonds—pair of aces wins!"

Wiley sagged in his seat, not knowing whether to be sorry at the loss of the saloon or happy to still be drawing breath.

"To quote the previous owner of this handsome establishment," Six Bits told Wiley with an insincere smile, "'get out of my saloon, you sorry bastard.'"

With surprising speed given the man's girth, Calvin Wiley vacated the premises.

"Drinks on the house!" Six Bits shouted.

The party was on.

———◆———

Memories crept up slow on Josh Lonigan and he didn't rush things. He lay as still as possible for a time, trying to make sense of the noises. A clangy piano fought for dominance over a crowd of rowdy voices.

He lifted one eyelid ever so slow, using all his concentration to keep the other closed and saw sunlight streaming through gaps in a warped greenwood wall. Lonigan allowed the other eyelid to lift, despite the fact that the air on his eyeballs was the consistency of crushed glass, and glanced slowly about.

Finally, he realized, remembered, where he was, but had only a fuzzy notion of how he came to be there. Where he was, was on a cot in a crib in the back of the C Street Saloon and Entertainment Emporium.

One by one, he activated his extremities and since none of his motion was hindered, concluded he was alone.

Except, that is, for the loud snores leaking through the curtain from the next crib. He knew the source of the snorts and wheezes and whistles was Six Bits Slater, Josh having spent more nights trying to sleep through that same racket than he cared to remember.

"Six Bits," he called weakly.

No response. Not even a change in rhythm.

"Six Bits!" he said, louder.

Same result.

Lonigan got himself upright, took a moment to accustom himself to the change in position, and shuffled slowly around the end of the curtain. There, in the next crib, Six Bits Slater was sprawled across the cot in every possible direction. One spurred and booted foot was on the floor, the other bent awkwardly and dangling off the opposite side. His arms were flung to the sides, palms upward and fingers twitching with every snort of every snore.

"Slater!" he said, grabbing Six Bits by the toe of his boot and shaking vigorously to punctuate the call. At that, Six Bits sat upright as if stung by a lightning bolt.

"What!? What the hell?"

"C'mon, get up. It's burning daylight."

"So?" Six Bits said, lapsing halfway back into whatever fog he had just been startled out of.

"Get up."

"What for?"

"Don't you remember? Hell, Six Bits, you've got responsibilities."

"Huh?"

"Why, you're the new owner and operator of the C Street Saloon and Entertainment Emporium."

"Oh. That. Oh, shit!"

Josh said, "What's the matter?"

"What you said—responsibilities."

Lonigan looked perplexed.

"Hell's bells, just think of it, Josh. I got this here building to worry about, and that ain't the half of it. I'm responsible for at least one barkeep I know of, that raggedy-ass piano player jangling away out there, and three whores."

"So?"

"So! Don't you see Josh, I'm the one that's got to see that all these people get paid, and come up with the money to do it. I don't know thing one about buying whiskey more than a bottle at a time, or how to put out a free lunch, how to take a rake from the card games, how to split the proceeds with the women—hell, I don't know nothing about a saloon except how to raise hell in one. I ain't never been nothing but a saddle tramp and never figured on being nothing but."

"But you're a businessman now, Six Bits! Hell, you could get rich."

"Not me. Not interested."

"What you gonna do?"

"Don't know. But I got six bits says I'll think of something by the time we hit them swinging doors on the way out of here."

The two cowboys slid through the door into the saloon proper and paused for a moment to survey Slater's recently acquired empire.

It appeared the party had been going nonstop since Six Bits called for drinks for the house. He had neglected to rescind the order before incapacitation set in, and it seems that word had spread far and wide across the Comstock mining district that drinks were on the house at the C Street Saloon and Entertainment Emporium.

So, in the absence of the boss, the piano man kept pounding. The barkeeper kept pouring. The saloon girls kept serving drinks to prospective customers who were more interested in free booze than anything else on the menu—which explains why Six Bits and Lonigan had slept undisturbed in the ladies' usual workplaces.

"Let's go," Six Bits said and set out through the crowd toward the batwing doors at the other end of the room.

They hadn't got far when someone in the crowd recognized Six Bits through the alcohol haze. Cheers, hurrahs, backslaps, handshakes, and all manner of drunken adulation accompanied them the rest of the way.

When they finally reached the front, Six Bits pushed through the swinging doors and said over his shoulder to Josh, "You owe me six bits. Be sure to mark it down."

"So what's your plan?"

"You'll see. Come on."

Six Bits, with his pal Josh in tow, scoured every nook and cranny of C Street asking after Calvin Wiley, erstwhile proprietor of the C Street Saloon and Gambling Emporium. They finally tracked him down, stabbing forlornly with a fork at a plate of chop suey in a three-table noodle parlor tucked between a barber shop and pool hall.

"What the hell you two want now?" he said, the words slurred by a recipe of flat beer and greasy cabbage. "Already stole the only saloon I got. Ain't you caused me enough trouble?"

"How about we end those troubles, here and now," Slater said.

"Whatever do you mean?" Wiley asked, to the accompaniment of a rattling throat hack and a misguided spit shot at a cuspidor.

Six Bits grimaced, his stomach too tender this day for such demonstrations, but he carried on. "Wiley, I woke up this morning— this afternoon—whenever the hell it is—realizing I don't want to be no respectable citizen nor a property owner nor a businessman."

"What's that got to do with me?"

"I propose to sell you back your saloon."

The fat man let go a disheartened laugh, then said, "How do you propose I pay for it? I ain't exactly flush with cash, you know. Every penny I got is tied up in that place already."

"Well, here's how I figure it. I walked through your doors after a pretty good run of luck in this town. More than doubled my month's wage—had eighty-four dollars in my pocket. If I was to walk away from the C Street Saloon and Entertainment Emporium with the same money in my pocket as I had when I walked in, I'd call it good."

Lonigan was too flabbergasted to do more than sputter.

Wiley was so dumbfounded he could only manage a single word: "Done."

"One other thing," Six Bits said.

Wiley waited, suspicion all over his face.

"I ever hear tell of you cheating at them card tables, faro or poker either one, I'll come back to this town and shoot your sorry ass. And I'll do it, too. I already got one killing coming to me where you're concerned. Don't make it two."

Wiley nodded his ascent then yanked out his shirttail to get at a moneybelt from which he extracted four twenty-dollar gold pieces and a five-dollar Half Eagle.

"Keep the change," he said.

Within minutes, Joshua Lonigan and Seth "Six Bits" Slater had fetched their horses from the livery and were heading back to the herd at a long trot. Once clear of the crowds of Virginia City they slowed to a lazy walk along the downhill dirt road. Ahead, a pair of magpies sat between the ruts pecking out bits of grain from a pile of droppings left lately by one of the well-fed horses that hauled freight wagons along the road.

"See them two magpies yonder?" Slater asked.

"I see them," Josh said.

"I got six bits that says the one on your side flies first."

THE DARKNESS OF THE DEEP

In 2003, Western Writers of America collected stories for an anthology, published by Forge Books, to commemorate the organization's fiftieth anniversary. Renowned author and editor Dale L. Walker titled the volume Westward: A Fictional History of the American West, *and selected stories based on actual people and events. "The Darkness of the Deep" is inspired by murderer and fugitive Rafael Lopez, object of the biggest manhunt in Utah's history. The criminal's fate was a mystery at the time the story was written. Evidence discovered since suggests Lopez was shot and killed by Texas Ranger Frank Hamer—the man famous for the bloody ambush of outlaws Bonnie and Clyde.*

———————◆———————

I fear darkness. At times it wrings sweat and squeezes the breath out of me as I lie abed wishing for the illumination of dreams. It has not always been so. I can trace the origin of my fright to a precise time and place: twenty-three years, seven months, thirteen days ago; the Alta Incline in the Minnie Mine.

The year was 1913. The "Wild West" was but a faded memory in most locales, but the narrow defile of Bingham Canyon was as raucous and rowdy as ever was any town at the end of the trail or the end of the rails. As you might have surmised, Bingham Canyon was mining country, a mountain filled with treasure but trapped in ore so low in grade that only large mining syndicates could afford the machinery and manpower required to extract paying quantities of metal. The mines needed men, so the town was awash in men. A regular stewpot, it was—Cousin Jacks, Chinks, Micks, Bohunks, Canucks, Greasers, Scandahoovians—every kind of man you can think of. Too many men, and too few women. Therein lies the beginning of this tale.

Rafael López, they say, was at the end of his one day off in the week. A day spent swilling what passed for liquor in the town's saloons. He stumbled and staggered through stupor and snowstorm uphill to the shack where his "sweetheart" lived and met a friend making his exit through the door López planned to enter. They argued. They fought. López pulled a pistol from his pocket and shot the man dead.

Now comes Police Chief J. W. Grant. "Dub" he was called. By the time he arrived at the crime scene, López was long gone. But there was no shortage of witnesses to the fact that the killer, sobered by his deed, had gone to his own quarters, loaded up with firearms and ammunition, and hightailed it out of town afoot.

Standing in fresh-fallen snow at the edge of town, Dub shivered as he eyed the trail.

"Well. He ain't likely to get too far too fast," he said. "I suppose mornin's soon enough to start after him. Sorenson!"

"Yeah, Dub," answered Jules Sorenson, Deputy Sheriff assigned by the County to the Canyon.

"Gather up Otto Witbeck and Nels Jensen and meet me here at first light."

Dub and the deputies followed the clear trail across the divide into Utah Valley, surprised as the sun climbed higher how much of the country López had covered. Crowding the western shore of Utah Lake, the Mexican led them all the way south into Goshen Valley. After spotting from his saddle some fresh footprints, Dub, keeping Sorenson at his side, sent two of the deputies on a small circle to attempt to corner the fugitive. He warned all to stay alert.

Too late. Rifle shots rang out from the willows.

"Dub, I'm a dead man!" Sorenson said. He looked surprised as he slid from the saddle.

The other riders, still but a short distance away, spurred up to ride to the defense of the Police Chief, whose horse was pitching and milling in the hail of bullets. Otto took a bullet just under the hat brim and rolled backward off his mount. Another shot hit Nels in the shirt pocket. With half his force shot out of the saddle and half of what was left mortally wounded, Dub controlled his horse, grasped the reins of the horse Nels was clinging to, and fled the field with appropriate haste.

Now begins my part in the hunt for Rafael López.

By the following morning, Dub had gathered a considerably larger posse for the pursuit. I was a member, one of twenty or so down from Bingham Canyon. While sincere in my intention to aid in the capture of the desperado, I confess a secondary ambition—to capture the excitement of the event for the readers of the *Canyon Chronicle*, for which I was employed as a reporter and typesetter. In spite of the mostly indoor nature of my vocation, I was not unfamiliar with the outdoor life, the squeak of saddle leather, or the use of arms. As the fourth son of the third wife of a polygamous Mormon father, my prospects of maintaining a livelihood in my family's livestock operations were nil. Being bookish by nature, I opted for a college education and the literary life. The education, at least, had panned out. Authorial success beyond the newspaper page was yet some distance into the future.

But I digress. Our posse was joined that morning by another dozen men from the nearby burg of Lehi, with small groups from elsewhere swelling our ranks as the day passed. We found nothing of López, despite scouring the shores of the lake in ever-growing circles radiating from the scene of the fugitive's ambush of Dub and the deputies. The snow had somewhat melted away and drifted so no trail was apparent. An uneventful day, all told. The next day started the same, save that there were now in excess of a hundred men in our camp, the perceived excitement of the chase having spread from village to town.

"Men, this Raphael López we're after is a bad hombre," Dub announced to the assembled mass. "He knows how to shoot and he's not afeared to pull the trigger. Most of you know by now that he's killed three good lawmen and a no-account Mick miner already. So be sharp. Don't do nothin' stupid. We don't need no dead heroes."

We rode out in contingents of twenty riders, directed by Dub to various parts of the lakeside mountains as if on a gather. Late in the afternoon, shooting broke out somewhere north of our location. We hastened over the intervening ridges until reaching the dry canyon whence the shooting originated.

López had ensconced himself in a jumble of boulders at the top of a steep draw that offered no access from any direction save below, due to surrounding cliffs and shale-covered slopes. From his eagle's nest, he could hold off an army, which is exactly what he was doing when we arrived. After the initial flurry, the noise of which had attracted virtually the entire posse to the area, those in pursuit realized they could not get a clear shot at the pursued, who, with a few well-placed shots, kept us at bay until nightfall.

Morning brought renewed attempts on our part to infiltrate the Mexican's lair. It soon was apparent that the site was undefended, our quarry having disappeared into thin air. Shell casings revealed that López had expended all available ammunition for his discarded rifle, and his use of pistols the evening before had been of necessity rather than choice. Finding no clue as to his current whereabouts despite hours of casting about for sign, the posse disbanded. Those of us from Bingham Canyon turned our mounts north.

"Dub, where do you suppose he's gone to?" one of our party asked the Police Chief.

"Well, I reckon he's on the way to California. There's a whole lot of nothin' between here and there but if anyone can make it, and plenty have, that pepper belly can sure do it."

"So you're not going after him?"

"Nope. Not unless someone reports seein' him somewheres. Like I said, there's a whole lot of nothin' out there."

"But Dub," I chimed in, "what can I tell readers of the *Chronicle* about the disposition of the case?"

"Hell, I don't know. You're the newspaper man, not me. But I guess you can say we got rid of López. Maybe it's not all neat and tidy like a trial and a hangin' but he's gone all the same."

Life in the Canyon had settled back into its routine of changing shifts, clanging hoist bells, the felt but not heard thump of blasting deep underground, and the ring of ore car wheels rolling on steel tracks when word reached the police that Rafael López was back in town.

"Bullshit!" Dub sprayed into the pale face of the store clerk standing before him. "You're nuts!"

"N-n-no sir," the clerk managed to force through rattling jaws. "It was h-him. He's carried an account at the company store since I been there. I've waited on L- López a dozen times at least."

"Well what the hell did he want this time?"

"B-b-bullets. He wanted bullets for a rifle and two kinds of pistols. And s-some food. You know, canned stuff. Stuff that would keep."

"And you gave it to him?" Dub asked.

"No sir. I didn't give it to him. I sold it to him on account. Like I s-said, he's on the books."

"Damn. A cold-blooded killer and known fugitive waltzes into the store pretty as you please for supplies and gets them, just like that. Lemme guess what happens next—he invited you up to his shack for supper in appreciation of your cooperation."

"No, D-Dub—ch-chief—sir. He didn't. He didn't go home. He went into the Minnie," the clerk said.

An interesting turn of events, I thought. I overheard the greater part of the conversation after beating a quick trail to the Police Station upon getting the news from a street urchin we pay to keep us informed of events.

So here we have Rafael López on the lam in a vast network of drifts, stopes, shafts, winzes, and inclines deep in the dark bowels of the earth. Knowing the Minnie mine well from his employ there, he would likely be able to elude capture for quite some time—or at least as long as provisions allowed. Dub, seeing no other course, opted to wait him out. Guards were posted at every point of egress from the Minnie, with simple instructions to be especially vigilant during shift changes, and to arrest López when he surfaced to replenish his supplies.

But he never resurfaced. Plenty of miners reported encountering him in the depths of the mine. Some claimed he robbed them of lunch buckets at gunpoint. Others reported food and water pilfered from places they had stowed it while working. As time passed, Dub was convinced the Mexican had accomplices—willingly or under threat—carrying supplies into the mine.

Finally giving up on his ineffectual siege strategy, Dub decided to smoke out the fugitive. Literally. He as much as ordered the mining syndicate to shut down operations for a shift at tremendous expense. Engineers closed off certain ventilation shafts to control airflow through the mine and Dub had huge bonfires built at all the intake vents. Additional guards were posted at every point of escape from the mine. Then piles of wet straw, moldy hay, and green juniper boughs were heaped on the fires. Clouds of greasy, acrid smoke poured into the mine and eventually found the outlets. Dub ordered the crews to keep the fires smoking and the sentries to keep a sharp eye. But, in the end, smoke was the only thing that came out of the mine.

"Well, hell. There's no way he's still in there," Dub opined. "If he ever was."

"But there have been eyewitness reports. Besides," I asked, "if López isn't in the Minnie where is he?"

"You ever been in a mine, copy cub?"

"No. I've never had occasion."

"Well, let me tell you somethin'. It's dark down there. Real dark. So dark it can make you see things that ain't there. And you hear things. Hell, I don't have any idea what them witnesses thought they saw."

"But what about the stolen dinner buckets?"

"That's easy enough explained. Come the day after payday, a lot of them miners down that hole ain't got two nickels to rub together. I don't suppose chowin' down on somebody else's lunch would weigh too heavy on their minds. As for your other question, I can't even guess where López is—but I don't intend to lay awake nights worryin' about it. There's plenty enough misbehavior out in plain sight in this canyon to keep me busy."

So, once again, the routine of changing shifts, clanging hoist bells, the thump of blasting deep underground, and the ring of ore car wheels on steel rails held sway. But not for long. One day a visibly shaken miner rushed into the police station. By happenstance, I was there checking arrest records for anything that might prove newsworthy.

"I have a message for the police chief," the miner said.

"And who might you be?" Dub said.

"My name is Gustav Mueller. They call me Dutchy. I am a timberman at the Minnie."

Dub perked up at the mention of the mine. "What's the message and who's it from?"

"The man, he said his name is Rafael López. He said to ask about the deputy he met by the lakeshore—if the deputy has a bad headache."

Dub mulled that one over, realizing that while it was no secret that Otto Witbeck had been shot and killed, not many knew or cared that his death resulted from a bullet placed dead center in his forehead. The chief's interest heightened.

"What else?"

"This López, he seems very angry. He said he wishes to meet Dub Grant at the Alta Incline in the Minnie between shifts tonight. He said he will kill Dub Grant."

"He says that, does he," Dub said. "Well, here's what we'll do, Mr. Dutchy. You're goin' to keep my appointment with Rafael López."

"Oh no, sir! I do not care to see this man ever again."

"But you'll do it Dutchy, or you'll find yourself behind bars for aidin' and abettin' a fugitive or whatever other reasons I can come up with to put you there. And by the time I decide to let you out on account of the whole thing being a big mistake, your sorry life will have passed you by. Now pay attention, and tell López this—tell him that that headache ain't botherin' that deputy no more, but that it's still likely to cause him—López—plenty of pain and sufferin'."

The reluctant miner attempted to deliver the message, he claimed, but the Mexican failed to show at the appointed time and place. Despite the futility of the previous attempt to smoke the renegade out, Dub considered another try to be a smarter approach than sending men into the Minnie to poke their noses into all the dark corners to see if López would shoot them off. So the miners showing up for morning shift were sent home and the fires were kindled again. Again, the result was a disappointment. As the final wisps of smoke vacated the mine, Dub decided to comb the Minnie despite the difficulty and danger.

Dub lined up a reluctant posse, recruiting as many miners familiar with the Minnie as possible to serve either as guides or deputies or both. At each of the mine's several levels, teams trooped outward from the shafts, breaking into ever smaller groups, following branching drifts toward working faces and raises that led to overhead stopes. I obtained permission to accompany Dub. Guided by Dutchy, we hiked directly to the place of the miner's reported encounter with López.

The Alta Incline is, in the jargon of the mining trade, a winze—a tunnel that angles upward from the 825-foot level to the 700 level. Dutchy led our parade upward by the light of a miner's torch he carried; our only light, as Dub and I had our hands full of armament. We had proceeded maybe a third of the way up the Incline when a rifle roared, effectively deafening us with its initial report as well as its echoes in that confined space. Dutchy pitched face downward and the lantern shattered, plunging us into instant and complete darkness save for the bright spots burned behind my eyes by the muzzle flash.

I could see nothing. I could barely sense my own presence in the pitch black let alone that of Dub, Dutchy, or our attacker. And while the feeling of isolation was frightening, the fact that I knew I was not alone was even more disconcerting. I did not know what had become of Dub. Perhaps the shot that downed Dutchy had taken the Police Chief out of action as well. I dared not speak, fearing my voice would betray my location and provide an effective, if unseen, target for the assassin. So I waited.

The blackness was so overwhelming that my very senses failed. Although I hugged a rock wall, I had no sensation of being upright. For all I knew, I may have been lying down or even upside down. I know not how long I sat in fear and silence. It seemed an eternity, but may have been mere moments—my ability to sense the passage of time no longer functional. There were sounds. Small sounds, strange and unfamiliar;

their source or location indecipherable. And the occasional rattle of pebbles falling, or rolling.

"You there, scribbler?"

Had I known up from down I would have jumped a foot in the air. The voice of Dub Grant boomed out of the silence, although he spoke barely above a whisper.

"I am here. Are you wounded?"

"Nah, I'm fine. You?"

"I have not been shot. But I am not fine."

"I know what you mean," Dub said. "This is a strange fix I find myself in."

"At least you can find yourself. I am not even sure I am me."

Dub did not respond. The darkness that had seemed to lift with our conversation once again weighed on me.

"Dub?"

"Yeah?"

"Do you think he's still here? López?"

"Can't say for sure, but I don't think so," he said. "I've been listenin' and I can only hear the two of us breathin'."

"I guess that means Dutchy is dead."

"I fear so. The last thing I saw was the back of his head turnin' inside out."

Having no response, I allowed silence to descend. I heard nothing except my own breathing, unable even to detect the sound of Dub's, though he could mine, he had claimed. After an interval that seemed interminable came the sound of pebbles dribbling down.

"What does that noise mean, Dub?" I asked.

"Beats the hell out of me. Rats, maybe. Might just be the ground shiftin' a bit and shakin' things loose. I've heard miners tell stories about tommyknockers. Maybe it's them."

"How are we going to get out of here?"

"We ain't—at least until someone misses us and hunts us up. We try walkin' around blind down here we'll be bumpin' our heads and bouncin' off walls or fallin' down holes. We had best just stay put. I do believe a smoke will help pass the time."

Dub rustled about a bit, rolling a cigarette, I assumed.

"Aren't you worried that you will betray our position?"

"Nah. I'm pretty sure that pepper belly has crawled back in his hole. Care for the makins'?" Dub asked as he scratched a match to the wall.

"No, thank you. I don't—

The explosion of rifle fire would have drowned out my next words, had there been any. The sound of the shot reverberated up and down the Incline as I watched Dub's toes turn upward in the feeble light of the dropped match fizzling out. I heard deliberate footsteps retreat; whether up or down the Incline I cannot say. Then, only darkness.

Later—how much later I do not know, but had it been much later than it was it would have been too late—I heard voices and detected a faint glow. Then I could see three men, two carrying lights, standing above—I assumed at the point where the Alta Incline connected with the 700 level.

"Dub!" someone shouted. "Dub?"

"Down here!" I replied. "Be careful! López was here—but I believe he has gone."

"We heard shooting. Anyone hurt?"

"Dutchy is dead. And Dub is shot. He may be killed."

No one found Rafael López that day. No one has found Rafael López since. Reports drift in from time to time of sightings in other mining regions—Colorado, Idaho, California, Nevada—reports carried by gyppo miners who claim to have known him in those parts.

And there were—and still are, from time to time—sightings of the Mexican in the Minnie. He is blamed yet for stolen dinner buckets, misplaced tools, misfired rounds, and any number of other misdeeds. For a time, I followed up every report, and can say without equivocation that the whereabouts of Rafael López are unknown. Perhaps he did escape from the Minnie and departed for parts unknown. Maybe he remained underground, victim of an unknown accident—blown apart in a powder blast, I like to think, mucked up with the ore and burned away as dross in the mills; a refiner's fire, of sorts.

As it turned out, I was in the darkness in the Minnie that day for a mere forty minutes, more or less. Just long enough for other searchers, who had heard both shots, to track down their source. Forty minutes from which I have yet to recover. Sometimes my dreams are illuminated by the sight of the toes of Dub's boots turning upward as he died. But, always, the light fades and there is only darkness.

It is the darkness that haunts me.

WHITE FACE, RED BLOOD

When it comes to Utah outlaws, no one enjoys the fame—or infamy—of Robert LeRoy Parker. Although relatively unknown by his given name, he is, thanks to a movie, well known by his favorite alias—Butch Cassidy. Other than the occasional theft of cattle and horses, this story pre-dates his life as a bandit. Not long after the actual events recounted in this story, however, Robert—Bob—Butch—and his saddle pals, Utah outlaw (and later lawman) Matt Warner and Tom McCarty, robbed a bank in Telluride, Colorado, launching the crime career of one of the West's most notorious desperados. Editor Robert J. Randisi included this story in the 2013 e-book anthology from Piccadilly Publishing, Livin' on Jacks and Queens.

---◆---

The bullet from Tom McCarty's pistol punched a hole in the forehead of the horseback Ute Indian. He slipped sideways off his startled mount and if he had any life left in him it drifted away with the cloud of dust raised when he hit the ground.

Once the remaining Indians settled shying, skittering horses, a pair of them dismounted and hoisted their fallen leader belly down over the back of his trembling horse, remounted, and led a parade of disheartened Utes out of the canyon cove that concealed the cabin. McCarty, Warner, and Bob Parker followed the Indians' progress with the business end of their guns.

As the last of the Utes rounded the bend, Parker jammed his Colt into its holster. "Sonofabitch, Tom! What did you go and do that for?"

"I'm damned if they was gettin' out of here with White Face."

"They wasn't gonna get the horse. No way was that gonna happen. But it didn't take killing to prevent it!"

McCarty lowered the hammer on his pistol and slowly holstered it. "We worked too damn hard to get that pony. I ain't takin' any chances. Not after yesterday."

"Bullshit," Parker said as he spun on his heel and stomped off toward the cabin.

"He's right, you know," Warner said, almost in a whisper.

"Don't you start with me, Matt!"

Warner stared at McCarty until the silence grew uncomfortable. His face did not betray what he was feeling when finally he spoke. "You'd best rein in that temper of yours, Tom. I don't hold with needless killing. Even if it's only an Indian. Next time you pull that pistol it better be worth it, 'cause if it ain't, you'll be ridin' on."

———◆———

The Ute pony called White Face came into Matt Warner's possession, with a lesser share each to Bob Parker and Tom McCarty, at the end of a long Colorado summer. At the beginning of the season, neither Parker nor McCarty had been in Warner's string.

It was in Telluride where he and Parker first shared a beer. Warner was new in town, having drifted into the country from a ranch in the shadows of the LaSal Mountains in the Utah Territory west of there. On the end of his lead rope when he rode into town was Betty, a mare Warner figured could outrun anything with hair and four legs. Trailing behind were twenty head of broke horses from his ranch string, and his saddlebags were stuffed with all the money he could muster—all of which he was willing, eager, to gamble on the brown mare.

Telluride, being a thriving metropolis fat with money mucked out of the mines that gave the city a reason to be, seemed to the Utah cowboy a likely place to get up a match race and fill his pockets with silver, for Warner had heard tell of a fast colt owned by a man named Mulcahy. That horse's reputation was such that Warner figured its owner ought to be ripe for picking.

The noise, the crowds, the size of the city overwhelmed Warner, accustomed as he was to wide-open spaces, peace and quiet, and miles and miles of high, dry Colorado Plateau between his outfit and the nearest neighbor. The cowboy and his remuda attracted little notice as he made his way through the streets, crowded as they were with horses, mules, oxen, cattle, sheep, freighters, delivery wagons, carriages, carts, buggies, riders, and all manner of folks afoot. Rows of stores, shops, eating houses, and saloons—mostly saloons—lined the busy streets, more commerce than Warner had ever seen in one place at one time.

He managed to wrangle his horses into a pen at a combination livery stable and wagon yard. The hostler there stabled Betty and Warner's preferred saddle mount, and offered to pasture the other horses out of town. A place in the corner of the hayloft above the stabled horses for the cowboy himself—upon his sworn promise not to smoke—finalized the negotiations. Warner hefted his saddle and bedroll into the loft, unpacked the bundle of cash money from his saddlebags and watched as the hostler locked it in the office safe, then joined the crowd in the streets.

For the remainder of the day and into the evening, Warner wandered from saloon to saloon. He sipped a few beers and filled his belly at the free lunch boards. But, mostly, he watched and listened. Before retiring to his nest in the hayloft, the cowboy had learned which saloons catered to miners, where horse-and-cattle folks bellied up to the bar, and which drinking establishments were frequented by the town's merchants, businessmen, high-stakes gamblers, and other moneyed types.

Come tomorrow, Warner would start down the road leading to riches.

———◆———

Mulcahy wasn't too hard to find. Warner bummed around the saloons for a day or two, asking questions when it wouldn't arouse suspicion or create curiosity. The day Mulcahy came to town Warner learned in one saloon that his man was in another grog shop holding court. He had been up north running a match race and told the tale of his colt's easy victory to anyone who would listen and everyone else within earshot—which was quite a distance, as Mulchay was of the Irish type that bloviated long and loud, with a double helping of boastfulness thrown in for seasoning.

Warner eased into the crowd and heard the story a time or two. When Mulcahy wore out the ears in that particular whiskey mill, he tipped his hat to his audience and announced business elsewhere before strutting out the door.

"Mr. Mulcahy?" Warner said, hustling to catch up to the clomping boots along the Telluride board sidewalk. "Mr. Mulcahy!"

The man stopped and eyed the ragtag cowboy but said nothing.

"Mr. Mulcahy—" Warner said again, then seemed at a loss for words to follow.

"You know my name. But you have me at a disadvantage there, as I know not who you are. Or why you have stopped me. Spit it out, man. I have business to attend to and haven't time to dawdle."

"Well, Mr. Mulcahy, sir," Warner said in his long Utah drawl. "It's about that horse of yours. The one you was talking about back there."

"Yes?"

"Sounds like he can run."

Mulcahy laughed. "For certain sure you are not from around here! Everyone knows that colt of mine. What's your interest?"

"Well, you see, I've got this little mare . . . ."

"And?"

Warner scrubbed at the dust on the boardwalk with the toes of his boots, cleared his throat, clasped his hands behind his back, dropped them to his sides, hitched one onto his waistband and used the other to tip back his hat. "I ain't sure, but I believe Betty can run pretty good . . . " he managed to say amid all the fumbling.

Mulcahy laughed. "Betty? You've a pony called Betty and you think she can run—is that it?"

"Yes, sir. And, well . . . ."

Mulcahy laughed. "It's a race you're after, is it?"

Warner swallowed hard. "Yes, sir."

Mulcahy laughed. "C'mon boy-o. Let's find a place to sit and I'll stand you to a drink and we'll talk business."

The pair turned into the next saloon along the walkway. Several patrons greeted Mulcahy as he made his way through the crowd, shaking hands and slapping backs and exchanging pleasantries along the way. They reached a table in the back corner, occupied by three men who looked to Warner like cowboys from local ranches enjoying an evening on the town.

"Gentlemen," Mulcahy said to them, "I've a bit of business to attend to and wonder will you give me the table. Drinks on me if you do."

As if choreographed and rehearsed, the three dusty men pushed back their chairs, telling, in their various ways as they stood, that they would be happy to relinquish their seats. Mulcahy pulled a half eagle coin from his pocket and flipped it toward one of the men, saying, as the cowboy snatched it out of mid-air, "Thank you, boys. Have yourselves another beer, and, if you'd be so kind, have the barkeep draw one for me and another for my friend here, and tell one of the ladies to bring them by."

Mulcahy and Warner sat and soon a pair of beer mugs, overflowing with foam, landed on the table, placed there, not by a serving girl, but by one of the cowboys with a, "Here you go, Mr. Mulcahy." He then backed away, holding his own full mug, to lean against the wall. And while the cowboy watched the goings-on in the saloon, Warner had the distinct impression the man was eavesdropping on their conversation.

"So you've got this horse . . . " Mulcahy said after foaming his walrus-like mustache, letting the invitation to speak trail off as he took another drink.

Warner sipped from his mug then set it back on the table where he slid it around in a circle, spreading a wet film across the marred surface.

"She's a little brown mare, like I said. I call her Betty."

"Not a name likely to strike fear into the hearts of the competition."

"No sir. I reckon not. But it fits, as there's not much to fear with that mare. She's just a ranch-raised cow horse, is all. She can run, though."

"Ranch raised, you say. Where is this ranch?" Mulcahy asked.

"Over in Utah. I got a place over toward the Spanish Valley. Just there at the base of the La Sal Mountains. Do you know that country?"

"No, sir, I don't." Mulcahy drained his beer in a few long gulps and waved the mug to attract the attention of a bar girl. "Another one for you?"

Warner's mug was still three-quarters full. "No thanks, Mr. Mulcahy."

"I'm still at a disadvantage, here. Your name, sir?"

"Warner. Matt Warner," he said, extending a hand across the table.

Mulcahy shook, then said, "So this mare of yours. You say she's fast. Have you raced her?"

"Not to speak of. There ain't much in the way of competition over my way. Meaning there's not all that many horses to run against or many folks wanting to run them. But she's held her own the few times I've raced her."

"And you want to match this mare, this Betty, against my colt?"

"Worth a try, I guess."

"You're a brave man, Mr. Warner. Either that, or plain stupid."

Warner cocked an eyebrow.

"You've ridden a long way just to lose your money. My colt is known far and wide. Even in Utah Territory, it would appear. Yet knowing he eats horses like yours for breakfast, you come all this way for a race."

This time, Warner laughed. "You've got it all wrong, Mr. Mulcahy. I didn't come here for no horse race. I brought a string of ranch horses for sale. See, I'm a fair hand with horses and raise a few on my place. Fact is, there's more than a little demand for my cow ponies in our country. But there ain't much market for them this season, so I thought I'd try my luck shifting them hereabouts."

"I see. So the mare's for sale, then?"

Warner swirled his mug around the table a few times before answering. "Every horse is for sale if the price is right. But, no, I didn't bring Betty along thinking to sell her. Just thought some time on the trail might toughen her up. Build a little more muscle, you know. She ain't wet enough saddle blankets to be a good enough using horse yet." He sipped his beer. "Besides, I kind of like that mare."

"So what put you in mind to challenge me to a race?"

"Heard you talking about your horse and racing and whatnot in that saloon down the way. Figured, what the hell—be good for a lark, if nothing else. Besides, Betty might just run the legs off your colt."

Mulcahy laughed. "I don't race for fun, you know. I doubt you've the stakes to make it worth lathering my colt."

"I reckon I could muster up five hundred dollars. Would that make it worth your while?"

If the race-horse man had not been a veteran card player and gambler, his eyes might have widened at the amount. But he did not betray his surprise and said, "Maybe. It's not much. But I might could make up the difference with side bets."

Warner waited, again slowly swirling his nearly empty beer mug around the stained tabletop.

Finally, Mulcahy said, "I guess you've got a race, sir. But, your mare being trail weary and my horse just back from running up north, let's give the ponies a rest. Shall we say Saturday next? Maybe given the time I can scare up a little action on the side—but I doubt many will bet against me, knowing my colt as they do."

The Utah cowboy agreed and the men talked longer to agree on terms: straight-up stakes without odds, no limit on side bets, three furlongs on a straight track, and each side to provide a judge to ensure fair play. They shook hands to seal the deal.

Mulcahy stood and slammed his mug sharply on the tabletop three or four times to quiet the room. "Gentlemen!" he shouted. "The race is on! This fellow here, Matt Warner by name, has challenged my colt to a race. Come Saturday next, I say without fear of contradiction, his mare will be publicly embarrassed—but Warner here is willing to risk it. Drinks on me!"

With that, he peeled some bills off his roll for the bartender and headed for the door, again running a gantlet of handshaking and backslapping. Warner drained off the last of his beer and left a moment later with very little notice, save a few curious looks from people in the crowd.

The leaning cowboy watched Warner leave, then shouldered himself away from the wall and followed him out the door.

———— • ————

The stable was quiet, only the occasional snort of a horse to break the silence. Warner walked down the alley to Betty's stall and propped his elbows atop the door. The mare nickered and shuffled over to where the cowboy stood. He scratched beneath her jaw and rubbed along her neck, talking softly.

He barely heard the footfalls before pulling his pistol, dropping to one knee and turning toward the dim square in the distance that was the stable door.

"I don't know who's there, but you better stand where you are," Warner said.

"Take it easy," a voice from the faint silhouette said. "I mean no harm."

"State your business."

"Just wanted to take a look at this horse of yours."

Warner laughed. "Brown mare in a dark stall? Even with a lantern— which you ain't got—you won't see much."

The shadow didn't answer, but Warner heard his feet shuffle.

"So, what is it you want?" he said as he ratcheted back the hammer on his pistol.

"Just talk. Nothing that requires guns."

"Walk back out that door. I'll follow."

The darkness of night in the street was just enough brighter than that in the stable that Warner could see the face of the man, but did not recognize him. Pistol still in hand, he said, "What is it?"

The man, dressed in range clothing much like Warner's, glanced at the pistol. "I'd be obliged if you'd put that away."

Sensing no threat, Warner squeezed the trigger and eased the hammer down then slid the revolver into the holster on his hip.

"Buy you a drink?" the man said.

Something about the cowboy seemed familiar, and Warner realized he was one of the men at the saloon table Mulcahy had commandeered. "Already had one. But then you know that, don't you."

"That mean you can't have another?

"I suppose not. Lead the way."

Warner followed the cowboy along the street, bypassing the saloon he'd frequented earlier in favor of a smaller alcohol parlor on the opposite side of the street in the next block.

"It's quieter here," the stranger said as he pushed through the doors.

A few drinkers propped themselves on the bar, and a table surrounded by a quiet card game rounded out the patrons. The two men filled some of the empty space at the near end of the bar and ordered beers.

"So?" Warner said after sipping brew through the foam.

"Heard you say you was from Utah. Around the La Sals?"

"That's right. You know that country?"

"Some. I'm from Utah myself."

"That right? Whereabouts?"

"Born in Beaver. Grew up in Circleville. Worked a while for a stockman out west of Milford, but didn't hang around long on account of a disagreement with the sheriff there. You?"

"My folks is in Levan. Haven't been there in years. Got in a disagreement over a girl when I was just a button and brained a fellow with a rock. Never supposed I'd be welcome there anymore. Worked on ranches up in Brown's Park, got my own place and raised horses. Moved down to the Spanish Valley country a few years ago. What's your name, anyway?"

"Parker. Robert LeRoy Parker. Some folks call me Bob. Others, Roy."

"Matt Warner," he said as he extended his hand. "Good to meet another Utah boy."

As they shook hands, Parker asked, "How good is that horse of yours?"

"Good enough. Why?"

"You're gonna lose that race."

"You think?"

"I've seen his colt run. He fairly flies."

Warner thought for a time and sipped his beer before saying, "But you haven't seen my Betty run."

"True enough," Parker said. "But Mulcahy has taken on all comers and ain't never been beat."

"I guess I'll take my chances."

Parker drained his beer, said, "Just be sure you don't bet everything you got. Leave yourself something to get back home on."

Warner laughed. "How you gettin' home, Bob?"

The cowboy looked puzzled. "You mean back to the ranch? Horseback, naturally. I got a pony hitched to a rail down the street a ways."

"Your horse, or does the ranch own it?"

"He's mine. The place I work lets us keep a few horses of our own."

"How many you got?"

"Him and two others."

"You sure enough that this Mulcahy colt will beat my Betty that you'll bet them ponies against three of my horses?"

After mulling it over a moment, Parker agreed to the wager. "And if I had any money, I'd bet that, too."

Warner laughed. "What else do you own?"

This time, Parker laughed. "Nothing but my saddle and bedroll."

"I'll take that bet," Warner said.

Parker laughed again and the men shook hands on the wager.

———— ◆ ————

The next morning, Warner rubbed down Betty, gave her a good brushing, saddled up and rode out of town. He checked his saddle stock in the pasture, saw they were doing well, and rode on.

Somewhere, well out of sight and sound of the busy city and those coming and going there, Warner snugged up his saddle cinch and heeled the brown mare into an easy lope. Once she settled into the gait, he leaned along her neck, kissed his lips, and urged the pony into a run, then with another kiss and a light slap on the rump with the tail end of the bridle reins, pressed the mare into an all-out run. Although unchallenged and running alone, Warner had spent enough time horseback to know that few horses could match Betty's pace.

He pulled her up into a gentle lope for a time, then again to a trot, letting the mare catch her breath and cool down slowly, then reversed direction and headed back to town.

Warner followed much the same pattern for the next day or two, tending to his horses and keeping the brown mare well exercised. The rest of the time found him bumming around the saloons, talking with townfolk and arranging side bets with his saddle horses for stakes. So many were eager to bet against him that Warner was able to ratchet up the odds in his favor. Should the mare win, he would not only double his money from the $500 bet with Mulcahy, he would do better than he ever dreamed with the cash and horses bet against his ranch ponies.

A smile lit up Warner's face when he wandered into one of Telluride's saloons one afternoon and saw Johnny Nicholson standing with his back to the bar, propped on his elbows with a beer in hand, surveying the goings-on around him. "Johnny!" he said. "Glad to see you made it!"

Nicholson returned the grin. "You think I wasn't coming?"

"Oh, I figured you'd be here if you got my message. I'm damn glad you made it in time."

Telluride was busier than usual. As word of the race spread throughout the area, people from outlying ranches and nearby towns drifted into the city, filling the hotels and rooming houses and occupying every likely looking camping spot in the surrounding coves and canyons.

"How's the mare?"

"She's prime, Johnny. I hope you brought something to wager. Folks are falling all over themselves to bet against us. I've taken bets against every horse in the remuda, my saddle and bridle—hell, some fellow fancied them buckskin-bottomed riding britches of mine, so I took that bet, too. And you know what, Johnny? I got a feeling I'm going to win that bet."

"This horse we're running against—must be something, if people are so willing to bet on him."

"That's so. He ain't never been beat and no one figures our little Betty will be the one to do it. Except me. And you, I guess."

Nicholson swallowed the rest of his beer. "I've been in the saddle so long my butt's numb. Besides, I ain't eat in so long my stomach thinks my throat's been cut. Feed me."

As Warner and Nicholson wandered the main street of Telluride looking for a suitable bean parlor to take their supper, they crossed paths with Bob Parker.

"C'mon, Parker," Warner said. "We're about to strap on the nosebag."

The three cowboys found a table in a likely looking hash house and fell to eating. "Bob, this here is Johnny Nicholson. He ain't a Utah boy, but he's been around long enough he might as well be. He lives up Brown's Park way and is a hell of a hand with a horse. He's ridden jockey for me some, so I sent him word I was coming here and to come ride Betty. Damn glad he made it."

Parker studied the man. "You've got your work cut out for you. That Mulcahy colt can run."

Nicholson only nodded and kept eating.

"Good luck to you," Parker said.

Nicholson nodded and kept eating.

"Parker here, he's betting against us," Warner said. "But I don't hold it against him. He just don't know any better."

Parker laughed and watched Nicholson eat. "The way your boy's packing it in, that little mare ain't gonna be able to pack him. If I had anything more to wager, I'd up my bet."

Warner laughed, then got serious. "Listen, Parker, I got to provide a judge for the race. I want you to do it."

"Me? Why me? Hell's bells, Matt, I'm betting against your horse!"

"That don't make no never mind to me. I don't know a soul in this town and don't know who's worth trusting and who ain't. You seem a good sort to me, and being a Utah boy you can't be too bad. Some of that Mormon upbringing likely stuck to you."

Parker thought it over for a time. "You got any objection?" he asked the jockey.

Nicholson shook his head in the negative and kept eating.

"Then I guess I'm your man."

And, again, Parker and Warner shook hands on the agreement.

———— ◆ ————

Race day was festive around Telluride, with picnics along the race course, makeshift bars with tapped beer and whiskey kegs set up here and there to feed the greater-than-normal thirst, lemonade and sarsaparilla vendors to satisfy gentler tastes, and food mongers of all kinds hawking their wares up and down the route. Pickpockets and thieves infiltrated the throng, plucking anything of value they could lay hands on.

And, of course, betting. Men stood atop powder boxes calling out odds. Others elbowed through the crowds seeking takers for their wagers. Few were willing to bet against the Mulcahy colt but some did—willing to risk the odds simply for the thrill of the gamble, figuring a losing bet was better than no bet at all.

Down near the starting line, Mulcahy supervised the saddling of his colt. Excited at the prospect of a run, the horse reared and pawed, making the job difficult. Mulcahy's jockey stood by quietly, needing no instruction and unconcerned about the horse's nerves—he knew from experience that when a pistol shot started the race, all that nervous energy would translate to speed.

Betty stood as unconcerned as her rival's jockey. As Warner and Nicholson adjusted latigos and cinch, headstall and bridle reins, the horse seemed not to notice. The pony stood so still, in fact, she might be asleep.

"Let the Mulcahy colt set the pace, Johnny," Warner whispered to his rider. "When you reach the third furlong, push her into the lead—but don't run away from the colt. Win the race, but by no more than half a length if you can manage it. If we want more races, we can't let them see how fast this mare is."

Nicholson merely nodded. He and Warner had discussed all this at length and he knew the drill. Mulcahy invited Warner to share his buggy and the two hustled to the other end of the course where Mulcahy backed the buggy into the place reserved for the owners at the finish line.

No sooner had Mulcahy set the brake and one of his men hung a tether weight from the buggy horse than a gunshot rolled down the course, signaling the start of the race. The already loud murmuring of the crowd erupted into yelling and hollering, deafening everywhere, but with a wave of increased volume preceding the horses down the track.

The race unfolded much as Warner ordered, with Betty staying with the Mulcahy colt, nosing ahead toward the end, then pulling away enough to ensure the victory as the other jockey laid the whip to his horse to no avail.

Nicholson immediately stood in the stirrups and reined in Betty. Mulcahy's jockey sawed at the reins to slow his mount. The noise and excitement along the race course was replaced by stunned silence. Then, Matt Warner let loose a war whoop and, taking the cue, the spectators exploded into wild cheering. They knew they had seen a real horse race and considered the money they'd lost wagering a fair price for the spectacle.

———— ♦ ————

Warner and Nicholson hung around Telluride for a few days, collecting their bets and counting their winnings. Mulcahy handed over the five hundred dollars he owed Warner, and offered him many times that amount for title to Betty. Warner refused.

Bob Parker came back to town riding one horse and leading two others and handed the reins and lead ropes to Warner. "Here's your horses, Matt. My bedroll's tied on the back of the saddle. It's all yours."

"Oh hell, Bob, I don't need your horses. I already got a saddle, and I can't sleep in but one bed."

"Not my problem. I gambled and I lost."

Warner said, "Well, I'm giving it back to you. Consider it payment for your acting as my judge."

Parker laughed. "Race horse judges don't get paid. You know that as well as I do. The stuff's yours."

But Warner had other ideas. "Listen, Bob. Don't be hasty. I've got a proposition for you. Me and Johnny are figuring on traveling around this country for a while, see if we can scare up some races. We're thinkin' that Betty will make us a bundle. You know this country. Why not partner up with us and ride along? I'll deduct the price of them horses of yours and that worn-out saddle and smelly bedroll from your share of the winnings."

"I don't know, Matt. I was thinking to stick around here till I could raise a stake. I ain't in no position to be a traveling man just now—couldn't even afford to cross a toll bridge should I come to one."

"You let me worry about that. I could use a good hand, and I've got a feeling you are one. What the hell—you ain't got anything better to do anyhow."

Parker thought it over, but not for long. Once again, the two Utah cowboys shook hands.

Meanwhile, since the race, Johnny Nicholson had become something of a celebrity around Telluride. And, as was usually the case in the West, there was no shortage of challenges to test his horseback skills. He topped off several rank bucking horses to the appreciation of gathered crowds. But one particularly nasty bronc proved his undoing.

A long-legged, spindly strawberry roan gelding couldn't unseat the cowboy with his usual repertoire of lunges and twists and turns, bogging his head, kicking his heels, and dropping his shoulders when his front feet hit the ground. So the horse panicked, unaccustomed as he was to anyone staying on his back so long, and lunged blindly into the round corral fence, a solid row of stout cedar posts with their bottoms buried deep and tight. He tried to scrape Johnny off against the posts and when that failed, reared over backwards slamming the cowboy into the fence, then rolled sideways over the top of his rider. Johnny's leg snapped like a stick of kindling.

And so ended his season aboard Betty. And so, almost before the pressure of his handshake with Warner dissipated, Bob Parker became a jockey. Although bigger and heavier than Nicholson, it wasn't enough to burden the brown mare. His long experience horseback, along with his experience, if limited, racing the animals, suited him for the job.

Warner and Parker weaved a web across southwestern Colorado that summer, racing Betty wherever and whenever they could get up a match. In Durango, they outran a mare called Gypsy Queen, in Mancos the Cavanaugh Stud, and other local favorites elsewhere in the region. Since they usually got where they were going ahead of Betty's reputation, at least for a time, betting was often heavy against them, meaning Warner, Parker, and Betty seriously damaged the economy of several Colorado towns.

But no matter how much money the trio took in, two of the three seemed incapable of keeping their hands on any of it. While Betty's spending habits are unknown, her keepers were famous spendthrifts, given to high living whenever their pockets weighed heavy. Practically every drink they purchased in every saloon was accompanied by a round for the house, and the generous pair treated everyone they met like an old friend in need of a good time.

Most of the winnings, however, were lost because both men were soft touches. More than one down-on-his luck rancher, any number of widow women with hungry kids, farmers with unpaid store bills, prospectors in need of a grubstake, and many others down on their luck for whatever reason benefitted from the racers' generosity.

Late one summer day Warner and Parker rode into Cortez. Tired and thirsty, they tied their saddle mounts and Betty to a hitch rail in front of a saloon and staggered inside. Standing next to the bar, Parker flexed his back muscles while Warner ordered beers. The grog shop, nearly bereft of other customers, was so quiet they could hear the beer foaming into the mugs as the bartender pumped them full. A voice from behind the men shattered the quiet.

"Matt Warner, you are one sorry sonofabitch."

Parker pulled his pistol as he turned, but saw no danger in the relaxed cowboy leaned back in a chair propped against the stained and tattered wallpaper. Warner, on the other hand, spun around and started across the room.

Confused, Parker watched his partner grab the seated man by a handful of shirtfront, pull him to his feet, then fold him into a hug and start laughing and slapping the man on the back.

"Tom McCarty, you useless sack of shit, what are you doing?"

The men exchanged pleasantries and insults for a few minutes.

"Bob, come on over here and meet Tom McCarty. Until my sister died, this saddle tramp was my brother-in-law. I hate to speak ill of the dead, but marrying him was the dumbest thing Tennie ever did. And while I was sorry to see her go, if it took dying to get Tom out of the family, well, at least some good came of it."

Warner laughed the whole time he told the tale, with McCarty laughing along with him. Soon, Parker and McCarty were fine friends and the more beers they irrigated it with, the stronger the bond grew.

After a lengthy spell of sudsy beers and inflated stories, the three men mounted up to ride to McCarty's ranch. "Ranch" overstated the case. McCarty had a cabin and a few corrals hidden away in a canyon where he held rustled cattle and horses. Warner and Parker admired the layout, being no strangers to that trade themselves. But they were not in the livestock business at present and grilled their host about the possibility of a horse race thereabouts. By now, Betty was known and Warner and Parker were unable to find a race anywhere. McCarty had heard tell of a fast Indian pony owned by a Ute out in McElmo Gulch so Warner and Parker saddled up and, along with their new partner McCarty driving a buckboard, led Betty in that direction.

The place lay some two dozen miles west of Cortez, nearly to the Utah border. McElmo Gulch was a wide, dry canyon, populated by sparse grass and brush, with cedar and pinyon trees lining the slopes. Strange pictures—geometric designs, fanciful animals, bizarre creatures—were pecked into rock walls along the way, evidence of ancient people that lent the canyon a ghostly aspect.

Soon after arriving at the Ute village—a well-populated place, home to maybe 200 of the Indians—the men learned the rumored horse was there. He was called White Face for his distinctive bald face accented by one glassy blue eye. The Utes, being natural and enthusiastic gamblers, were eager to wager on a race, even given their poor circumstances.

Despite repeated stumbling over the language barrier, the cowboys and the Utes finally came to terms. White Face and Betty would race head to head, with the winning owner taking possession of the losing horse.

While Warner worked out that deal, McCarty and Parker negotiated with other men for odds on Navajo blankets against cash. Sure of their horse, the Utes dragged practically every wool blanket they owned out of their wikiups and tipis. As the pile of blankets grew, so did the angry looks on the faces of the women; they, apparently, were less enthusiastic about risking what little they owned than their men were.

As usual, a gunshot started the race and Betty and White Face flew off the line and pounded down the course. The Ute rider crowded Betty, leaning White Face into the mare. But Parker reined up, throwing the Indian pony off its stride. As Parker jockeyed around the other side and pulled even, the Indian tapped the brown mare sharply on the muzzle with his quirt.

Parker, tired of the Indian's tricks, let loose with a holler and laid the spurs to Betty. The brown mare liked to have leapt right out from between his legs, such was the surge of speed she mustered. That ended the race for White Face, as Betty lengthened her lead with every stride.

The Utes' shock soon turned to anger. None of the cowboys could understand the nature of their objections, but there was no doubt the Indians were displeased. As fast as McCarty could load the blankets into the buckboard they'd be pulled out again. Parker and the Indian jockey fought over White Face's hackamore rein. Warner climbed atop the buckboard and jacked the lever on his Winchester and fired into the air.

"Now, your horse lost that race, fair and square," he told the angry Utes. The leader of the band argued, saying they did not want to give up the horse. While they parried back and forth, McCarty got the pile of blankets loaded. Parker rode Betty through the crowd, dragging White Face with the Indian rider still aboard. McCarty grabbed the Ute jockey and pulled him off the horse and when the man got to his feet and lunged at him, the cowboy laid into him with the quirt strung onto his wrist.

"Tom! That's enough!" Warner yelled. "Climb aboard my horse and let's get out of here," he said. "Bob—" Warner tossed the carbine to Parker, still aboard Betty, and pulled his pistol. By now McCarty was mounted and his pistol, too, was trained on the angry crowd. Warner took the lines in his free hand and slapped the offside horse on the rump, keeping the barrel of his pistol and his eyes on the seething Utes as he drove out of the village. The horse Parker rode in on trailed along, tied to the back of the buckboard. McCarty and Parker followed, riding forward but looking backward, firearms at the ready, with White Face following at the end of a taut rein dallied around Parker's saddle horn.

Once clear of the village, the men urged the horses into a run, meaning to put as much distance as possible between them and the hornet's nest before the angry Utes swarmed after them.

But the Indians never came and the cowboys traveled long into the night to make it back to McCarty's cabin.

———•———

The late night led to a late morning and the day was well underway before Parker hauled himself upright and lit a fire in the cabin's small pot-bellied stove. He poured fresh water and dumped a handful of grounds into the pot that sat atop it and as the brew boiled, the smell of coffee rousted Warner and McCarty out of their bedrolls.

They sat on sawlog stools around the rough-hewn table that comprised the cabin's only furnishings, sipping the hot coffee from chipped mugs as their sleep-smeared faces reorganized themselves.

Parker cleared his throat, opened the stove and spat into the fire. "You boys reckon there'll be trouble?" he asked. "Will them Utes go to the agent or something and file a complaint?"

McCarty laughed. "Hell no," he mumbled. "They go to the Indian agent and admit they've been gambling it'd be nothin' but trouble for them. Ain't nothin' gonna happen."

"You're wrong, Tom. There'll be trouble, but it won't be from no Indian agent," Warner said softly. "Beating that warrior like a dog is about as bad a thing as you could do to one of them. Nothing but disrespect in that—it violates their honor. Worse, even, than had you killed him. You ought to take up thinkin' before you act, Tom. At least try it, for heaven's sake."

McCarty yawned and stretched. "Well, I ain't gonna worry about it. That blanket-ass wants trouble I'll accommodate him. Whole damn bunch of them, for that matter."

Later that day, along toward evening when the sun hung low and turned the air a soft shade of ochre and stretched the shadows of trees and even sagebrush long toward the east, the Utes rode into McCarty's ranch.

As the cowboys came out of the cabin the Utes—fifteen of them by Warner's count—spread before them. Warner stood his ground while

Parker and McCarty sidled away, putting some distance between them and forcing each Indian to choose a single target rather than a crowd.

In his broken English, the Ute leader made it clear to Warner that they would forget about yesterday's incident at their village if the cowboys would return White Face.

"The hell you say," Warner replied. "We won that race fair and square. You put the horse up for stakes and you lost. It's as simple as that."

"We want White Face."

"Well, you ain't going to get him. A bet's a bet and there ain't no going back on it," Warner said, all the while calculating the odds and trying to decide in his mind which of the Utes it would be his responsibility to shoot if it came to that. He heaved a sigh and hoped it wouldn't.

"White Face," the Ute said. "Give us back White Face and you will live. If not, you will die."

"I already told you. He ain't your horse. He might have been yours yesterday, but he's mine today—and you damn well know it. Like I said, a bet's a bet."

The Ute did not reply, but when he shifted—only slightly, a barely noticeable move—the battered rifle he carried across his lap, the bullet from Tom McCarty's pistol punched a hole in his forehead.

SHORT FUSE

Although the man himself barely appears in this story, Butch Cassidy is ever present. Many will remember the exploding boxcar scene in the movie that made the outlaw famous. "Short Fuse" is built around the same event, and while it takes liberties as fiction will do, it adheres more to the known facts than the movie did. Rough Country, *a 2014 anthology published by High Hill Press and edited by Spur Award-winning author Brett Cogburn, included this tale.*

———— • ————

For reasons Charlie Woodcock could not understand, the world had gone dark and silent. The vacuum inside his head struggled to come to terms with the smell of dust and smoke and the gloom that engulfed him.

He lay still in his confusion for a time; how much time he could not say.

As awareness crept through his body he felt a heaviness upon his chest and prickles of pain in other parts. He first wiggled a finger, then a hand, and finally raised his right arm and shoulder. The weight upon him shifted and the smothering black retreated into the dark of night.

The emptiness in his ears gave way to high-pitched ringing and the odor of dust and smoke intensified. Left arm still trapped, he pawed with his right at whatever was atop him. Finally able to shift the unhinged side of the packing crate, he struggled to sit upright and swept broken boards and paper and other unidentifiable debris from his legs.

Rolling to one side, Woodcock kicked away the remaining clutter, shifted to his hands and knees and pushed himself slowly to his feet, grasping for balance a splintered plank hanging from the side of the express car. As he attempted to focus, he felt his face and found his spectacles dangling from one ear. He wrapped the wayward stem around the other ear, finding one lens blurred with a web of cracks but the other intact.

"Woodcock?"

107

He heard his name, the call muted as if filtered by sleep; one ear pressed against a feather bed and the other burrowed under a pillow filled with down. Turning toward the sound, straining to see through a night dimmed by drifting haze, he realized where he was, and why.

———— ♦ ————

Just after two o'clock on an early June morning in 1899, the locked-up wheels of the Union Pacific Railroad's Overland Flyer squealed to a stop in a part of Wyoming where trains had no business stopping. The fireman aboard the engine released his death grip on an overhead rod, found his balance and spewed a stream of profanity in the direction of the engineer.

"Shut up, you damn fool," came the reply.

"What the hell we stopping for? We ain't to Medicine Bow for another twenty miles."

"Open your eyes. There's two signalmen on the track out there. Must be the Wilcox bridge washed out in the storm."

That explanation proved false when a man with a lantern in one hand, a pistol in the other, and a wildrag wrapped around his face stepped into the cab. Even above the engine's racket, the train men heard the ratcheting of the hammer as the intruder cocked the revolver. A second man of similar description followed into the confined space, further lengthening the odds against the two railroad men.

"Pull 'er ahead!" one of the bandits said.

The engineer, crossed eyes locked on the black hole in the end of the pistol barrel an inch from the bridge of his nose, did not respond.

"Now! Get this train across that bridge and damn quick, or it'll be too late."

The engineer stood as if paralyzed until the masked man drove home his point with the pistol, laying the barrel sharply above his ear.

"Move it!" the bandit yelled as the train inched ahead, finally gaining traction and rolling over the muddy wash. No sooner had the caboose cleared the span than a blast rocked the night, turning the trestle to flinders.

"Stop."

The engineer braked again and the robbers escorted him and the fireman back along the tracks past the tender and mail car and express car and watched as they uncoupled the passenger cars.

As the parade made its way back to the engine, one bandit grabbed a handful of the other's shirt sleeve and jerked him to a stop. "What for did you hit that guy, Harvey? You know Butch don't like no violence."

"Butch ain't here. Besides, Butch wouldn't be none too happy if we left that train sitting on the wrong side of a blown-up bridge. Or piled up in the bottom of the ravine. I had to do something to wake him up and get him to drive the train."

"You should have strung out more fuse."

"Well, I didn't. Don't make no never mind, now. Let's get on with it."

From his desk in the express car, Charlie Woodcock wondered what was up when the train stopped and started again and again. The explosion offered sufficient explanation. As the train steamed ahead, minus the cars behind his, he reassured himself the safe was secure, checked the locks on the express boxes, tidied up his desk and waited.

A few miles down the track the outlaws again ordered the train to halt. As he braked to a stop, the engineer watched four more masked men carry lanterns out of the darkness. By the time he and the fireman made their way back to the mail car at gunpoint, one of the outlaws was already banging the butt of a pistol against the door.

"Come on, open the damn door," he called out, then set to pounding the door again. "Open up! You know damn well we're coming in, so let's do this the easy way." No response. "All right," he said. "Looks like we'll have to blow it. Have at it, Harvey."

The man called Harvey said, "You got it, Sundance."

The engineer's eyes widened and he stammered, "Sundance! You the Sundance Kid?"

The outlaw laughed. "You think I'm going to answer that?"

"Well. No. I guess not."

The trainman watched the bandit called Harvey stringing fuse from a stick of dynamite wedged in the mail car door. "Hey, Sundance?" the engineer said, and grinned as the robber turned in response. "So, if that's who you are, one of these others must be Butch Cassidy."

Lantern light reflected in the outlaw's sharp blue eyes.

"No," the Sundance Kid finally said as those assembled backed away from the train. "Haven't you heard? A few years back, the governor of this shithole state gave Butch a pardon in exchange for a promise that he wouldn't rob any more trains in Wyoming. Butch ain't the kind to go back on his word." Exploding dynamite punctuated the statement.

Not far away, but too far away to be awakened by the blast, Butch Cassidy lay curled in his bedroll near the glowing ashes of a dying campfire. While the unfolding robbery followed his plan, and while he would ride with the Wild Bunch as they fled the country, and while a share of the loot would weigh heavy in his saddlebags as they did, he slept well in the knowledge that he had not, not really, violated the terms of his pardon.

Harvey Logan pulled his fingers from his ears and stood watching the smoke clear. The sliding door on the mail car was splintered and knocked off its track, but mostly intact.

"Ben, News, give me a hand," he said. The three of them jerked and jammed the door and finally rattled it loose. "Sonofabitch," Ben gasped. "They must of reinforced these damn doors."

"Throw down your weapons and come out of there!" Flatnose Curry yelled to the still-smoking hole left by the open door. A shotgun and two pistols arced out of the dark car to land on the roadbed, followed by two men wading through the haze wafting at the smoke. Their hands shot into the air upon seeing the rifle leveled in their direction by the masked outlaw. "Get over there," he said, motioning them with the barrel of his rifle to join the engineer and fireman.

"All right, boys, see what's in there," Sundance said. The Logan brothers and Ben Kilpatrick, the Tall Texan, entered the car. Soon enough, mail sacks came flying out the door and News Carver and Flatnose Curry started dumping their contents on the ground while Sundance covered the trainmen.

"The famous Sundance Kid," the engineer said. "You as handy with that gun as folks say you are?"

The sound of the pistol cocking and the look in the bandit's blue eyes in the lantern light stifled the railroader's curiosity.

"Anything?" Sundance said.

"Not much," came the reply from the men by the mail car. "Hardly anything."

"Shit. News, watch these yahoos."

Carver took over the guard as Sundance walked to the express car. Expecting the worst after hearing the mail car explosion, Charlie Woodcock had wedged himself between two tall packing crates well away from the door. Despite knowing it was coming, the sudden pounding on the door gave him a start.

"Hello in there!" Sundance yelled.

No response.

More pounding.

"Come on, you can't hide! Open this door or you're likely to get hurt."

No response.

More pounding.

"I ain't asking again. Open the damn door. You ain't going to like what happens if you make me open it for you."

"Sorry," came the muffled reply from somewhere inside. "I can't do it."

"Can't do it? You trying to tell me you don't know how to unlock a door? Hell, mister, you locked the damn thing so I'm betting you can unlock it."

Silence.

More pounding.

Sundance called to the engineer. "Who the hell's in there?"

"Woodcock. Charlie Woodcock."

More pounding.

"Woodcock!"

"Yes sir?"

"Open the door."

"No sir."

"Shit," Sundance said under his breath. "Come on Woodcock. You can do it."

"Sorry, sir. If I was to open that door it could cost me my job."

Sundance laughed. "Hell, Woodcock, leave it closed and it could cost you your life."

"That's all right, sir. I've got life insurance."

Silence.

"So that's it then, Woodcock?"

"Yes sir."

"Well, hell, Woodcock. You better hope that insurance pays off." Sundance called out to Logan, "Blow it, Harvey. And don't spare the dynamite."

As Charlie Woodcock wedged himself tighter into his hole, Harvey Logan bundled up a handful of dynamite sticks, fused a blasting cap, stuffed it into the bundle, reeled off a short length of fuse, and put a match to it.

"Fire in the hole, boys," he said as he hotfooted it away from the train.

He didn't get far enough soon enough. The explosion lifted Harvey off his feet and flung him head over heels. Shattered boards sprayed the air and splinters stung the huddled train robbers and trainmen. Inside the car, all five of Charlie Woodcock's senses were blown away in the blast.

The outlaws were soon on their feet, save Harvey, brushing debris from their clothing and picking out slivers. Sundance and Carver helped the stunned powder monkey to his feet. His attempts to walk were stumbling at first, but soon enough smoothed out. Shaking his head to clear the cobwebs, Logan accompanied Sundance to the express car to see if the blast had successfully breached the door. And to see if there was still a Woodcock.

"Woodcock!" Sundance hollered.

No reply. But the outlaw heard rustling inside and leaned in to see the express car agent crawl out of the debris and struggle to his feet. Again he yelled, but the man seemed not to hear him, instead looking around as if lost. Sundance passed his lantern through the door space and set it on the littered floor and followed it in.

"Woodcock!" he yelled again.

The man turned, regarded him without recognition, then widened his eyes in sudden realization of his surroundings and the masked bandit he faced. Sundance hoisted his lantern and looked around the express car, finding the safe against the far wall and toward the corner.

"Woodcock," he said, "You and me are going over to that safe and we're going to open it." Woodcock's eyes looked lost and vacant. Sundance dragged him over to the safe, set his lantern atop it and, with his pistol as a pointer, encouraged him to open it. The man looked at the safe, looked at his captor, repeated the action, and shook his head.

"What? Come on Woodcock, don't cause any more trouble. Open the damn thing."

Struggling to find his voice, the addled man finally managed to say, "Can't."

"What do you mean, 'can't'? Damn it man, open it!"

Woodcock bobbed his head, pursed his lips, swallowed, and took a deep breath, trying to remember how to talk. "I don't . . . " he said, " . . . can't . . . " he said, " . . . re . . . mem . . . . Think of the . . . numbers," he said.

Sundance stuck his pistol in the man's face. Woodcock drew back instinctively. "I . . . I'm sorry, mister. I can't. Think. Right."

Grabbing Woodcock's shirtfront, Sundance pulled him forward, changed his grip to the back of the man's collar and forced him to his knees before the safe as if praying for memory. Woodcock reached for the dial, drew back, reached again, his hand trembling, no, shaking uncontrollably. The shaking stopped when finally he grasped the dial, but his mind could not make his fingers turn the wheel.

Exhausted, he bowed his head. "I'm sorry. The combination is gone. Just gone. I can't . . . ."

"Shit," Sundance said, ratcheting back the hammer on his pistol. "Shit!" again, as he lowered the hammer and jammed the weapon into its holster. "Shit!" yet again as he grasped Woodcock's collar and hoisted him to his feet. He pushed the man ahead of him across the littered floor and did not stop until Woodcock stepped off into emptiness and fell to the ground.

"Harvey! Looks like we'll have to blow this damn safe. Damn Woodcock's either gone stupid on us, or is too smart for us."

Sundance noticed a lightening of the eastern sky, thinking their troubles on this raid were putting them well behind Butch's schedule.

"Come on, Logan, get it open, and get it done quick-like."

Perhaps it was because he felt rushed. Maybe his mind, like Woodcock's, was a bit discombobulated by the earlier explosion. Whatever the reason, Harvey Logan overestimated the charge required to rupture the express vault. For when the men, bandits and Union Pacific employees alike, watched the blast—this time from a safe distance—they saw, as if in slow motion, the sides of the car billow outward and disappear while the roof swelled like a bubble then burst. The shock wave ruffled whiskers and pressed garments tight against skin, and the men rocked back on their heels in unison, as if nailed to a row of saplings in a wind gust.

Again in unison, all eyes turned upward. Falling and drifting, drifting and falling, sheets of paper floated lightly downward, defying gravity as long as possible as they seemed to sparkle and shine in the dim of an early summer dawn. While the biggest and brightest pieces of flotsam were assorted papers of unknown value, many, most, of the sailing papers were legal tender; currency of various denominations backed by the full faith and credit of the government of the United States of America.

Acting again as one, the men—at least those with masked faces—snapped out of the trance and set to gathering greenbacks by the handfuls, stuffing them inside shirts and hats, piling rocks atop piles on the ground, and stowing bills any place they could find, no matter how poorly suited to the purpose. Although ill-advised, the Tall Texan ripped the wild rag from his face and turned it into a sack of sorts to stuff with money.

The Sundance Kid climbed onto the floor of the former express car, which was about the only part of it still functional, but could not find any remnant of the safe. He finally found what was left of it—most of the back, the bottom, and part of one wall—lying on the ground on the opposite side of the train. Still inside were three heavy bags of gold coins, a bag of silver dollars, and a sack of stacks of currency wrapped in bands. Two other bags of paper money lay nearby, ripped open but with most of the bills still inside. Most of the money was terribly scorched and much of it torn, several stacks had corners sheared off and otherwise suffered the effects of the explosion.

The boys in the Wild Bunch managed to get the haul divvied up into manageable loads and aboard their horses before sunrise. They rode off toward the rendezvous with Butch and the fresh horses that would keep the gang a step ahead of the posse that was sure to come.

Official accounts from the Union Pacific Railroad claimed the bandits got away with but a few thousand dollars. Those in the know put the take somewhere just south of $50,000. What cannot be disputed is that for years afterward, blackened, tattered currency, and bills with missing parts, were slapped down on poker tables, saloon bars, bean parlor tabletops, grocery store counters, the palms of soiled dove's hands, and everywhere else in the West where money would spend.

Except, perhaps, church collection plates.

———◆———

Just over a year after the Wilcox train robbery, in the early evening of a hot August day in 1900, the locked-up wheels of the Union Pacific Railroad's Number 3 train squealed to a stop in a part of Wyoming where trains had no business stopping. As the engine ground to a halt somewhere between Tipton and Table Rock, the man in the express car expected trouble. It wasn't long in coming.

All too soon, he heard pounding on the door. And a voice: "Open up!"

"Sorry," he replied. "I can't."

"Can't?"

"No sir. If I was to open that door, I could lose my job."

A moment of silence.

Then: "Charlie? Charlie Woodcock? Is that you?"

More silence.

"C'mon, Charlie. Open the door."

Silence.

"I ain't askin' again Charlie. But you had best understand that Harvey's here with me and he's got a big handful of dynamite. You know how Harvey is with dynamite. And I gotta tell you, Charlie—it's a damn short fuse."

"Sorry, Mr. Sundance. But I guess I'll risk it. I can't afford to lose my job."

"Damn it, Woodcock! Do you really think the Union Pacific Railroad wants you dead? Would your boss let himself get blowed to hell if he was in there with you?"

Woodcock said nothing.

But, discretion sometimes being the better part of valor, the door started slowly sliding, sliding slowly, as if it were shy, even embarrassed, about surrendering.

THE NAKEDNESS OF THE LAND

The well-made but short-lived quarterly magazine, Out West, *edited by Sam Hawken, featured this story in its Spring 2007 issue. If the general outlines of the story seem familiar, crack open your Bible and read chapters 37 through 45 of Genesis.*

————◆————

I thought I'd seen the last of my little brother the night I left him for dead in Cold Spring Draw. But here I am, fettered to a cast-iron stove in his house and having no idea what happens next.

At least it's warm, which is something I haven't been much lately. And the food's good. Which is something else I haven't been seeing enough of. The cook's culinary skills surpass her conversational abilities, if the fact that she hasn't spoken six words to me in all the days I've been here is any indication.

Being stuck in this room has given me plenty of time to try to figure out Joey, but I'll be damned if I can find any sign I can read. He looks to be well off, or at least living like it. There are books all over the walls and a big desk with papers poking out the cubby holes and a safe off in the corner bigger than this stove I'm chained to.

Of course none of it's his.

He runs the ranch, but says it belongs to some rich man Back East who only shows up in the summer. Nonetheless, I'd have to say my little brother has done well for himself these dozen years we've been apart.

————◆————

"Joey, you better get started. It's a long enough ride and Ruben is probably needing these supplies by now. I hope you'll find him up on Blacktail

Ridge but if the feed gave out, he probably pushed the herd over into that valley toward the Pyramid Peaks."

Looking more and more at seventeen like the man his father hoped he'd become, the boy checked the cinch one last time and swung into the saddle as the old man tightened the diamond hitch on the packhorse.

"You ride easy. This old mare's not as young as she once was," the man said. "And get back here soon as Ruben turns you loose. There's work to be done."

The boy nodded and rode out to find his brother. It was hard to think of Ruben as his brother. He was well past thirty, and had no use for a baby brother. He especially resented the favored treatment young Joey got from their parents.

The way Joey looked at it, he didn't ask to be a surprise—blessing, as they put it—in his folks' declining years. And he had to admit that they doted on him. Take the summer herding, for instance. Ruben hated being stuck out in the hills, far away from the town and the saloon and the dance hall girls, while Joey would have taken his place in an instant. But Dad—Ma, really—liked to keep him home at the ranch.

He knew Ruben considered him spoiled. To Joey, it seemed more like smothered. He craved long days horseback in the hills, tending the cattle and exploring the world inside his head. He was determined to enjoy this trip as long as it lasted.

Riding across the flatland, he looked with satisfaction upon the stacks of hay here and there in the grassy meadows that held the sagebrush at bay. He thought of how when cold winds scoured the land and the cattle bunched up in the low places to shelter from snow blowing dry as sand, they'd undo the summer's work and dump the grass back on the meadows.

It was a delicate balance, ranch life on this high desert. Without the mountain pastures and hay patches, cattle would be forced back to the green, humid country they came from.

Through the clear air, the plateaus in the distance seemed near enough to touch but Joey knew the sun would be well up in tomorrow's sky before he started his climb.

———— ◆ ————

From before he had a tooth in his head, the kid could do no wrong in Ma and Dad's eyes.

I was mostly grown when he was born, and it was bothersome to be out working my tail off and come home to see them fawning all over the little brat. Truth be told, he was a good kid.

And me being such a disappointment, looking back I can see where they'd put all their hopes in Joey.

After all those years of watching him grow up smarter than me, better with cattle and horses, more willing to work, I guess I'd had a bellyful.

Still, I doubt I'd have done what I did if I hadn't been looking at the world through the bottom of a whiskey bottle for three or four days straight. But being out in those mountains with nothing or no one for company but a bunch of mangy cows for weeks on end, who could blame me for trying to improve my outlook with a little liquid?

———◆———

Riding along the spine of Blacktail Ridge toward the divide, Joey could see the cattle had been gone from here for several days. He topped out and set his course toward the Pyramid Peaks, figuring to cover most of the distance by nightfall and hook up with Ruben sometime the next day.

Ruben would for sure be needing the supplies, more so than Dad suspected. But what the packhorse was carrying wasn't what needed replenishing so far as his brother would be concerned.

Joey knew Ruben had dumped one of the sacks of flour Ma had packed for him back into the barrel and refilled the bag with bottles of whiskey from his stash. No matter how far from town he got, Ruben wasn't one to deprive himself of the thing he enjoyed most.

Shadows lengthened and clouds stacked up against the horizon. He rode through stands of quakies and across parks painted with lupine and yarrow. Dark evergreen trees climbing the slopes provided contrast for the glowing sun-struck colors of the alpine meadows.

Joey found it hard to imagine a better time or a better place.

All the same, he had this gnawing feeling that all wasn't as it should be. From the scattered sign he'd seen, it looked more like the herd had merely wandered through here, rather than being moved. And even though cattle tended to roam and disperse across the hills by nature, as many cows as they had up here ought to have left more trace than he could see.

As he unsaddled and unloaded and made camp near Cold Spring Draw, he figured he'd be taking up the subject with Ruben soon enough.

THE DEATH OF DELGADO

―――――― ◆ ――――――

When I saw the fire down at the other end of the valley, I hoped—hell, I don't know what I hoped. But it had to be another human and I hadn't seen one in a spell.

So I pocketed a bottle of hospitality, saddled up and rode down there.

I stopped a good ways off to study the situation and saw it was Joey— wide awake and dreaming. While not exactly my choice of company on a summer evening, I figured I'd have to see him sooner or later so decided to go ahead and get it over with.

―――――― ◆ ――――――

Firelight reflected off Joey's face as he stared into the flames lost in thought. He didn't hear the horse's approach. Was unaware of advancing footsteps. So when the man stepped between him and the fire, a startled Joey scrambled to get up.

A heavy hand halted his progress, pushing him back to the ground.

"Sit down, you little turd," a voice growled. "No need to get up on my account."

"Ruben?" Joey sputtered. "Is that you, Ruben?"

"Yeah, it's me," he replied as stepped past the boy and squatted at the edge of the fire's glow. "And, sad to say, it's you. I was hoping for some worthwhile company when I saw the fire."

"I brought supplies."

"Yeah, little brother. But you ain't supplying what I'm needing."

Joey studied Ruben's haggard appearance and figured he was pretty well supplied already. His eyes were so red he suspected they'd glow without benefit of the fire. And the way his face sagged it appeared gravity—or lack of sleep—was about to get the better of him.

"Where are the cows, Ruben?"

"Oh, they're around. Here and there. They haven't wandered too far."

"You let them stray like this, it'll take too long to gather them. And we'll likely not find some of them at all. Dad ain't going to like that."

Ruben finished off the bottle he carried and threw it across the fire at Joey.

"Yeah, well, I'm sure he'll have confidence in you to get the job done." He staggered to his feet and started for his horse.

"Where you going, Ruben?"

"Back to my camp. I don't care much for the company here."

He missed the stirrup. He got it on the second try and heaved himself into the saddle.

"You best just leave the grub here and head on back at first light. We don't want Ma and Dad to miss you. It'd be pretty hard on them if they thought something bad happened to their baby boy."

"Dad will want to know about the cows."

"Well, you can just tell him they're fine."

"Ruben, it appears they're scattered from hell to breakfast and I'll tell him so."

"You'd be well advised to mind your own damn business, little brother."

"It is my business. Dad's too. He ain't going to be too happy about you laying around up here drunk."

Without thinking, Ruben unstrung his lariat and shook out a loop.

"That's a piece of news he won't be hearing anytime soon," he said as he cast a loop over Joey, jerked the slack, took a turn around the horn, wheeled his mount and spurred him madly into the darkness.

As the boy bounced and caromed off rocks and bushes, the horse veered sharply to avoid plunging over the edge of the draw. Joey, cracking at the end of the whip, dropped into empty air. The tail of the rope burned through Ruben's hand as his dally gave way.

———◆———

To tell the truth, I didn't even think about what I'd done to Joey. I rode to my camp, all but fell off my horse and collapsed.

It was late in the day when I finally woke up. The next day, I guess. Maybe the day after. Hell, I don't know.

I rolled over and raised up on my hands and knees. My horse was grazing a little way off, still saddled. As the fog in my aching head thinned, a wave of sickness washed over me, either from all the liquor or the realization of what I'd done.

I hauled my sorry self into the saddle and rode toward Cold Spring Draw, my backbone stabbing my brain with every step that horse took. I couldn't find any trace of the boy. Maybe he walked away.

Then again, I could have been looking in the wrong place altogether.

His camp was pretty much as we'd left it. Ashes gone cold in a ring of rocks. Bedroll on a mattress of pine boughs. Horses—thirsty by now—staked out. Supplies strung up in a tree.

It struck me that even abandoned, that campsite was a lot better organized than my thoughts. I had to figure out something.

———— ♦ ————

With the one arm and leg that still worked, it was all Joey could do to push himself backwards downhill. Which, with the box end and steep sides of the draw through there, was the only way to go.

For parts of two nights and days—the parts when he wasn't passed out from pain or blacked out from the after effects of the blows his head had absorbed—he crawled down the draw.

Some ways below, a trail from the plateau above wound into and out of the draw. The small stream from the spring above spread into a shallow pool at the crossing and it was here the boy gave up. Lying in the cool water, he was barely breathing when the prospector found him.

Doubting it would save him but feeling obligated nonetheless, the old man bound up the boy's arm and leg then lashed together a travois to drag him down to the flat land. He figured if no one could help him, at least someone might know where the boy ought to be buried.

The first stop was the Dream Ranch. The prospector was afraid it would be the boy's last.

———— ♦ ————

Sooner or later I'd have to face the music with Ma and Dad and I figured on sooner, if for no other reason than to get it over with. Besides, leaving the herd to bear the news might be explanation enough for the cattle being scattered hither and yon.

I strung together his saddle horse and the old pack mare and headed for the ranch, concocting a story along the way.

The way I figured it was this: Joey never did make it. While riding out to check the herd one morning, I came across his horse, wandering free and dragging a lead rope from a halter. The packhorse was staying close and was spooked. When I found the camp, it looked like hell had been through it, scattering goods and groceries to the four winds.

Bears got it, I figured.

And while I never found any trace of the boy, I figured they must have got him, too.

It was worth a try.

———◆———

Only eighty or so miles as the crow flies from Joey's home place, the Dream Ranch might as well have been across the sea.

The only wagon roads through the rugged plateaus required a long drive to mountain passes far to the north or south, so there was little travel and no commerce to speak of between the regions.

The land itself little resembled the high desert Joey came from. The Dios del Sol Valley was a greener, wetter, and altogether gentler country.

The ranch, centerpiece of the valley, was the result of a rich Eastern gun maker's dreams of being a cattleman. A few long weeks horseback each summer was the extent of the owner's involvement, so operations and the big house fell to a hired manager.

Joey's care fell to the ranch cook. She tucked him into a back bedroom and nursed him until a doctor was fetched from town. He set the broken leg and arm as best he could, wrapped the banged-up rib cage, and did all he could for the battered head—which was hope for the best.

Then, as doctors are wont to do, he pronounced Joey young and strong and likely to survive, took up the lines and headed back to town.

So it was back to the cook. She spoon-fed the boy, changed his dressings, and slowly but surely coaxed him out of bed and back to life.

Once Joey was up and around, he started helping out with chores around the place and it seemed natural somehow for him to stay on to do some cowboying when the offer was made.

He had no idea what Ma and Dad knew of his fate. And although he worried about them, months had passed and he felt no urgency to return to his former life. Riding over the ranch's vast range tending cattle seemed an ideal way to spend his days for the time being.

———◆———

Bad as it sounds, losing my little brother was the best thing that ever happened to me.

I swore off the sauce. I took an interest in running the ranch. And I tried, through being a better man, to fill at least a piece of the hole losing Joey left in Ma and Dad's lives.

And things did seem to get better after a while. I settled into my lot as a rancher and took as much of the burden off Dad as he'd allow.

Still and all, life does have a way of catching up with you.

———— ◆ ————

The years on the Dream Ranch were good to Joey. The ranch manager came to rely on him. The owner liked riding with him summer days. Through hard work and savvy, he worked his way up to cow boss.

But there was a fly in the ointment, and one summer the Dream Ranch seemed more like a nightmare.

For starters, the owner found out his manager had had his hand in the till for years and sent him packing.

Then one evening Joey stopped by the big house to report to the owner, who was still out riding. While waiting in the shade of the side porch, he and the man's pretty young wife flirted like they always did.

But this time, she wanted more than talk.

She parked her pretty little backside on Joey's lap as he sat in the porch swing, swept his hat aside and planted a kiss on him.

Scared near to death, the young man did the only thing he could think of on short notice.

He ran.

And, as he rounded the corner on his way to the steps, practically ran over the owner.

"What on earth is his hurry?" he asked his wife.

She blushed in reply, on top of the flush that already colored her face.

"What's been going on here?" he asked, angrily.

He'd had occasion to suspect his wife more than once. Then, seeing the hat on the swing, he assumed he had reason to suspect Joey.

"I don't know," she said. "Nothing. We were talking. He just came at me. Oh! Thank goodness you got here when you did! I don't know how much longer I could have held him off."

He found it hard to believe. He felt like he knew Joey from the hours they'd spent together horseback. He knew his wife, too.

But what could he do? What could he say?

"Well. I suppose I better talk to him," he finally said. "At best, it'll be a matter of sending him down the road. At worst, I might have to call him out."

Her "Thank you!" was muffled as she threw her arms around his neck, face pressed to his chest. "Oh, thank you!

"Now," she said shakily, "if you don't mind, I'm going to my room. I'm in such a state!"

She left him alone, hat in hand, deep in thought. He stood as if rooted for several minutes, mulling over his options.

"Sir?" a voice asked tentatively, breaking the spell. He looked around and saw the cook standing in the kitchen window.

"Sorry. A bit preoccupied," he said. "What is it?"

"Well, sir, it ain't my place to say anything and you know I seldom do. But I've known that young man from the day he showed up here all busted up. And I've gotten to know him right well since. And I'll just say this. If you sack that fellow, or shoot him, or anything else, you'll be punishing an innocent man."

With that, she turned away from the window and back to her work.

And with that, he realized he'd found a man he could trust as his new ranch manager.

———◆———

All that first spring we kept supposing it would rain any day.

Nobody worried much through the summer, because other than an occasional thunder bumper, it seldom storms then anyway.

But when fall passed without the usual rain, Dad saw cause for concern.

Very little snow fell in the high country that winter, which didn't bode well.

And when the seasons repeated themselves the next year with little relief, it was real trouble.

The cattle were poorer than usual coming out of the hills, and throughout the fall they cropped what little grass there was right down to dirt. The hay meadows hadn't even greened up that summer, so hay was scarce. Any blade of grass that dared to rear its head was fought over by hungry cattle.

But things sure changed that winter.

Overnight, the brown, denuded landscape was turned into a white wasteland, empty as the naked thigh of a crib girl.

THE DEATH OF DELGADO

Snow. Deep snow. Accompanied by cold that cracked your spit before it hit the ground.

What little hay we had was soon gone.

Snow kept coming and the cold never let up and our sorry stock started dying. Cattle drifted in close to the houses and barns and bellered night and day as if begging could produce fodder. The racket was enough to drive you crazy.

We skinned out what dead cows we could to try to get something out of them in lieu of the calves that would never be born, and frozen stinking hides piled up all around the place.

With no hope left and nowhere to turn, Dad and I hatched a desperate plan.

We'd hire as many wagons and drivers as we could from town and I'd try to lead them across the desert and over Crooked Canyon Pass to the Dios del Sol Valley. The thinking being that conditions there had been better, and there may be hay for sale.

We knew we could never haul enough to save all the cattle still standing. But we could save some.

If I'd known how the trip would turn out I'd have never set out. But we got here.

———◆———

The sound of wagons rolling into ranch headquarters woke Joey from a dead sleep. He pulled on his pants and boots, lit a couple of lamps in the house, slid into a coat and stepped onto the porch.

He recognized Ruben the moment his brother pulled the scarf from his face and spoke. Sensing an advantage, he stayed where he was, silhouetted against the open front door.

"We left a herd of starving cows on the other side of the mountains. We're looking for hay to take back," Ruben offered for openers.

"It's a long way to haul hay."

"That it is," Ruben said. "But we didn't see any choice in the matter, other than let the rest of the herd die off. That whole country is covered with snow—and the only thing under that snow is dirt. Naked as an innocent babe."

"What ranch you come from?"

125

"The Compass"

"Wasn't that Jacob Stone's place?"

"Still is. Although he's along in years to the point that giving advice is about all he can do. Jacob's my dad. I'm surprised you know of him."

"Used to have dealings over that way. But it's been years," Joey said. "We've got hay enough to fill your wagons. Stable your horses in the big barn. You men can put up in the bunkhouse tonight. We'll fix you up come morning."

———— ◆ ————

Before sunup, when the only other thing stirring on the ranch was the cook—who somehow knew she had extra work this morning—Joey huddled with his foreman.

He outlined the terms of the sale, which the foreman thought were too favorable to the buyers given the circumstances, but Joey held firm. He followed up with detailed instructions on how the first wagon—the one on which the man named Ruben held the lines—was to be loaded.

Several hours later, Joey watched from the shadows of the porch as the laden wagons rolled away.

Once they were well out of sight, the foreman and a couple of hands took up their trail, soon overtaking and halting the procession.

"What's the trouble?" Ruben asked, unnerved at the display of weapons.

"It seems you gentlemen are hauling away more than just hay," said the foreman.

"I don't know what you mean."

"Maybe we'll just have a look at your load."

As he expected, but much to Ruben's shock and surprise, the foreman found the wallet full of the money that purchased the hay tucked into the supply box.

Ruben, bound with a catch rope, started back toward the ranch afoot, the two cowboys following along.

Saying he saw no need for the cattle to suffer any longer than necessary, the foreman sent the wagon train on its way.

"We'll keep the law out of this if we can," he told the departing drivers. "But tell the ranch owner he'll have to come fetch Ruben himself. If he wants him back."

THE DEATH OF DELGADO

———— ◆ ————

Even in broad daylight, we were well into our conversation before I realized who it was I was talking to.

Knowing I hadn't taken that money, I suspected little brother was up to something. But I couldn't figure out for the life of me what it might be.

We talked some as the days passed. For the most part, though, he's left me rattling around this living room chained to the damned stove. Waiting.

For what, I do not know.

———— ◆ ————

You could see the lone horseman coming from a long way off.

Joey went inside and watched through the window as the old man covered the last little way. He slid cold and stiff from the saddle, looped the bridle reins around the hitching post and climbed the porch steps.

Invited into the house, he removed his hat and blinked and rubbed his watery eyes to rid them of snow glare.

Jacob found his focus. And found himself face to face to face with his sons.

THE CHICKEN AND THE BULL

This little story, set in modern times, is written for young readers, but its theme, it seems, is appropriate for all ages. The dirty little trick that launches the tale actually happened during a spectator event at a college rodeo—or so I was told many years ago. "The Chicken and the Bull" appears here for the first time.

———— ◆ ————

Flat on his back, Jeremy sucked wind and wondered if he'd ever catch his breath. If I live to be one hundred, he thought, I'll never forgive Mitch. He rolled over, hoisted himself to hands and knees, spitting dust and mud and wondering how he could have been so stupid.

He should have known better. If there was one thing he'd learned about Mitch these past few days it was that he couldn't be trusted. Give him the smallest chance, and he'd take advantage. Still, it seemed innocent enough when Mitch told him about the bull.

"See how that bull's eyes are set wide," Mitch said, "way out there on the sides of his head? What that means is, he can't see nothing that's right in front of him. Get a little off to one side or the other and he'll mow you down. But long as you stay right in front of him, he don't even know you're there."

Mitch should know. He was a cowboy, and lived on his uncle's guest ranch every summer. Helped out, too, even though he was only fourteen. Jeremy had seen him feeding cattle, saddling horses, and helping out in the livestock pens at the nightly rodeo. So, when he offered advice on how to snatch the ribbon from the hump on the bull's shoulders to win a prize, Jeremy listened.

The look in the bull's eyes told him he'd been had. But, by that time, it was too late.

It happened at the rodeo Jeremy's fourth night at the guest ranch. He'd only watched the first few nights, and wasn't sure he wanted to try any of the contests for guests the ranch mixed in with the regular rodeo events for real cowboys. In fact, he thought the "Ribbon Race" looked especially scary.

What they did was tape a big red ribbon on a bull's back, right on the hump of his shoulders, then turn him out into the arena with the "racers." Whoever pulled the ribbon off the bull won the prize. The bull wasn't all that big, as bulls go—just a year old and nowhere near fully grown. Jeremy watched the bull snort and paw up dust and spin around to face the racers as they darted in and out snatching at the ribbon. The bull was fast, and even charged a few times. Finally, a girl who looked to Jeremy to be about seventeen, dashed in from the side when the bull turned toward someone else, pulled the ribbon, then ran around cheering and jumping and holding it high like a red flag.

No one had been hurt, but still . . .

"Thing is, you gotta get in there quick," Mitch said. "The longer he's out in that arena, the madder that bull gets. If you stay in front and go right at him, like I said, you can have that ribbon in your hand before that bull or anyone else knows it happened, and you'll be the winner."

"I don't know . . ." Jeremy said.

Mitch laughed. "What's the matter, city boy? You chicken? Heck, a girl won it last night! You ain't gonna let no girl show you up, are you?"

Jeremy felt the blush rise up his neck and color his cheeks.

So, he'd let Mitch shame him into trying, and this is what he got for it. He finally made it to his feet, and as he pulled out the front of his shirt to shake the dirt loose he could hear the cowboy laughing. Jeremy wiped the dust and mud from his teary eyes and limped toward the fence.

"Man, you really got freight-trained," someone said, patting Jeremy on the shoulder as stumbled through the arena gate. "That bull ran right over you. Are you all right?"

Jeremy blinked through the mud, but didn't recognize the boy. He looked to be about his age, thirteen, with black hair and brown skin, dressed in cowboy clothes.

"My name's Gustavo," he said. "You can call me Gus. If you can talk, that is."

Jeremy didn't answer, just spat out more dirt and mud.

"You OK? Can I help you?"

"I'm all right, I think. Thanks, Gus."

"No problem, man. Let me guess—Mitch got to you."

"How'd you know?" Jeremy asked.

"Ah, he does it all the time. Ever since I been working here cleaning barns this summer, he picks out one of the guests to pick on. He don't mean no harm."

Just then, Mitch came around the corner of the fence, still laughing. "What's the matter, kid? That bull get too close to you?"

Jeremy didn't know what to say.

Mitch slapped him hard on the back. "Don't worry city boy. You're a guest here, and guests ain't expected to be tough. You just take it easy and let the cowboys take care of the rough stock."

Jeremy's eyes got watery again as he watched Mitch head back to the stock pens.

"Like I said, he don't mean no harm," Gus said. "He just likes to think he's tougher than the guests."

"I'd like to show him I'm tough enough to be a cowboy," Jeremy said. "But I don't know how."

"How 'bout you ride that bull?"

Jeremy could feel his eyes get wide. "Are you kidding? Are you trying to sucker me into doing something dumb, like Mitch did?"

"Hey, no problem, man. It's just an idea. But I think you can do it."

They talked a while, and Gus filled Jeremy in on the art of bull riding. Kids their size didn't try the big bulls, just young ones like the one that ran over Jeremy, or maybe steers.

"It's simple, really," Gus said. "All you do is put one hand in the rope and squeeze, grip the bull's sides with your knees, and hang on."

"Well, it sounds easy," Jeremy said.

"No, no! I said it was simple, but it isn't easy."

"Does it hurt if you get bucked off?"

"Not as bad as what you've been through," Gus laughed. "After getting steam-rolled like you did, getting bucked off is nothing!"

Gus arranged to have the ribbon bull put into the chutes for the bull riding, and as he was helping Jeremy get ready, Mitch walked by.

"Well what've we got here?" he hollered. "The sissy boy—I mean city boy—thinks he's a bull rider! Ha! I say you'll chicken out."

Jeremy looked out through the fence rails at Mitch. He had to admit he was scared. Maybe Mitch was right.

"When that gate opens, I'm betting that bull comes out alone," Mitch said, "because you ain't tough enough to ride no bull. You're chicken!"

But Jeremy did come out of the chute on top of the bull, and stayed there through four bone-jarring jumps before being bucked off. Heck, he thought as he jumped up brushing off the dirt, that was even fun!

He heard Mitch laughing as he walked back toward the chutes, but this time the laugh was different.

"I gotta admit it, kid, you surprised me! I didn't think you had it in you," Mitch said as he patted Jeremy on the back. "You didn't stay on that bull for long, but by golly you got on him! You're a lot tougher than I thought."

Maybe—just maybe—Jeremy thought as wiped dust out his eyes and spit out another mouthful of mud, I'll forgive Mitch after all.

WORKING GIRL OF THE WILD WEST

This previously unpublished story is an experiment in "flash fiction"—the attempt to tell a story in less than a thousand words. Working girls were a fixture in the Old West, with the women involved in the trade often there involuntarily, but lacking any option. In this tale, the woman imagines a way out—sort of.

———— ◆ ————

There's comfort in walking into a room and knowing you've been to bed with every man in the place. Not comfort in the sense of satisfaction, mind you, but relief in knowing your night's work is over.

I tick them off in my mind as I survey the saloon—the drummer standing at the bar haranguing our hometown shyster-cum-land speculator; two ranch hands huddled over the green felt, passing what's left of their month's pay slow but sure to an itinerant gambler; and, alone in the corner, a henpecked farmer from down the riverbend who spends more time between my sheets than the ones on the bed his shrew of a wife occupies.

Then there's Gilpin, who tends bar and owns the place. Despite his best efforts, all the boiled shirts, shined shoes, and pomade-slicked hair on God's green earth cannot disguise the fact that he's naught but a lowborn lout.

"Gil," I says to him, "what say I turn in early?"

"Not on your life. It ain't but ten o' the clock."

"Aw, hell, look around! These men've had their horizontal refreshments already. There ain't none of 'em goin' to be wantin' seconds tonight, and no fresh meat is likely to be showin' up this late."

"So," he says, "you can serve drinks. Or maybe someone will want a tune."

"Nonsense. Even a sorry drinks-slinger such as yourself can handle a crowd this size. And they all know that piano's so far out of tune they couldn't recognize the song they requested on a bet. I'm callin' it a night."

"No," Gilpin says. "You stay put. It's your job."

My job.

If I had a stack of them fancy engraved calling cards, they'd read, "Katherine 'Little Red' O'Donnell, Whore."

None of them highfalutin euphemisms for me. I'm a whore, plain and simple. Not "Soiled Dove" or "Saloon Girl," neither "Fancy Woman" nor "Painted Lady." Just your common, everyday, run-of-the-mill whore.

(By the by, I was christened "Little Red" at a house in Last Chance Gulch in Helena, to distinguish me from "Big Red," a woman twice my size with tangled locks of a suspicious shade of orange. Me, I came by my auburn tresses honestly; brought them with me all the way from Ireland.)

Like so many on the old sod, our particular branch of the O'Donnell family starved out and so sought better prospects on America's distant shores. On the crossing, I met a boyo my own age—sixteen years—name of Liam, also O'Donnell, from the far side of our same county. The fact that we might have been, probably were, shirttail cousins did not hinder our striking up a shipboard romance.

But when Da found Liam squirming around on the quarterdeck with my legs wrapped around him, we got stood up in front of the ship's captain and declared man and wife, an event solemnized by the Holy Roman Church as soon as the gangplank hit solid ground in New York City.

Liam and I set up housekeeping among the many Irish there and attempted a life. It was clear after a few years there was no future for us in the city so we set out for the West. We'd intended to take up a farm somewhere—Colorado, maybe, or California. But Liam succumbed to the lust of the buffalo hunt and left me tending the stove and washtub at a trading post on the Kansas plains while he set out with one of the wagons for a season as a skinner, intending to make our fortune.

He hadn't been gone but three weeks when he took a fever and died. So, with my husband finding himself toes-up under the prairie soil, I soon enough found myself toes-up under a parade of stinking, lice-infested hide hunters; my only means of accumulating enough funds to get out of that fetid place.

It was much the same ever after.

I entertained the troops upstairs at a saloon near an army post. Trail-weary cowboys at a railhead town. Miners in cribs in the mountains of Montana. And, now, whoever drifts through the batwing doors of this one-horse-town's pestiferous poker palace with a dollar and a desire in his front pocket.

But, somehow, there never were and never are enough of those dollars to get a girl anywhere but the next bed in the next town.

And so I have decided to quit this life for a new one. My intention is to relocate to Great Salt Lake City and convert to the religion of the Latter Day Saints. (For appearance's sake only, mind you—being born Irish means being inextricably Catholic, and all the waters of baptism on earth cannot wash it away. Be that as it may, I shall journey to the Utah Territory and, for all practical purposes, become a Mormon.)

Despite these years of hard use, I believe my womanly charm and feminine wiles are as yet sufficient to turn the head of some gray-bearded patriarch and seduce him into inviting me into his harem. The work will be much the same, I suspect, but the hours much better—for I shall be but one among a richness of wives.

I can almost see it now—myself, seated at a long table lined with women, heads bowed as the husband we share intones a lengthy grace on the simple but hearty meal we are about to share.

"Amens" said, he raises his eyes to inspect his wealth. I suppose it's a comfort to an old man to look around a crowded room knowing he's been to bed with every woman in the place.

SILENT NIGHT

In 2012, Chila Woychik, publisher and editor at Port Yonder Press, put together an anthology of Christmas stories written by members of an informal online group of Western writers called The Campfire with the title, Christmas Campfire Companion. *My contribution to the collection is "Silent Night," the story of a Christmas that looks to be cold and lonely. Cowboy poet, writer, and entertainer Andy Nelson read this story on his 2014 CD of Christmas poems and stories.*

———— ◆ ————

It's no wonder they call them lucifers, the cowboy thought. *A man has a devil of a time gettin' one of the damn things lit.*

With stiff, shivering fingers he scratched another of the matches against a rock and watched it sparkle, hoping it would burst into flame. It did, and he shielded the wavering blaze with his hand and held it to the pile of dry pine needles. He dropped the match onto the tinder when it burned his fingers, and added twigs and wasted matchsticks one by one to the infant fire.

The fire wouldn't amount to much, he knew. The small dry branches he'd snapped from the bottoms of the evergreens overhead were the only fuel at hand. All else lay hidden beneath a three-foot blanket of snow. Only here, in a shallow, protected pocket beneath a tight grove of pine trees could he find bare ground. And while he had no hope the fire would burn out the bone-deep chill, the building of it kept mind and body busy, pushing aside the temptation to huddle down into a nap from which he knew he would not awake.

He knew he ought to keep moving, but stopped here in the trees because his horse was spent. The climb up the canyon was a steep one, made more strenuous by the snow. He and the mount took turns breaking trail, the cowboy hunched shivering in the saddle for a time while the horse lunged slowly ahead, then dismounting to wade thigh-deep through the powder snow, dragging the horse along by the bridle reins.

With every step, he cursed his stupidity at being here.

Another winter riding the grub line. As had been the case more often than not these past few years, he'd wasted his summer wages on drink and gambling. His prodigal habits meant bumming his way through the long season between fall and spring roundups, relying on the good will of ranchers. Given his age, wandering from ranch to ranch, trading odd jobs or simply company for food and shelter was becoming less attractive with each passing year.

But he loved the cowboy life and had no intention of giving it up for a town job until he absolutely had to. Just about now, with this fix he was in—cold and hungry in a mountain snowstorm—tending bar or selling ribbons didn't sound half bad. At least he'd be indoors. With a full stomach. And warm.

Some of that mush would taste pretty good right now. Even with the all the mouse tracks through it.

He'd last dined on oatmeal—or at least what passed for it. He suspected the meal, shaken from the wrinkles of a crumpled-up, gnawed-through sack on a dusty shelf, was as much mouse droppings as cereal. But, lacking any alternative, he'd boiled it to a somewhat palatable paste in an empty tomato can—which had been full of his second-to-last meal a day earlier.

Both were served up in an empty line shack where he'd sought shelter when this storm hit three days ago. The camp wasn't used in winter—abandoned each fall with the move of the cattle to the low country—so held no supplies. The rusty can of tomatoes and the discarded remnants of rolled oats were the only edible things on hand.

And the cowboy wasn't the only one hungry—he'd barely been able to scrape together an armful of musty hay for the horse.

Four days ago, he'd thanked the owner of the Slash-Seven for his hospitality and ridden away. He'd been a couple of weeks there, lazing around the bunkhouse jawing over coffee with the old cook, mending saddles and tack that didn't really need fixing, splitting firewood to add to the already substantial stack, and helping out with any other pretend chore he could put his hand to. Despite warnings about the approaching storm, he'd said his goodbyes before wearing out his welcome. He figured to clear Gunsight Pass ahead of the snow, drop down to, then cross, Davidson Valley and pay a visit to the Bar-Cross Ranch. Maybe even stop by that little town—Milagro, as he remembered it—and cadge a drink at the saloon. An easy two-day, ride he figured.

What he hadn't figured on was the speed or severity of the storm that overtook him in the canyon. Snow fell heavy and steady, piling up until bucking it wearied both him and the horse. He considered himself lucky to find the line camp, where he figured to spend the night and wait out the storm. Instead, the storm outlasted him.

The beef and biscuits the Slash-Seven cook wrapped up for him were gone in a matter of minutes after leaving the unsaddled horse under a shed in a small corral and stomping the snow from his boots. The only thing the camp wasn't short on was water—nearly two feet on the ground when he got there, with more added every hour. All it took was a bit of melting on the cabin's cookstove. But there was only a day and night's worth of firewood, and no food—save the rusted can of tomatoes and a meager handful of oatmeal and mouse crumbs.

So when the gray turned from dark to pale for the second time, he saddled up and rode on, knowing that while his chances of making it over the pass in the snow were slim, the odds of surviving at the isolated and empty cow camp in the continuing storm were even worse.

———— ◆ ————

By the time the weak fire consumed all the dry branches he could break from the bottoms of the trees, he figured the horse had had a long enough blow. He pulled the latigo tight, retied the cinch knot, and swung into the saddle. The trail behind him was still visible, but only as a depression in the powdery snow. There was no hint of a trail in front of him, but uphill was the only way to go.

Again, he and the horse alternated breaking trail until, after an exhausting two hours of an increasingly steep climb, they topped out at Gunsight Pass. The snow wasn't as deep inside the narrow, steep-sided V-shaped gap, so the cowboy again loosened the cinch and squatted nearly beneath the horse to rest. With every labored breath, geysers of steam erupted from the horse's nostrils. Despite the cold, runnels of sweat dripped from his flanks.

The cowboy alternately folded his arms across his torso, tucking hands into armpits, and swatted at his chest and cheeks, hoping for warmth as he waited for his mount to cool down. Finally, he stood, stomped, and slowly lifted his knee, poking cold toes into colder air until finding the stirrup, and swung slowly into the saddle.

The depth of the snow dwindled the farther down the lee side of the mountain he rode. But still the snow fell, and still it stacked too deep for easy riding. But his turns breaking trail for the horse grew less frequent; the time between rest stops lengthened. From time to time he caught a glimpse of the Davidson Valley through the dwindling storm.

He stopped at another cluster of pines, the ground beneath covered with needles rather than snow, and scraped together a pile for tinder. Another struggle between stiff fingers and reluctant matches finally resulted in another small fire—barely enough heat to melt snow to slake the horse's thirst. On the ride up to Gunsight Pass, a small but swift stream cut through the snow the length of the canyon, tumbling too fast to freeze even with the altitude, so thirst was easily slaked. No such luck on the downhill trip. Most streams on this side, the cowboy knew, ran only in spring.

By the time horse and rider reached the valley floor, the gray day darkened into night. The cowboy's destination, the Bar-Cross, was miles away yet, a bit north of west across the broad valley. Milagro, as he recalled, lay due south, tucked against the mountain range he'd just descended. The town being closer—it couldn't be more than five or six miles, he imagined—he set that as his target and reined the horse left.

I can bunk in the livery stable, if nothin' else, he told himself. *Be under cover and out of the wind, leastways. Maybe even do a little pearl divin' in trade for a hot meal.*

What he really wanted, though, was the warmth of whiskey. But that, he knew, was a pleasure he'd likely forego this visit for want of funds.

Then again, mayhap I'll find a softhearted barkeep in this burg.

Soon the cowboy's path intersected a road. Although snow-covered, it showed signs of recent traffic, a few wheeled outfits having passed not long since. The easier travel on the flatland soon rocked the cowboy to sleep in the saddle and if he dreamed he did not know it.

He awakened when the horse stopped in the main street of Milagro.

The storm had cleared and stars burned bright in the cold dark. The cowboy had no idea of the time, turned to find the Big Dipper in the sky behind him and figured it to be seven or eight o'clock, thereabouts. He rubbed the sleep from his eyes and studied the town. Deep snow covered every roof he could see. While there were tracks through the snow on the streets, whoever made those tracks was nowhere in sight—not a soul stirred, nor was there any noise to be heard.

A few lamps burned in windows here and there, but that—along with wispy smoke rising from some chimneys—was the only sign of life. Most every building was dark and looked to be locked up. No surprise for the stores, considering the hour. But the café he could see a few doors down on the right, the saloon across the street, even the town marshal's office and jail beside him on the right appeared oddly abandoned.

He sat waiting and wondering for a few minutes but nothing changed. Heeling the horse into motion, he rode to the hitchrail in front of the jailhouse and dismounted. The door only rattled with his push. He cupped his hands around his eyes to peer into the dim office and saw just what he expected—nothing and nobody.

Leaving the tied horse drinking from the trough next to the hitchrail, the cowboy worked his way down the boardwalk, gazing into windows and trying the doors at any buildings with light inside. All were locked, including the eating house. Across the street he found the same. The saloon doors were closed and locked behind the batwings, and the room was empty, despite being the most well-lit place in town. A few glasses and bottles glinted on tables and along the bar, and a poker game looked to have stopped mid-hand, with cards fanned before three of the seats, the rest of the deck stacked in front of one, and a small pot of colored chips in the middle of the green felt.

Whump!

The loud noise spun him around with a start. But the powdery snow rising from the street said it had only been a snowslab avalanching off the boardwalk roof. The cowboy shuddered; this time not from the cold.

Damn! This place is makin' me jumpy. Wonder what's goin' on around here.

He angled across the street, unhitched the horse, and continued on his way, walking past the empty buildings with the horse following. At each intersection—the few there were in the small town—he stopped and studied the side streets for any activity but found none. There were signs of travel through the snow; all converging on the main street down which he walked.

The commercial district of the town thinned out some four blocks along, as did the houses on the side streets. He skylined the roof of a large barn a half block to the west, and went that way on the assumption it would be a livery stable.

Ought to be a hostler on duty. Someone's got to watch out for the stock and such.

His first assumption was correct—it was a commercial stable, surrounded by stock pens and corrals and a wagon yard. The cowboy rolled back the main door, led the horse through and stopped to get his bearings and allow his eyes to grow accustomed to the deeper dark. A narrow strip of light gleamed under a doorway to his right.

Office, maybe. Or sleeping quarters for the hostler. Maybe both.

He looped the reins around a ring on the wall. He knocked on the door. Waited. Knocked again. Nothing.

A latchstring lifted a bar inside the door and he pulled it open. A rumpled blanket lay on a cot in the far corner, next to it on the floor a small safe. A rolltop desk, shoved against the opposite wall, bristled with rolled papers, pencils, awls, hoofknives, a shoeing hammer, and other odd implements. Piles and stacks of papers covered the writing surface. Next to the desk stood a sawhorse with a well-used, half-assembled saddle astride it. A few bridles and harness parts littered the floor. A door hung on the back wall, covering a hole he assumed led to a tack room, or maybe feed bins.

Lifting the lit lantern from a hook inside the door, he walked back into the alley for a look around. The cowboy climbed a ladder to the loft, raised the lamp high to spread the illumination but saw nothing unusual. Horses stood in several of the stalls along the alley, some standing hipshot and likely asleep, others munching hay or grinding grain. None paid him any attention or even seemed to notice his presence.

He spun around with a start when a stabled horse leaned into a wall, rattling the boards.

This town is givin' me the chilly quivers!

On down the alley in the far corner, he found an old watchdog curled up on a tattered horse blanket. He watched it twitch from time to time, probably excited by something in its dreams.

The cowboy lifted the lid from a barrel in a row along the wall; saw it was full of oats. He found a feedbag on a wallpeg and filled it with a bait of the grain, pulled the bit from his horse's mouth and let it dangle, then slipped the morral over his muzzle and buckled it behind the ears.

I'll muck out stalls to pay for that. If ever there's anyone to pay.

Rather than return to the office, he watched as the horse made short work of the feed then pulled off the *morral* and slipped the bit between its teeth, hung the lantern on a hook beside the sliding door, led his horse out and rolled it shut. Back on the main street he checked the streets in every direction. Still, nothing moved. He mounted the horse and continued his way south.

Something in the air prompted the cowboy to stop before he'd traveled a hundred yards. He reined up, wondering what it was, turning his head side to side, straining to hear.

He rode on. Stopped again. This time, he heard something. Music, maybe. The cowboy tapped his heels against the horse and listened for more of whatever he had heard as he rode. The road curved slightly westward as it left town, and just past the bend, maybe two furlongs ahead, he saw light spilling out the windows of a still indistinct building.

As he rode closer, the building resolved itself in the dim night. A schoolhouse. Grange hall. Church. Something like that. Maybe all those things. Carriages, buggies, wagons, and saddle horses surrounded the building. Now and then, as the cowboy approached, he heard snatches of sound floating away from the building and, once, what sounded like applause.

Once he reached the yard he reined up and studied the place. Seeing nothing threatening, he swung out of the saddle, tied the horse to a picket fence away from the other mounts, walked toward the double doors at the end of the building, climbed the steps, and stopped on the porch. The sounds from inside were more distinct now.

Some kid recitin' or somethin'. Maybe sayin' a poem.

Then another young voice, doing much the same.

He carefully opened the door to be faced with a wall of backs—men, lined up across the opening, all facing the front of the room. Through the gaps he glimpsed much the same along each side wall—rows of people two and three deep. In between, ranks of men and women on benches and chairs.

The man directly in front of the cowboy turned at the intrusion, noted the cowboy's hollow cheeks and sunken eyes. "Can I help you, stranger?"

"What's happenin'? Ever'one in town must be here. What's the occasion?"

The town man studied him, skepticism written on his face.

"Don't you know what day it is, friend?"

The cowboy furrowed his brow and pursed his lips. Said, after a few moments, "No, sir. I don't guess I do."

"Why, it's Christmas Eve! School kids is puttin' on a show. Sure, the whole town's here! Best come on in yourself and shut that door."

The cowboy followed the town man as he shouldered and elbowed his way through the standing crowd, leading his guest over to a table against the back wall. He ladled up a mug of hot spiced cider, and gestured an invitation toward a spread of plates and platters of pastries, cakes, cookies, and homemade candies. A steaming coffee urn at the opposite end of the table looked tempting.

The cowboy scalded his mouth in his hurry to get the cider inside him and attempted to smother the fire with an iced sweet roll. He turned to the scene at the front of the room. A girl, maybe twelve years old, in a long gown fashioned from a folded and draped bedsheet and wearing a crown of gold-painted rope, stood front and center on an elevated platform that stretched wall-to-wall across the room. She was reciting the Christmas story he recognized from childhood, the one his mother read from the Good Book. Book of Luke, he recalled.

Behind the girl to one side stood a row of similarly clad girls. Angels, he realized. Opposite them was a line of boys meant to be shepherds, for some held sheephooks and a couple held live ewes on tethers. Center stage rear, beneath a paper star hung to the wall stood an older boy draped in a blanket; in scattered straw at his feet knelt a girl holding a baby doll wrapped in a quilt.

The cowboy swallowed another pastry. "I thank you kindly, sir," he whispered. "I've been mighty cold and hungry."

"Help yourself to more, friend, and don't be thankin' me. Whole town did this, and you're welcome to it. Traveler, stranger, all the same. Ain't nobody ought to be left out this night."

Quite the place, this Milagro, the cowboy thought as he refilled his mug, this time with blistering hot coffee. The children on the makeshift stage eased into unaccompanied song, the townsfolk starting to join in by the second note . . .

Silent night, holy night . . .

GOOD HORSES

Cowboys are masters of understatement. While some are braggarts, many, maybe most, are more likely to downplay their accomplishments. The same can be true when they talk of horses. "Good Horses" is based on that premise. Back around the turn of the century there was a small journal, Literally Horses, *published and edited by Laurie Cerny that featured literary works about horses. This story appeared in its pages and, in 2001, was recognized by the publication with a Remuda Award for Best Short Fiction.*

———— ◆ ————

"That's a pretty good horse you're riding," McCarthy ventured, the first words out of either rider's mouth since leaving camp a quarter of an hour ago. Joaquin ruminated on the comment for a hundred yards or so.

"Si. He is a good one. But that caballo you are riding, my friend, *that* is a horse" he finally replied.

"Oh, he'll do. Sure enough the best in my string. But I've watched that dun you're aboard all the way up the trail and I don't think this sorry roan compares," McCarthy countered.

For three months and more, the two had helped push a herd up out of Texas but this morning's exchange represented more conversation than they'd shared in all that time. Each cowboy's days and his piece of the nights were spent riding herd and, outside of cussing cattle, the work offered little opportunity for talk. Evenings around the fire, each man, by nature, kept his own counsel while other hands swapped stories in the nightly lying contest.

Now, the herd was bedded down a few miles outside Ellsworth, waiting for a train. By lot, this was Joaquin's and McCarthy's day to pursue a little recreation in town. The sun had yet to make an appearance above the horizon. Such days were rare, and the pair intended to not waste a minute of it.

143

"Shoot," McCarthy continued. "This pony pitches every time I climb aboard, and has tried to pile me since the day I met him." Each man's thoughts drifted 700 miles south.

———————◆———————

The Crazy Heart Ranch spreads over a sizable chunk of the Texas plains southeast of San Antonio. Spring roundup starts tomorrow, the result of which will be a herd of market steers to be trailed north. Working cattle was fine with McCarthy, one of the dozen or so hands hired on by the outfit, but this day was more to his liking. The horse herd had been run in, and today the boss would pick out a string of maybe a dozen horses for each cowboy to ride on the gather and as a remuda for the drive. Getting on horses was why McCarthy was a cowboy. He relished the thought of forking a string of unfamiliar mounts, getting to know them during the roundup, and spending long days in the saddle on the trail.

He watched the wrangler drop a loop around the neck of an ordinary-looking roan horse, and stepped up when the boss called his name.

"McCarthy!" he hollered. "This one's yours. See if you can get him saddled."

Most of the horses were green broke—they'd been ridden enough not to be strangers to the saddle, but were far from what you could call trained for cow work or even riding. Noting how the roan trembled, McCarthy figured he could be trouble. Nonetheless, he slid the split-ear headstall over the horse's head, wedged the curb bit between its teeth, and put the blanket and saddle in place as the animal sidestepped away from him. Giving the cinch an extra tug, he tied off the latigo, picked up his reins, grabbed the left ear of the quivering horse, and swung into the saddle. McCarthy found his right stirrup, released the ear, and squirmed into the lowest seat he could find.

Much to his surprise, the horse didn't explode. The roan just stood there, all atremble, front legs stiff and hind legs in a slight squat. "Well hell," he thought. "Here goes nothing." McCarthy touched rowels to the horse's belly. The result, those in attendance would later say, was the stuff of legend. The horse leapt into the air, swapped ends, and landed stiff-legged with bone-crunching, teeth-rattling force. Almost before he had time to feel the impact, McCarthy was airborne again, the result of a spring-loaded skyward lunge of the horse's front end, followed by a high kick that put his hind legs well over his head. Shaken and surprised at the violence of the roan's attack, McCarthy was still aboard, but barely. He weathered the next few jumps and found his balance, but knew he was far from having this horse rode. The animal knew all the tricks. He sunfished, dropped shoulders, walked on his front feet, sucked back, jumped one direction and kicked the other, twisted and spun, anything and everything in the equine repertoire. But he couldn't unseat the determined McCarthy. The rider never raked or quirted the horse, partly because the roan needed no encouragement to work out the kinks but mostly because it wasn't McCarthy's way. He had never believed that antagonizing horses helped in the long run.

After what seemed to McCarthy to be about five minutes less than forever, the horse finally lined out into a lope. The pair of them, breathing hard, made a wide circle across the plain; the man, for now, still in the saddle and in control.

———— ◆ ————

"Man, that was some bronc ride," Joaquin said, admiration in his voice.

"Yeah, I guess I lucked out that time. You'd think after all that pitching, one or the other of us would have learned something, though," replied McCarthy. "If I was any kind of cowboy, I'd have realized right then that this jugheaded roan would never make much of a mount. And if he was any kind of a horse, he'd have realized he wasn't going to buck me off and would have quit trying."

"Oh, my friend, the trail is at its end. The time for tall tales is over."

"Why, Joaquin, whatever could you mean by that?"

"I have seen many caballeros, and you are one of the best. I think you know that. I think, too, that your horse knows it."

"So?" McCarthy asked.

"So, you should save your lies for the campfire, and confess that the bucking is a sign of your horse's spirit. He wants to make sure you are awake when you ride him, so the fine horseman will appreciate the fine horse."

"Joaquin, mi amigo, you've gone loco. Now, that horse you're aboard— compared to him, this one I'm on can't tell a steer from a tree stump."

"It is true, this one understands the cattle. I think maybe it is because he is as stupid as they are."

"Be that as it may," McCarthy said, "if it wasn't for you and that little dun horse this whole outfit would still be sorting steers at the Crazy Heart." Once again, their thoughts turned back down the trail.

———◆———

"Joaquin!" the boss shouted as the wrangler led the dun forward. "Try to teach this one which end of a cow to chase!"

The horse didn't look like much, even among this herd of scrubs. Maybe 13 hands high on his tiptoes, and light enough that Joaquin figured it would be as easy for him to carry the horse as the horse to carry him. He was a claybank-colored dun, roman-nosed and paddle-footed. His ears were bigger than average and a bit floppy, tipped by fuzzy tufts of black hair. But it soon became evident to Joaquin that what the little dun lost in looks he more than made up for in cow sense.

He had a long, easy stride riding circle and ate up the miles with unflagging energy. Almost automatically, he headed into the thorny clumps of brush where cattle hide, knowing where to look better, even, than the cowboy on his back. Let a calf or mossy-horned steer or ornery cow cut and run and the dun was always a step ahead, turning them back into the herd without effort.

When it came time to road brand the steers, there wasn't a horse on the outfit that could keep up with the dun. He'd slide quietly into the herd, ease a critter to the fringes then cut it out and move it toward the desired bunch, pivoting quick as a cat to block its path should it try to turn back. His every move was so precise it seemed effortless. Joaquin proved to be a poet with his reata, due to the combination of his skills and the ability of the little horse to put him in perfect position for the toss, whether a horn or heel shot.

Those days on the drive when Joaquin rode the dun were pure pleasure. The other drovers could only watch the pair in wonder. The horse and cowboy seemed to always know what the cattle were thinking before they knew it themselves. Trouble was avoided more often than not because Joaquin and the horse were there to prevent it. The dun was tireless, and as eager to be under the saddle and working the herd as McCarthy's roan was to buck. And, much as McCarthy was a born caballero, Joaquin was a natural vaquero.

———•———

"Yep. That horse under you ain't much to look at, but he's damn sure a good one."

"You are right about one thing, friend," Joaquin replied. "He is not much to look at. If I could choose a name for him, I would choose 'Tequila' I think."

"And why would that be?"

"Because looking at this horse is like taking a drink—it burns all the way down."

McCarthy, stifling laughter, offered "Surely you'd agree, though, that your ugly dun could outrun any horse in the cavvy. I'd bet a month's pay that you'd even outrun that big fancy eastern-bred stud horse in the boss's string."

"I think not. I think that horse runs faster for sure, and maybe a couple of others. Your roan, too, will beat us. That is what I think."

"Well now I know you're plumb loco, Joaquin! This sorry bag of bones might out-buck yours, but he couldn't keep up on the run on his best day."

"Ah, but I know different, McCarthy. Have you forgotten the day we all raced for our lives?"

McCarthy knew well the incident of which Joaquin spoke.

———•———

The herd was at the crossing of the Canadian River in Indian Territory. With a storm on the horizon, the boss wanted to be on the opposite bank before rain swelled the stream and caused a delay. It took a lot of whooping and hollering, but the crew got the animals across by mid-afternoon and bedded them down to wait out the storm. The boss didn't expect that the steers, tired from the crossing, would stampede, especially in daylight. But with clouds rolling in and lightning flashing, he opted to keep every hand horseback and take no chances.

It's a funny thing about a stampede. One second the herd is lying quiet and the next they're on the run. Without communication any human ear can detect, they rise as one and take flight. And the only sound in a stampede is rumbling hooves, rattling hocks, and clattering horns; not a beller or bawl is heard. The stampede at the Canadian was true to form.

Quick as a lightning bolt, every cowboy was on the run, racing for the front of the herd. The only way to stop a stampede is to turn the leaders, and keep turning the herd back on itself until the cattle mill. It's a dangerous race. A false step, a wash, a prairie dog hole, a tangle of brush, a spot of slippery mud—all this and more can upset a horse, the result of which is almost-certain death for horse and rider since the stampeding cattle, running blind, pound everything in their path into the ground.

Joaquin watched as McCarthy, aboard his usually skittish roan horse, outpaced everything on four feet to gain the lead. His pressure to turn the herd slowed things just enough to allow other riders on fast horses— including Joaquin himself—to reach the fore and get them turned. The stampede was over sooner than most. Neither man nor beast was killed or unaccounted for. And the outfit's esteem for McCarthy's competence in the saddle and the speed and agility of his roan bronc climbed a notch or two.

———— ◆ ————

"I saw how your horse runs, my friend. We all saw," Joaquin continued. "You left my little dun and every other horse in the dust—or mud, that day."

"Oh, that was nothing but luck. I just happened to be practically in front of the herd when the excitement started. Besides, you were stuck over there on the side closest to the river."

"Que?"

"Well, you know, Joaquin! All those little washes and arroyos leading down to the bottoms made for a rougher ride. More dangerous, too. That dun picked his way through there like a night horse, only twice as fast. If my roan hadn't of been on smoother ground, you'd have run circles around us."

"I do not think so, my friend. This poor little crooked-legged horse can barely walk, let alone keep up with your roan."

"You really think so?"

"That is what I think."

"Hell, this sorry excuse for a horse is as likely to light into bucking as look at a man."

"Perhaps what you say is true, McCarthy. But I believe your fine caballo could cover the country faster while bucking than my dirt-colored, big-eared pony can at the run."

THE DEATH OF DELGADO

The cowboys rode on in silence for a time. Eventually, a grin spread across McCarthy's face and he burst out laughing.

Joaquin looked at McCarthy.

McCarthy looked at Joaquin.

Without a word, each rider spurred up his mount and the race on the road to Ellsworth was on.

HORSE THIEF MORNING

Another story featuring my favorite Old West character, Porter Rockwell. The historical incident behind this tale was mentioned in an earlier story, "Separating the Wheat from the Tares." Here, we cover the bloody event in greater detail, with the description of the gunplay based on recorded history—at least one version.

————— ◆ —————

Brown Sal was a darn good horse, even if she was a mare. She could outrun every horse in the valley—leastways every one that ever cared to race against her. She was good to ride, real smooth-like, and could walk out at a right quick pace and do it all the day long. And when I rode out to the far pastures to move the cow herd, I could knot the reins and let them hang on her neck and that horse would handle them cattle without so much as a blink of an eye from me. Why, she'd even submit to the harness and pull Pa's buggy around the streets of Salt Lake when he took a mind to go into the City sporting with Ma.

You can see why Pa thought so much of that horse.

So when that scapegrace Lot Huntington stole her, Pa did not hesitate one minute before sending for his pal Porter Rockwell to get her back. How old Port went about it makes for a pretty good story and I will get to it by and by. But first, you got to know about Lot Huntington.

See, Lot was a known rowdy who got into more trouble than his upbringing would lead one to expect. His daddy, Dimick Huntington, was kind of a big deal. He was one who Brigham Young relied on and had answered any number of callings over the years. Mostly, he was the man to see if you wanted to know anything or do anything when it came to the Indians hereabouts. Brother Huntington had been an interpreter with the Utes and the Shoshonis since coming west and all them Indians trusted him and knew him to be a solid and reliable sort.

His boy Lot, now, he was a different story.

He must have been within two or three years of reaching age thirty when he stole Brown Sal. And already he had been up to more no-good in his life than he ought to have been. Still, Lot was a likeable sort. He always had a friendly smile and a good line of talk, especially when it came to the ladies. I have to say that with all the trouble he was involved in, he never mistreated no women. On the other hand, he was known to defend their honor whenever he saw the occasion required it.

As I said, folks liked Lot. Most men were happy to share a drink with him, whether in one of the saloons or roadhouses, or out of a jug or pocket flask around a campfire. He probably drank more than a Mormon boy ought to, and that might be to blame for some of his misbehavior, but it wasn't uncommon in those days for a man to imbibe. Fact is, they say he had been on a big bender that time he shot Wild Bill Hickman on Christmas day back in '59.

Wild Bill is another interesting story, but I won't go into it just now. Suffice it to say he more than earned the moniker "Wild Bill." He was a sometimes lawman and sometimes outlaw. He rode under orders from Brigham Young from time to time, and other times Bother Brigham would as soon he never heard of the man and wished he could be rid of him. For a time, Hickman ran a gang of thieves and rustlers known as Hickman's Hounds, and Lot Huntington was known to have ridden with him now and again. In fact, Hickman kind of took young Huntington under his wing and showed him the ropes of the outlaw trade, according to some.

Anyhow, the way I heard it, some of Hickman's bandit pals, including Lot, without his knowing it, stole a herd of horses from one of Wild Bill's friends, who was a freighter. Hickman found out who the thieves were and reported it, which resulted in a standoff when a bunch of them thieves caught Wild Bill out of town one night and threatened to shoot him. Never one to shun a fight, Wild Bill pulled his pistols and faced down all seven of them, and they turned tail and ran, shouting threats as they went. Lot was among them. Must have been they was drunk enough to feel brave but not sloshed sufficient to want to shoot it out with Wild Bill.

Them boys kept drinking and arguing for days, trying to talk one another into taking on their friend Wild Bill. Lot finally got up the courage on Christmas morning and found Wild Bill Hickman outside the Townsend Hotel at the corner of First South and West Temple Streets, right in the heart of downtown Salt Lake City.

Lot walked up to Wild Bill, they say, spewing obscenities the like of which ought not come out of any mouth a mother kissed. He drew his pistol, but Wild Bill, being no stranger to shooting scrapes, grabbed Huntington's hand and pushed the gun aside even as he slid a pig sticker out of his belt fixing to gut Lot.

The way Hickman told it, he held up for a second as he didn't want to kill his young friend. One of the men with Lot yelled "Don't kill him!" and stepped between the two. As Lot backed off, he dropped the hammer and shot Wild Bill, then shot him again whilst Hickman was pulling his own pistol. Lot turned and ran down the alley before Hickman could return fire, which, when he finally did, landed a bullet in Lot's backside. Lot let out a yelp, turned and threw some more lead in Wild Bill's direction, and ran again.

Wild Bill, meantime, was barely able to stand, having been smote by bullets in hip and thigh. Some folks on the way home from Sunday school—not only was it Christmas, it was the Sabbath as well—carried Hickman inside and a couple of sawbones went to work on him, picking chunks of lead out of him. Seems one of the bullets had shattered and ripped him up inside pretty good, even getting some pieces stuck in his bones. Them doctors gave Wild Bill up for dead, but him, being a contrary sort, wasn't having it.

He was laid up for weeks and barely breathing. One of Huntington's pals sneaked into Wild Bill's room one night intending to do away with him, but Hickman had Jason Luce there standing guard, and Luce sliced up the intruder pretty good with his Bowie knife—stabbed him a dozen times, they said.

Anyway, thanks to Lot Huntington, Wild Bill Hickman hobbled around on crutches clear through that summer and walked with a limp the rest of his life—every day of which was painful on account of all that lead Lot left in him.

But you got to remember that Lot wasn't drunk all the time, and when he wasn't on a toot he was as nice a fellow as you'd care to meet, even if he was a thief and an outlaw. Fact is, he was the kind of guy that young boys could admire, what with his easy smile and his swagger and the way he wore his hat—cocked at a just a little more of an angle than most men would be comfortable with. And when he had money—probably stolen—he always spread it around, buying drinks for grown men and licorice sticks for kids, which he would pass out in the street to any tike who happened by. Of course many a mother refused the offer on behalf of their kids, then gathered their skirts and shuffled themselves and their little ones away from the evil influence as quick as they could manage.

But I better get back to my story.

Lot Huntington's theft of Brown Sal didn't just happen on its own. It came near the end of another of his drunken sprees. Let me catch you up on that, then we'll get to the horse stealing. And what happened after.

It all starts with Utah's governor at the time. Now, you got to remember that there was no love lost between the United States and Utah Territory in them days. We had barely avoided a shooting war with the government a few years earlier, and they kicked Brigham Young out of the governor's office and put Alfred Cumming in, who didn't know thing one about Utah or Mormons or anything else so far as I could see. Turns out Cumming was a real peach compared to his replacement. But I'll get to that.

Anyway, when the Civil War broke out Back East the Army that had come out here to fight us was sent to fight the Southerners—except those who quit the Army to join up with the South and fight against their old comrades in arms, which more than a few of them did, including General Albert Sidney Johnston, who had been in command out at Camp Floyd. But no sooner were those soldiers gone than the government sent more soldiers—these from California, under Colonel Patrick Edward Connor— to keep an eye on us Mormons. I guess they was afraid we'd join up with the Confederates, which wasn't all that farfetched a notion seeing as the United States of America had never done the Latter Day Saints any good and had allowed our fellow citizens to do us a good deal of harm when we was back in the States.

Abe Lincoln replaced Cumming with John Dawson—that would have been along about the end of 1861—who was the sorriest excuse for a politician I ever heard of, and that's saying something. First thing, he got up on his soapbox and demanded Utah Territory fork over a passel of money to help the Union fight the Civil War. Which suggestion Brigham Young soon laid to rest, and rightly so.

Most folks wrote that off as politics and didn't pay it much mind. But what Dawson did next got folks stirred up but good. What he did was, he made rude and unwelcome advances of an improper nature towards a woman, whose name I will not mention, who was doing some sewing for him—and he did it right in her own front room, if you can imagine. She told him to leave off and that she planned to report his uncouth behavior to the police. When he offered her a sizeable sum of money to keep quiet, well, that really put a bee in her bonnet and she took up a fireplace shovel and went to work on him; drove him right out the front door, she did.

Once word about that indiscretion got out, Dawson was rightly concerned for his safety so he abandoned his office and absconded for the East. He'd only been governor for maybe three weeks, a term in office that was three weeks too long if you ask me. He made his way up the canyon to Mountain Dell to Ephraim Hanks's stage station to catch an eastbound coach.

But who should find him there in the cold and snow of New Year's Eve but Lot Huntington and half a dozen other yahoos who ran with him at times—I can't name them all, but Moroni Clawson was there, as was Wil Luce and Wood Reynolds. Wood Reynolds, by the way, was kin to the woman the Governor attempted to compromise and it might have been him who agitated the others to go after Dawson. Not that it took much encouragement, to my way of thinking.

Them boys just hung out at the station drinking and raising a ruckus whilst Dawson cowered in the corner trying to keep warm and out of sight. He came back from visiting the backhouse and saw that someone had lifted the fancy beaver robe that had been covering him. He protested, they say, and Wood Reynolds shut his mouth with a balled fist. Knocked him right to the floor, Wood did, and while he was down the rest of the pack lit into him, kicking and punching and giving him what-for as a reminder of his lapse of manners. There were rumors that them boys turned Dawson into a steer, but I think that was just a tall tale. Not that I'd put such a mutilation past them boys, if they were drunked up enough. They had the know-how, for certain, having performed that very operation on many a bull calf every spring.

Someone dumped Dawson onto the stagecoach when it came through and he went back to Washington and raised all manner of uproar for his treatment out here but so far as I know nothing ever came of it. The courts swore out warrants against Lot and them others, but there wasn't a policeman or sheriff or marshal in the Territory inclined to go after the boys, at least for that offense.

Given what happened to Lot Huntington a couple weeks later, it might have been better had he been arrested and lounging in jail. That way, he would not have been accused, right or wrong, of lifting an Overland Mail cash box with $800 in it from Townsend's Stable and getting another arrest warrant with his name on it for his efforts. Nor would he have stole Brown Sal and got my Pa in a huff, who put Porter Rockwell on his trail.

Here's what happened.

Pa rode Brown Sal into town one evening—not the City, but Jordan Mills, nearest where we lived—to see Bishop Swenson on a tithing matter. He tied the mare to the fence and came out hours later to find her gone—or not find her, I guess I should say. He studied around as well as he could in the dark but the tracks in the snow and the streets were so muddled he couldn't make any sense of them.

So, it being late, and Pa not being the kind to inconvenience a neighbor by waking them up late at night for the borrow of a horse, walked on home. Which was no short distance, by the way, and it was darn cold besides, like a January night is likely to get. The trip took him most of what was left of the night and he was in no shape to do anything but take to his bed when he got to the house.

My big brother Sam was right upset with the situation.

"I'm goin' after 'em, Pa," he said as he pulled on his boots.

"Going after who? You don't know who stole Sal any more than I do."

"It won't take me long to find out," Sam said. "Them thieves leave tracks just like anybody else does."

"I told you there was no trail I could make out."

"Well, everybody in the Valley knows Brown Sal, so whoever it was sure ain't stickin' around here or headin' for Salt Lake. That means about the only thing they can do is head south past Point of the Mountain then west into the desert on the stage road."

"Maybe you're right. But you just leave it be. I'll send for Port."

"You do that Pa. And get him out here in a hurry. Meantime, I ain't waitin' around."

Pa thought for a minute while Sam threw what cooked food he could scare up into his saddlebags. Pa said, "If you're going south you'll likely find Port at the Hot Springs. That's where I'd look, anyway."

See, at that time Porter Rockwell owned a roadhouse down at the Point of the Mountain called the Hot Springs Brewery and Hotel. He had a house a little farther on in Lehi, and a big ranch way out west of there at Government Creek. And he had a place in the City as well. Ol' Port's interests were pretty spread out, and you'd likely find him anywhere. But on a cold winter day or night, the Hot Springs Brewery and Hotel was as good a guess as any and better than most.

Sam and me and two of Sam's pals swung into the saddle and headed south. Pa wasn't keen on me going along, but Sam said another gun could make a big difference if it came to shooting. As it happened, I was pretty well-heeled with a .36-caliber Navy Colt percussion-cap revolver that came to me when the Army abandoned Camp Floyd. Guns were not among the things they auctioned off to the public when they shut down the fort, so my owning it was not exactly on the up-and-up, but I was not the only one back then in possession of a firearm courtesy of the United States Army.

I could shoot, too. Better than Sam, even. But plinking peach cans off a fence post ain't the same as shooting at a man so there's no telling how I would do in a gunfight. Truth be told, I was curious about it. But, at the same time I was not all that eager to test myself. You know how it is. A young feller like I was is always wondering how he stacks up, if he's fit to be called a man, that sort of thing.

Anyway, when we got to Draperville down at the south end of the valley we found out three men had been through way late the night before, one of them on a horse that matched Brown Sal's description right down to the bulldog tapaderos on Pa's saddle. Which meant Sam was likely right in his notions about where they'd go. And it meant they had the best part of a day's lead on us. But the man we talked to said they didn't seem to be in much of a hurry.

We rode on to Rockwell's roadhouse and found Port there. He'd ridden up from his house in Lehi that morning so did not see the horse thieves when they rode through, but the barkeeper heard them go by in the wee hours and wondered why they didn't stop for the night or at least come in to warm up.

Port was on his way to the City, but did not hesitate half a second to change his plans when we told him Pa wanted his help to get his favorite horse back. Not only did Port favor horses and hate horse thieves, he and Pa were saddle pals from way back and either would most likely do anything the other asked, short of breaking the law. Come to think of it, in Port's case going outside the law wouldn't have mattered much anyway. It was well known he was willing to do darn near anything to accomplish his purposes or fulfill whatever assignment he'd been handed.

"It's Brown Sal they took, you say?" Port said.

"It is," Sam said.

"Damn. That mare's too good a horse for any lowlife horse thief to have his hands on. You reckon she was took on purpose by someone who knew who she was, or do you suppose they just happened on her?"

"Couldn't say. She was tied to the fence outside the Bishop's house in town. So it could be either way, or both. The thief might have just come by and saw the opportunity. Could be he recognized Sal and that made the chance even harder to pass up."

"How many?"

"Man in Draperville said three."

The barkeep nodded agreement. "Sounded like three horses that went by here. Not much traffic on the road, cold as it was last night. Only that outfit and one wagon came by here all night, and the man in the wagon stopped for a beer and a bowl of beans."

"Were them horsemen in any hurry?"

This time the saloonist's head moved side-to-side rather than up and down. "Nope. Just walking along."

"That's what they said in town, too," Sam added.

Port thought for minute or two, sipping at a mug of beer and tugging at his beard. "All wheat, boys. It's all wheat. We'll get them."

"Wheat," if you don't know much about Porter Rockwell, is a word he used when he meant everything was fine. Nobody knows for sure why, but some folks thinks it's because of that Bible story in the Book of Matthew about the wheat and the tares; the wheat, of course, being what was good and the tares what was bad. Not that Port was much on scripture, mind you. Fact is, the man couldn't read a word, scripture or otherwise, and if he ever paid attention in Sunday school you'd never know it. Still and all, even given his lack of observance, Port was as good a man as ever set foot on the earth. Of course some folks would beg to differ and claim there was never a worse man to walk the earth, but most of them didn't know ol' Port and relied on rumors for their opinions.

We set out from the Hot Springs Brewery and Hotel and once we cleared the gap where the Jordan River cuts through the Point of the Mountain we started bearing west along the wagon road. That road was well traveled and had been for years, being the route of the Overland Stage and Express, the way to Camp Floyd when the Army was out there, and had been the trail the Pony Express followed. Not that we knew it at the time, but that meant Lot Huntington—who was the one who stole Brown Sal, but which we didn't find out till later—knew the country well, him having been a

Pony Express rider and all. Besides, Brown Sal probably wasn't the first stolen horse he had ridden or herded along that road.

We pushed our mounts at a pretty good pace for about twenty miles or so until we got to the Stagecoach Inn. That place, as you might could tell from the name, was a stage station. The big hotel was built a few years earlier when the Army pitched their tents at Camp Floyd, which happened to be just across the road.

There wasn't much there anymore, but when the soldiers was at Camp Floyd, Frogtown—what they called the settlement that sprung up—had more than seven thousand folks living in it, they say. Except for Salt Lake, it was about as big a town as you could find anywhere in Utah Territory. Hardly anybody lived there when we went after Brown Sal, but darn near everyone on the Overland Road stopped there. If you were westbound it was about the last place of any note before setting out into some serious desert, and if you were eastbound you knew civilization wasn't far off once you got there.

The station agent was a good friend of ol' Port's and he stood us to a hot meal and even hotter coffee. He told us, too, that our quarry was a young man he believed to be Lot Huntington and two others he did not know but had seen around, and they had passed through not so many hours ago, so we knew we were gaining on them. Port figured if we borrowed fresh horses we could catch them at Faust's Station, another twenty miles or so down the road. But the Overland Stage man went him one better, offering Port the use of a coach and driver.

Now, I know you're thinking a man who worked for the Overland Stage wouldn't be giving the loan of a stagecoach to just anybody, but Porter Rockwell wasn't just anybody so far as the Overland Stage was concerned. See, ol' Port, as a Deputy United States Marshal—did I mention he was a lawman?—had recovered more stolen money and rustled horses for them than they could ever repay him for.

All of us was happy with that development. Having been horseback darn near every minute of a long, long day, sitting in a stagecoach offered a nice respite for our backsides. Besides, the inside of that coach was considerably warmer than what it was outdoors that night.

The driver whoaed up the team a ways shy of Faust's Station on account of Port didn't want to alert the outlaws of our presence if they were there. So we stomped the life back into our feet and hoofed it on in to the station while it was still dark. Port sent Sam to look under a shed in one of the corrals to see if Brown Sal was there and he came back and said she sure enough was.

"Wheat," Port said. "Looks like we outguessed them horse thieves."

We backed off a ways and waited while Port figured out how he wanted to handle things.

"Here's how this is gonna go down, boys," he finally said. "I don't want any gunplay if we can help it, so check your loads and be ready but don't shoot unless your life is in danger."

I nodded in agreement, and I suppose the others did too, although I don't guess Port could have seen us much in the dark. But he went on, accustomed as he was to being obeyed in such situations.

"Come the morning, them thieves will walk out the door and when they do I will be ready for them. With any luck, they'll throw down their guns. I have my doubts about what Lot will do, as that boy don't always use his head as God intended. I don't want to shoot him, or anyone, but if they start burning powder you all jump in and make your aim true. We'll have the advantage on account of we know what we're shooting at and where they are and they won't."

I nodded again and we all listened as Port told us where to conceal ourselves. He took up the position nearest the station, behind a pile of cedar fence posts stacked end up, sort of like a stubby Indian tepee.

We shivered out there for a good long while waiting for the sun to rise and take the chill out of the air. But before it did, in the gray light of dawn, things heated up all on their own. First sign of life we noticed was smoke coming out the chimney atop the little log building that served as the stage station and Doc Faust's abode. I don't know what the others thought about that smoke, but it made me wish I was indoors sitting next to that fire, even if it meant horse thieves for company.

After what seemed like a glimpse of eternity, we heard the door rattle then swing open. Without even meaning to, I took a quick breath then could not let it out again. My pistol was already in my shooting hand, but I shifted it to the other and flexed my fingers and rubbed them against my pants leg to get the frost out of them and some fresh blood into them. As I passed the Colt back to my shooting hand I stole a glance to make sure all my caps were seated.

By then we could see it was Doc Faust coming out. Port waited until he closed the door then stepped out from behind his post pile. Doc's eyes got as big around as coffee saucers. But he hotfooted it right over to where

Port waited and the two of them stepped back out of sight of the shack should anyone else happen out the door. From where I sat I could see Port and Doc talking but could not hear them. Doc talked a lot and waved his hands about and nodded his head up and down and side to side and flapped his hands around some more as he worked his jaw. Port just stood there with his hands in his coat pockets—where, I happened to know, he kept his pistols, their barrels sawed off short so they would fit better—as calm and cool as the morning, his only movement an occasional blink of his eyes.

Port told us later that Doc Faust told him for certain it was Lot Huntington and Moroni Clawson and John Smith who had ridden in the evening before and that just then they were inside eating breakfast. Port told him to go back in and inform the outlaws we had the station surrounded and to toss out their guns and follow them out the door with their hands up.

Doc more than likely passed along the information just like Port said. But those boys in there must have had a different idea, for nothing at all happened for what seemed like the longest time but couldn't have been more than a few minutes.

Then the door opened again and Lot Huntington walked out with a pistol in his hand, him pointing the barrel of it here and there in search of a target. I don't know what kind of gun it was, exactly, but it looked to me to be about the size of a mountain howitzer.

"Throw down that gun and throw up your hands!" Port said.

Huntington looked around but saw nobody.

"Like hell I will," he said to the post pile.

"I don't want to shoot you, Lot. I'd hate to have to explain to your folks why I killed a boy of theirs I'd known since his baby days."

"Shut up, old man! You show your face and I will put a bullet in it."

"C'mon, kid. You ain't got a chance. Nobody has to die here."

Lot kept his pistol pointed at the post pile and walked as calm as you please toward the corral and ducked between the rails.

"Stop right there, Lot!"

"Shut the hell up, old man. I'm leaving here and there ain't you nor nobody else going to stop me."

Port stepped out from behind the pile of posts and stood watching as Huntington rounded the corner of the shed and went out of sight.

He walked toward the corral, as if unconcerned or uncaring that at any moment Lot could step out of the shed and shoot him down.

Lot did step out of the shed soon enough. He had Brown Sal by the cheek piece on the bridle and walked her toward the gate so that she was between him and Port. I thought at the time that was a pretty cowardly thing to do, hiding behind a horse, but I know it was the smart thing to do and I wouldn't have thought a thing of it had the horse he was hiding behind been any other but Sal.

"Stop!" Port hollered as Lot walked Sal toward the gate.

"I already told you to shut up, Rockwell."

"I'll shoot you, Lot, sure as I'm standin' here."

"You're welcome to try, old man. I ain't afraid of you for one minute. You've outlived your reputation as far as I'm concerned."

Had I been breathing, I imagine the fog of it on that cold morning would have clouded my view of what happened next, but as I was not breathing at the time my view was clear as the winter air. By then, Lot had reached the corral gate, which was nothing more than fence rails like the rest of the corral, except these weren't pegged into place. So, all you had to do was slide them back a ways and let them drop. Which was just what Huntington was doing, but it was pretty slow going, what with him having to keep his gun and Sal's bridle reins in one hand and both eyes on Rockwell while he nudged the rails along with the other hand.

It looked like Port was just going to watch him do it, and I wondered if I was seeing the last of Brown Sal.

Lot had worked his way up to the top rail by then and as it slipped free he lost his grip and it dropped to the ground and bounced into Sal's foreleg. Now, Sal is even-tempered as horses go, but something like that will spook any horse, especially when the tension has got the air so thick you could slice and stack it.

Sal shied then reared up on her hind legs and Lot Huntington was exposed for those few seconds. But that's all it took for Port to pull the trigger three times. The horse thief staggered and fell into the fence rails and as he keeled over backwards his left leg got hung between two of the poles and that kept all but his head and shoulders from reaching all the way to the ground.

When the gunsmoke around Port cleared, he wasn't paying any attention at all to Lot, knowing from experience, I suppose, that there would be no more trouble from that quarter. Instead, his pistol pointed toward the station.

"The rest of you come on out of there," he said. "Send out the guns first."

The door cracked open and a rifle and three revolvers arced out the hole and clattered to the ground. Moroni and John walked out acting both sheepish and afraid, their wide eyes riveted to the hole in the end of Rockwell's gun barrel, which was still wisping a bit of smoke. Port called the rest of us out of our hidey-holes and had us tie up the two horse thieves.

In the few minutes it took all this to happen, Lot Huntington hung there on the fence rails bleeding out and didn't move an inch. I know, for I cast more than a few glances that way while all this was going on.

There's not much more to say. Rockwell's shooting proved to be as accurate as his legend claimed. The middle of Lot's chest was ripped to shreds by eight balls of double-ought buckshot. I know, because I counted the holes. I suppose it's best to say that Porter Rockwell often charged his pistols with buckshot. He claimed it more forgiving if your aim is a mite off, and more deadly—sort of like hitting a man with six or eight or however many bullets from a .32 caliber pistol, as opposed to one .44 or .45 caliber bullet. Myself, I wouldn't know. But that's what Port said.

There wasn't anything more to do but wrap Lot's body in a canvas sheet and stow it atop the stagecoach, load up the living and head back toward home. We didn't even stop for a cup of coffee before setting out. The worst part was riding along in that coach as it rocked back and forth, knowing Lot Huntington was riding up top, colder than we were.

Brown Sal didn't seem bothered by his death as she trotted along behind, tied to the back of the stagecoach. When I stuck my head out the window to check on her from time to time, I swear there was a smile on her face.

THE PASSING OF NUMBER SIXTEEN

"The Passing of Number Sixteen" is a "long" short story, written and originally published as a three-part serial. Author Dusty Richards, as editor of a new online Western magazine, Saddlebag Dispatches, *requested a story that could be serialized in the debut issues of the publication. This is the result—a modern-day Western mystery with a rodeo setting.*

———— ♦ ————

The horse hadn't started to bloat when the feed crew showed up that morning. But, left to lie in the summer day, it would have swelled in the sun until stiff legs spraddled at impossible angles.

"Number Sixteen" was the only name the horse had ever known. Bred and born to buck, home for his nine years of life had been pastureland owned by the Rough String Rodeo Company. And, of course, the catch pens at countless rodeo arenas and the stock trailers that carried him and the other broncs in the bunch there.

"Well, there ain't no doubt what killed him," Andy Bowen, Number Sixteen's owner, said as the chains binding the horse's hind legs to the bucket of the front-end loader tightened and the tractor dragged the carcass from the pen.

"The question is, who."

"And why," said the deputy from the county sheriff's office.

The eight other horses in the pen huddled as deep into the far corners as they could, snorting and pawing and trembling as their dead corral mate's neck and head snaked through the gate, a thick stream of dried blood crusted from the scorched hole in the center of Number Sixteen's forehead to the dull, dead eye dragging through the dust.

A veterinarian was on hand, but nobody needed his expertise to tell them it was a bullet from the barrel of a pistol that felled the horse. "Fired at close range," he had told them earlier, attempting to add something to the conversation.

But Bowen and Hugh Morgan, the deputy, could see that for themselves. For that matter, so could the hay hands who first found the dead bronc and the two cowboys who rolled out of their sleeping bags to see what the commotion was all about.

"Damn," one of them, face still smeared with sleep, said. "Number Sixteen. Best bareback bronc in the bunch."

The other cowboy only nodded. But the comment caught Bowen's attention and he turned to study the two cowboys. He recognized them both as regulars this summer at the rodeos where he provided stock. The one who had spoken, Wes Simms, entered the bareback and saddle bronc riding and rarely earned his entry fees back. But the other, Tanner Lambert, was already making a name for himself aboard bareback horses, regularly winning money in this, his first rodeo season.

"Hell, Tanner, this is bad business for you," Bowen said. "You had Number Sixteen drawed in the bareback riding this afternoon."

Again, the young cowboy only nodded. He knew, and Bowen knew, the killing of Number Sixteen put a cramp in his chances to win the buckle at this rodeo. Whatever replacement horse drawn for him from the re-ride pen, no matter how good, wouldn't hold a candle to Number Sixteen. Lambert knew drawing that bronc was as close as it gets to a guaranteed paycheck for the cowboy who could ride him. And he could—he'd done it last month at the rodeo in Cedar Ridge.

Across the fairgrounds, unnoticed by the men behind the bucking chutes in the pen just vacated by the carcass of Number Sixteen, Rowdy Galvin sat on the trunk of his battered car, sock feet propped on the bumper, watching.

Galvin, too, was a regular at rodeos in the region. A few years back he'd been a top hand in the bareback and bull riding, and even managed to win money at the big shows against the top riders. Plenty of those in the know believed he could have hit the road in a serious way and won a place at the National Finals, the biggest rodeo of them all, especially in the bareback riding. But Rowdy Galvin was undisciplined, with a wild streak as wide as the gap in his spur lick, and so he worked at odd jobs and entered what rodeos he could get to, usually winning his share of the purse but never getting ahead, owing to his reckless habits.

His dissolute nature started innocently enough, hitting the rodeo bars after the shows. Beer and whiskey were bad for him, and with a bellyful of either or both Rowdy lived up to his name. But when a buckle bunny—one of those wayward girls in every town whose goal, at least for that weekend, is to catch a cowboy—introduced Galvin to harder stuff, he really went off the rails. Crystal meth was his demon at present. He had snorted, smoked, and injected enough of it that his teeth were already paying the price. The effects were obvious in the rodeo arena, as well.

What the hell, he thought as he slid off the back of the car, opened the rear door and flopped onto the back seat, wallowing himself a nest in the dirty laundry, food wrappers, and filthy blankets and stolen motel pillows, hoping against hope to get some sleep. But the lingering effects of smoke from the latest glass pipe probably would not allow much of it.

"Any idea where to begin looking into this?" Deputy Morgan asked the stock contractor.

"Not a clue," Andy Bowen said. "Who'd want to kill a horse?"

"Wonder why nobody heard it. There was folks here all night." Morgan chewed on the toothpick poking out the corner of his mouth. "You boys—what'd you say your names are?"

"Wes Simms."

"Tanner Lambert."

"You two was sleeping here, wasn't you?"

"Yessir," Simms said. "Right over yonder under them trees. That's my car there—the green Ford with the gray front fender."

"You didn't hear anything? No gunshot?"

Lambert shook his head. "Nosir," Simms said. "'Course we didn't get back here to bed till twelve-thirty, maybe one o'clock."

"Where were you before that?"

"We was in town. Had supper after the rodeo then just hung out for a while."

"Hung out?" Morgan said. "Hung out where?"

Simms squirmed. Finally, Tanner Lambert answered.

"We was in the parking lot at the Longhorn Bar."

"Parking lot?"

"Yup," Lambert said. "See, we ain't of age to go inside."

Simms butted in with, "But all them girls goin' to the bar, they got to get there through that parking lot, so we thought we'd take our chances on meetin' some."

Morgan chewed his toothpick some more. "I don't suppose any of them girls—or anybody else—might have slipped you a bottle of beer or two, maybe?"

Simms squirmed.

"Hell, Deputy, leave the boys alone," Bowen said. "They're good kids. And it seems to me like you got bigger fish to fry here than worrying if some cowboy might have, just maybe, licked a little foam off his lips last night. Find out who shot my horse, dammit."

Tossing the toothpick into the bloodstain in the dirt, Morgan followed the drag rut left by Number Sixteen's carcass out the gate and down the alley. He opened the door of his patrol car, paused for a look around, then climbed into the car and drove away.

"You boys sure you didn't hear or see anything?"

"No, Mr. Bowen, we sure didn't," Lambert said.

"Time we got back," Simms added, "we was so tired we coulda slept through a lot more than one little ol' gunshot. Leastways I coulda."

Tanner Lambert nodded in agreement.

"Well, if you boys would keep your eyes and ears open I'd sure appreciate it," Bowen said. "Anybody dumb enough to shoot a horse might just be dumb enough to brag on it."

"Sure thing," Simms said. "C'mon, Tan—let's go into town and see if we can't find us some fried eggs at that choke 'n puke café where we had dinner."

As the boys drove through the fairgrounds gate, a tricked-out cherry-red pickup truck passed them going in. Jacked up high on oversized tires with a row of lights decorating the roll bar, the truck's most distinguishing feature was a sound system blasting low-frequency thumps from sub-woofers that shook the leaves on the cottonwood trees, loud enough to drown out the deep rumble of the engine, amplified by custom headers and straight pipes.

Lambert cranked his head around to watch it pass by. "Little early in the morning for that kind of thing, don't you think?"

"Guy must have a permanent headache," Simms said.

The truck pulled up behind Rowdy Galvin's junk car, stopping only when the grill guard added another crease to the rusty heap's trunk lid. The driver's side door popped open and a pair of pointy-toed boots with contrasting leather toe caps swung out, topped by faded jeans with frayed slits and holes up the legs, and dropped the distance to the ground. The man wore a plaid western-style shirt with the sleeves torn out at the shoulders, snap-front undone and gapped open to reveal a crude, homemade, obscene tattoo on his bare chest. The tough-guy attire ended with a flat-billed cap, cranked around backward with a forelock of greasy tangled hair hanging out the hole above the adjustable plastic strap.

Out the other door dropped an oversized man dressed in multi-color athletic shoes, camo-print cargo shorts and a solid black t-shirt two sizes too small. Although the sun had yet to clear the horizon, a pair of dark glasses wrapped around his shaved head. The big man leaned casually against the fender of the truck and folded his beefy arms. The driver, jerky and erratic like an anxious, broody hen, strutted to the open door where Galvin's feet hung out and pounded on the car's roof.

"C'mon, asshole! Outa there! Haul your sorry ass out here and don't forget to bring your wallet!"

Galvin shot upright and out the door in such a hurry he neglected to duck, and his head bounced off the top of the door frame with enough force to knock him back into the car. The driver grabbed him by the leg and jerked him out, and the rough landing knocked the wind out of the dazed cowboy as efficiently as a buckoff would. The driver dropped to his knees astraddle Rowdy's chest, yanked his head off the ground by a hank of hair and proceeded to jerk the head side to side. He slammed the head down then alternately slapped one cheek and backhanded the other until streams of saliva tinged with blood from loose teeth threaded out of Rowdy's mouth.

"I want my two hundred dollars," the driver yelled, much louder than necessary even given the addled state of Galvin's brain in the circumstances. He grabbed a fistful of Galvin's shirt and hauled him upright as he stood, then slammed the stumbling cowboy against the car's fender. "Where is it? Where's my money?"

Galvin lifted his sagging head and looked into the fiery eyes of his attacker. "I ain't got it yet, Wolf. You know I ain't got it. I done told you tomorrow."

The driver poked a finger into Galvin's chest. "Listen, asshole, I drove all the way over here from Crawford City to get that money and I ain't leaving till I get it. I'll take it out of your sorry hide if I have to—won't be able to spend it that way, but I'll trade it for the satisfaction of pounding you to a pulp."

"Look, Wolf, I'm up in the bareback ridin' tonight. I think I can win it. You'll get your money then."

Wolf laughed and snarled at the same time. "Hell, I was here last night, Galvin, and saw that bull pile drive your ugly head. Don't look to me like you're in line to win a damn thing. You didn't last but maybe three seconds."

"That's all right, Wolf. I've always done better in the bares. And I think my chances just got better."

"How's that?"

"This kid, this upstart name of Tanner Lambert's been ridin' real good. He was drawed up in this afternoon's perf on ol' Number Sixteen, which made him damn near a shoo-in to win it all."

"Yeah, we heard that from some of your idiot cowboy friends in town last night. So what?"

"Well, they just dragged that horse off to the byproducts plant a while ago. Which means Lambert won't be gettin' on him. I drawed a pretty good horse, so no matter what that kid does this afternoon there's a good chance I can outscore him on the horse I drawed for tonight."

Wolf all but burned holes in Galvin's eyeballs with his stare. "Lucky for you. See you do it."

The driver turned to go, but Galvin grabbed him by the elbow. "Wait, Wolf," he said. "Look, I ain't feelin' too good. I can't ride worth a damn like this. How 'bout you stand me to an eight-ball of glass?"

After another of his snarly laughs, Wolf said, "Listen, asshole, you're already into me for two hundred bucks. You want to more than double that debt?"

"I got to, Wolf. Like I said, I can't ride like this."

Wolf thought a minute. Then, "How much you stand to win—assuming you can stay on long enough?"

"Can't say exactly. With the added money, I'd guess the purse for first place will run about six hundred."

Wolf thought again. "All right. But here's the deal. You win, I get five hundred. And you damn sure better win."

Galvin swallowed hard. "I'll do my best, Wolf."

"Get the man an eight-ball," Wolf told his passenger.

The big man fetched a baggie from the truck's jockey box and carried it around behind the truck and up to where the pair stood and handed it to Wolf.

The driver dangled the bag in front of a hungry Rowdy Galvin. "Now you listen to me, asshole. I'll have my money before I leave this pissant town or you'll answer for it."

"Like I said, I'll do my best."

"It better be good enough. If it ain't, I'll beat you to within an inch of your life."

Galvin swallowed hard as he stared, as if hypnotized by the dangling bag of meth.

"And when I'm done with you, I just might hand you over to Bubba here. And you ain't likely to survive that."

The driver and his passenger boarded the big truck, backed away from Galvin's car and ripped a doughnut through the grass and dirt, spraying the cowboy and his car with debris as they roared away, stereo pounding some unrecognizable, tuneless thump, thump, thump that hung in the morning air as the pickup tore through the fairgrounds.

As if awakening from a bad dream, Rowdy Galvin dove into the car, jerked open the hatch in the center console and pulled out a black Walther nine-millimeter semi-automatic pistol, jacked a shell into the chamber, and stood holding it as he listened to Wolf's truck disappear, the sound lingering long after the vehicle was out of sight.

"Shit," he said, staring at the pistol. After a moment he reawakened, tossed the pistol back into the console and rooted around in the mess in the back seat for a glass pipe.

Down at the all-night café, Tanner Lambert used a triangle of buttered toast to mop up the last of the egg yolk and shove the few remaining strands of hash browns onto his fork.

"You boys like some more coffee?" the waitress asked as she made her rounds with the steaming glass decanter.

"Yes, ma'am," Wes Simms said.

"Scoot on over, honey," the waitress said. "I need to take a load off. I been up all night."

"Sure thing," Simms said, sliding against the wall to make room. "We remember you was here last night when we come in."

"You boys in town for the rodeo?" she asked as she filled their china mugs.

"Yes ma'am," Simms said. Lambert nodded in agreement.

"Been lots of you guys in here the last couple days. What's you boys's names?"

"I'm Wes Simms. That feller over there, that's Tanner Lambert."

"Tanner Lambert? Why, I heard your name mentioned here last night, right at this very table!"

"How's that, ma'am?" Lambert asked.

"Well, there was a bunch of cowboys having a late supper—or early breakfast—after they'd been to the bar, you know. And these other two came in—not cowboys, them two, even though one of them wore boots, but not the kind like any real cowboy would wear if you know what I mean. Other guy, he looked like a side of beef. Anyways, they started asking the cowboys sittin' here all about the rodeo—how much money there was to be won, who was most likely to win it, like that. Seems like, Mr. Lambert, you're the odds-on favorite to win the bareback riding."

Crimson climbed up Lambert's neck and flushed his cheeks before he found his voice. "I . . . I sure hope so, ma'am. But you never know. You just do the best you can and hope them judges' pencils is sharp."

"Ol' Tanner here just got some bad news about that, though," Simms said around the lip of his coffee mug.

"Talk on."

Simms set the mug down after a sip. "See, he was all fixed to ride the best bronc in the string. Horse called Number Sixteen. Thing is, somebody shot that horse last night."

"Shot a horse?"

"Yes ma'am. Right in a pen out at the fairgrounds."

"I never heard of any such thing."

"We only just found out a while ago. The law's looking into it, so I reckon word will get around soon enough."

"So what about you, Mr. Lambert? Now that you don't have a horse to ride, I mean."

"Oh, they'll draw me another mount out of the re-ride pen. It won't be as good as Number Sixteen, but I hope it'll be good enough to win some money on."

"Well, best of luck to you. Say, you boys might know this other cowboy they was askin' about. Rowdy . . . Allen?"

"That'd be Rowdy Galvin, ma'am," Simms said.

"Them two was mighty interested in him. His chances of winnin' and all."

"Rowdy's a passable bull rider and darn good bareback rider when he's on his game. Which he ain't been, too much of, of late. So what was the verdict on Rowdy?"

"Oh, them cowboys said much the same thing. Told that pair he wasn't likely to win no buckle, what with Mr. Lambert here in the competition. They might have even mentioned that horse you were talking about—the one that got killed. Anyways, they wasn't too happy when they left here. Stomped out in a huff and drove off in this big nasty red pickup truck I'd need a stepladder to get into. Not that I would.

"Well, I best be gettin' back to work," the waitress said. "Nice talkin' to you, and good luck at the rodeo." She topped off their mugs again before shuffling back to the coffeemaker behind the counter.

"What do you suppose that was all about? Them boys askin' all them questions?" Lambert asked.

"Hell, Tan, I don't know," Simms said as he stifled a yawn. "Let's get back out to the fairgrounds. I got half a mind to stretch out under one of them cottonwood trees and stare at the insides of my eyelids for a while."

Deputy Hugh Morgan was back at the fairgrounds when they arrived, in a huddle with Andy Bowen, the stock contractor. When the lawman saw their car, he waved them over.

He spit out a chewed-up toothpick when the cowboys climbed out of the car. "Where you boys been?"

Simms wrinkled his forehead and said, "In town, is all. Havin' some breakfast. Why?"

"Just wondering, that's all," the deputy said as he pulled another toothpick from his hatband and stuck it in the corner of his mouth. "I aim to keep track of everyone who was here last night until we get this sorted out."

"So what've you learned?" Bowen said.

"Not much. The vet fished the slug out of that horse's skull. Nine millimeter. After filing a report at the office, I talked with all the folks camping out over here. No one noticed anything out of the way. Some said they heard outfits coming and going in the night, but nothing more than you'd expect.

"One thing, though. What do you know about the guy in that wrinkled-up Chevy over there?" Morgan paged through his notebook. "Bruce Galvin?"

"Bruce? That his name?" Bowen said. "Only name I ever knew he had was Rowdy. What about him?"

"He seems a mite suspicious to me. Tweaker if I ever saw one."

"Tweaker? What the hell's a tweaker?"

"Meth head. Speed freak. Sketcher. Druggie."

"Beats the hell out of me. Wouldn't know what the stuff looks like if it was sittin' on my dinner plate. Wouldn't surprise me, though. Rowdy's always been prone to overdoing whatever it is he's doing. And the folks he runs with ain't likely to invite him to attend church with them."

"What about you boys?" Morgan said as his back teeth frayed his toothpick. "You know if he's into drugs?"

Neither Simms nor Lambert had an opinion. "We're just small-town boys," Simms said. "Ain't none of that stuff where we grew up."

The deputy laughed. "The hell you say. You boys just don't know what you're looking for. Drugs are everywhere."

Lambert said, "I ride against Rowdy all the time, but I ain't never seen nothin'. He does seem changeable when it comes to moods. Sometimes he seems fine, other times he's wound up like a pocket watch. Now and then he walks around half asleep. One time at Castle Bluff, he flew off the handle at the flank man and shoved him right off the back of the chute 'cause he didn't like the way he was hangin' the flank strap. Couple of fellows had to hold him back when he climbed down off the chute threatenin' to beat the old man. Weren't nothin' to it—no reason for him to get in a huff at all. But, far as I know, that's just Rowdy. I ain't never seen him before this summer."

Morgan nodded. "Sounds like he's tweaking to me. I think I'll have another talk with him. Shooting a horse just for sport ain't out of the question for a meth head. Even if he's not involved, he might know more than he's saying."

The deputy was back within minutes. Rowdy Galvin stared out the back seat window of the patrol car, sitting awkwardly with his hands cuffed behind his back. Morgan brought over a pair of plastic evidence bags to show Bowen and the boys.

"Just as I suspected," he said, holding up a bag with a short glass tube with a glass ball on one end, all tainted with brown soot, and a little bag of what looked to the boys like rock salt, inside. "This is the stuff. Meth. They smoke it in that glass pipe."

But the other evidence bag set the stock contractor and cowboys back on their heels. Inside was a semi-automatic pistol. "Nine millimeter," the deputy said.

---◆---

The breeze flowing through cottonwood leaves sounded like water rolling in a gentle mountain stream. The soft rustle was like a lullaby to the napping Wes Simms, stretched out in the shade of the trees with his hat propped over his face. Tanner Lambert sat cross-legged nearby, riding glove strapped tight around his wrist and bareback rigging in hand. As he worked rosin into the glove and handhold, the squeaks and creaks sounded like rusty nails pulled out of weathered planks on a barn wall.

Absorbed in the work, Lambert barely noticed the approaching thump, thump, thump as the jacked-up red pickup rolled slowly across the fairgrounds until it braked to a stop not ten yards away. The driver cut the ignition, silencing the thumping stereo system and rumbling exhaust pipes as Lambert looked on.

"You Tanner Lambert?" the driver asked as he slid out of the tall truck and walked toward the young cowboy. Lambert set the bareback rigging aside and nodded.

"Word is, you're a pretty good bareback rider."

Again, Lambert only nodded.

"You ride this afternoon, right?"

Another nod.

Stirred by the visitor's arrival, Wes Simms sat upright and seated his hat. Sensing trouble, he started to stand. But halfway up, the passenger from the truck, having eased himself around behind, grabbed Simms by the collar of his shirt and jerked him back to ground.

"You'd best just stay put, cowboy," the man behind the hand said. "This ain't none of your business."

Simms cranked his neck around, knocking his hat askew, and stared up at the too-big man in the too-small black t-shirt, decided his advice was good, and made no further attempt to reach his feet.

The driver squatted in front of Lambert as the cowboy said, "Who are you? And what do you care?"

After a cold stare that lasted too long, the driver said, "Call me Wolf. I ain't goin' to bother tellin' you why I care. Just know that I do—a lot." Again, the stare.

"So?"

"So, today might just be one of those days where your luck ain't so good."

Lambert furrowed his brow in confusion. "What do you mean?"

"You ain't winnin' the bareback ridin' at this rodeo, cowboy."

Lambert repeated the question.

"I don't care if you fall off the horse or get disqualified somehow or do whatever else it takes to see that you don't win. Just see that you don't win."

"What the hell? I won't do no such thing! I came to ride, and to win, and, God willing, that's just what I aim to do."

Wolf's stare discouraged any further argument. "Listen, kid," he said, repeatedly jamming his index finger into Lambert's chest. "And listen good. You can lose the bareback riding today. Or you can lose a few teeth. And who knows? Big ol' Bubba over there might just step on that riding hand of yours—by accident, of course—and mash all them bones inside that glove there to mush. Get it?"

Now it was Tanner Lambert's turn to stare.

"I don't get it," Wes Simms said as Bubba twisted the collar of his shirt, tightening it around his neck. "What the hell does it matter to you if Tan wins or not?"

Wolf turned slowly and stared at the restrained cowboy. He stood, took off his backward cap and raked his fingers through tangled, greasy hair and plopped the cap on again.

"Here's the thing, asshole. I don't really give two shits about Lambert here. But he ain't goin' to win no bareback ridin' on account of somebody else has to."

"Who?"

"Not that it's any of your business, but there's another one of you sorry-ass cowboys who's needin' that prize money real bad right now. You probably know him. Rowdy Galvin."

Even the choke hold of a further twist on his shirt collar couldn't stifle Simms's laugh.

"What's so damn funny?" Wolf said.

Simms grabbed at his collar. Bubba loosened his grip at Wolf's nod.

"Rowdy ain't winnin' nothin' at this rodeo," Simms said with a chuckle.

"Why the hell not?"

"Sheriff's deputy hauled him out of here in handcuffs a couple hours ago. I reckon he'll be locked up."

Bubba tightened his grip on the boy's collar and jerked him upright, lifting him a good six inches off the ground and shaking him like the bell on a bull rope.

"Bubba! Leave off!" Wolf hollered. The big man dropped Simms and he stumbled but kept his feet. "Tell me what you're talkin' about. And make it damn quick."

Simms told Wolf how Number Sixteen had been found dead in his pen early that morning, shot in the head. And how Deputy Morgan, in the

174

course of his inquiries, found Rowdy Galvin in possession of illegal drugs. And how, unexpectedly, he found a pistol of the same caliber that killed the horse in the cowboy's possession. And, finally, how the deputy had arrested Galvin for the drugs and taken him into custody for questioning about the shooting.

"Sonofabitch," Wolf said under his breath. Then, "They think Rowdy shot that horse?" to no one in particular. He strutted around in erratic circles talking to himself and waving his hands around, acting more like an anxious chicken than his namesake. "C'mon Bubba," he said after a few minutes of fitful parading around.

The two hauled themselves into the high cab and the motor—and pounding stereo—roared to life. The driver's door swung open and Wolf's left boot dropped to the chrome running board and his head popped up above the door.

"You listen to me, Lambert. This don't change nothin'. You make damn sure you don't ride your horse today, or it'll be the last one you ever ride."

He ducked back into the truck, slammed the door and hit the throttle, cranking the truck into a tight turn and spraying divots and dirt as it thundered away.

Wes Simms plopped back down on the rolled-out sleeping bag he'd been napping on and pulled on his boots. "Put that stuff away, Tan," he told his friend with a nod toward the bareback rigging. "We better go have a talk with Andy Bowen."

They found the stock contractor in the alley between the catch pens cutting stock—moving the bareback and saddle bronc horses and bulls that would buck in that afternoon's rodeo performance, now but a few hours away, into separate pens for ready access when each event came up on the schedule.

Bowen left the rest of the job to his chute boss and other helpers to hear what the boys had to say, squatting with them behind the bucking chutes in the shade under the announcer's stand. After hearing the story, he pulled his mobile phone from its hand-tooled leather holster on his belt and dialed up Deputy Hugh Morgan. He must have been nearby, for it was only a matter of minutes until his patrol car skidded to a stop next to the arena.

The stock contractor sketched out the story for the deputy, who proceeded to pump the boys for details.

"He didn't say why Rowdy Galvin needed the money, then?"

"Nosir," Simms said.

Morgan chewed on his toothpick a moment, then said, "Well, I reckon it's easy enough to figure out. See, this Wolf fellow lives over in Crawford City. Raised as an ordinary town kid, from what I've been told. But when the drill rigs started showing up over there goin' after all that oil and gas they got, he got into drugs with some of them oilfield boys he worked with. I guess he was bright enough to see there was more money to be made peddlin' dope than workin' as a roughneck, so he worked his way into the trade. Nowadays, they say he's top dog in this part of the country. Word is he's done away with a few folks here and there to get to that position and stay there, but nobody's ever been able to pin anything on him that'd stick. Still, he's on every lawman's list around here, from the D.E.A. and F.B.I. to the local police. Then again, some say he's got more than a few cops on his payroll and that's why he never gets caught with dirty hands."

After mulling it over a bit, Bowen said, "Then I guess Rowdy Galvin must owe him money—a drug debt—and he wants Rowdy to win so he'll get his money."

"That's my guess. Galvin ain't sayin' nothin' but what you say makes sense to me—that's the same direction my thinkin's been runnin'."

"Hell's bells, the man must be stupid," Wes Simms said. "It ain't easy to fix no rodeo. Even if Tan don't do no good, then Rowdy's still got to ride good enough to win. And if he's all hopped up on drugs like you say, then there ain't no guarantee he could make a bronc ride. And with Rowdy locked up and all, there ain't even no guarantee he'll get to try."

Tanner Lambert swallowed hard. "How far you think he'll go—Wolf?"

The deputy pulled the shredded end of the toothpick from his mouth and tossed it into the dirt. "Couldn't say. But he's a ruthless bastard, I'm told. Don't know that he'd kill you, but he wouldn't hesitate to rough you up good."

"Think he'd go so far as to kill Number Sixteen?" the stock contractor asked.

Morgan slid another toothpick from his hatband and gnawed on it a few times before answering. "Don't know that he'd even think of it. He ain't no cowboy. Doubt he's been any closer to a rodeo arena than the bleachers. Can't see he'd know enough about how a rodeo runs to figure something like that out."

"But he was askin' about it," Lambert said.

"What do you mean?" Morgan said.

"Down at the café. Lady there told us at breakfast Wolf had been in there, talkin' to some cowboys. Asked them about the bareback ridin' and who was likely to win it. Lady said those cowboys told 'em I had the best shot on account of drawin' Number Sixteen."

Another toothpick, this one barely chewed, hit the dirt and was replaced by another. "I'll be damned," he said. "I suppose it's possible. But it seems to me Rowdy Galvin's the more likely culprit. He'd know better than Wolf how much difference the draw makes in rodeo."

"I can't see that," Bowen said. "Dumb as Rowdy is, even when he's hopped up on drugs, he's still a cowboy. Hell, he'd give his eye teeth to climb on Number Sixteen at any rodeo. He's won his share of money over the years on that bronc. If he killed him, he'd never get that chance again. I just can't see it."

"Meth does some pretty strange things to folks," the deputy said. "Not to mention fear. Wouldn't surprise me in the least."

"Still, it don't seem like anything a cowboy would do."

Wes Simms cleared his throat. "What say we forget about Rowdy Galvin for a minute. What about Tanner here? What's he supposed to do?"

"Whaddya mean what am I supposed to do?" Lambert said. "Hell, I'm gonna get down on whatever horse they draw for me and spur the hair off of him. I'm here to ride for the money, Wolf or no Wolf."

"Tan, you saw that stud horse with him. That guy liked to have pinched my head off and he never even broke a sweat."

"Be that as it may, I'm ridin' my best. I can't see them two causin' me any trouble. If anybody should come after me, everybody knows right where to look for who done it."

"I don't know, kid. I'd think awful hard on it," the stock contractor said.

"You sayin' I shouldn't give it my best?"

"No, Tanner—no! What I'm sayin' is there's no shame in drawin' out. Havin' lost a chance to get on Number Sixteen, nobody'd think twice about it. They'll just figure you decided to go to another rodeo somewhere where there's a better shot at the money."

The young cowboy tipped his hat back and thought for a minute.

"Naw, Mr. Bowen. I can't do it. I'm gettin' on this afternoon."

"That might not be the best idea you ever had, Tan," Simms said.

"He's right," Morgan said. "I'd advise against it. Wolf is just too unpredictable."

Tanner Lambert stood up and pulled his hat down tight. "Well, gentlemen, I'm awful sorry, but I'm fixin' to ride. See you boys at the rodeo." The young cowboy headed off across the fairgrounds to the makeshift campsite under the cottonwood trees.

"Well, Deputy," Andy Bowen said as they watched Lambert walk away, "I guess that's another item to add to your list—protectin' young Lambert. Boy's got more guts than good sense."

Morgan gnawed on the end of his latest toothpick and said, "We'll try to keep an eye on him. But the Sheriff Department's stretched mighty thin as it is with the rodeo in town. City police, too."

"Why don't you just arrest Wolf?" Simms asked.

"For what?" the deputy said. "He ain't done nothin' yet 'cept talk. Can't arrest a man for that. You find me some probable cause and I'll lock him up."

"Can't you bust him for drugs?"

Morgan laughed. "He's too smart for that. Like I said, nobody's been able to convict him on anything, yet. Not that they haven't tried."

"Well, I'll put the word out among the cowboys," Bowen said. "They'll watch out for the boy."

"Might help," Morgan said. "Just make sure they don't do anything stupid."

"Back to work," Bowen said. "I've got a rodeo to put on." Already, rough stock riders were showing up behind the chutes to begin their pre-ride preparations, while timed-event hands were warming up roping and bulldogging horses out in the arena.

By the time Wes Simms made it back to the shade of the cottonwood trees, his friend was zipping his gearbag shut. He'd already peeled off the t-shirt he'd been wearing and snapped on a long-sleeve shirt.

"Here, Wes, give me hand," he said, passing Simms his contestant number and a safety pin.

"Long as you're doin' it, do it up right," Simms said as he pinned the paper square to the back of Lambert's shirt. "Whatever horse they run in for you, you lay back and kick him high, wide, and handsome. You go on ahead. I'm gonna get me a rodeo burger and I'll see you behind the chutes in time to stretch your latigos."

Back at the arena, the judges had just gathered in the rodeo office with the rodeo secretary and Andy Bowen to draw a horse for Lambert from the mounts assigned earlier to the re-ride pen. "Buster Brown," the judge said, reading the name from the unfolded slip of paper he'd drawn out of Bowen's upturned hat.

"Good enough horse," the stock contractor said. "He's no Number Sixteen, but I think he'll buck hard enough to make that kid pay attention."

Bowen left the office and hoofed it to the arena. He grabbed some chute helpers and went out back to the pens to cut Buster Brown out of the bunch in the re-ride pen and move him in with the bareback horses. Then that bunch was pushed down the alley and into the chutes. Cowboys scrambled up and down the back of the chutes to identify the horses, while the chute boss did the same on the arena side, calling out the names of the horses and reading from his list the names of the matching cowboys.

Locating Tanner Lambert in the crowd behind the chutes, Bowen informed him of the draw and pointed out the horse.

"Don't know him," Lambert said. "What's he do?"

"Oh, he'll go out there and jump and kick a little."

A cowboy standing nearby laughed. "Hell, Andy, that's the same thing you tell everybody." Then, having seen Buster Brown, or "Brownie" for short, buck a few times, filled his young competitor in on the horse's tendencies. "He's a bucker, Tanner. Not a lot of rhythm to him and he'll duck and dive some, but if you get past the first couple seconds, when he usually takes a big sideways jump to the left, you'll do all right. Too bad about Sixteen—hell of a deal, that. But, good luck anyway."

The ride went pretty much as the cowboy predicted. Brownie jumped out and took two stiff-legged hops then lunged to the left and lit with the force of a pile driver. Lambert felt it all the way to the top of his skull. But then, Brownie lined out across the arena jumping first to the left and then the right with his front legs, while he twisted and rolled his hind end to the opposite side. The rider found himself reaching for the shoulders with his spurs in fits and starts, as the bronc's moves were uneven, mixing long leaps with short lunges.

Still, even in less-than-ideal conditions, Lambert's instincts kept him in the middle of his mount and his spur licks, while irregular, were, as Wes Simms had suggested, "high, wide, and handsome." When he heard the buzzer through the cacophony that always accompanies a bronc ride, Tanner reached for the front of the rigging with his free hand and pulled himself upright. He opened his riding hand to pull it loose, and the rosined glove, wedged tight in the handhold, jerked loose just as the pickup man rode alongside and pulled the release on the flank strap wrapped around the bucking horse. The cowboy wrapped his arms around the horseman's waist and slid from Brownie's back as the pickup man smoothly applied the brakes to allow Lambert to lower himself to the ground.

As he walked back to the bucking chutes, Lambert heard the announcer's call. "The judges liked that ride, ladies and gentlemen—they gave Tanner Lambert a score of eighty-six points, moving the young cowboy into first place in the bareback riding. Let's let Tanner know how much you liked that ride," he said, spurring the crowd into wild applause.

Wolf, however, sitting on the front row of the bleachers near the bucking chutes, did not join the enthusiastic ovation. He glowered at Lambert walking along the fence, not ten feet away, unwrapping the tie strap on his riding glove. "C'mon, Bubba," he said, and he and the big man walked away from the arena and into the fairgrounds parking lot. A few minutes later, heads turned in the crowd in an attempt to identify the source of the deep thump, thump, thump and rumbling exhaust pipes as the red pickup truck drove away.

A couple of hours later, the rodeo reached its climax with the crowd favorite—bull riding. Deputy Hugh Morgan stood near the narrow gate that allowed the cowboys behind the bucking chutes and watched the bulls rattle their way between the rails as slide gates slammed shut behind them. With all the clatter, he barely heard the ring of his mobile phone. He listened with the phone at one ear and a finger in the other, then used the same finger to poke angrily at the button on the phone's screen that said "END."

Fumbling to get the phone under the flap and back into his shirt pocket, he stormed through the gate and bulled through the cowboys crowded behind the chutes looking for Andy Bowen.

"He's out," he said after grabbing the stock contractor's shoulder and spinning him around.

"Out? What the hell you talkin' about, Deputy?"

"Rowdy Galvin. Somebody bailed him out of jail!"

"The hell you say. Well, I hope he's feeling up to it, 'cause he's got a bronc to get on this evening."

———— • ————

Wes Simms sat in his bronc saddle with his feet in the stirrups, as if sitting on a horse rather than on the ground in the shade of the cottonwood trees at the fairgrounds. Using a knotted sock like a powder puff, he dusted rosin onto the swells, pressed against them with his thighs, and rocked the saddle fore and aft. The motion and pressure heated the rosin, which created a sticky bond between the saddle and his chaps as it squeaked and creaked.

His friend Tanner Lambert sat nearby fiddling with his bareback rigging and tinkering with his spurs, even though his work at this rodeo was done. His score of eighty-six points earlier that afternoon would likely earn him a paycheck and, depending how this evening's riders fared, he might even hold his first-place position and take top money and the championship buckle.

"I reckon I'm as ready as I'll ever be, Tan," Simms said, unbuckling his chaps. "Let's wander on over to the hamburger stand at the arena and get us a cool, refreshing beverage and a gut bomb."

"You're gonna die of a rodeo burger overdose, as many of them things as you eat."

"Aw, hell, Tan—them things is good for you! Look what a fine figure of a man I've become on a diet of little else but burgers and ice-cold sody pop." Simms rolled his chaps and stuffed them in his gear bag, laid the stirrup leathers over the seat of the saddle and threaded one stirrup through the other to make a nice, tight package.

Satisfied with its condition, Lambert zipped the last of his gear into his war bag, rose and hitched up his britches. He undid the big shiny buckle on his belt and drew it up a notch. "Well, good or bad, I guess I need something in my stomach. My back bone is rubbing the inside of my belly button plumb raw."

Stock contractor Andy Bowen squatted against the wall of the cinder-brick hamburger shack, taking advantage of the scant shade it offered as he sipped beer from a bottle dripping with condensation. Standing above him was Deputy Hugh Morgan, with the County Sheriff himself standing at his side. Sending Simms to the window with his food order, Tanner Lambert sidled up to the wall beside Bowen to listen in.

"There wasn't a thing we could do about it, Hugh," the sheriff said. "That cowboy produced a witness as to his whereabouts most of last night and the judge let him go."

"What about the drug charge?" the deputy said. "Wasn't that enough to hold him?"

"You know better than that. Simple possession. He made bail and that was that."

The deputy tossed his gnawed toothpick aside.

Bowen sipped his beer, and asked, "What about my dead horse? Morgan here thinks Rowdy did it."

"Like I said," the sheriff replied with an impatient sigh, "he has an alibi."

Morgan laughed and bit into another toothpick. "Alibi my ass. Some skanky drug ho who'd swear under oath the moon was made of green cheese if it would get her a fix."

"Still, she claims Rowdy Galvin was at her place partying till near morning—long after that horse was shot. Besides, she wasn't the only witness."

"More meth heads," Morgan said.

"How the hell did Rowdy come up with bail money?" Bowen asked. But before anyone could offer an answer, the red pickup with a case of 'roid rage announced its presence with a low rumble of exhaust pipes and the incessant thump, thump, thump of stereo speakers. The small crowd beside the concession stand watched the truck slink across the parking lot and roll to a stop next to Rowdy Galvin's wreck of a car. The driver's door opened and Wolf, almost instantly, appeared on the ground beside it.

Bubba lowered himself out of the passenger door in a more deliberate manner, reached back inside and pulled out Rowdy Gaines, lowering him by his shirt collar to the ground. The big man pushed and carried the cowboy to his car, opened a rear door and shoved him into the back seat. Wolf leaned into the car through the opposite window, screaming at Galvin loud enough to be heard over the noise of the truck, but not loud enough to be understood by the audience at the hamburger stand.

"Well, hell," the stock contractor said. "I'll bet cut diamonds against cow dung that's the answer to my question, right there."

The sheriff instinctively set his hand atop the service revolver holstered to his belt. "I don't think you'd find anybody to take that bet."

"Hmmph!" The deputy said. "I'd almost bet somethin' more than bail money passed from Wolf's hand to that judge's."

"You had best mind what you say, Morgan," the sheriff said.

"Aw, hell! Everybody knows he's got half the legal system in this part of the state on his payroll."

"That's no cause for you to be making unfounded accusations."

Another frayed toothpick hit the dirt, and another found its way between Morgan's molars.

Tanner Lambert and Wes Simms sat and watched and listened and sipped soda pop and chewed hamburgers. Andy Bowen stood up, drained the last of his beer, and tossed the empty bottle into a nearby trash can where it landed with a clang. "Well boys," he said as he wiped his lips with a shirt sleeve, "much as I like your company I got work to do. The stock for this evening's performance ain't goin' to sort itself."

Across the parking lot, Rowdy Galvin half cowered and half relaxed in the back seat of his car, his awareness dimmed by the euphoria of the meth smoke that swirled inside his head. Through the haze, he could hear Wolf's nonstop harangue. While he couldn't quite string it all together, he knew it went something like this: "I'm tellin' you, asshole, my charity in your direction is more than used up. Now you got bail money on top of what you already owe me. There ain't enough prize money in this here rodeo to cover it—if, that is, you can win any of it. But I'll tell you this, asshole, you better win enough to put a good-size dent in your debt or I'll turn Bubba loose on you."

And so on.

And so on.

Right now, Rowdy Galvin wasn't sure he could remember how to find the bucking chutes, let alone manage an eight-second ride on the hurricane deck of a feisty bareback bronc. *Maybe*, he thought, *just maybe, I smoked a bit too much this time.* And he wondered if he even cared.

He was still wondering the same thing later as he glided across the parking lot toward the brightly lit rodeo arena. The last of the horses in the grand entry were tailing their way out of the arena when he finally found his way behind the bucking chutes. His bronc was easy to find—it was the only one in the row of chutes without a bareback rigging already on its back.

"Damn, Rowdy!" Tanner Lambert said. "Get a move on! The chute boss has already threatened to turn your horse out."

Galvin only stared. Lambert pulled the gear bag off the cowboy's shoulder, ripped open the zipper and handed Galvin's bareback rigging to Simms. "Wes! Get this cinched up on Rowdy's horse!" he said as he unfurled the chaps from the bag. Galvin stood as Lambert strapped the chaps around his waist and fastened the buckles inside his thighs.

"Rowdy, you think you can ride?"

Galvin laughed. "Hell, kid, I was ridin' broncs when you was still shittin' yellow. Help me with my spurs. I can ride anything with hair on." The cowboy sat down with a plop and wrenched at his boots. Lambert brushed his hands aside and jerked the boots off, then helped him pull on his bronc-riding boots and tightened the spur straps and ankle straps.

"Where's my damned horse?" Galvin said. "Put me on him and I'll show you boys a thing or two about bareback ridin.'"

"You sure, Rowdy? You don't look so good."

"You ain't much to look at yourself, Lambert. You just hide and watch— I'm gonna ride that bronc and win this sumbitch."

Given his condition, Galvin's confidence was misplaced.

He wedged his gloved riding hand into the handhold, set his spurs and nodded for the gate. By instinct alone he marked the horse out. When the powerful lunge of the horse's second jump popped his spurs loose he let them roll up the horse's neck all the way to the front of his rigging then reached back down to grab another spur hold over the points of the bronc's shoulders.

Then, it all went wrong.

Galvin's timing and reactions, dulled by the drug, could not keep pace with the speed of the horse's moves. When his spurs next rolled high toward the horse's withers, he did not react quickly enough to grab a new hold. So, when the horse dropped its head and dove to the left on the way back to the ground, Galvin's left foot flopped over the neck and he found himself with both feet on the right side. The bronc's next upward leap left the rider's head and shoulders behind, and Rowdy Galvin was helplessly hanging nearly upside down.

Fortunately, he was dangling on the side of his riding hand—had he been over his hand, his wedged glove could not release from the rigging's handhold and he would have been hung up and flung around like a stuffed bunny in a dog's jaws. Instead, he opened his hand and the horse's next lunge jerked it loose and he hit the arena dirt on the back of his neck and shoulders. Unable to catch his breath, the stunned cowboy lay there until the rodeo clown reached his side, but waved off the help, rolled over, struggled to his hands and knees and managed to find his feet.

"No score for Rowdy Galvin," the announcer said. "All that cowboy will take home is the appreciation you give him, so let's hear it for Rowdy!" Applause filled the arena as Galvin shuffled back to the bucking chutes and through the narrow gate to the contestant area behind.

There was no applause, however, from Wolf or his sidekick Bubba. The drug dealer sat with no reaction save a surly stare. Before the chute gate opened for the next bareback rider, the pair left their seats on the front row of the bleachers.

Wolf pushed his way through clusters of people and barely noticed the police officer guarding access to the area behind the chutes as he bulled his way past him.

"Hey!" the cop said. "You're not allowed back here!"

But Wolf paid no attention, shoving his way through the bronc riders until he found Rowdy Galvin, sitting against a rail fence pulling off his boots.

"You sonofabitch!" he said, grabbing the fallen bareback rider by the front of his shirt and hauling him upright. "You were supposed to ride that horse! You were supposed to win!"

As the startled cowboys looked on, Wolf slapped Galvin on the side of the head, rattling his jaw and knocking his hat to the ground. Several cowboys moved to intervene, but hesitated when Bubba made himself big.

"Knock it off, Wolf," Galvin said.

"I'll knock it off all right, asshole! I'll knock your head off!"

Wolf's fist drew back, but before he could unleash the blow, Galvin, still clutching the riding boot he'd pulled off, swung it in a wide arc and landed it upside the drug dealer's head. This time, it was his hat that was knocked askew, the backward cap spinning off his head and landing in the dirt. But it was his cheek that felt the brunt of the blow, as the long-shanked bareback-riding spur ripped a bloody gouge.

Turning loose of Galvin's shirt, Wolf staggered backward. As he stopped, he reached behind his back, swept the tails of his unsnapped shirt aside, and pulled a semi-automatic pistol from the waistband of his pants.

"You stupid asshole," he said through clenched teeth and fired a round at the dazed cowboy.

Bubba or no Bubba, one of the watching cowboys dove for Wolf's waist while Wes Simms grabbed him around the chest and shoulders from behind. As they all tumbled in a heap, Tanner Lambert reached out and grabbed Wolf's wrist and wrenched the pistol from his grip. Enough diminutive bronc riders lined up in front of Bubba to make him think twice about intervening to rescue his boss.

"Best give that to me, Tanner," Andy Bowen said softly to Lambert. The young cowboy looked at the gun in his hand as if surprised to find it there. He passed it to the stock contractor.

By that time, the local policeman was in the middle of it, his unholstered weapon wavering between Bubba and the confined Wolf. Soon, Deputy Hugh Morgan rushed onto the scene, shoving cowboys out of the way as he came. He found Rowdy Galvin bleeding on the ground with a couple of cowboys tending to him—one holding him off the ground in his lap, the other applying pressure to the wound, both hoping the paramedics in the ambulance outside the gate would get there soon. Wes Simms sat spraddle-legged on the ground with Wolf sitting in front of him, held tight in the cowboy's strong arms.

"How's he?" the deputy asked with a nod toward the gunshot cowboy.

"How the hell do I know?" the cowboy pressing against the hole in the hollow below Galvin's collar bone. "He's bleedin' like a stuck pig."

"Serves the horse-killing sonofabitch right," Morgan said.

That drew a burst of laughter from Wolf. "Morgan, you dumb ass. That idiot cowboy never shot no horse and you know it."

Morgan snarled and pulled his county-issued Glock 17 service revolver from its holster, but before it cleared, Andy Bowen leveled Wolf's Sig Sauer pistol inches from the deputy's nose. "I wouldn't do that if I was you, Morgan," he said between clenched teeth.

"What the hell?" the startled deputy said, his hand frozen on the Glock's grip.

"Rowdy never shot that horse," Bowen said. "I told you that."

Morgan's eyes shifted toward Wolf and back. "Maybe it was him, then," he said, prompting another burst of laughter from the drug dealer. "He might have done it. That's his Sig in your hand, ain't it? I'd say it takes a nine-millimeter round, same as what killed that horse."

More laughter from Wolf.

Andy Bowen didn't even blink. "What about that pistol of yours, Deputy?"

Again Wolf laughed.

"What about it?" the deputy spat as he viciously gnawed at the toothpick clenched between his jaws.

"Unless I miss my guess, it's a nine-millimeter, too."

"It sure as hell is," Wolf laughed. "And if you look around in Morgan's car, I'm bettin' you'll find a not-altogether-legal suppressor that'll fit that Glock like a glove."

"How do you know that?" Bowen asked.

Again Wolf laughed. "On account of I bought it for him for another job a while back. Right off the internet. I didn't want anybody hearin' anything when I sent him to shoot that stupid horse, so I told him to be sure and use it."

"So you put him up to it? You got Morgan to shoot Number Sixteen?"

"I sure as hell did. Even recorded the call on my cell phone."

Andy Bowen's brow furrowed and his eyes squinted as he turned his full attention to the deputy, reaching out with the pistol until it was so close to the lawman's face his eyes crossed as he stared, wide-eyed, at the hole in the end of the barrel.

Things were quiet the next morning at the fairgrounds. Hamburger wrappers skittered around beneath the bleachers as a gusty breeze kicked up clouds of dust in the arena. The hamburger stand was closed up tight, the panel that had shaded the customer window now lowered from its props and locked down. The only activity was behind the catch pens, where a diesel truck and trailer, with "Rough String Rodeo Company" painted on the sides, was backed up to a loading chute.

Tanner Lambert and Wes Simms, lacking anything better to do, stood beside the ramp next to stock contractor Andy Bowen as a stream of bucking horses clopped up the chute and into the trailer, rocking it on its springs as they jostled for position inside. Now and then Bowen popped a stock whip, the noise reminding the animals to keep moving as a couple of helpers urged them through the alley from behind.

When the county sheriff's patrol car rolled to a stop a few feet away, Bowen and the boys left the others to see to the loading and walked to the car. The sheriff stepped out with a tall foam cup of coffee in hand, and the quartet squatted in the shade of the cruiser.

"Morning, gentlemen," the sheriff said. "Had I thought, I'd have brought you all some coffee."

"Already been topped off, Sheriff. Think nothin' of it," Bowen said. The young cowboys eyeballed the cup with a look that said they had yet to have breakfast, or even coffee.

"Thought you might like to know what's up," the sheriff said.

Bowen nodded. Lambert and Simms settled in, knowing that breakfast would wait a little longer, but not minding the delay.

"That cowboy, Rowdy Galvin, is going to be fine. Bullet didn't really do much damage, hitting him where it did. He'll be in the hospital a few days and laid up a while longer."

Simms said, "I don't guess he'll be gettin' on any broncs for a while."

"No, he won't. But if the man's got a lick of sense, he'll use the time to get off that damn meth." He turned his attention to the stock contractor. "How is it you were so sure he didn't shoot your horse?"

"Like I told Morgan, Rowdy's a bronc rider. Sometimes a damn good one. Ain't no cowboy would shoot a horse that way—especially one like Number Sixteen."

"So what made you suspect my deputy? If it wasn't Galvin, Wolf looked more likely."

"Maybe so. Especially after he was askin' around about who was likely to win the bareback riding, and why. So while it was his idea—spur of the moment kind of thing; had he thought it through he might have realized it was a bad idea—I figured he wouldn't want to get his hands dirty. People like him get to thinkin' they're important, and they pay others take on the unpleasant tasks."

The sheriff tipped his hat back and scratched his forehead, then sipped his coffee. "But why Morgan?"

"Don't know. Didn't really dawn on me until last night in that mess behind the bucking chutes. He just wouldn't leave off tryin' to blame Rowdy, never mind that it didn't make sense. So I figured there had to be a reason he wasn't willing to look any further. Like you say, Wolf was in the mix but up until then, Morgan hadn't shown any interest in bracing him for anything—even pushin' drugs. The man had to be hidin' somethin'. Then when Wolf 'fessed up and said he put your deputy up to it, I realized my suspicions was right."

After another sip of coffee, the sheriff said, "Morgan's made a pretty good deputy over the years. It never occurred to me he might be in Wolf's pocket. But, like he said himself, that dealer's got a bunch of law enforcement folks around this part of the country on his payroll. All that aside, Wolf is damn sure going to prison this time. And maybe he'll be willing to use some of the dirty cops in his network as bargaining chips."

"What about your deputy?" Wes Simms asked.

"He's locked up. Transported him to the jail over in the next county. Wouldn't do to house him with criminals he might have arrested. Though I admit I was tempted. The county attorney will be drawing up charges first thing tomorrow morning when he gets to work. It'll be a long list. I don't think we'll be seeing much of Hugh Morgan for quite a few years."

"Just make damn sure shootin' Number Sixteen is on the top of that list of charges. And don't let him bargain his way out of it—horses like that don't come along every day."

The sheriff stood and scuffed at the dirt with the toe of his shoe. "One more question, Bowen—could it have worked?"

Bowen thought for a moment before replying. "I suppose it's possible. But only just. In the first place, Rowdy would've had to be in shape to ride, which he wasn't, thanks to Wolf. On top of that, all the other bareback riders, including Tanner here, would have to put up poor scores. Gettin' Number Sixteen out from under Lambert might have helped some in that regard, but the boy's got it in him to win money on damn near any horse that'll go out there and jump and kick a little."

"What about Wolf's threats?" the sheriff asked the young cowboy.

"Oh, no doubt him and that ox that follows him around could've messed me up pretty good. But they'd have to catch me first. Besides, if it was to come down to it," Lambert said with a smile, "I'd have fed them ol' Wesley, here."

NOTES FROM THE FERAL HEN RESCUE SOCIETY

This silly, strange, satirical little story appears here for the first time. It was prompted by the ongoing debate over wild—feral—horses on public lands. While I favor their presence in reasonable numbers, there's little doubt their numbers have grown beyond reason, both in confinement and in the wild. That set me to thinking—what if, rather than horses, some other critter was overrunning the range. And, what if an organization formed to agitate for their protection . . . .

————————— ◆ —————————

No one can say with certainty when *Gallus gallus* first appeared in the American West. We know chickens arrived in the New World as early as Columbus's voyages, but since his visits were restricted to islands of the Caribbean, it is unlikely any of the birds now running free in the basin and range country or elsewhere in the Intermountain West descended from that chicken stock.

However, virtually all Spanish sailing ships carried domestic fowl on their voyages, and as the regions now known as Central America, Mexico, and the American Southwest were colonized, hens and roosters, along with cattle and horses, spread with Spanish settlement. Inevitably, chickens escaped captivity and wandered into the wilderness. Flocks were scattered as villages were destroyed in wars with the natives. And birds were abandoned at outposts deserted for other reasons. Later, as American emigrants crossed over and settled the interior West, some domestic chickens from the East likewise flew the coop to join what were, by then, significant flocks of feral, free-ranging fowl.

It is important to note at this point that although these Western birds are commonly referred to as "wild" chickens, that is an incorrect designation. As all of these now "wild" animals are descended from once-domesticated birds, "feral" chickens is the correct term. (Feral being defined by Webster as "having escaped from domestication and become wild.")

THE DEATH OF DELGADO

Habitat and Lifeways

Feral chickens once roamed valleys and plains throughout the West. Prime chicken habitat closely coincides with that most attractive to human settlement. But, as coexistence with humans is impossible over extended periods, today's feral flocks are increasingly pushed farther and farther into remote, marginal areas. Thus, while small numbers of feral chickens can be found most anywhere in the West, the only stable, viable populations are restricted to the Great Basin of Utah and Nevada, the high plains of Wyoming, and a few scattered concentrations in western Colorado, southeastern Oregon, and regions bordering Idaho's Snake River Plain.

Feral chickens are social beasts. They naturally congregate in flocks for reasons of safety and reproduction. Flocks usually number from four to twenty hens, with one dominant rooster. Immature birds, both male and female, stay with the group. Pullets, or prepubescent hens, usually mature and integrate with the flock until its size exceeds the management ability of the rooster, then the flock "moults," so to speak, and a number of younger birds leave to form new extended family units.

Within these forming flocks, as well as within existing groups, young males mature and grow increasingly cocky, challenging the dominant rooster for leadership. Fierce fighting often ensues, with death occasionally the result. Aged, defeated roosters who survive these challenges (which most do) are driven off to wander alone, scratching out a living as best they can.

Hens tend to coexist more peacefully within family units. A "pecking order" establishes, mostly through intimidation but also with brief bursts of intense violence, determining which hens are first to water, win first choice of feeding area, and earn a respite from gathering chicks under their wings—leaving this and other child care tasks to younger, more vigorous hens and older, nearly mature pullets.

Symbolism and Iconography

While many dismiss the existence of feral flocks of chickens as an irrelevant historical accident, there is little doubt that these feral, free-ranging hens and roosters have come to symbolize much of what we in America love about our Western heritage. Who, upon seeing a group of these birds running through sage and prairie grass, long necks held low, tails cocked skyward, wind ruffling feathers, doesn't feel a swell of pride, a touch of envy at these noble, colorful creatures. Feral chickens have become icons of Western independence, of wrestling a livelihood from a hard land.

Indeed, it can be said that to many Americans, these feral flocks *are* the West, *are* America, and that their loss would represent a loss of values we all hold dear.

On a larger scale, feral chickens are an example to humans. Accepting, tolerant, and inclusive by nature, these birds do not discriminate on any basis—neither color of feathers, flock of origin, grooming and appearance, nor breeding and brooding preferences. All are welcome and nurtured within the group, save hens whose age and infirmity put the flock at risk, or roosters defeated in combat for dominance. (Sometimes, too, chicks with hatch-defects that prevent their keeping up with flock migration or unable to scratch and peck enough chickenfeed for sustenance, are abandoned for the safety of the chicken congregation.) Even in these instances, those excluded are not victimized or humiliated. Rather, they are simply driven off and allowed to fend for themselves.

Occasionally, those left behind encounter other wandering fowl in similar situations and form *ad hoc* family units. This, however, is rare, as lone chickens—especially those whose ability to flee is compromised—are easy prey for chicken hawks, coyotes, human hunters, and other predators and are often killed before the opportunity to meet others in similar circumstances presents itself.

THREATS AND OUTLOOK

While huge numbers of feral flocks once wandered the West, numbers have dwindled and are dwindling. Townfolk once saw feral chickens as an easy source of food and hunted them intensely. Others captured birds, both hens and roosters, confining them for both egg-laying and to raise as meat.

During one sad period of our history, feral chickens were hunted commercially. Vast numbers of fowl were driven for miles, by men afoot or horseback, later in airplanes and helicopters, herded into makeshift brush enclosures, then trucked to slaughterhouses for processing as pet food, with even bones and beaks ground to meal used as protein supplements for domestic flocks in a distasteful, cannibalistic practice of industrial agriculture.

While meat from feral chickens was never commercially marketed for human consumption in the United States, certain slaughter operations did ship whole carcasses and chicken parts to some European nations (primarily France) as well as China and Southeast Asia for the high-price restaurant trade. Feral chickens from America are considered a delicacy by some who are willing to pay vast sums to dine on exotic, free-range fowl from the Wild West.

(On a side note, even eggs pilfered from nests in the wild are in demand in certain markets. Those who enjoy such fare claim a delicate hint of sage in every bite, and that the natural leavening ability of alkali—absorbed by the hens from soils in the West—gives eggs laid in the wild a lighter, fluffier texture.)

While feral flocks now enjoy federal protection (thanks, largely, to lobbying efforts of the Feral Hen Rescue Society), illegal hunting yet exists, and initiatives to halt the export trade have met with limited success. A few tenacious fowl processors continue to operate, often under cover, and, in at least one case, across the border.

Efforts to legislate further safeguards are met with resistance on many fronts. Some in the rural West claim scratching by feeding flocks leads to erosion; others say the seeds they consume interferes with natural reseeding of rangelands traditionally used for cattle and sheep production; still others fear the spread of disease from feral chickens to domestic flocks, particularly those in large-scale factory-type confinement operations where captive chickens are exploited for both eggs and meat.

Only a concerted effort and outcry by those supportive of maintaining the presence of feral flocks in the West will prevent these feral-chicken haters from prevailing in the court of public opinion.

Your Support is Needed

How can you help? First and foremost, contact your political representatives at every level and voice your support for protecting feral chickens.

Involve yourself and your family in federal rescue and adoption programs, which humanely capture surplus hens and roosters and make them available to families and individuals who promise to provide good homes. (Surprisingly, chickens make good pets and their presence is becoming increasingly acceptable, even in urban environments.)

Finally, familiarize yourself with this irreplaceable resource. Include a visit to feral chicken territory in your next family vacation. Or join a tour group for one of many increasingly popular excursions that bus visitors in commodious motor coaches to locations that provide opportunities to view and photograph feral flocks in their natural habitat.

In whatever ways you are able, lend your support to efforts to save our dwindling flocks of feral chickens. For, in the last analysis, if we lose these feathered symbols of the Wild West, we will, in a very real sense, lose the West itself.

THE DEATH OF DELGADO

In 2012, this tale won the Western Writers of America Spur Award for Best Western Short Story. Although the people and particulars in "The Death of Delgado" are imagined, the incident at the center of the story is real, as told in "The Land is Free," a 1961 True West *magazine article by Colen Sweeten as told to Colen Sweeten, Jr. Originally published by Western Fictioneers in an anthology entitled* The Traditional West, *it was a Finalist for that organization's Peacemaker Award for short fiction and has also appeared in their "Peacemaker" anthologies.*

———— ◆ ————

I came face to face with my future the day Christian Delgado rode onto our ranch. At least I hoped—dreamed—I had.

Delgado was a cowboy.

Oh, there were plenty of cowboys in our part of the county. But Delgado was a different sort. Flashy isn't the right word, but there was a certain amount of sparkle to the man and his trappings. He was some strange crossbreed of what nowadays we'd call Californio, buckaroo, and vaquero. Heavy-roweled Mexican spurs, high-topped boots with tall, underslung heels, short chaps that covered his lower legs with nothing but leather fringe, wool vest up top.

His saddle was especially eye-catching. Unlike the plain and practical kacks around our place, his slickfork was silver mounted with conchos, buckles, and bands; his other tack and horse jewelry likewise festooned.

As I said, I was enthralled the minute I saw him. He filled the dreamy eyes of this eleven-year-old Idaho ranch kid with a near-perfect vision of what a cowboy ought to look like.

Mind you, he wasn't anything outside of ordinary from a physical standpoint. He wasn't tall, maybe seven inches above five feet, hung on an average frame that was neither slender nor stocky. Not particularly handsome, I'd say, but neither was he hard to look at. His face, save for a sharp-trimmed mustache, was so clean-shaven it always looked as if he'd just now toweled off the last flecks of lather. He was, I suppose, in his twenty-third or -fourth year that summer.

Even though Christian Delgado had never seen the south side of the Rio Grande, he was, to folks hereabouts, a Mexican. (Some called him a greaser, but never within his hearing.) But he claimed descent direct from the Spaniards of old, and offered deep green eyes and the pale skin on the inside of his forearms as proof of his genealogy. And, to this fascinated boy, he did carry himself with the elegance of a conquistador, a caballero, a Don. There's no doubt he was the kind of man folks paid attention to— the focus of attention in most every crowd, with the quiet confidence of one accustomed to that attention.

He showed up in the Curlew Valley because he heard that Dad had horses that needed rode. He'd heard right.

Dad and Uncle Evan had a sizeable ranch and raised a good many horses for sale. Nothing fancy, mind you, just good solid cow horses and some heavier stock for driving. We also put up a considerable amount of winter feed cut from hay meadows, and ran cattle on range that required the beef to graze at a fast walk just to get to enough grass to work up a cud of a size worth chewing.

And so Delgado went to work. Most of the time he spent horseback, either tending the cow herd or breaking horses. His means of training was simple: a good horse is the result of a lot of wet saddle blankets. When he wasn't sweating the edge off green-broke colts on long trails up and down the hills and canyons of our rocky, brush-covered country, you'd find him starting even greener colts in the round pen. He'd sometimes have half a dozen tied up outside waiting their turn.

Every chance that summer, you'd find me hanging by my elbows from the top rail, eyeing his every move. On a lucky day, I'd ride beside him through the brush, doing my best to handle one of his graduating students like a real hand—like Delgado—would. While abroad on the range we'd see to the cattle; doctoring any that needed it and drifting them back toward home if they wandered too far. Lucky days, for sure, for a kid with cowboy dreams.

But I wasn't all that lucky all that often that summer.

Dad, you see, was digging a well up in the corner of the south pasture. Water was scarce in Curlew Valley, and the stream through that end of our place, while wet enough in springtime, flowed only shallow dust by late summer. A reliable water supply was always to be desired, and always to be realized when chance presented itself. So when Dad watched a forked willow stick in the hands of an itinerant water witch take a nosedive, he dedicated his summer to digging a well.

Digging a well in those days and in that place wasn't a complicated job—you just grabbed the handle of a shovel and put the business end of it to work. The only thing you needed to worry about, Dad always said, was to fill up the back half of the shovel—the front half would take care of itself, he said.

He also told me that when you stood in the deep bottom of the long hole the well was becoming, you could look up at the narrow opening and see stars shining in the middle of the brightest day.

But all I could see those long days helping out at the well was lost opportunities—squandered time, wasted time, time I wanted to be with Delgado.

Instead, I spent my time daydreaming about what I was missing. Now and then, in answer to Dad's call echoing up the hole, I'd pull the well rope off the stake it was anchored to and knot it to the clevis on the singletree, then kiss ol' Socks into a shuffling walk, watching the rope feed its way through the squeaky hand-carved wooden block lashed to the top of the cedar pole tripod over the hole. When the heavy bucket cleared the hole I'd whoa-up Socks, swing the laden tub over to solid ground and call the horse back to slack the rope until the bucket landed. Ol' Socks didn't even need a jerk line to control, just voice commands.

Bucket settled, I'd walk over to the horse, unhook the rope out of the clevis, walk back and two-hand-heft-and-grunt the bucket over to the pile and dump out the hole it held. Hand-over-hand all along the length of the rope, I'd lower the bucket back down the well, careful not to let it fall too fast for Dad to grab before it beaned him, then take another hitch to the anchor stake. As Dad commenced putting more of the hole in the bucket, I'd bring Socks around and back him up close to the hole so we'd be ready to haul up the next load.

Mostly, the big bucket would be heaped with dirt and rocks, but for a few days now it had been showing more and wetter mud so Dad was feeling like the bottom of the well couldn't be far off.

A couple of times a day, besides the trip up for dinner and the one at the end of the day, Dad would ride the bucket up for a rest and some fresh air. Sometimes the air down there would get pretty thick, he said, and that meant more trips up the hole and longer stretches in daylight before going back down.

From time to time he would fashion a bundle of grass hay about the size of the hole, tie it to the rope, and plunger it up and down the well to force the heavy air out. A trick he learned, he said, from an old "Cousin Jack" miner who lived in town.

Dad sensed my fascination with Christian Delgado, and knew I saw in the young man the realization of my cowboy yearnings. And, of a normal summer, he would not have objected to my making of myself a full-time apprentice to the horseman. But he needed my help at the well, what with Uncle Evan and the hired hands busy with haying from dark to dark those long hot days. And he often enough made me to realize he appreciated my help, and promised there'd be a time for cowboying.

Truth be told, Dad wished he could be out cowboying too, for he was a man who loved horses and cattle. I knew, too, that he admired the touch Delgado had with horses. Not as much as I admired him, maybe, but even through eyes wrinkled with experience Dad saw something beyond the ordinary in that cowboy's ways.

The day Delgado died dawned like any other.

He haltered and tied that day's mounts to the rail outside the round corral.

Uncle Evan and the hay hands hitched up a team and hayrack and rolled out for the meadow.

And Dad and I and ol' Socks shuffled slow toward the hole in the far corner of the south pasture.

"It's getting pretty boggy down there, son," he said.

"How much deeper you gonna have to go," I asked through a wide yawn as I fisted some of the sleep out of my eyes.

"Can't say. The mud makes for a messier job, but the water does cool it down some."

The past day or two he'd been coming out of the hole muddy above his knees, and he'd said the bottom got softer with every shovelful he hefted out of it. We were threading a good sixty feet of rope down the hole by then.

"I hope, in another day or three, to have to tread water down there. Then I'll know it's a good well. If it draws water enough in the dead of summer, it ought to serve year round. And, near as I can tell after straining the mud through my teeth, it's going to be good, sweet water."

THE DEATH OF DELGADO

Being a kid, and lacking proper appreciation for such things, I answered with another yawn.

We soon settled into the day's routine, and it did not appear anything would be along to break it. As usual, a breeze kicked up as the day warmed then grew gusty and dusty as the air got hotter. A dust devil whipped up out on the flat and I watched tumbleweeds spin around and around and up and up and eventually peel off to roll back to earth.

"Up!" Dad hollered from down the hole, but his call didn't register.

"Up!" he said again, louder, jolting me back into the present.

I worked the rope off the stake, knotted it through the clevis, and kissed Socks into motion. Unlike me, he'd paid attention to Dad's call and was ready to lean into the harness. By now, the both of us could practically do the job in our sleep and I was soon back on the powder box I used for a seat with barely any recollection of having left it.

This time it was the wind that woke me from my daydreams—heavy, hot gusts peppering me with dirt and debris. I squinted over my shoulder to see that dust devil right there and bearing down on us. With arms wrapped around the top of my head, I fell to my knees and made myself small.

Through the blow I could hear, barely, rattling harness and ol' Socks snorting and blowing. I peeked past a bent elbow in time to see the horse sidestep then shy backward, haunches down and head up as he tried to back away from the swirling wind.

It was gone in an instant, but by then Socks was caving off the raw rim of the well, raining dirt and pebbles down the hole. Upset all the more, he kept snorting and shuffling until his hind legs slipped and he rolled onto his back and into the shaft.

He couldn't fall far—he wedged tight against the sides no more than six or eight feet down, all the while thrashing and screaming. He skidded another few feet and settled there.

"Dad?" I squawked with what little voice I could find. Socks blocked the echo I was used to hearing in the hole, and I thought maybe he blocked my voice as well. Beyond the horse there was nothing to see but darkness. The falling dirt must have broken Dad's coal oil lantern or knocked it into the slop.

"Dad?" again, louder this time.

I didn't even realize I'd been holding my breath until it rushed out with relief when I heard Dad's reply.

"Honey?" he yelled. "What happened up there?"

"Socks fell in the well!"

"I see that. Think you can help him out?"

Our yelling upset the horse again, and his scratching and thrashing sent another rain of dirt and stones rattling down on Dad.

"I don't think so," I said. "He's too far down. And he's upside down."

"Damn!" I heard Dad say—the first foul word I'd ever heard out of his mouth, the hearing of which shocked me almost as much as the mess we were in.

"We'd best be quiet so's not to spook him any worse than he is," he said. "Check the rope, see that it's tied off tight."

I hustled over to the stake and took another double half hitch around it just to make sure.

"Is it all right?"

"I think so."

"Now, son, you just sit tight." I heard him working the shovel as he chinked a ledge in the shaft where he set the bucket to get it out of the way. "What I'm going to do is try to climb out of here. Think there's room for me to squeeze past ol' Socks if I can get up there?"

"Maybe," I said. "I don't think so."

The horse took another fit and in the squirming and straining slipped another foot or two. The block lashed to the tripod started to sway and rattle, the rope jerking rhythmically as Dad pulled himself steadily upward. Dirt and rocks splashing in the bottom said he was using his feet to help claw his way out of the well.

The rope stopped jerking from time to time as he wedged himself against the sides to rest. Soon, the pulse of his grasping hands would travel up the rope again and before long I could hear his breathing, and the strain in it.

Then the horse must have sensed Dad's presence beneath him, and not known what to make of it. In a renewed bout of heaving and clawing, twisting and straining, ol' Socks came loose of a sudden and slid down the well scraping rocks, dirt, and Dad off the sides and taking it all down with him. They bottomed out with a thick splash and heavy thud that reverberated all the way to the surface. A few more pebbles and dirt clods trickled down, falling into silence along with the fading echo.

I wasn't there to hear the quiet.

THE DEATH OF DELGADO

After crossing the pasture at a dead run, I stumbled to a stop, the rails of the round corral the only thing keeping me from tumbling all the way down.

Delgado had seen me coming and waited quietly across the fence atop one of the colts, which shied and scrambled backward when I hit the fence. When the colt stopped, Delgado flexed his hips and kissed his lips to urge it forward, finally touching it with the spurs. A soft haul on the hackamore reins stopped the colt's sudden lunge and Delgado settled down into the saddle as I struggled for breath.

"It's, it's Daddy," I said. "He's down. The well. Socks fell in. On top. Of him."

The corral gate was already swinging open. Delgado had dismounted in an instant and already he and the colt were on my side of the fence. Without a word, he grabbed me by the waist and swung me aboard the skittish colt.

"You hurry. Tell Evan to bring the team and his men to the well. They are unloading. Tell him to bring the derrick cable. Hurry. I will go to your father."

That horse was only half under my control, if that, on the run to the hay yard. Once or twice he kicked up his heels and tried to bog his head, but by sawing on the reins I was able to prevent a come-apart or complete runaway.

He didn't want to stop when we tore out of the hay meadow and into the stackyard. I cranked his head to one side until it was practically in my lap and he finally came around in a circle and stopped as Uncle Evan and the three workers looked on.

Before the story was half told, Uncle Evan had scrambled down off the stack of loose hay, chopped the derrick cable in two with a hay knife and was pulling it screaming through the pulleys on the derrick. The hay hands lit into the load like windmills, forking it off every side of the wagon. They kept at it even as Uncle Evan heaved heavy coils of derrick cable over the rack on the front of the wagon then climbed up, hooked a leg over and whipped up the team with the lines.

As the haywagon clattered and bounced out of the stackyard, I tapped my heels to the colt's sides and hoped he'd do something other than go to pitching. He snorted some and flung his head around, but another soft kick in the belly convinced him to line out and walk. Once he settled in, I urged him into a long trot and figured to let it go at that.

Delgado was just clearing the lip of the well when I rode up. Any hope I had for Dad washed away in the tears streaming down his muddy face.

He'd stopped only long enough to grab a lantern from the milking stall and an ax and shovel and pry bar from the tool shed—whatever was at hand, I guess. By the time Uncle Evan arrived, Delgado was already at the bottom of the well, having slid down the rope with the lit lantern in his teeth. But all he could find to do was pull the bucket out of the mess, tie it to the rope, and ask Evan to haul him up—which he did, by hand, with help from the three men on his hay crew.

The cowboy stepped out of the bucket as it reached the surface and plopped down on my box.

"I cannot find him," he said as he absent-mindedly scratched with a fingernail at the mud that covered his chaps, then unbuckled and peeled them off. "The hole is full of nothing but broken horse and mud. I felt around as much as I could. Nothing." He unbuttoned and pulled of his vest then tugged his shirt over his head.

Delgado unsheathed his knife and went to whittling on the ax handle. It seemed a poor choice of activities in the circumstances. I said "What—"

"There is no room to work the ax in the hole," he said, cutting off my question. Although his voice was quiet, anger, frustration maybe, was as evident as if he had shouted. "It is too tight."

Still unsure what he was doing, I thought it best to keep my peace.

Snapping off the handle, he shaved the raw edge to smooth the splinters as best he could. To Uncle Evan, he said, "I guess we won't be needing that cable. There is no way we'll lift that horse out of there without caving in the sides. He will have to come up in the bucket. Lower me down, then get your team ready. It will be too much lifting to do by hand."

Evan and at least one of his hay hands were years older than Delgado. It didn't occur to me at the time, but I have since wondered why it was the younger man giving orders in that tense situation, and why the others complied without question or comment.

It did not dawn on me, either, what Delgado was doing down there until the first bucket came up. Blood sloshed over the sides as Uncle Evan swung it away from the well. The horse's head hung over the rim, muzzle stained scarlet and nostrils dripping gore.

I hit my knees as that red mess splashed to the ground and I heaved up what was left of breakfast and kept heaving until there was nothing left to come up and then I heaved some more. And even after that, the sound of Delgado and his ax at work down the well would set me to gagging all over again.

One front quarter, then another, came out of the hole in poorly butchered pieces. Then Delgado came up. Blood-spattered and gasping, he sat flat to the ground and sucked in air.

"Anything?" Evan asked.

"No. Nothing."

Uncle Evan asked no more questions, simply stared vacantly at the hired man on the ground.

"You're spent. I'll go down," he finally said.

"No. There is no room. I can hardly get any leverage myself, and I am smaller than you. I will finish the job."

He said the lantern kept flickering out from lack of air, so he gave up trying to keep it burning and did his awful work in the dark. Worst of all, worse than the dark, worse than the heat, worse than the mud, he told us, was the stink. Even in the open air the stench of blood and torn flesh was overpowering when the wind swirled it your direction. It got worse when broken entrails and smashed organs topped the pile.

Finally, the second hind leg, broken at an odd angle, plopped out of the bucket and onto the pile dripping mud and blood and that was the end of ol' Socks.

Standing with hands grasping spread knees, Uncle Evan bent over the lip of the well awaiting word from Delgado. From time to time he would hear him sloshing around down there, or the occasional splash.

Finally, "I have found a hand."

Later, "I have freed as much of him as I can, but he is stuck fast. You will have to send down the cable."

From the hay wagon, Uncle Evan fetched a steel pulley and short length of chain and hooked it to the tripod next to the wooden block through which the well rope was threaded. As he tested the strength of his work, his men stretched the kinks out of the cable. He threaded it through the pulley, quickly clamped a clevis to the end, and shoved the wire rope down the shaft an arm's length at a time.

It seemed an eternity until Delgado asked to be lifted up in the bucket. He stepped out, cut the well rope from the bail, then pulled the end through the block and tossed it out of the way so it would not tangle with the cable.

"I don't know. He is stuck pretty tight. I got a loop around him but I don't know," he told Evan as they watched the hands hitch the cable to the doubletree harnessed to the team. "I never could feel his feet. Too deep."

As the slack slowly came out of the cable he said, "I hope he doesn't come up like that horse."

Uncle Evan took over the team, and with his easy hands at the lines they leaned slowly into the load.

Nothing.

He urged the horses on—tugs creaked, singletrees cracked. The cable hummed, the pulley trembled. The heavy cedar posts in the tripod groaned and their thick bottoms pushed up ridges in the dirt as they tried to spread wider, threatening collapse.

The team grunted and strained and leaned harder into their collars as Uncle Evan, in desperation, slapped one horse then the other on the rump with the lines. Slowly, almost imperceptibly, they moved ahead. Half the length of a hoof. Another. And then, with a release felt deep in the belly of every one of us, the team was walking free.

The pulley from the hay derrick squealed as it slowly rotated. Uncle Evan handed the lines to another of the men as the team's distance from the hole increased and he quickly followed the cable back to the well to stand beside me and Delgado.

Dad came up belt buckle first. Uncle Evan collapsed in a heap when he saw his broken brother, bent double, backwards, swinging slowly from the derrick cable.

I stared, uncomprehending. I guess my day's ration of distress was long since used up, to be replaced by shock and resignation.

Like I had done so many times, Delgado swung the load away from the hole as the team backed slack into the cable and settled it to solid ground. He pulled the pin out of the clevis and cast it aside and carefully, gently, gathered Dad's limp body in his arms and carried him to the hay wagon. Then he turned for the house and walked away.

———— ◆ ————

Delgado did not die that day.

At least not like Dad was dead.

But the spirit was gone out of him as surely as if it had been his body we pulled out of that temporary grave at the bottom of the well.

In a way, I guess it was.

He didn't stop at the bunkhouse any longer than it took to stuff his few belongings into his war bag. I don't know what he wore on his feet when he left our place. His soggy high-topped boots with the blood-and-mud-encrusted Mexican spurs still strapped to them were left standing outside the door, abandoned to the well as surely as Dad's were; his sucked off in the muck in the bottom of that hole where, I suppose, they still are.

So far as I know, ol' Socks was the last horse Delgado ever touched.

For years, he stayed around these parts setting his hand to a variety of jobs—sacking wheat at the feed and seed, clerking at a grocery store, tending bar, that sort of thing. Last I heard, he was somewhere off in Wyoming pushing folks around in wheelchairs in a convalescent hospital.

I led that green-broke colt he'd mounted me on that day back to the yard and pulled off Delgado's silver-mounted saddle and hauled it inside the tack shed. It has been there ever since, hanging from a rafter on a rawhide tether.

ABOUT ROD MILLER

Born and raised in Utah, Rod Miller turned a lifelong interest in the history and culture of the American West into numerous poems, stories, magazine articles, and books.

He is winner of three Western Writers of America Spur Awards—for a novel, a poem, and a short story ("The Death of Delagado," which appears in this collection, along with Spur Award Finalist, "A Border Affair").

His novels include Spur Award Winner *Rawhide Robinson Rides the Range* and *Rawhide Robinson Rides the Tabby Trail* (Five Star), Western Fictioneers Peacemaker Award Finalist *The Assassination of Governor Boggs* (Cedar Fort), *Cold as the Clay* (High Hill Press), and *Gallows for a Gunman* (Pinnacle).

The Lost Frontier: Momentous Moments in the Old West You May Have Missed (TwoDot) is his latest book of history. Others include *Go West: The Risk and the Reward* (Range Conservation Foundation), *Massacre at Bear River: First, Worst, Forgotten* (Caxton Press), and *John Muir: Magnificent Tramp* (Forge).

A collection of Miller's poetry from Pen-L Publishing, *Goodnight Goes Riding and Other Poems*, includes the Spur Award Finalist poem, "Song of the Stampede," and the book won the Westerners International Fred Olds Poetry Award. An earlier collection, *Things a Cowboy Sees and Other Poems* (Port Yonder Press), won the same award as well as the Academy of Western Artists Buck Ramsey Book of the Year Award, and one of its poems, "Tabula Rasa," is a Spur Award Winner. He is also author of a chapbook of poems, *Newe Dreams* (Laughing Mouse Press).

Miller writes for magazines, and has been featured in Ranch & Reata, American Cowboy, Range, True West, Western Horseman, and other

Rod Miller

periodicals. He served as Guest Poetry Editor for *American Cowboy* and Contributing Editor for *Roundup*.

A graduate of Utah State University where he earned a degree in Journalism, Miller also rode bucking horses for the intercollegiate rodeo team and competed for several years in rodeos throughout the Intermountain West.

Visit Rod Miller online at

WWW.WRITERRODMILLER.COM

WRITERRODMILLER.BLOGSPOT.COM

WWW.AMAZON.COM/AUTHOR.RODMILLER

3

For those learning it is okay to be themselves.
In the end, you are the one who remains.

Chapter One

Navi Vale's mornings were calibrated.

She woke before the alarm, not out of discipline but habit. The body learned faster than the mind when repetition was rewarded. Light filtered through the narrow window in a pale, indifferent band. The city was already awake but not yet asking anything of her.

She dressed in the same range of tones she always did— colors chosen for their refusal to stand out. The fabric sat comfortably against her skin, familiar enough that she did not need to look at herself while fastening it. Mirrors were efficient tools. Nothing more.

Breakfast was simple. She ate standing at the counter, reviewing the docket for the day. Three assessments. One renewal. No disputes flagged in advance. It would be a clean day.

That knowledge settled her.

The walk to the offices followed a fixed route. Three streets. One footbridge. A gradual incline where the city widened just enough to suggest scale without demanding engagement. Navi liked this stretch best. It belonged to no one. Not yet work. No longer home.

People passed her without comment. A nod here. A brief acknowledgment there.

She was recognized without being known, which suited her. Visibility invited expectation. Expectation complicated judgment.

At the offices, the air changed subtly—cooler, flatter, carrying the faint mineral scent of stone and processed light. Navi paused long enough for the threshold to register her presence, then stepped inside.

Colleagues greeted her with the quiet ease reserved for those who did not disrupt flow. Someone handed off a case without explanation, trusting her to see what mattered. A supervisor inclined their head, already moving on.

This was competence as currency.

Navi settled at her desk and began.

Records opened smoothly beneath her hands. Names aligned. Dates behaved. The system responded the way it was meant to when handled correctly.

Midday arrived without ceremony. Navi ate late, as usual, alone and standing. Hunger was a distant signal, easily postponed. The work mattered more than comfort; comfort could always be earned later.

By afternoon, her docket was nearly closed. She felt the familiar easing in her shoulders that came with completion. The day had gone as planned.

The final assessment was routine. Lineage second order. Maternal. No prior complications. Navi reviewed the preliminary fields without concern.

She rested her hands on the slate.

It warmed beneath her palms.

The sensation was ordinary. Expected.

Still, something in her chest tightened, just slightly, an involuntary hitch she dismissed as fatigue.

"State your name," she said.

The petitioner did.

The slate paused.

Not enough to matter.

Enough to be felt.

Navi blinked once and continued.

The day had been calibrated.

She had no reason to expect otherwise.

(The record would disagree.)

Interlude I

Internal Balance Log – Auto-Generated

Classification: Minor Irregularity Confidence Threshold: Maintained

The system does not think in moments.

It thinks in patterns.

A single pause is not a concern. A fraction of delay falls within acceptable variance. Bodies hesitate. Hands warm. Attention fluctuates. These are known quantities.

The record from Assessment Cycle 4417–V registers a latency of 0.43 seconds between input and confirmation.

This does not exceed tolerance.

No alert is issued.

The name resolves. The archive stabilizes. Balance holds.

A secondary notation appears in background processing.

Not an error.

A deviation.

Deviation requires comparison.

The system retrieves prior interactions associated with License: VALE, NAVI.

Findings:

- Consistent completion times
- High compliance rate
- Minimal appeal history
- No ideological drift detected

Deviation is isolated.

The system archives it as context.

Language protocols adjust imperceptibly.

Future records routed through this license will:

- Confirm alignment twice instead of once
- Delay finalization by a fractional margin
- Record biometric response data for trend analysis

These adjustments are preventative.

They are not punitive.

The system does not assign intent.

Intent belongs to individuals.

Patterns belong to Balance.

Balance remains intact.

For now.

End Log

Chapter Two

Navi did not feel different when she woke.

That unsettled her more than pain would have.

The morning followed its usual sequence. Light through the narrow window. The quiet click of the kettle. The familiar weight of clothing chosen not to argue with the world. Her body moved efficiently, without protest.

She stood at the counter and reviewed the day's docket.

There was an additional note attached to her first assessment.

Not a warning.

A clarification request.

The language was careful—neutral in tone, generous with procedural courtesy. A request for verification of lineage markers associated with a previous case. Standard follow-up. Entirely reasonable.

Navi read it twice.

Her chest tightened.

She told herself this reaction was irrational. Clarifications happened every day. They were safeguards, not judgments. She approved them herself when they crossed her desk.

Still, the sensation lingered, low and insistent, like pressure beneath the sternum.

She closed the slate and prepared for work.

The walk felt longer.

Nothing about the route had changed. Three streets. One footbridge. The incline that opened the city just enough to remind her she was not alone.

Yet her steps slowed without instruction. Her breath shortened. The space around her felt subtly mismeasured, as if the world had shifted by a fraction and refused to settle back.

At the offices, the threshold registered her a beat later than usual.

She noticed.

No one else did.

The assessment room was the same one she had occupied the day before.

The familiarity should have steadied her.

Instead, the stone felt closer. The light harsher. Her skin prickled with awareness she could not justify.

The petitioner entered. Different face. Different posture. A routine clearance renewal.

Clean.

Navi rested her hands on the slate.

It warmed.

Too much.

She pulled her hands back immediately, heart thudding. The heat lingered anyway, blooming across her palms like an afterimage.

She pressed her fingers together beneath the desk until the sensation dulled.

"State your name," she said.

The slate responded instantly.

No pause.

No resistance.

Relief should have followed.

It did not.

As the assessment progressed, Navi became acutely aware of her own body.

Her breath required attention. Her shoulders ached from holding themselves too precisely. A dull pressure gathered behind her eyes, neither pain nor fatigue.

The record was flawless.

That was the problem.

Nothing tugged. Nothing resisted. Nothing pushed back against her touch.

The absence felt deliberate.

When she marked the clearance approved, the slate accepted it without warmth, without hum.

The room did not exhale.

Navi did.

Afterward, alone, she stood at the desk longer than necessary.

Her hands tingled faintly, as if waiting for a sensation that refused to return. She turned one palm upward, then the other. The skin was unmarked. Ordinary.

She should have been relieved.

Instead, a quiet certainty settled in her chest.

Whatever had happened the day before had not resolved.

It had been noted.

Later, reviewing records from the afternoon docket, Navi noticed something small.

A fractional delay.

Not in the slate.

In herself.

She hesitated before finalizing a file that required no hesitation at all.

The moment passed. The mark set. The record closed.

But the delay remained.

She understood, then—not as a conclusion, but as a pressure she could no longer ignore—that the system had adjusted.

And so had she.

The difference was this:

The system knew why.

Navi did not.

That imbalance settled into her bones and stayed.

(It would not be corrected quietly.)

Interlude II

Protective Guidance Circular – Revision Notice

Distribution: Internal Audience: Licensed Personnel, Tier II and Above Tone: Reassuring

Recent reviews have indicated minor inconsistencies in how historical materials are interpreted during assessments.

These inconsistencies do not reflect failure.

They reflect engagement.

As a reminder, the purpose of the archive is not to reproduce the past in full detail, but to preserve those elements of it that remain useful to present stability.

Accordingly, the following clarifications are issued:

- Historical records may contain redundancies, emotional artifacts, or localized narratives that no longer serve communal balance.
- Absence within the archive should not be interpreted as erasure, but as resolution.
- Lineage gaps are an expected outcome of prior harmonization efforts and should be treated as settled.

Personnel are encouraged to rely on validated summaries rather than peripheral markers when conducting reviews.

Extended attention to anomalous data can cause unnecessary strain.

For your protection, access to unharmonized materials will now be limited to personnel with demonstrated resilience and consistent alignment metrics.

This adjustment is temporary.

It will remain in effect only as long as needed to ensure clarity, efficiency, and well-being.

The Balance is maintained not by remembering everything, but by remembering what matters.

End Circular

Chapter Three

The reassignment notice arrived without ceremony.

Navi read it standing in the corridor outside her office, the slate balanced in one hand, the other resting against the cool stone of the wall. The language was precise. Courteous. Designed to sound like opportunity.

Temporary Adjustment of Duties.

No cause cited.

No duration specified.

Her new assignment would begin immediately.

She was to report to Peripheral Review.

The word peripheral lodged beneath her ribs.

Peripheral Review occupied a lower tier of the complex, closer to ground level where the light filtered in unevenly and sound traveled less predictably. Navi had passed the doors many times without reason to enter.

Inside, the pace was slower. The work less visible.

Cases here were already decided.

Her role was not to assess, but to confirm that prior outcomes remained intact.

A maintenance function.

She understood the message.

By midday, she felt it.

The difference in how people moved around her.

Colleagues who once handed her files without comment now hesitated, conversations trailing off when she approached. A supervisor she had worked under for years offered a polite smile and nothing else.

Her name still opened doors.

It simply no longer invited confidence.

At midday break, Navi discovered her access tier had been adjusted.

Not revoked.

Refined.

Several archive paths returned a neutral denial. No explanation beyond a reminder that access levels fluctuated according to current assignment needs.

She stared at the notice longer than necessary, pulse thudding faintly at the base of her throat.

This was not punishment.

This was management.

The real cost surfaced at the end of the day.

Her housing clearance had been updated.

Not rescinded. Reclassified.

Her apartment—assigned, efficient, close to the offices—now exceeded proximity guidelines for her revised role.

She was offered alternatives.

All farther out.

All temporary.

Navi walked home slowly.

The familiar route no longer belonged to her. The footbridge felt exposed. The incline steeper.

At her door, she paused, hand hovering over the entry seal.

Inside, everything was exactly as she had left it.

Orderly.

Aligned.

The space did not receive her the way it once had.

She sat at the table and opened the reassignment notice again, searching for language she might have missed.

There was none.

No accusation.

No error.

Just adjustment.

That night, as she reorganized the shelves she had already aligned a hundred times before, her hands began to tremble.

Not from fear.

From effort.

She stopped.

For the first time, she let the disorder stand.

The imbalance pressed gently against her chest.

It did not correct itself.

And no one came to make it so.

Chapter Four

The new apartment was farther out than she expected.

Not distant enough to be unfamiliar—just far enough to break habit.

Navi carried her belongings herself. There were not many. The relocation notice had described the move as temporary, and temporary things did not require ceremony. A single bag. A box of records she told herself she might need.

The building sat between two transit lines that did not quite meet. The street below was louder than she was used to, voices overlapping without resolving into anything she could follow. Children ran the length of the walkway, their movement unpredictable, uncorrected.

No one here waited for permission to exist.

Her new unit was narrower, the ceiling lower. The light came in from the side instead of above, catching dust she could not immediately place. The entry seal accepted her credentials without warmth.

Inside, the space felt unfinished.

Not poorly kept—simply uninterested in her.

She set her bag down and stood for a long moment, unsure what order should come next.

That evening, Navi walked the surrounding blocks.

There was no fixed route.

She passed a woman selling food from a cart that operated just beyond permitted hours. The woman glanced up, met Navi's gaze, and did not look away. Navi felt an old instinct rise—to nod, to reassure, to smooth.

She did none of it.

Further on, a group gathered near the transit stairs. Not organized. Not protesting. Talking too loudly. Laughing without modulation. One voice carried a cadence she felt in her chest before she understood it.

Her pace slowed.

The sound tugged at something behind her ribs, a low pressure she had learned to ignore. She paused, hand brushing the stone rail, steadying herself.

No record opened.

No slate warmed.

The sensation lingered anyway.

At a small vendor stall, Navi hesitated before ordering. The menu was handwritten, inconsistent. Prices rounded differently from line to line.

She almost asked for clarification.

Instead, she chose at random.

The food was unfamiliar. Spiced in a way she could not name. It unsettled her stomach and grounded her at the same time.

The vendor watched her eat.

"You're new," they said.

It was not a question.

"Yes," Navi replied automatically.

The vendor nodded once. "You'll get used to the noise," they said. "Or you won't."

They turned away without waiting for her response.

Navi stood there longer than necessary, holding the empty dish.

That night, the building did not settle.

Sound traveled through the walls—arguments, music, footsteps overhead. The order she usually imposed on space failed her here. Shelves did not align. Corners refused symmetry.

Her hands shook as she tried to reorganize the small kitchenette.

She stopped.

The pressure in her chest eased slightly when she did.

She sat on the floor instead, back against the wall, knees drawn up.

This was not how she ended days. This posture had no sanctioned purpose.

From somewhere nearby, a voice began to sing.

Not clearly. Not beautifully.

Persistently.

Navi closed her eyes.

For the first time since the reassignment, she did not attempt to correct the sensation rising in her body.

She let it pass through her.

It did not resolve.

It stayed.

And in that staying, something in her loosened—just enough to make room for what she had never been permitted to hear.

Chapter Five

Peripheral Review did not feel like punishment.

That was its design.

The room was wider than those used for active assessment, its ceiling higher, the light less controlled. There were no petitioners here—only records that had already been decided, sealed, and filed away from public challenge.

Navi's role was confirmation.

She was to ensure outcomes remained consistent with prior determinations. Not to reopen. Not to reconsider. To verify that nothing had drifted.

She sat at the long table with three others she did not know well. No introductions were offered. Names were unnecessary. The work did not require trust—only compliance.

The first file opened without resistance.

A relocation clearance from seven years prior. Approved. Archived. Harmonized.

Navi read the summary. She read the summary again.

The language was familiar. Protective. Regret-minimizing. It framed loss as inevitability and called it balance.

She marked confirmed.

Her palm tingled faintly.

The second file carried a supplemental tag.

Post-Decision Stabilization.

Navi hesitated. The hesitation was small—no more than a breath—but she felt it register in her shoulders, the subtle tension of being observed even when no one looked at her directly.

She opened the file.

This one included peripheral materials: testimonies excluded for clarity, lineage threads deemed unresolved, notes flagged as emotionally saturated.

She was not meant to read these.

The system had included them anyway.

Her chest tightened.

A name surfaced in the margins—misaligned, lightly anchored, familiar in the way of a half-remembered tune. Navi did not touch it. She read around it, keeping her hands folded, posture impeccable.

Her body reacted regardless.

Heat bloomed beneath her collarbone. A pressure pressed forward, insistent but contained. She focused on her breathing, counting silently until the sensation dulled.

The summary concluded with a clean line:

Outcome maintained.

Navi marked confirmed.

The tingling in her palm intensified.
Across the table, one of the others shifted.
Not enough to draw attention. Enough to be noticed.
Their gaze met Navi's for a fraction of a second. There was no accusation in it. No solidarity either.
Only recognition.
Navi looked away first.

By midday, the pattern was unmistakable.
Files routed through Peripheral Review did not erase contradictions.
They contained them.
They stored what could not be resolved and labeled it complete.
Navi felt the weight of it settle into her arms, her neck, the base of her spine. Each confirmation left a residue she could not shake —a faint sense of pressure, as if she were holding something closed with her own body.
During the break, she stood by the window and watched people cross the courtyard below. None of them looked up.
She understood, then, what Peripheral Review protected.
Not truth.
Finality.

The last file of the day resisted her.
Not openly.
The slate warmed and cooled in uneven pulses, like breath held too long. Navi kept her hands still and read with her eyes alone.
The outcome was older. The language harsher. A decision made before the system learned how to soften its voice.
The confirmation required her mark.
Her hand trembled.
She let it.
Across the table, the person who had looked at her earlier did not move.

Navi pressed her thumb to the slate.

The mark set.

The pressure in her chest did not ease.

It spread.

That evening, as she left the building, she realized something simple and devastating:

Peripheral Review was not a holding space.

It was a reservoir.

And she had been placed where the weight would accumulate.

Chapter Six

The woman waited until the others had left.

Not conspicuously. She gathered her things at the same pace as everyone else, slate tucked under her arm, movements economical. She did not look at Navi again until the room was nearly empty.

Then she said, without turning, "You hold it in your shoulders."

Navi froze.

The remark was not accusatory. It wasn't even directed, not fully. It was the kind of observation people made when they were naming weather.

"I'm sorry?" Navi said.

The woman faced her. Older than Navi by a few years, maybe more. Her license pin was scuffed at the edges, the engraving dulled by time or habit. Peripheral Review had done that to things—worn them without breaking them.

"When a file resists," the woman said, "you lift here." She raised two fingers, hovering near her own collarbone. "Most people don't notice. They just breathe shallower and call it focus."

Navi felt heat rush up her neck.

"That's not—" She stopped herself. Correction required authority. Authority was not being offered.

The woman gave a small, unencouraging smile. "You're new to this tier."

"Yes."

"And very careful."

Navi waited for the rest.

"It doesn't last," the woman said instead.

They stood in the wide room, the long table between them cleared of files, surfaces immaculate. The system preferred clean exits.

"I don't know what you mean," Navi said.

The woman nodded, as if that were the expected response.

"You will," she said. "Or you won't. Depends how long you stay."

She reached into her bag and withdrew a folded slip of paper.

Paper.

Navi's eyes flicked to the door. No one was watching. No alerts sounded. Peripheral Review rarely required urgency.

The woman set the paper on the table and did not slide it closer.

"If you find yourself holding more than you can set down," she said, "don't try to organize it. That only teaches the weight where to live."

She picked up her bag.

"What is this?" Navi asked.

"A name," the woman replied. "One the archive doesn't like very much."

She left without waiting.

Navi stood alone for several breaths before approaching the table.

The paper was plain. Unmarked. No seals. No identifiers.

A single name had been written by hand.

The script was uneven, the letters pressed too hard, as if the act of writing had required resistance.

Navi did not touch it.

Her body reacted anyway.

The familiar pressure gathered beneath her breastbone, sharp enough this time to steal her breath. Her vision narrowed. Sound receded to a dull interior hum.

She closed her eyes and counted.

When she opened them again, the room had not changed.

The paper remained.

So did the pressure.

That night, in her new apartment, Navi placed the paper on the small table near the door.

She did not attempt to align it with anything.

She sat on the floor instead, back against the wall, and waited for the sensation to pass.

It did not.

The name pressed at her awareness—not as memory, not as command, but as invitation.

For the first time, Navi understood that containment was not the same as silence.

Some things grew louder the longer they were held.

She did not sleep well.

In the morning, the paper was still where she had left it.

So was the pressure.

And somewhere beneath both, something in her had begun to listen.

Interlude III

Alignment Support Notice – Confidential Draft

Distribution: Internal (Supervisory Review) Status: Provisional Tone: Supportive

Recent trend analysis indicates elevated somatic engagement among a small subset of licensed personnel.

This engagement does not imply noncompliance.

It reflects care.

However, prolonged exposure to unresolved archival material can produce strain responses that, if unaddressed, may compromise clarity and well-being.

To support continued effectiveness, the following optional measures are now available:

- Voluntary Alignment Consultations with certified facilitators
- Memory Streamlining Sessions to reduce cognitive load
- Temporary Reassignment Adjustments to encourage recalibration

Participation is encouraged but not required.

Declining support will not affect current standing.

(Continued trend divergence may necessitate review.)

Facilitators are trained to preserve professional identity while easing internal conflict.

Outcomes are confidential.

Records of participation will be maintained only for quality assurance.

The Balance protects those who protect it.

End Draft

Chapter Seven

The name appeared without warning.

Not fully.

Navi noticed it first as absence—a place where the air seemed thinner, as if something had been removed but the space still remembered it. The room smelled faintly of warmed stone and recycled light, the mineral tang that clung to every lower tier. She drew a breath and felt it catch halfway in.

Peripheral Review files were not supposed to surprise her. They were summaries, compressions, decisions already resolved into stillness.

This one resisted that stillness.

She leaned closer to the slate. Its surface held the day's heat, a dull warmth that seeped into her palms without her touching it. Somewhere behind the walls, a ventilation cycle shifted, the low sigh of air flattening sound until the room felt padded, private.

Her chest tightened. The familiar pressure gathered low and sharp, testing for give.

She did not touch the slate.

The field shimmered—not visually, but the way heat unsettled air above stone. Half-letters surfaced. A consonant pressed too deeply into the margin, darkened as if written with too much force.

The rest blurred, harmonized into neutrality.

Her breath caught.

It was the same name.

Not written.

Contained.

Navi forced herself to continue reading.

The case involved a housing displacement, approved years prior under emergency stability measures. The summary language was immaculate. Protective. Regret-neutral. Each sentence lay flat, smoothed of edges.

The body of the text made no mention of resistance.

The margins did.

Her palm tingled even without contact, a crawling warmth that climbed her forearm and settled into her shoulder with a dull ache. She became acutely aware of her own breathing, of the faint rasp of fabric as she shifted, of the quiet click of another slate somewhere down the table.

Across from her, a reviewer shifted. Not the woman from before—someone younger, hair pulled tight, eyes already tired. Their gaze flicked to Navi, then away.

Too fast to be coincidence.

Navi swallowed and scrolled.

The name flickered—never fully visible, never fully gone. The pressure beneath her breastbone sharpened, a precise insistence that stole a fraction of her breath. She tasted metal at the back of her mouth.

She thought of the folded paper in her apartment. The dry rasp of it between her fingers. The way it had refused silence, even in sleep.

This was not invitation.

This was proximity.

A prompt appeared at the bottom of the slate.

Confirm archival resolution.

The system waited.

Navi's thumb hovered above the mark. Her shoulders lifted without permission, the old reflex to brace. She lowered them deliberately, feeling the effort echo down her spine.

The pressure intensified.

She understood then that this was the point of Peripheral Review.

Not to decide.

To condition.

She pressed her thumb to the slate.

The mark set with a soft, final click.

The name vanished completely.

The room's air seemed to thicken. Her vision swam, edges blurring, and she gripped the table until the cool stone steadied her. The ventilation sighed again, indifferent.

Across the room, no one spoke.

The system exhaled.

Later, alone, Navi returned to her apartment. The corridor smelled of cooking oil and damp concrete, a human heat that lingered. She stood before the small table near the door.

The paper lay where she had left it.

The handwritten name did not flicker.

It did not harmonize.

It did not disappear when she looked directly at it.

Her chest ached.

For the first time, she understood the difference between erasure and survival.

One required permission.

The other did not.

Chapter Eight

The invitation arrived as a courtesy.

That was how it was phrased.

Not a summons. Not a directive. An opportunity to recalibrate.

Navi read the message in the early light, the apartment still heavy with last night's warmth. Somewhere down the corridor, someone was already cooking—oil heating too fast, garlic catching just before it burned. The smell pressed into the room without asking.

She closed the slate and stood for a moment, breathing through it.

The consultation suite occupied a middle tier—not central, not peripheral. The corridor leading to it smelled faintly of citrus cleanser layered over stone, an attempt at freshness that never quite erased what lay beneath. Sound softened here. Footsteps dulled. Voices lost their edges.

A facilitator met her at the door.

They were dressed neutrally, their expression practiced into something that suggested attentiveness without intimacy. Their voice, when they spoke, carried the faintest echo, as if the room had been designed to listen back.

"Thank you for coming," they said.

Navi nodded. Gratitude was implied.

Inside, the space was warm. Intentionally so. The light diffused through fabric panels that shifted slightly with the air cycle, never quite still. A low hum vibrated through the floor—steady, almost soothing.

"Please," the facilitator said, gesturing to a chair that cradled rather than supported.

Navi sat.

The chair adjusted beneath her weight, subtle changes aligning her spine, her shoulders. She felt herself exhale without deciding to.

"We've noticed elevated engagement," the facilitator said. "Nothing concerning."

They smiled gently. The kind of smile meant to reassure people who had already begun to doubt themselves.

"Sometimes," they continued, "those who care deeply experience strain when exposed to unresolved material. Our role is to help ease that load."

As they spoke, the hum beneath the floor shifted pitch— barely audible, but enough that Navi's chest responded before her mind could.

"What does that involve?" Navi asked.

"Mostly listening," the facilitator said. "Guided reflection. Alignment exercises."

They placed a small object on the low table between them.

Smooth. Oval. Warm to the touch.

Navi did not reach for it.

"Have you experienced lingering sensations after work?" the facilitator asked.

Navi hesitated.

The hesitation stretched, thin and visible.

"Yes," she said finally.

The facilitator nodded, as if she had confirmed a preference.

"That's very common," they said. "The body holds on when the mind is asked to let go too quickly."

They leaned forward slightly. The citrus scent intensified.

"With your permission," they said, "we can help redistribute that weight."

Navi felt the pressure rise beneath her breastbone, sharper now in the controlled quiet. The chair responded, shifting again, encouraging her shoulders to lower.

"What does redistribution mean?" she asked.

The facilitator's smile did not change.

"It means you won't have to carry what isn't yours."

They began with breathing.

Slow. Counted. The room adjusted to her rhythm, the hum synchronizing until it was difficult to tell where her breath ended and the sound began.

Images surfaced unbidden—not memories exactly, but impressions. Stone corridors. Hands passing papers. A name she refused to picture fully.

The pressure eased.

Just a little.

Relief washed through her, sudden and almost painful in its sweetness. Her eyes stung.

"There," the facilitator said softly. "Do you feel that?"

"Yes," Navi whispered.

"That's alignment," they said. "When friction resolves."

Something in Navi tightened.

The relief had come too easily.

She thought of the paper on her table. The way the pressure there never resolved, only stayed.

"What happens to what's released?" she asked.

The hum wavered.

The facilitator's pause was brief. Practiced.

"It integrates," they said. "Into the system that's built to hold it."

Navi's breath faltered.

"And if I don't want it integrated?"

The room seemed to lean in.

The facilitator's smile softened further, shading into concern.

"Then we would want to explore why holding on feels safer than letting go," they said.

When Navi left, the corridor felt colder.

The citrus smell clung to her clothes, faint but persistent. Her body felt lighter—unsettlingly so, as if something had been skimmed from the surface of her awareness.

Outside, sound rushed back in: footsteps, voices, the scrape of carts against stone. The world felt sharper at the edges.

She walked home slowly.

At her apartment door, she hesitated before entering.

Inside, the paper lay where it always had.

The pressure surged the moment she saw it, fierce and grounding.

Navi sagged against the wall, breath coming fast, relief and fear tangled together.

Whatever the consultation had taken, it had not taken this.

She understood then that support did not mean safety.

It meant selection.

And she had just learned how close she had come to being edited.

Chapter Nine

The change did not announce itself.

Navi noticed it first in the woman from Peripheral Review.

They were seated two places down the table, posture still correct, slate angled precisely as before. Nothing about her appearance suggested difference—until she looked up.

Her eyes did not hesitate.

They moved from file to file with a smoothness that felt practiced in a new way, like someone who had learned how not to linger. When a name surfaced that once would have drawn pressure into the room, the woman's shoulders remained level. Her breath did not change.

Relief, Navi realized.

Permanent.

The file in front of Navi vibrated faintly.

Not the slate itself—the air around it. A subtle displacement, like sound traveling through water. The sensation gathered in her chest, familiar and sharp, but when she glanced sideways the woman did not react.

"You went," Navi said quietly.

The woman did not look up. "I did."

"And?"

A pause. Brief. Efficient.

"It works," the woman said.

The words landed without emphasis. Not relief. Not warning.

"What does it cost?" Navi asked.

This time the woman looked at her.

Something essential was gone from her expression. Not kindness. Not intelligence.

Friction.

"I don't wake up heavy anymore," she said. "I don't carry things home. I sleep."

"That's not an answer," Navi said.

The woman smiled, apologetic. "It is where I am now."

The system adjusted around them.

Files moved faster. Confirmations set with less resistance. The room felt lighter, the hum beneath the floor settling into a consistent, unobtrusive rhythm.

Navi's body responded by doing the opposite.

The pressure intensified.

By midday, it sat behind her eyes like a held breath, sharp enough to blur the edges of her vision. She pressed her feet flat to the floor, grounding herself, and felt the stone vibrate faintly in response.

Someone else was holding less.

She was holding more.

The handwritten name surfaced again.

Not in a file.

In a voice.

She heard it as she passed through the lower corridor that connected Peripheral Review to the transit level. The space smelled of damp stone and old metal, the air warmer here, crowded with movement.

A man stood near the wall, speaking to a child whose attention kept slipping toward the stairwell.

He said the name casually, as one might say come here or not yet.

Navi stopped.

The pressure surged, fierce and grounding. Her vision narrowed. Sound dulled around the edges.

The man noticed her then.

Not with fear.

With recognition.

"You hear it too," he said.

It was not a question.

Navi's throat tightened. The system's training rose in her— deny, deflect, disengage.

She did none of those things.

"Yes," she said.

The word left her mouth before calculation could intervene.

The child watched them, eyes wide, curious rather than afraid.

"That's new," the man said softly. "They usually take longer."

Navi felt the world tilt.

"What usually?" she asked.

"Before the weight makes you visible," he said.

A chime sounded down the corridor.

Not loud.

Directional.

Navi felt it register in her bones the way the consultation hum had—not painful, but insistent.

The man stepped back.

"They don't like it when we gather," he said. "Even like this."

He took the child's hand.

"Don't let them tell you the quiet is kindness," he added.

Then they were gone, swallowed by the stairwell traffic.

Navi stood alone, heart racing, the pressure still blazing in her chest.

She understood three things at once:

The support measures worked.

They changed people.

And she had just been seen by someone the system had failed to erase.

When she returned to her slate, a new notification waited.

Alignment Follow-Up Recommended.

The words pulsed gently.

Navi did not acknowledge them.

She closed the slate.

For the first time since her reassignment, she left work without confirming her final file.

The omission would be logged.

The pattern would register.

And the system, which did not think in moments, would begin to narrow.

Chapter Ten

he system responded the way it always did.

Not with urgency.

With scheduling.

Navi's housing review was set for the following week.

The notice arrived mid-morning, nested among routine updates, its language indistinguishable from maintenance advisories and transit adjustments. **Proximity Reassessment. Occupancy Optimization. No action required at this time.**

She read it once. Then again.

The pressure beneath her breastbone sharpened, then steadied, as if her body had learned the rhythm of this kind of approach.

At work, the room felt different.

Not louder. Not quieter.

Closer.

The ventilation cycled more frequently, the citrus cleanser cutting sharper through the stone's mineral damp. Chairs adjusted faster. Slates warmed and cooled with brisk efficiency. Everything worked.

Which meant everything was watching.

Navi took her seat at Peripheral Review. The long table bore faint scratches she had not noticed before evidence of previous configurations, past bodies arranged and rearranged until alignment was achieved.

She opened the first file.

No resistance.

The second.

Still none.

By the third, her shoulders began to ache, a dull burn from holding herself still against an absence that felt intentional.

Across from her, the woman who had accepted support completed confirmations with effortless speed. Her slate barely warmed. Her breath remained even.

Navi did not look at her.

Midway through the morning, a facilitator appeared at the edge of the room.

They did not interrupt. They waited until a natural pause—until the system itself provided a seam.

"Just a brief check-in," they said softly. "When you have a moment."

Navi nodded. Declining would have required explanation. Explanation created texture. Texture drew attention.

The consultation alcove smelled faintly of eucalyptus this time, a cooler note layered over the familiar citrus. The lighting adjusted as she entered, lowering fractionally.

"How are you feeling today?" the facilitator asked.

"Functional," Navi said.

The facilitator smiled. "That's good."

They placed nothing on the table this time. No oval object. No tactile invitation.

Progress, Navi thought.

"We noticed a delayed confirmation yesterday," the facilitator continued. "Nothing concerning. Just a pattern we like to understand early."

The word pattern settled into Navi's spine.

"I was interrupted," she said.

"Yes," the facilitator replied, pleasantly. "Interruptions happen."

They did not ask what kind.

When Navi returned to her desk, the file she had left open had closed itself.

A small courtesy.

She reopened it.

The name was not there.

But the space it left pressed against her awareness, as tangible as a held breath. She felt it in her jaw, her wrists, the soles of her feet against stone.

She finished the day without incident.

Which was, she understood now, an incident in itself.

That evening, in the outer district, sound met her before light.

A train braking too late. Laughter spilling from an open doorway. Someone arguing in a language she did not know but felt in the chest anyway.

She climbed the stairs to her apartment slowly, hand grazing the rail worn smooth by years of unsanctioned use.

Inside, the paper waited.

She did not unfold it.

She sat on the floor and listened to the building breathe— pipes ticking, voices drifting, a radio somewhere below slipping in and out of tune.

The pressure eased just enough to let her think.

She understood something then, with a clarity that did not feel like relief:

The system would not confront her.

It would reposition her.

And repositioning required consent only once.

After that, gravity did the rest.

Chapter Eleven

The relocation did not require her presence.

That, Navi realized, was the point.

She learned about it through a courtesy update delivered to her slate just before midday. The message appeared briefly, then folded itself into the day's administrative flow.

Reassignment Confirmation: Housing Optimization Complete.

No address listed.

No date emphasized.

Just a note that her belongings would be transferred by authorized personnel to minimize disruption.

Minimize disruption to whom, the message did not specify.

At Peripheral Review, the work continued uninterrupted.

Files arrived. Files closed. Outcomes confirmed.

The system did not wait for her reaction.

Navi noticed, however, that the table had been reconfigured. The spacing between seats adjusted by inches—not enough to warrant comment, enough to alter sightlines. She now sat closer to the window, farther from the door.

Containment through geometry.

Mid-afternoon brought a support notice.

Not new.

Reiterated.

Alignment Follow-Up: Strongly Encouraged.

The language had softened further, padded with assurances. Participation would ease transition. Participation would support continuity. Participation would ensure that recent changes did not feel abrupt.

Navi did not respond.

The slate logged her silence without comment.

When she returned to her apartment that evening, the door seal accepted her credentials but did not welcome her.

Inside, the air felt wrong.

Not colder.

Emptier.

Her shelves were bare. The small table by the door was gone. The paper was not there.

She stood very still, listening to the building breathe around her pipes ticking, voices muffled by distance she had not noticed before.

Her chest tightened, then steadied.

Authorized personnel, the notice had said.

A secondary message arrived as she stood there.

Items Successfully Rehoused.

A location identifier followed.

Not her own.

The transit ride was efficient. Quiet. Cleaned recently, judging by the sharp scent of disinfectant layered over metal. The city passed in flattened segments, light breaking unevenly across glass and stone.

Her new building rose where districts thinned and oversight blurred. Taller. Narrower. The entry seal hesitated before admitting her.

Inside, the air carried dampness and old heat. Voices echoed unpredictably. Someone was crying somewhere above her. Someone else laughed too loudly below.

Navi found her unit.

Smaller.

Lower ceiling.

No table by the door.

Her belongings had been arranged efficiently. Aligned without regard for habit. The shelves held what she owned, but not how she had placed them.

The system had learned her shape.

It had not learned her rituals.

She sat on the floor.

Not because there was nowhere else to sit, but because standing felt like performance.

The pressure beneath her breastbone rose, sharp and grounding. Her breath shortened, then slowed.

She waited for the paper.

It did not appear.

Whatever had been taken had been taken cleanly.

Later, a final notification surfaced.

Transition Support Available Upon Request.

Below it, smaller:

Declining Support May Extend Adjustment Period.

Navi closed the slate.

For the first time since the system had begun to reposition her, she understood the shape of the offer.

Support was no longer about ease.

It was about return.

And return, she knew now, would require her to agree that nothing essential had been lost.

She did not make that agreement.

The omission settled into the system.

It would be noted.

And noted things, in this world, had a way of accumulating.

Chapter Twelve

The request arrived framed as an accommodation.

Navi received it late in the evening, after the building had settled into its uneven quiet. Pipes knocked somewhere above her. A voice down the corridor rose and fell, punctuated by laughter that felt a little too loud for the hour.

She sat on the floor, back against the wall, slate resting dark in her lap.

When she activated it, the light bloomed gently.

Assistance Requested.

Not required.

Requested.

The case involved a single occupant.

Recent transition. Proximity adjustment completed. Minor resistance noted during relocation.

The system language was careful, almost apologetic. The individual had expressed difficulty settling. Support had been offered. Support had been declined.

The request was simple:

Navi was to conduct a **Post-Transition Confirmation.**

Not an assessment.

Not a review.

A confirmation that the repositioning had achieved its intended effect.

The address was close.

Too close.

Navi felt it register in her body before she understood why.

The building was older than hers, its stone darkened by damp and time. The entryway smelled of mildew and old oil, the scent thick enough to taste. The seal admitted her with a reluctant buzz.

Inside, the light flickered.

Someone had tried to fix it recently.

The unit door was already open.

A woman stood just inside, arms folded tight across her chest. Her eyes tracked Navi's approach without hostility, without welcome.

"You're not support," the woman said.

The statement was flat. Observational.

"No," Navi replied. "I'm here to confirm your transition."

The word tasted wrong.

The woman laughed once, short and humorless. "Of course you are."

The apartment was sparsely furnished. Not empty paused. Boxes stacked but unopened. A chair positioned facing nothing. A window that refused to close all the way, letting in street noise and damp air.

Navi's chest tightened.

The pressure gathered fast here, sharper than it had been at work, as if the walls themselves resisted containment.

She became acutely aware of her badge, the quiet authority it carried.

"Have you been sleeping?" Navi asked.

The woman shrugged. "Sometimes."

"That's common after transition," Navi said, hearing the system speak through her mouth. "It takes time to recalibrate."

"Recalibrate to what?"

Navi hesitated.

The hesitation filled the room.

She opened her slate.

The confirmation form populated automatically, fields ready to be marked.

The woman watched her hands.

"If you say I'm fine," the woman said, "they'll stop coming."

Navi's breath caught.

"They'll stop helping," the woman corrected herself. "Sorry. Wrong word."

The pressure in Navi's chest surged.

"Yes," Navi said quietly.

"And if you don't?"

Navi did not answer.

The silence stretched.

Outside, a train screamed along distant rails, the sound raw and unfiltered.

The woman sat down heavily on the edge of the bed.

"They moved me twice," she said. "First time I told myself it was temporary. Second time they told me I should be grateful."

Navi felt something shift inside her, a subtle tearing sensation she had no language for.

"They said you'd understand," the woman added. "That you were reasonable."

The word landed like a weight.

Navi looked at the confirmation fields.

Stability: Pending.

Compliance: Pending.

Adjustment Successful: Pending.

Each required a mark.

Each would make the woman disappear into administrative calm.

"Yes," Navi said quietly.

"And if you don't?"

Navi did not answer.

The silence stretched.

Outside, a train screamed along distant rails, the sound raw and unfiltered.

The woman sat down heavily on the edge of the bed.

"They moved me twice," she said. "First time I told myself it was temporary. Second time they told me I should be grateful."

Navi felt something shift inside her, a subtle tearing sensation she had no language for.

"They said you'd understand," the woman added. "That you were reasonable."

The word landed like a weight.

Navi looked at the confirmation fields.

Stability: Pending.

Compliance: Pending.

Adjustment Successful: Pending.

Each required a mark.

Each would make the woman disappear into administrative calm.

Navi lowered the slate.

"I can delay this," she said.

It was not refusal.

It was not compliance.

It was the narrowest possible opening.

The woman stared at her, searching.

"For how long?"

Navi swallowed. "Long enough for it to be noticed."

That night, when Navi returned to her own apartment, the pressure did not ease.

It spread.

Not pain.

Responsibility.

She understood now what the system had done.

It had not asked her to choose sides.

It had asked her to **confirm reality for someone else.**

And in doing so, it had taught her the cost of being reasonable.

Chapter Thirteen

At first, it felt like inconvenience.

The transit gate hesitated before opening, long enough that Navi glanced at the indicator to check her credentials. The light turned green. The delay resolved itself. She stepped through and told herself not to catalog it.

The second time, the platform assignment changed without notice. A reroute. A temporary measure due to maintenance she could not see. She followed the arrows and arrived only slightly later than expected.

None of this required response.

At work, her schedule adjusted by minutes.

A meeting shifted forward. A review pushed back. A corridor marked temporarily closed funneled her through a longer path that passed fewer doors.

She noticed, distantly, that she no longer crossed the central atrium.

The realization did not settle.

The third adjustment arrived as assistance.

A message appeared on her slate mid-morning, phrased with practiced ease.

To reduce fatigue, your movement between tiers has been streamlined.

Below it, a highlighted route. Familiar enough to feel generous. Narrow enough to be specific.

Navi accepted it without thinking.

Later that day, she attempted to visit a building she had accessed for years.

The request did not deny her.

It paused.

A prompt surfaced.

Please specify purpose.

She stared at the words longer than necessary, then entered a reason that had always been sufficient before.

The gate opened.

The pause remained with her.

It was not until the end of the week that the pattern surfaced.

She stood at the edge of the transit platform, watching a train depart she had intended to board. The indicator listed her route as active, but the door did not reopen.

Another train followed.

Then another.

By the time she arrived at her destination, the building was closed for the evening.

She sat on a bench and waited for the pressure in her chest to settle.

It did not.

That night, she mapped her movements without meaning to.

Not formally. Not on a slate.

In her body.

The way her shoulders tightened at certain intersections.

The ease she felt only within a narrowing set of corridors.

The absence of places she used to pass through without thought.

She realized she had not been to the outer district in days.

Not because she had chosen not to go.

Because she had not been routed there.

The understanding arrived quietly, without ceremony.

No message announced it.

No policy named it.

She was not being stopped.

She was being *kept*.

The system had not restricted her movement.

It had learned it.

And once learned, it had begun to prefer where she was easiest to contain.

The realization did not bring anger.

It brought clarity.

Containment, she understood now, did not begin with walls.

It began with paths.

And by the time you noticed which ones were missing,

you had already been walking the rest for some time.

Chapter Fourteen

The first record finalized without her.

Navi learned this not from an alert, but from absence.

The file should have been waiting when she arrived—a routine confirmation she had delayed earlier in the week.

She opened her slate, expecting the familiar pending marker.

The docket refreshed.

The case was closed.

She read the summary twice.

Outcome confirmed. Transition stabilized. No further action required.

The language was clean, compacted, relieved of excess detail. Dates aligned. Signatures nested properly. The system had done careful work.

It had not needed her.

Navi scrolled.

The deeper layers did not open.

Where once there had been expandable fields—testimony fragments, contextual notes, peripheral materials—there was now only a validated synopsis.

She checked her access tier.

Unchanged.

She attempted again.

The slate warmed, then cooled. A brief courtesy delay.

Nothing opened.

A notice appeared at the bottom of the screen.

Secondary Confirmation Applied.

Below it, smaller:

This measure supports continuity during periods of adjustment.

Navi closed the slate.

Her chest tightened, then steadied, the pressure settling into a familiar ache.

At Peripheral Review, the rhythm had shifted.

Files arrived already smoothed. Questions resolved upstream. Decisions presented as facts rather than processes.

Her role, she realized, had narrowed.

She was no longer asked to *decide*.

She was asked to *witness*.

Midday brought a case she recognized.

Not by name.

By residue.

The address matched the building from her post-transition confirmation. The one with the flickering light. The open door.

Her fingers went cold.

She opened the summary.

Outcome: Adjustment Successful.

Compliance: Achieved.

Stability: Confirmed.

The words lay flat, unquestioned.

She searched for the woman's remarks. The hesitation. The boxes unopened.

None of it remained.

Navi felt the pressure surge, sharp and immediate. Her breath shortened. She pressed her feet flat to the floor, grounding herself against the stone.

Across the table, no one looked up.

The system did not pause.

It only needed to ensure that when harm occurred,

it happened already complete.

By the time she arrived,

there was nothing left to touch.

Chapter Fifteen

People began to arrive pre-aligned.

Navi noticed it in the pauses that no longer happened.

At Peripheral Review, files passed through her hands with a practiced smoothness that left no residue. Petitioners were no longer routed to her, not even for confirmation. Instead, she received prepared outcomes—decisions already shaped, questions already answered somewhere upstream.

She was thanked for her consistency.

The first reassignment of personnel occurred quietly.

A colleague she had shared a table with for years was moved to a different schedule. Another was assigned to a remote tier "for continuity." Their departures were logged as operational improvements.

No one said goodbye.

Navi found herself seated between two new faces who spoke only when required. Their slates chimed at identical intervals. Their confirmations landed with synchronized precision.

They did not look at her.

A support liaison was introduced.

Not attached to her directly.

Embedded.

The liaison attended Peripheral Review "to observe workflow efficiencies." They asked no questions of Navi. They spoke only to supervisors, quietly, with the confidence of someone whose presence had already been approved.

When Navi stood to leave the table, the liaison rose as well.

"Just walking," they said, smiling.

Outside of work, the narrowing continued.

Neighbors in her building began to shift schedules. The voices she recognized disappeared, replaced by others who kept their doors closed. The food vendor on the corner stopped operating at her usual hour.

A notice appeared on the public board:

Community Rebalancing Underway. Thank You for Your Patience.

Patience had become a civic virtue.

One evening, as Navi returned along her approved route, she passed a familiar doorway.

She slowed.

The unit was dark. The window that had once refused to close was sealed now, its frame newly reinforced. A small placard had been affixed beside the door.

Unit Vacated. Adjustment Complete.

The words were precise. Finished.

Navi stood there longer than necessary, the pressure in her chest sharp but contained.

A passerby glanced at her, then away.

No one stopped.

At home, her slate chimed.

Mentorship Opportunity Available.

The message described a junior reviewer recently reassigned due to "elevated engagement." Navi's experience made her an ideal stabilizing presence.

Participation would demonstrate leadership.

Participation would support communal balance.

Navi closed the slate without responding.

Later, as the building settled into its uneven quiet, she realized something with slow certainty:

The system was no longer trying to correct her.

It was reorganizing the world around her so that her presence did not matter.

Containment, in its final form, did not isolate.

It **thinned**.

And thinning, she understood, was how influence disappeared without leaving a trace.

Chapter Sixteen

The mentorship request did not expire.

It adjusted.

Navi noticed the change three days later, folded into a routine notice about workflow alignment. The language had softened again, as if patience itself were a resource being spent carefully.

Mentorship Session Scheduled.

Time preselected.

Location assigned.

Participation confirmed.

The room was small and windowless, its walls paneled with a fabric that absorbed sound too efficiently. The air smelled faintly of citrus and clean metal, a neutral blend designed to disappear once noticed.

The junior reviewer arrived early.

They sat with their hands folded, slate untouched, posture rigid in the way of someone who had been told this meeting was for their benefit.

"I'm glad you're here," they said when Navi entered.

The phrase sounded rehearsed.

They spoke first.

About fatigue. About difficulty settling after reassignment. About how the records sometimes felt louder than they should.

Navi listened.

The support liaison stood near the door, not facing them, not quite turned away. Their presence registered as pressure more than sight.

"Everyone says you're steady," the junior reviewer said. "That you make things feel manageable."

The word manageable pressed against Navi's ribs.

She thought of the woman in the damp building. The sealed window. The placard that had replaced a life.

She thought of the paper that had been taken cleanly.

Navi spoke carefully.

Not about resistance.

Not about harm.

She spoke about weight.

"How it doesn't always mean something is wrong," she said. "Sometimes it means something hasn't been finished."

The junior reviewer frowned slightly. "Finished how?"

Navi hesitated.

The liaison shifted.

"There are things," Navi said, "that the system closes before the body does."

The room felt suddenly smaller.

The junior reviewer's breath caught. Just once.

The liaison turned.

"That's not guidance," the liaison said mildly.

"No," Navi agreed.

She did not look at them.

"It's experience."

Silence followed.

Not alarmed.

Attentive.

The junior reviewer nodded slowly, as if something had aligned and misaligned at the same time.

"I feel that," they said.

The liaison made a note.

The session ended on schedule.

No reprimand.

No warning.

Just a gentle reminder to rest.

Later that evening, as Navi walked her narrowed route home, her slate chimed.

Mentorship Feedback Recorded.

Below it:

Language Divergence Noted.

The pressure in her chest did not spike.

It settled.

At home, she sat on the floor and let the building's uneven sounds move around her.

She understood then what she had done.

She had not refused.

She had not exposed.

She had not disrupted process.

She had **left a residue in another person**.

That could not be retrieved.

That could not be summarized.

That would require containment beyond thinning.

Navi closed her eyes.

For the first time since the system had begun to reorganize her life, she felt something like direction.

Not toward escape.

Toward consequence.

Chapter Seventeen

The system answered with inclusion.

Not immediately.

First came a recalibration notice, folded into a weekly digest that thanked staff for resilience during a period of collective adjustment.

Integration Review Scheduled.

The phrase carried a warmth that felt rehearsed.

The review was not held in a consultation suite.

It took place in a common room Navi had passed a hundred times without entering—a space designed for overlap. Long tables. Shared light. Plants chosen for their endurance rather than beauty.

The air smelled faintly of soil and citrus.

Several people were already seated when she arrived. Not supervisors. Not facilitators.

Peers.

Some she recognized. Others she did not.

They greeted her with polite familiarity, the kind that assumed shared purpose without requiring disclosure.

A coordinator spoke.

They thanked everyone for attending. For flexibility. For continued commitment to balance.

"This is not corrective," the coordinator said. "It's connective."

Navi felt the pressure in her chest adjust, not spike.

The exercise began gently.

Each person was asked to describe a moment when their work had felt heavy—not harmful, not wrong. Just heavy.

The framing mattered.

Weight without blame.

One by one, people spoke. Briefly. Carefully.

A delay that lingered. A name that stayed longer than expected. A case that followed them home in fragments.

The coordinator nodded at each contribution, recording nothing visible.

When it was Navi's turn, the room waited without pressure.

She chose her words the way she always had.

"I notice when things close before they settle," she said.

Several people nodded.

The coordinator smiled. "That awareness is a strength," they said. "Unprocessed engagement can be tiring. Integration helps distribute it."

The word *distribute* moved through the room.

They were asked to place their hands on the table.

The surface was warm. Not unpleasantly so. The light above dimmed a fraction, enough to soften edges.

A low hum emerged—not sound exactly, but synchronization.

Navi felt the familiar easing begin at the margins of her awareness.

Not relief.

Alignment.

Across from her, the junior reviewer's shoulders dropped.

Someone else exhaled sharply, then laughed, surprised.

The room felt lighter.

Too quickly.

Navi withdrew her hands.

The hum faltered, just slightly.

A few heads turned.

The coordinator's expression did not change.

"Everything alright?" they asked.

"Yes," Navi said.

Her voice was steady.

She placed her hands back on the table.

The hum resumed.

But it did not fully settle.

When the session ended, people lingered.

They spoke more freely than before, trading small confidences framed as relief.

"I didn't realize how tense I was," someone said.

"It's easier when you share it," another replied.

Navi listened.

She felt the pressure in her chest thin, spread across the room like heat dispersing.

Not gone.

Shared.

As she left, the coordinator walked beside her.

"We'd like you to participate again," they said. "Your presence helps others integrate."

"Integrate what?" Navi asked.

The coordinator paused, as if considering how much honesty the room could hold.

"Experience," they said finally.

That night, in her apartment, Navi sat on the floor and waited for the pressure to return to its usual shape.

It did not.

Instead, it felt distributed, less sharp, less hers.

She understood then the system's final strategy.

Not erasure.

Not thinning.

Absorption.

If everyone carried a little of the weight,

no one would name it.

And naming, she knew now,

was the last thing the system could not integrate.

Chapter Eighteen

After the integration review, the quiet changed.

Not in volume.

In texture.

Navi noticed it first in herself.

The pressure that had once gathered sharply beneath her breastbone no longer spiked in isolation. It spread more evenly now, a low warmth that surfaced in shared spaces and receded when she was alone. The edges of it were harder to find.

This should have felt like improvement.

Instead, it felt like dilution.

At work, conversations softened.

People spoke in the same careful register, offering small recognitions without anchoring them to anything specific.

"I felt lighter after," someone said in passing.

"It helps to know you're not the only one," another replied.

No one named what had been shared.

No one asked what remained.

The coordinator's invitation followed two days later.

Not a summons.

A continuation.

Integration Session II: Optional Participation.

Below it:

Your presence has been noted as stabilizing.

Stabilizing what, the message did not specify.

That evening, Navi walked her narrowed route home more slowly than usual. The city moved around her with practiced ease—doors opening when expected, transit lights changing on time, voices flowing along approved paths.

She passed the sealed doorway again.

The placard remained.

Adjustment Complete.

The words had begun to fade at the edges, the adhesive loosening just enough to curl.

She stood there, listening to the hum of the street.

The pressure in her chest warmed.

Not sharp.

Shared.

At home, she sat on the floor and placed her hands flat against the stone.

She tried to recall the exact shape of the pressure as it had once been—before containment, before thinning, before integration.

The memory resisted.

Not erased.

Softened.

She understood then what absorption required.

Not forgetting.

Agreement.

Agreement that what could no longer be clearly felt did not need to be named.

Her slate chimed.

A message from the junior reviewer.

No subject line.

Just a line of text:

I don't feel it as much anymore. Is that good?

Navi stared at the words.

The room felt very still.

She thought of the integration table. The hum. The warmth spreading outward.

She thought of the woman whose confirmation had been finalized without her.

She thought of the name that had survived only when spoken aloud.

Navi typed slowly.

What do you feel instead?

The reply came quickly.

Relief, the junior reviewer wrote. And a kind of quiet. I can focus again.

Navi closed her eyes.

The system offered quiet generously.

She understood the choice with sudden clarity.

If she continued to integrate, the weight would disperse until it no longer belonged to anyone.

If she stopped, the weight would gather again, sharper, lonelier, undeniable.

Either way, the system would continue.

The difference lay in whether anyone could still point to what it cost.

Navi opened her slate and drafted a response.

She did not mention harm.

She did not name the system.

She wrote only this:

Pay attention to what the quiet lets you ignore.

She sent it.

The message was delivered.

No alert followed.

No correction.

But as the night settled, Navi felt the pressure begin to gather again, slowly, deliberately drawing itself back into a shape she recognized.

Not because the system had failed.

Because she had chosen not to let it finish.

Chapter Nineteen

The system closed the loop with care.

Not immediately.

Firsl, it acknowledged her.

A commendation appeared in Navi's weekly digest, positioned between transit updates and resource advisories.

Recognition of Service: Your contributions during recent integration efforts have supported communal steadiness.

No name attached.

No audience specified.

The language carried a mild warmth, the kind meant to settle nerves rather than stir pride.

Her schedule adjusted again.

Not tighter.

Simpler.

Fewer transitions between spaces. Longer blocks assigned to observation tasks. Her slate populated with summaries rather than files, outcomes rather than processes.

She was thanked for her reliability.

The word rested uneasily against her ribs.

The junior reviewer did not attend Integration Session II.

The absence was not remarked upon.

Later, a note circulated about attendance flexibility and the importance of pacing.

The system did not correct divergence.

It absorbed it.

That evening, Navi returned home to find a small package by her door.

No seal.

No delivery record visible.

Inside was a thin binder, its cover unmarked. The paper smelled faintly of dust and old glue.

She sat on the floor and opened it.

The pages held fragments.

Not records.

Margins. Handwritten notes. Partial transcripts. Addresses without outcomes.

Materials unsuited for archiving.

She recognized the hand.

The woman from Peripheral Review.

Tucked inside the back cover was a note.

They can distribute weight, it read. They can't store it forever.

No signature.

Navi closed the binder.

The pressure in her chest steadied, familiar and precise.

She understood what the system had done.

It had given her quiet.

It had limited her reach.

It had praised her restraint.

And in doing so, it had assumed that what could not be archived would disappear.

The next morning, Navi altered her routine.

Not drastically.

She left five minutes earlier than usual. Took a longer corridor. Paused where she had been encouraged not to linger.

No alert sounded.

The system adjusted.

At work, she placed the binder beneath her slate.

She did not open it.

She did not share it.

She let its weight remain exactly where it was.

Later, during a scheduled observation block, a case summary flickered with a familiar kind of absence.
Navi noticed.
She did not reach to finalize.
She wrote nothing.
She waited.
The delay registered.

By evening, the city felt unchanged.
Transit ran on time. Lights held steady. People moved along preferred paths.
Containment remained intact.

In her apartment, Navi placed the binder beside the door, where the paper had once rested.
She did not align it.
She did not hide it.
She let it be seen by anyone who knew how to look.

The system would respond.
It always did.
But not everything required response.

She let its weight remain exactly where it was.

Some things only required presence.

And presence, Navi understood now, was not the opposite of compliance.

It was what remained after agreement ended.

She sat on the floor and listened to the building breathe.

The pressure held.

Not shared.

Not erased.

Held.

(End.)

Interlude – Epilogue

The quiet did not last the way they promised it would.

At first, it felt like relief.

The junior reviewer noticed it in the mornings—how easily their breath settled, how the familiar tightness behind the eyes no longer greeted them upon waking. Work moved smoothly again. Files opened and closed without resistance. The day ended where it was supposed to.

They told themselves this was health.

Still, something had shifted.

Not absence.

Orientation.

Certain summaries now left an afterimage. Not discomfort, exactly. More like a faint question that lingered at the edge of thought, impossible to articulate without sounding ungrateful.

They had learned the language well enough to know which thoughts not to finish.

One evening, leaving later than usual, they took a corridor they had not used in weeks.

No alert sounded.

That surprised them.

The hall smelled faintly of dust and old paper, a scent they could not place but felt oddly steadied by. Halfway down, they noticed an object near a doorway—unremarkable unless you were looking.

A thin binder.

Unmarked.

Resting where someone might see it and decide not to.

They did not touch it.

Instead, they stood there, feeling something gather—not sharp, not overwhelming. Just present. A familiar pressure they had almost forgotten.

It occurred to them, then, that the quiet had not erased the weight.

It had simply moved it somewhere harder to notice.

They returned to work the next day with this understanding unsettled but intact.

During a routine observation block, a summary passed across their slate that felt wrong in a way they could not name. No errors. No omissions. Just a smoothness that asked too little of them.

They paused.

The pause was brief.

But it was real.

Later, they found themselves standing in the common room where integration had once felt generous. The plants still held their shape. The tables still carried warmth.

They placed their hands flat against the surface.

Nothing happened.

No hum.

No easing.

Only the awareness of their own breath.

They understood something then—not fully, not yet.

Quiet was not the absence of weight.

It was the decision not to ask where it had gone.

That night, passing the doorway again, they noticed the binder was still there.

Untouched.

Patient.

They knelt this time.

They did not open it.

They rested their hand beside it, close enough to feel its presence without claiming it.

The pressure gathered.

Not unbearable.

Locatable.

The next morning, the junior reviewer arrived at work five minutes early.

They sat at their desk and opened the first file of the day.

They did not finalize it right away.

They waited.

The delay registered.

Somewhere, the system would notice.

They were no longer sure that mattered.

They had learned, quietly, what remained when agreement loosened.

Not defiance.

Attention.

(End.)

www.ingramcontent.com/pod-product-compliance
Lightning Source LLC
Chambersburg PA
CBHW060829250626
47162CB00005B/2003